THE VECTOR

Published by 1889 Labs Ltd.
Visit our website for free books and other fun stuff:
http://books.1889.ca

FOR RIE:
Thank you for not hating this.

THE VECTOR

BY MCM

1889 BOOKS

NOVEMBER 21 - 27

01

Paint peeled off the swing set in the front yard, yellow flakes drifting like sunburnt snow to dead grass. No wind for some time. The air smelled of rank summer sweat, still and stagnant, seeping out of the parched soil. There were no birds in the barren trees.

A nightmare had come to town.

It walked down the road with methodical pacing, long cloak swaying gently with each footfall. The worn machete on its belt clanked against armoured gloves. No hint of skin or hair suggested it was human: overlapping layers of cloth, metal and rubber took care of that. The mask over its face hissed softly, taking in air to process. In every way, inhuman.

From behind cracks in shuttered windows, anxious eyes watched it pass, breaths held until it was safely out of sight, superstitiously certain it could smell fear in the air. There weren't many to see it this day. Some houses had long-open doors, others were boarded shut with black paint splashed from afar.

A ghost town, by will or fortune.

The chain fence around number 37 was untouched, a lone tire leaning precariously against its gate.   The closest anyone dared come.   From a tiny half-frosted window in the door, Kurt saw the thing pause at the end of the walkway. He swallowed slowly, adjusted his view to see better.

It was staring right at him.

It rolled the tire away, carefully leaning it against the fence post, and unlatched the gate. Halfway up the interlocked stone path, the thing stopped, turned, stared at the cross in the lawn. Four graves beneath its soft shadow, all roughly dug in the cold November soil. Nothing moved for some time, and Kurt gripped the trim round his small portal with bloodied fingernails, waiting.

Finally, the thing turned away from the graves, climbed the steps to the porch, and without a pause, opened the front door. Kurt stumbled backwards into the foyer, falling against the banister as the dark figure stopped before him.

"Are…" Kurt stammered, his voice weak and creaky. "Are you…"

The thing looked at him without emotion. Air hissed.

"Are you a Healer?" Kurt gasped.

It watched him a moment, then carefully bowed a 'yes'.

Kurt collapsed down on the steps, covered his head with his frail empty arms, and began to sob. He heard the soft crunch of thick boots grinding dirt into the Persian rug. He hesitated, looked up, saw the mask, his reflection in the dark oval goggles. He looked so *worn*.

The Healer held out a hand to him, and he took it, stood, let himself be led into the living room. He sat in his father's soft armchair, awkwardly, like a stranger in his own home, being hosted by someone who'd only just arrived.

The Healer sat on the sofa to the right, and removed two cloth packages from a pouch on his belt: one blue, one black. He placed them gently on the coffee table, and unrolled the black one to reveal a small plastic device, and an assortment of vials.

Kurt closed his eyes, shuddering.

The Healer put a long vial into the base of the device, clicking it into place. Kurt studied every move with his arms pulled close to his chest, like a child expecting a shot at the doctor. When it was time to draw his blood, Kurt's face was already streaked with tears.

The Healer didn't force him, but it was clear there was no escaping it.

Kurt exhaled loudly, held out a trembling arm, and the Healer's hand gripped his elbow firmly. A quick sting shot through him as a tiny blade hit, and he yelped, closing his eyes tightly as his blood filled the vial.

His elbow jerked free, a cotton swab pushed against the wound. The Healer slid a panel down on the device to reveal a small LCD screen.

Kurt looked out the front windows, saw the tip of the cross on the lawn, and just stared. It was like the room was empty again, and he was alone there, sitting, watching, waiting for a resolution. Absolution.

The creak of rubber beside him shook the daydream away.

"They… they died because of me?" he asked, not so much a question as a need for confirmation.

The Healer didn't shift his gaze from the device, and the callousness of it pushed Kurt into hysteria: he grabbed the monster's wrist, thick with metal, shook it, and got the attention he needed.

"They died because of me!" he shouted.

The Healer placed a hand atop Kurt's, squeezed gently, and he calmed, his breathing ragged but slow.

"W-w-was it me?" he whispered.

A moment passed where neither moved, as if the answer had to be read from the air rather than repeated as fact.

But then, the Healer nodded.

"No!" Kurt screamed, curling against the chair. He cried again, till he had no air in his lungs at all, and gasped a horrible raspy breath against the floral fabric, like he was drowning out of water.

He felt the cold tap of metal against his neck, a hiss and a sting, and his eyes shot open at the shock of it. He pushed his face into the cushions, stopped his theatrics, and started to mouth a prayer in his few last seconds.

A fire shot through his veins, and he flailed back, onto the floor, and convulsed so hard he bit the edge off his tongue. He gagged on the blood.

A strong hand pushed down on his chest, keeping him from rolling, and in the moments before his vision gave out, he saw the Healer over him, an expressionless mask, watching.

"Not your fault," it said to him in a rough, processed voice from the darkness.

On his way out of the house, the Healer closed the door quietly, respectfully. As he made his way past the graves, he paused as harsh static struck his ears.

"Home to Green Four," came a voice, Mandarin Chinese distorted by an overcast sky, as if spoken through a digital waterfall. "Do you copy, Green Four?"

The Healer took the heavy satellite phone from his belt, unfolded the antenna, then let it hang by his side again.

"Green Four to Home," he said, fluent in his native tongue. "Sigma5 is neutralized."

A pause. Static again.

"Understood," said Home. "We will send you the co-ordinates of a safe location to leave the blood sample."

The Healer nodded to the empty air.

"Your next assignment is identified," said Home, without a hint of emotion. "You will be leaving at once."

The Healer turned west, the afternoon sun nearly invisible in the haze.

"Understood," he said again.

"Profiles and identification algorithms will be sent to you en route. We have intelligence indicating a living host at the Motol Hospital in Prague."

The Healer stiffened slightly as the line devolved to static. He turned around, straight behind him, and stared into the darkening sky, back where night was already falling. He turned a bit more, south-east.

"Home," he said carefully, deliberately. "I am already west of Prague. Please confirm."

Static. The faint sounds of a discussion away from a microphone.

"Confirmed, Green Four," came the reply. "Maps and speaking guides will be relayed before you cross the border."

The Healer glanced back towards the setting sun, then stared headlong toward his objective. A weak wind tugged his cloak, and a speck of rain hit his mask, between his eyes. His suit whined faintly, warning of moisture contact, gently quieting as the drop slid down and away. He did not react.

"Understood," he said once more.

Another raindrop glanced off his shoulder.

He was stirred back to life at the sound of the incendiary grenade exploding in the house behind him. He retracted his steps down the interlocked path, opening the front gate as the black smoke started to pour out of the windows, and into the sky above. He left the tire as he'd found it.

Another raindrop hit the train's window and dripped slowly downward. Eva watched it, her head against the glass, as the sky darkened. She shivered in the cold, pulled her thinning denim jacket tighter, her arms substituting for the buttons long since torn from the front. Her tank top was too threadbare and worn for this weather, but she had no bags, no clothes to change into.

She peered down the side of the train, as far as she could, but saw no movement. The fields outside were abandoned, half-turned soil waiting for another pass with a tractor.

"Forty minutes," she muttered to herself, checking her watch. She looked back the way they'd come, saw nothing there but hostile sky.

A knock at the door startled her. She sat straight, adjusted her jacket, tried to fix her poorly bundled hair. The door opened a moment later, and a uniformed officer with a surgeon's mask entered the suddenly cramped compartment. He took a quick look around, but seemed bored by the action, like he'd done it one too many times before.

Eva tried not to move, kept a smile on her face that felt fake no matter how she adjusted it. The officer made no attempt to establish eye contact, only said gruffly in Czech: "Ticket. Passport. Photo identification."

Eva slid a small worn manila envelope from her right breast pocket, holding out the contents with shaking hands. The officer took the papers and cards, started running them through his hand-held with casual expertise. He nodded towards her jacket as he worked.

"Not the safest place to keep these things," he said.

"I know," she said, nodding anxiously.

"Stolen passports go for, what, €65,000 in Barcelona?"

"Eight-five—" Eva began, then stopped very abruptly, and stared at the ground. She could hear the officer had paused his work. She tried not to shiver during the awkward silence.

"You should get a better jacket," he said, and the work resumed.

"I will," Eva said, relaxing a bit, but still on guard. "It's been a long trip."

"I can see that," he muttered, flipping through the pages of her passport. He turned it sideways, flicked his eyes over at her, then snapped it shut and slipped it underneath the handheld while he worked on her health card.

"You look young for twenty-three," he said, though he wasn't looking at her.

"Th-thank you." she stammered.

"It's not a compliment. Under the circumstances, nothing I say is going to be a compliment. Let's see your eyes."

She looked up at him, nervous. He squinted at her.

"Nice shade of blue. What's that, azure?"

"I think it's called brandeis, actually."

"Really. Never heard of that before. It's funny, the odd facts and trivia you learn from these encrypted health cards."

There was an awkward silence.

"A border guard in Switzerland told me," Eva said.

The officer cocked an eyebrow.

"What else did he tell you?"

"I looked old for twenty-one."

The guard smiled at this, but it wasn't a warm smile. He had very hard features, and the mask didn't sit well on his face. The metal bridge for the nose was snapped in half where he'd tried to reshape it too often, and the spaces around the sides fogged his glasses in slow, steady bursts as he breathed.

"Ms Kolikov," said the officer, gruffly but wearily, like he was repeating a lecture for the thousandth time, "your passport is Russian. Your name is Russian. And unless you're going to claim you've been living under a rock until recently, I'm pretty sure you know the Czech Republic closed its borders over two years ago, *especially* to our cousins in Russia."

Eva lowered her gaze, appropriately chastised. The officer continued. "Unspoken policy says we don't even do the small talk with people who carry Russian passports. Last guy who did ended up dying from boils the size of a fist on his neck, because — and I don't mean to generalize — even though you people *started* it, you *still* don't seem to grasp how big a shitstorm it's become. Don't know when to quit. And we're sick of trying to make you understand. Like spitting into the wind.

"Now, I could list you about fifteen regulations covering the rights of refugees and amnesty claimants as they relate to UN containment policies, but the bottom line is this. I'm fully within my rights to grab you by the scruff of the neck and toss you off this train before you even have a chance to think of a way to convince me otherwise."

Eva held her breath. The officer scrolled his handheld briefly.

"This is the part where you convince me otherwise," he sighed.

"Oh!" Eva stammered. "Well, I used to have dual citizenship, so while I'm not *technically* Czech anymore, my mother *is*. She lives in Prague right now and I—"

"You've been in *Paris*," he interrupted.

Eva nodded. "A few years ago. At school."

"Computer science," noted the officer.

"No, fine arts," Eva corrected.

"Says here 'computer science.'"

"I switched majors."

He glanced at her again, eyes unflinching.

"Computer science in Paris is all I see. Let's move on."

"I haven't been in Paris for years. You can check my passport... I left before —"

"Ms Kolikov," said the officer, staring her down, "your mum's a citizen. You cleared the first hurdle. Congratulations. Now trust me when I say this: if you are lucky enough to continue on this train, you will want to have saved your impassioned speeches for the Immigration agents at the station. Words don't change your documents, and from here on out, all we care about are your docu..."

He trailed off, frowned at the screen, and looked back at her sharply. She froze, unsure what he'd read. He pocketed her ID and his handheld, leaned out the door and called down the hallway.

"What's a 17-5?" he said, his voice scratchy when loud.

There was a brief pause, some clattering, then a voice mumbled something back that Eva couldn't make out. The officer sighed, leaned further out the door, cupped his hand to his mask and shouted again: "What's a 17-5?"

He glanced back at Eva, then walked out of her cabin, sliding the door half-closed, and disappeared down the hall. She was left there with no papers, painfully alone in a space meant for four. The wind outside was picking up, and the sky was darker still.

A sudden scream from the hallway broke her stare, and she turned round to see a woman being shoved down the narrow passage. The officers on either side kept pushing her forward, their faces cold behind creased masks.

The woman grabbed the bar outside Eva's door and tried to resist, but the larger of the two officers planted a hand on her face and pushed so hard it seemed as if her neck might break.

The woman reached inside her jacket and pulled out a passport, a Euro ID card, tried to hand them back. One of the officers smacked them out of her hand, onto the ground, as if they meant nothing to him. They meant everything to her, and she gasped in horror, lost her grip, and was pushed out of view.

Eva carefully leaned closer to the door, trying to see where they'd gone. She heard the echo of screaming, frantic banging, and then the sound of the heavy doors to the train slamming shut.

The woman's passport lay on rug in the hall, cover bent and tread upon. Bulgarian. Eva glanced out the window again, felt the cold through her jacket more intensely now. She touched her empty pocket, bit her lip.

"A long way home," she said to herself, then risked another peek at the passport. Her hands clasped together, white fingertips trembling, working up the nerve to snatch another lifeline. It would only take a second to pull it in. All it would take is a second and she'd have a back up plan after months of—

A knock at the hallway window jolted her back to attention. The officer had returned, holding her passport and rapping the glass again with scarred knuckles.

"Up!" he called.

Eva quickly obeyed, slipped out of the cabin without a word. The officer watched her with callous eyes, squinting unhappily. He grabbed her chin and turned her towards him, making sure he had her attention. He waved her passport, health card, and ticket like a magician about to perform a trick, then shoved them into her pocket. Eva flinched at the contact. Her jaw was aching from being clenched so long.

"Back of the train," he said, shoving her slightly.

She caught her balance just in time, stared at him desperately.

"What's at the back of the train?"

"Quarantine," he said coldly, thumbing the safety off his pistol.

03

"Wait!" Eva pleaded as the officer closed in. "I'm Czech!"

He aimed the gun squarely at her head.

"I've got forty *other* so-called Czechs back there who say the same thing."

Eva's face lost colour.

"Forty?" she gasped. "But if one of them is sick..."

"Less paperwork for me," he grunted.

Eva bumped into the wall. The officer half-smirked, like he was begging her to make a move, so he'd have an excuse to shoot. There was nothing to fight back with, nowhere to run, and no hope if she tried. She slowly raised her hands above her head.

There was a flash of movement, and suddenly a pair of arms wrapped around his neck from behind, pulling him back and off-balance. He thrashed to the side, swung a fierce elbow back into his assailant's stomach, but still couldn't get free. He was slammed into the wall, cracking the window to the compartment, but not giving up his gun.

He swung his elbow back again, once, twice, and the third blow connected with a crack. The grip on his neck loosened, and he pulled forward, free, face red with fury and stress.

Eva's fist hit him so hard he slammed into the wall. For a moment, he had a look of confusion, like it didn't make sense, what had just happened. But only for a moment. She finished him off with a blow to the face. He collapsed to the ground, glasses broken, eyes rolling and shut.

Eva looked up, saw a lean, scruffy man with ruffled blond hair, wincing at the pain in his ribs.

"Where'd you learn to do that?" he grunted.

"Here and there," she smiled. "Thanks, I think."

"Don't take it personal," he grinned, crouching quickly, scooping the gun out of the guard's limp hand and giving it a once-over appraisal. "He'd be getting to me next, and I'm not even Czech. You coming?"

She glanced down at the unconscious guard, then to the back of the train.

"Not much choice anymore, is there?"

"Great! I'm Anton, by the way."

"Eva," she said.

Anton smiled back, then took off on a skittish, exploratory journey, down to the heavy doors at the middle of the train. A bright yellow sign warned them not to leave until they were sure it was safe outside; a friendly biohazard symbol served as the point below a question mark.

"I hope you like walking!" Anton beamed, and pulled the door open, just a crack at first. The cold air beat Eva in the face, making her squint. The rain was coming down fiercely now, the horizon a blurry mess of heavily slanted sleet pounding into the farmland.

Anton saw it first. He gripped Eva's hand tighter.

The Bulgarian woman in the fur coat was backing away from the two guards who had shoved her outside. They had their pistols aimed, but the way they were closing in on her said they were doing more than just threatening.

The woman turned to run, covering only a few metres before two shots rang out, and she dropped to the ground in a heap, her coat spread out in the mud like the wings of an angel.

"Oh shit," Eva and Anton said at once.

The guards turned back, holstering their weapons, but paused at the sight of the open door. The gruff one reacted faster, his eyes open wide as he charged at them, drawing his gun and taking aim.

"Don't move!" he shouted, and Anton slammed the door, threw down the locking bolt just as a loud *thump* hit it. He and Eva dashed back to the unconscious officer, who was on the verge of waking up when Anton viciously kicked him across the head and into the wall.

"What are we going to do?" Eva asked.

"I don't know yet," Anton said, glancing up and down the corridors. "Let me know if you think of something. Now come on!"

He took off towards the front of the train, Eva close behind. The other passengers watched them go, some looking ahead, some looking back, waiting for the guards to calm the insurrection. None made a move to follow them.

Eva and Anton ducked into a small compartment at the rear of a car, closed the door and flicked on the lights. He started rifling through cupboards like mad, dropping food packets, sterile pillows and sealing tape all over the ground as Eva peeked outside, trying to hear signs of trouble.

"Why are they shooting people?" Anton hissed. "Whatever happened to *deporting*?"

"Border's wide open," Eva replied. "You get thrown off the train, what'll you do? Give up and go home, or finish the trip on foot?"

"I guess," he conceded.

"The only way for them to be *certain* is to make sure we don't make it *anywhere* on foot. I should have known this would happen, when they didn't do the check at the border. We're too close to Prague to just boot us out."

"How far do you think it is?"

Eva shrugged.

"Close enough to try."

Anton let out a gasp of joy and yanked a pair of heavy brown wool blankets from a low drawer, folding them over and tucking one under his arm. He shoved the other at Eva.

"Take this, and move fast!" he said, pushing his way out into the corridor, glancing back briefly before racing down to the end of the car, to another outside door.

"I have them!" came a distant shout, and Anton angrily slammed a fist against the wall, then turned his attention to a ladder instead.

"Let's go! Quick!"

They climbed fast, up onto the slick steel roof. It was ridged to make it easier to scale, but the gentle curve was still steep enough that it was dangerously easy to fall, especially in this weather. Anton pointed back towards the tail end of the train.

"We'll double back, get into the fields, muddy up the blankets and stay put till they give up and leave."

Gun in hand, he led Eva down the length of the train, rain raising a deafening roar all around them. It was so noisy she wouldn't know if someone were calling after them, not until a gunshot at least… But they were past the point of warning anyway, so she dashed forward, trying to keep her feet on course while the slick metal threatened disaster.

She felt a quick tug at her arm, and in an instant, Anton was falling sideways off the train, smacking his shoulder before disappearing off the edge. Eva dropped to her knees and leaned over the side, watching him roll to a painful stop in a ditch by the muddy field. He reached desperately for the gun, which had fallen a short distance away.

Behind her, guards were starting to get onto the roof, their loud shouts of co-ordination echoing past. She gripped her blanket tightly, and without pausing, jumped off the train, landing next to Anton. She flinched at the impact, felt like her legs might have broken.

"Anton!" she gasped, scuttling over to him. "Anton!"

He got hold of the gun, wiped it across his shirt to clean off the mud, and lurched to his feet.

"Blankets! Fast!"

She shoved the blankets into the mud, dragging them around. Before she could get very far, Anton grabbed her by the arm and pulled her further into the field, past a watery pool. She let the blankets collect all the filth they could along the way.

"We need them now!" Anton called urgently.

"Almost there!" she shouted back, but he wasn't listening anymore. The guards had caught up with them, were starting to climb down ladders, urgent but confident.

Anton checked the safety.

"Leave my blanket. I'll catch up."

"Anton, wait—"

But her voice was drowned out by two sharp shots as Anton clipped the closer guard in the thigh. He fell, hard, into the tracks, and his comrade quickly slung his gun out and fired wildly towards the escapees.

Eva had cleared nearly ten metres when she tripped into the mud with a splash. She checked behind herself to see if anyone had noticed, but all she saw when she looked was a quick image of Anton, cornered by the enemy, receiving a bullet to the chest, and toppling backwards.

04

OUTSIDE PRAGUE, CZECH REPUBLIC
NOVEMBER 26

Eva lay still, rain blurring her vision, as the echo of the gunshot disappeared into the bitter air. She was shivering violently, whether from the cold or from fear, and she drew slow, ragged breaths to keep from sobbing.

The blanket was beside her, disappearing into mud that was flowing free like a river, and she knew she, too, was sinking in, out of sight. Just how far, she couldn't tell.

The guards were yelling back and forth to each other, terse military barks that she couldn't make out. Two more skirted the roof of the train, looking out into the fields with guns drawn, hunting her. It was impossible to tell how much they could see, so she tried to shove herself further into the muck, to disappear.

"Hey! He's still breathing!" came a shout from near the train, and Eva dared to look up that way. A pair of guards were standing over Anton, guns holstered. She couldn't see any movement, couldn't hear any signs of life, but all the same she felt the pit of her stomach hollow out with terror.

"We've gotta move him," one said to the other.

"I'm not touching that. He's bleeding all over the place."

"We've got gloves."

"Then *you* do it. Better yet, next time shoot 'em out in the field like you're supposed to."

Eva heard a slosh close by, held her breath. Another slosh, and she could faintly hear the sound of feet trudging through the mud behind her. Slow, methodical, searching.

She sunk her face lower, closed her eyes, and pushed as far down as she could, until her nose was half-submerged, pulling in foul-smelling filth every other breath. The footsteps stopped, but she heard the sound of sleet pounding a guard's waterproof jacket.

"Listen," continued the guard close to the train. "If we leave him here, people are going see him, and we'll have a panic on our hands the last half hour of the trip."

"As if Holik's leg won't do that anyway. Or the half-dozen gun-shots they've all heard by now."

The guard behind her was moving again, but she couldn't tell if he was coming or going. She became aware of the feeling of rain hitting her left calf directly, and she realized the mud was flowing off her, that she was slowly becoming uncovered as she lay there.

She tried to shift her leg until the mud wrapped around her, but then the footsteps stopped again. They were still close by.

"Fine," grumbled the first guard. "One way or another, it's got to be done. Thanks a lot, though."

Eva felt pressure on her right foot… The rough tread of a boot on her skin! She bit her lip to keep from making noise, felt her ankle scream with pain.

Then: *crack!*

A gunshot echoed out, and everything lost meaning.

"Jesus!" gasped the first guard, and Eva swore she heard mad gur-gling. The guard behind her leapt over her, giving her ankle one last crunch as he did. She whimpered into the mud, but it was quickly drowned out by the sound of another gunshot, then a quick series in return.

"Jesus! Oh Christ, I'm hit! I'm hit!" wailed the first guard.

Radios were buzzing all around, footsteps sprinting through water, and Eva heard the heavy doors to the train crash open. She peeked up, over the mud, blinking back the rain.

"One, two, three… Up!" called an officer, and the first guard was hauled up on a stretcher, and carried to the door.

She saw the other guard propped up against a comrade, his eyes blank and a gushing wound in his neck. They closed his eyes and lifted him gently up and away.

One of the younger guards spent a good two minutes sloshing the mud around with his foot, trying to hide the blood that had pooled there.

Even when she was finally alone, Eva stayed perfectly silent in the rain, for longer than she could keep track of. The deluge didn't let up, kept pounding her bare head, so cold it was like tiny blades smashing into her skull.

She looked ahead, tried to see Anton, see if he was still alive; though that wasn't likely anymore. She tried sliding forward on her stomach, crawling flat on the ground, but she knew it was too risky, and she stopped, rested her head on the side and waited.

Then, after an unbearable wait, an older, senior-looking officer came out the door, trudged near where Anton had fallen, and lit a cigarette. He looked out into the field, right towards Eva, blowing smoke against the wind.

A minute later, he was joined by the officer she'd beaten, his glasses gone, bruised face, an ice pack on the side of his head. He leaned against the train, looking winded.

"All set," the hurt one said. "The cars are sectioned and we're ready to move."

"How's Karel?"

"As long as he doesn't pick up anything, he should make it. We've got him in isolation with the doc."

"Good. We'll get going once I finish this."

There was a pause as Eva's officer looked out over the field too. They stood there in silence, and Eva shivered at the thought she might be seen.

"How about the girl?" her guard said.

"She's 17-5, right?"

"Yeah. Hadn't seen one of those before."

The smoking officer stared out at the setting sun. His cigarette glowed brightly.

"She's either dead or going to die. I'm not wasting any more lives on her."

The other man nodded solemnly, then kept quiet for the time it took his superior to finish smoking and toss the butt into the mud. They climbed aboard the train, slammed the door shut, and within a few minutes the train's engine roared back to life, and it started to slide down the tracks.

Eva waited until it was a faint shimmer on the horizon before crawling to her feet. Her ankle seared with pain, but she kept walking on it until the sensation disappeared into her general discomfort. After a few kilometres she was barely limping at all.

*   *   *

The woman stood behind a fence near the train tracks, her wide hat drooping uselessly in the rain, a lantern by her side, sending light across the field as far as the weather allowed. She hadn't moved the entire time Eva had seen her there, and the only motion she made up close was to maintain lazy eye contact with the only other living creature for miles. She was gaunt, like a skeleton with a thin layer of skin holding it together.

"Nice night for a walk," said the old woman as Eva passed by.

Eva stopped, turned back. It was sometime after midnight, and she was bleary-eyed and shivering madly.

"Excuse me?" she trembled.

"No rain lately. This is good for the crops."

Eva smiled weakly, nodded, started back on her way.

"You're going to the city?" asked the woman, interrupting again. "I came from the city. Had a flat there, a nice big television. Watched imported films every Friday night. You ever seen *Midnight Cowboy*?"

Eva shook her head.

"Me neither. It was top of the queue when my husband died. Moscow 9."

Eva just watched. The old woman was talking more to herself now, fiddling her thumbs, staring at the ground as a waterfall poured off the brim of her hat.

"I couldn't go back. They sealed my flat, and I had nowhere else to go. My sister wouldn't see me, my parents wouldn't answer the phone. They may have been dead already. I'm not sure. It's always hard to tell."

Another minute passed with just the sound of the rain, and when Eva decided it was time to move on, the woman looked up at her directly.

"Are you good at farming?"

"Sorry?"

"Do you know anything about growing food? Keeping animals?"

"No. No, sorry, I don't."

The woman nodded, looked back to the ground.

"I live in the barn, way back there. The farmhouse is sealed. Tape all over. No idea why. I won't go in. But the barn is nice. I… I thought it was a waste of land, you know? All this land, and no one alive to use it? Such a shame. I just… I'm not very good at growing things. I need some help."

Eva looked back, saw nothing in the darkness. No farmhouse, no barn, no crops.

"I'm going to stay with my mother. She's got a place in the city," Eva said, and the woman nodded as if she'd expected it.

"That's good. That's very good," she muttered, turning around in a circle, then settling back where she'd been. "Well then, I won't keep you. Good luck in there. Good luck indeed."

Eva nodded again, then started back towards the city. When the woman's lamp was no longer helping light her way, she heard a coarse cry:

"Oh! And if you find any books on farming, bring them out for me! I'll make us tea!"

Eva didn't turn to reply. She just kept walking into the cold.

SKIPTON HOUSE, LONDON, ENGLAND
NOVEMBER 27

William Carey stubbed his toe on a concrete barrier, and his coffee promptly dumped itself all over the sidewalk. It took him a moment or two to fully process what he'd done, by which point the hot liquid was well on its way to searing his hand, which made him throw it away in a hurry, cursing quietly under his breath.

"'Morning, Mr Carey," said a patrolman, tight rubber mask hiding a warm smile. "Trouble with your beverage, sir?"

Carey smiled pathetically, shrugged.

"I seem to lose them daily, don't I, Claude?"

"That you do, sir."

Carey wiped his trousers off with his free hand, his leather briefcase barely counterbalancing the effort. He stood up, sighed loudly, and pushed his wire-rimmed glasses up his nose. Luckily, there was no one else in the area to see his disaster.

Somewhere off in the distance, a lone motorbike zipped down another empty street, piercing the morning quiet and sending a storm of pigeons off the rooftops all around Skipton House.

"One day I'll make it to my desk without tripping over things."

Claude shrugged, then caught sight of a young woman in a grey skirt and a yellow wrap-around mask on her way to work. She ably flashed him an ID badge as she passed, and took no notice of Carey at all. The two men watched her card-swipe her way through the front doors and disappear inside.

Carey's coffee-soaked clothes were starting to give him a chill. He wiped at them some more.

"It's a waste of a good drink, is what it is," he grumbled.

"You'd have to dump it out at the first checkpoint anyway, sir," Claude said, checking down the street this way and that, like he was waiting to get on with more important business.

"No. Really?"

"Yes sir. No outside substances past checkpoint A."

"Oh dear. I… I guess I never got far enough to find out about that rule."

"Yes sir."

Carey began staring at the ground, embarrassed, started shifting the briefcase to his other hand and back. He refused to meet Claude's eyes, though Claude wasn't paying attention anyway.

"Well, have a good day, then!" Carey said with a deflated kind of cheer.

"And you, sir."

Carey hopped onto the street, crossed over to the other side, and caught sight of himself in the polished brass of the 'Containment Office' sign: he looked like a fool, and he wanted desperately to go home.

*   *   *

The coffee machine at Skipton House was deep inside the building, in a hallway where the lights barely functioned and stacks of boxes overflowed dot-matrix pages all over the floor. A patchwork system of notices on the wall instructed employees how *not* to brew coffee, complete with a warning that two scoops of the Colombian Dark from the mini-fridge on the left might very well constitute a biohazard.

Carey kept his briefcase perched between two fingers on each hand, waiting patiently while the 'quick brew' light died a meandering death.

The fluorescent bars above him, which had been no brighter than a candle to start, gave out midway through the process, leaving Carey in utter darkness for a few minutes while he tried to tap it back to life with the heel of his shoe. A woman with a black skirt and a white cotton mask stared uncertainly as the light came back on, him standing there on his toes, his worn leather loafer in his fingertips, madly swatting at the ceiling.

After a moment of awkward silence, he stepped aside so she could pass.

His coffee still wasn't done.

Down the hall, in the great sea of cubicles that made up the first floor of the Client Service Department, he heard the chatter of a few dozen workers speaking in calm, soothing tones to the panicked masses.

"No sir," said one woman, her northern accent cutting through the rest. "we have not absorbed the Immigration Office. You still need to clear things with them before filing papers with us. No, no sir, I won't be able to transfer your file. They gather rather different information there. Did you... oh you *have*? And they still told you to... Right, let me save you some time, then. You're going to have to fill out a BCO-193 form and mail it in to our Liverpool branch, and they'll... yes, that's right, four months. I wish I could, sir, but as you can imagine, there's a substantial backlog of late..."

The coffee machine beeped gently, bringing Carey back to the task at hand. He picked up his cup and turned round, carefully navigating the crowded hallways to his office in the Corporate Accountability (Foreign Affairs) section. Off to his left spread a large room filled haphazardly with desks, stacked thick with wires, papers and dossiers.

Each of the thirty-odd employees there looked up to him as he came through, nodding respectfully and muttering their 'Good morning, Inspector's in a way that was not entirely convincing.

Carey tried waving to them, but the motion spilt coffee on his hand. His eyes twitched at the heat, and he smiled weakly and darted into his office.

He set the cup down on his desk, sloshing even more around, sucking the drops of coffee off his hand, then clasped it tightly and tried to contain himself.

His flailing was interrupted by a sharp knock at the door that sent him scrambling for tissues, scrap paper, anything to soak up the mess. He got things reasonably tidy, leaned back in his chair, faking an expression that only half-resembled authority.

"Come in," he called, picking up a pen and searching his desk for a paper to be writing on, though all such papers were now in the trash.

"Excuse me, sir," said a woman, leaning in the cracked-open door. "I wish this could wait. We seem to have a very serious problem on our hands, and we need your help."

"What kind of problem?" Carey squeaked, motioning her to come in.

She slipped into the room, and Carey immediately remembered her name: Janice. She was possibly the most gorgeous subordinate in the entire government. Carey knew her name thanks to the ID tag she wore on her too-tight sweaters, which oddly reminded him of the actress in the sexual harassment video he'd been shown as part of orientation.

"It's something we caught last night," she said, sitting cautiously across from him. "It might be nothing, but—"

"But then you wouldn't be in here with that look on your face," Carey interrupted, and Janice's expression went as blank as she could manage.

"Quite right," she conceded. "It's urgent."

"Where's that David fellow? He's your manager, isn't he? Shouldn't he be here too? I mean, not that I mind. I'm sure you're capable."

Janice's eyebrow twitched.

"I'm sorry, sir, didn't you hear? David had a cough last night. He's under house arrest till spring."

"*Spring*?" Carey gasped. "For a cough? What do we do here in flu season?"

"Honestly, sir, we lose half the workforce through the winter. I only clocked six months of time last year. The Department takes it very seriously."

Carey nodded uncertainly.

"Well then," he said. "Lacking David, I guess *you'll* have to walk me through this."

"My pleasure, sir," she said, handing him a block of pages from deep inside the stack of folders. He scanned it quickly to try and gather context, but got nowhere. It was filled with columns of numbers and codes, none of which made sense to him. All he recognized was the subject line at the top.

"Zemus Pharmaceuticals," he said. "Are we... I wasn't aware Zemus used foreign workers."

"Oh, they don't, sir," Janice said. "This was sent to us by Revenue, actually. A bit outside our usual scope. They had some questions and thought we should take a look."

"Oh, I see," Carey said, nodding broadly. "Co-operation among the branches of government. Good to see." He flipped to the second page, then the third, frowned. "I'm still not following, I think," he said.

Janice's face lit up, and she quickly dashed round the desk, her perfume strong. She pointed to the first of the highlighted entries on the second page, following the line across with her pen, resting on the code 'EAB', in the 'Testing/Approval' column.

"These are the additions to the next Zemus booster shot, due for manufacture in December," she said. "You see there are nearly twenty cases of Executive Approval Bypass already. Revenue was wondering if that's normal."

"And... um... is it?" Carey smiled nervously.

Janice pointed to one of the other entries, its 'Testing/Approval' column full of letter codes.

"The average patch in a booster release is based on a live virus," she said. "Zemus researchers crack a strain and put it into the testing process, working their way along until the vaccine is proven to be safe for general consumption."

"Ah," sighed Carey. "so they're bypassing all the testing. Um. Executively."

"They have a process built specifically to let them bypass testing," Janice said, her eyes twinkling as she avoided looking at him. "It's supposed to be used when they make a deal with another certified British company, so they can pass their treatments back and forth without reinvesting in the testing that's supposedly taken place. It saves time and money, and keeps all boosters as up-to-date as possible."

Carey nodded.

"I'm following," he said. "But... er... why is this a problem, exactly?"

Janice pointed to one of the highlighted entries, tapped it gravely.

"None of these strains have been identified within Britain," she said. "They're all continental."

"Right!" he said. "Continental is certainly no good. So should we... should I assign someone to start the paperwork on... I mean... discipline or somesuch? Is that what we'd do here?"

Janice shook her head, and it was increasingly obvious to both who was better suited for the chair Carey now occupied. She closed the folder, crouched next to his chair, spoke in a near-whisper.

"This needs careful handling, sir," she said. "I'd like permission to bring it to the Director, if you don't mind."

"The *Director?*" Carey gasped. "Janice, listen, I've been here almost a month and I've only met the man once. I don't think we should be... you know... bothering him about some *import violations.*"

"Sir, Zemus *hasn't been* importing anything," she whispered urgently. "There would be stacks of paperwork as tall as this room for each one of these entries. There would be hundreds of man hours dedicated to confirming them. And more importantly, there would be some evidence that there are actually Continental companies *behind* each of these cures in the first place. We've looked, and there aren't any. Half of the strains here aren't even registered with EU Health."

"Maybe they're from the Chinese…?" Carey offered meekly.

"The Chinese use a whole other system. They go through the government first, trickle down to the corporations at the end of testing. And anyway, Zemus puts so much effort into dodging Chinese vaccines, it's highly unlikely they'd suddenly start adopting them under the table like this.

"No sir, these bypasses are being implemented blindly. There's a concerted effort here to add new elements to the Zemus boosters in such a way as to dodge the usual inspections… and we have *no idea* what's actually in them. It's not a matter of regulations. This is true public safety on the line."

"Oh," said Carey meekly. "All right then, *we'll* go see the Director straight away. And you'll do the talking."

Janice smiled, stood up and almost immediately changed her composure: she stood taller, held her face more sharply, reeked of middle management.

"Just… what are you planning to say?" Carey asked, and she stared down at him with intense focus, her jaw set.

"I'm going to explain that someone could very well be using Zemus' booster shot project to distribute viruses globally. And unchecked."

It was midday before Eva saw the peak of the church on Nepomucká, and it took another hour before it looked anything like the photo she'd carried in her wallet all these years.

Even when she got the angle right, the differences were striking. The sky today was a light grey rather than bright and blue, and Eva looked nothing like her younger self, wearing a University of Paris t-shirt, plump, with a hearty smile. The photo was creased and faded, looked worse for wear; but not as bad as Eva.

She rounded the corner to Píseckého, past a row of houses she only half-remembered, and paced quickly down to #1 with the kind of stiff-moving determination that only comes from a fear of the elements.

Sometime around dawn the weather had changed from a kind of rainy-cold to a winter-cold, giving Eva's exposed skin a sharp, prickling sensation that she knew would feel like a blazing fire the second she got warm. *If* she got warm. The last of the mud had washed off her some time ago, but it took with it whatever insulation she might have had.

She leapt up the building stairs and pushed on the front door. It swung open eagerly, and Eva felt a tiny pocket of warm air blow past her, out into the rain. Beyond the threshold, she found it was colder inside than outside, so she dashed up the stairs to the third floor, down the hall to #303, and knocked with a reddened hand.

No answer. She tried again, as a shiver shot up her spine, eating away any lingering patience. She made a fist and pounded on the door, her teeth rattling audibly.

"She isn't home, dear," said an old woman from next door. She was peeking out of her apartment, shawl pulled around her short, thick frame. She wore glasses nearly a third the size of her face, yet her eyes were squinted like she couldn't see.

Eva tried to control her breathing so she could speak clearly, but had little luck.

"How long has she been gone?" she called out feebly.

The woman cocked her head a bit, came out into the hall with a cracked fibreglass cane and wobbled towards Eva.

"I wouldn't know, dear. I don't like to snoop. But I remember that young fellow from this morning was knocking at the door like such a madman, I nearly called the police!" The woman paused a short distance away, inspecting Eva carefully. "You look cold."

Eva closed her eyes, thought of warm places.

"I... I had to walk from... from the train station," she said. "it's raining."

"Poor thing," said the woman. "Here... take my shawl. You don't want to catch a cold in a place like this."

Eva put out a hand, smiled weakly.

"No... no thank you," she said. "Too wet right now. I... I just have to get inside and warm up."

"Inside? Do you know Mrs Kolikov? I didn't know she..." The woman gasped. "Oh my... you're not *Eva*, are you?"

Eva winced at the woman, nodded.

"Oh my dear... I had no idea... in the photos you always look so radiant and..." she trailed off, realizing what she was saying. Eva laughed.

"Been a hard few years," she said.

"For us all," the woman sighed. She reached out her hand, as if waking back into polite society. "I'm Bachida Novacek. I live next door. It's so wonderful to finally meet you."

Eva took the woman's hand with icy fingers, shook gently.

"Hi," she said, then pulled her arm back in a vain attempt to stay warm. Mrs Novacek rubbed Eva's shoulder, the air of a kind grandmother about her.

"You must have been out there a long time to be this wet. Why don't you come to my place and warm up?"

Eva shook her head. "No, really, it's okay. I just really want to get inside. Did my mother leave a key around here, under the mat or s-s-s-something…?"

Eva collapsed against the door as a shiver swarmed over her, and she pressed her head down and shut her eyes tight, trying to ride it out. But before long the weight of the past few days slammed into her, and she started sobbing uncontrollably, one hand covering her eyes, the other desperately trying to twist the doorknob.

A warm hand rubbed her back, up and down, and she felt a comforting nudge under her arm.

"Come along, dear," the old woman said. "let's get you fixed up."

Eva stumbled, head sunk low, into the humid, homey embrace of Mrs Novacek's living room. She was guided down onto a too-soft sofa, between a pair of ochre-and-mustard knitted pillows, a warm blanket wrapped over her shoulders. It took her a full minute to control her crying.

"I'm all wet," she said, keeping her eyes to the ground.

"Things dry," Mrs Novacek said, digging under a pile of blankets, hunting for the second of a pair of thick furry slippers. "When did you eat last?"

"I can't eat now. Too cold."

"Tea, then," and she shuffled off into the kitchen, cane creaking with each step.

The living room was packed, but tidy. There were countless photo frames lining every available surface, showing a full range from glossy colour to dusty black-and-white. There were a handful of frames lined with wilted flowers, set aside from the rest, a single scented candle burning before them.

Above the fireplace was a large painting, done in oils, from Place de l'Alma in Paris, looking over the Seine. The sky was a rusty colour, not the merciless, bright orange that came in more recent days. Eva knew the image intimately.

"You have one of my paintings?" she called out.

"Your mother gave it to me. She's very proud of you, dear. It's not every child who's so gifted in the arts! My late sister had two of your paintings in her dining room, she loved them so much. When they unseal the house, I'll see if I can't spirit them away."

"How bad is it here?" Eva asked. "News is hard to come by on the outside."

"The Old Town Square closed last month. The vandals had run wild for too long. It was necessary, but it... it took the spark out of us. The radio said the old clock's keeper has fallen ill. His son, too. Only the daughter seems safe, and who knows for how long? Sometimes you wonder... when is it too much? When do we stop being who we are?"

"I hope it takes more than that," Eva said.

"But it can't be as bad as where you've been," the old woman replied. "Paris must have been terrible. I know your mother has been worried sick about you."

"I know," Eva said, lowering her head, "I know. I made a mess of things."

"Why did you stay out for so long, dear? Excuse me for saying, but why didn't you come back home, come back and take care of your mama?"

Eva shook her head, bottom lip trembling.

"You know that feeling you get, riding a bike down a steep hill? You know it could go so wrong for you... it *should* go wrong... but you still hope you'll be okay? You'll survive unscathed?"

Eva ran her fingers through her hair, gripped her head, tried to control the shivering. All the shivering.

"I guess I thought I could survive the trip," she said.

"You *did* survive, dear," said Mrs Novacek as she paced back into the room, a pair of tea cups rattling on their saucers. She handed one to Eva, who took it with trembling hands. The warmth made her fingers prickle, but it was a good pain to be feeling, after all that cold.

"Drink slowly," Mrs Novacek said, lowering herself into a chair across from Eva. "You've got a lot of cold to undo, and it will take a while."

"Thanks," Eva said, sipping the camomile quietly. Her host blew into her own cup and looked out the window.

"It's colder this year than it has been since I was a girl," she said, grim. "They say it never snows in Prague until February, but I think this year is different. There was no autumn at all. A parched summer to a bitter winter."

"It's like that everywhere," said Eva. "They say it's the lack of cars on the roads, messing up the ozone layer. Or... or the other way around, maybe."

"They say a lot of things," harumphed the woman.

Eva looked out the sliding glass door, into the pale water-colour sky over the city. A few browned leaves, untouched by the rain, blew across the balcony to the left, and under the divider to—

"That's it!" she gasped, and quickly put her tea down on the coffee table. Keeping the blankets wrapped tight around her, she scurried to the balcony, and leaned over the edge, peering down the row. A smile grew on her face, and she looked back at the confused Mrs Novacek.

"My mother never locks the balcony door!" she exclaimed, just before the cold air brought her shiver back full-force. "If I can swing around this partition, I can get in through the back!"

Mrs Novacek observed the situation through her thick glasses.

"I think you ought to wait for her to get home," she said, but Eva had already handed her back her blanket, and was climbing up on the balcony ledge, holding the partition tightly with reddened fingers.

She glanced down below herself as she straddled the two sides, as the wind bit her re-exposed skin. There were gardening tools down there: a rake, push lawn mower and an assortment of pruning shears, half-buried by a scattershot pile of leaves. Three storeys down. Eva's sneakers slid slightly on the ledge.

She moved herself enough to be able to swing around the rest of the way in a quick motion, and she landed on her mother's balcony and toppled to the ground.

"Eva! Eva, dear, are you all right?" cried Mrs Novacek from the other side.

Eva got up awkwardly, brushed the grime and dirt off her knees, and gave the sliding glass door a little nudge. It slid open easily.

"I'm great, Mrs Novacek. No trouble at all. I just…"

Her voice trailed off into nothing as she looked into the apartment, and saw the blood splatter on the kitchen wall.

"Hold on a second," Eva called to Mrs Novacek, and walked into the apartment with careful, silent feet.

It was cold inside, and dry, like the inverse of Mrs Novacek's place. The walls were stark and bare; the glass-topped coffee table had a solid layer of dust to it. At the division between the living room and the kitchen, Eva noticed the glistening remnants of a pair of wine glasses, the white carpet stained burgundy, next to a dried pool on the tile floor.

A knife lay on its side on a cutting board, a rotting carrot half-chopped, alone on the counter. Eva rounded it without breathing, her eyes locked on the blood sprayed on the far wall, dripping down along the baseboards into an area she couldn't — and didn't *want to* — see.

After a last, hesitant step, she saw a thick pool of blood, glassy almost, rubbed about on the clean tile floor. But no body. Nothing at all, as if someone had bled all that, standing up, and left only a fading set of footprints to the front door and beyond.

Eva touched the toe of her shoe to the pool of blood. It stuck slightly, but not much. She rubbed it off on the ground next to her, looked around anxiously.

"Mama?" she called out into the flat. A sharp echo repeated it.

She carefully padded down the hallway to her mother's bedroom on the right, peered in cautiously. She held her breath and listened for a sound for any sign of life. She reached in, flipped on the lights, and saw nothing but more of the same sterile blankness as the rest of the place. The bed was made up the way it always was.

Further down in the bathroom, Eva instinctively switched on the heat as she entered the room. The thermostat clicked quietly as the baseboard heaters woke from a yearlong slumber, sending the smell of hot metal into the air.

Aside from the medicine cabinet being half-open, there was nothing of note. The expired prescription bottles were still neatly arranged, labels out. The shower mat drooped neatly from the edge of the bathtub.

The last room at the end of the hall had been Eva's, briefly. But when she opened it, she found none of her old things. Instead, there was a heavy oak desk, covered with piles upon piles of papers, folders and random stationery. A laptop screen peered through the mess, its base buried beneath a sea of physical things. A pair of hulking bookshelves overflowed with medical journals, binders of reports and university textbooks Eva had never seen.

The floor, too, was littered with crumpled papers, notes and sketches. Molecules, DNA strands without notation, coded scribblings in her mother's handwriting. A red pen cracked under her foot as she made her way across the room, to the small end-table that held a thick cardboard box. There was a smear of blood on the side, the bottom corner badly bashed in, crumpled.

Inside, she found a dozen smaller boxes, about the size of a can of soda, with blue-and-white labels in Finnish, French and Russian. Eva turned one and read the Russian:

GENESIS INCUBATOR

REFILL CAPSULE

220MG (55MG X 4)

She put the package down and stepped back, looking around. She dashed back to the kitchen, grabbed the phone off the wall, and turned it on.

Her finger hovering over the keypad, Eva listened to the dial tone. She looked at the drying blood on the ground, saw her passport peeking out of her jacket pocket, stained with mud. The empty room sucked the warmth out of her.

She turned off the phone and left it on the counter.

Just then, a knock at the door sent Eva back into the wall. She stayed there, quiet, listening. After a short pause, there was another knock, quick and agitated, and Eva carefully slid towards the door, her thumping heart making it hard to concentrate on whatever sounds she could discern from out in the hall.

She found her voice, squeaky with fear.

"Hello?" she called to the locked-and-chained door.

"Eva?" asked Mrs Novacek anxiously, and Eva exhaled so deeply she nearly fainted. She undid the chain, threw the lock and opened the door enough to peek out.

"Hi, Mrs Novacek," she said, trying to sound as calm and nonchalant as she could.

"Oh, you made it! I was worried! You sounded as if something was wrong!"

Eva bit her lip.

"Oh, I… I just thought the oven was left on. Optical illusion. My eyeballs are probably frozen."

She faked a smile, but the half-blind old woman didn't notice. She just rubbed Eva's arm kindly, patted her gently.

"You *look* frozen, too. Go take a warm bath, dear, and stay here until your mama gets home. She'll be so happy to see you."

As Eva shut the door, she looked around the desolate room, cold and empty and alien, and shivered again.

"Until she gets home," she repeated.

*   *   *

Lean arms wrapped round Eva, warmer than the bath water, and she turned her head back and kissed a rough, unshaven chin, eyes closed. Past the scented oils, she smelled him. Familiar. She felt breath on her neck, so at peace, and slowly drifted lower in the water, but he held her tight, and she smiled.

"Rhodri," she moaned.

Then she choked on cold water.

She sat up suddenly, her arms locking tightly on the edges for support. She was alone in the room, in the bath especially. The water was frigid. She sat there a moment, not moving, till things stopped rippling around her.

She glanced to the side, out into the empty hallway.

"Stay out of my head," she said to no one present.

*   *   *

She awoke some time in the night feeling winded, like she'd been running for hours, but unable to sleep any more. It took all her willpower to down a foil-wrapped package of 'Safe Food' she'd found stashed in the closet. The wrapper boasted 'Czech Government Certified', which made Eva smile.

She spent half an hour on her mother's sofa, wrapped in two fleece blankets, staring away from the TV at the empty fireplace. There was wood to the side, a lighter too, but she just watched the dark hole instead. The baseboard heaters went *click click click click* as they came back to life, trying to keep the November air at bay.

She was peripherally aware of the programme guide appearing on the screen, informing her of all the great classics that would be coming up on Prague's #1 station. The easy-listening music made her eyelids heavy, and she swayed a bit, but stayed awake.

The news came on, and she found herself watching, though her head didn't turn.

"We are following a developing story at this hour," said the newscaster, a pristine blonde whose cheeks still had the marks from the edge of a filter mask. "A six-year-old boy thought to be lost in the east-end housing projects last week has been found, and re-united with his grandparents following an exhaustive search by local police.

The boy, who cannot be named due to patient confidentiality laws, was last seen by neighbours nearly eight days ago. According to sources, he has survived on breakfast cereal in the attic of a neighbouring building since disappearing."

Eva reluctantly turned her head to the screen as the boy's grandfather carried a blanket-wrapped child past the news camera.

"It's a miracle we have him back," said the old man, tears in his eyes. "It must have been so hard for him, alone, out in this weather, especially after his mother—"

"That's all for questions," interrupted a police spokesman, hand across the lens, pushing the cameraman away. "Give them some privacy. Go on."

Eva turned off the TV, threw the remote across the room. She took a long, slow breath. The air was still cold.

She rummaged through her mother's drawers until she came out with another layer of sweaters, long underwear and socks, and found the biggest, heaviest boots she could to throw on her icy feet. She stomped around the living room a bit to get her blood flowing again, and turned all the thermostats up as high as they'd go.

A knock at the door gave her a start, but also something to do. She sprinted over, undid the chain and the lock.

"Thank god you're here, Mrs Novacek, I was…"

But it wasn't Mrs Novacek at the door. A heavy gloved hand grabbed the front of her shirt and yanked her off balance.

"*There* you are, Ms Kolikov," said a woman in a heavy winter coat, holding a police badge over her thickset partner's shoulder. "We were wondering when you'd show up."

NOVEMBER 28

Dr Fanta Anouma adjusted the stethoscope on a frail, pocked arm, and checked her watch with a frown. A drip of sweat trickled down her ebony skin, and she brushed it with her free arm, careful not to touch her sterile gloves. The sound of the heaters all around the room was hard to overcome; she strained to hear, wrinkling her brow with concentration.

"Know what you're doing?" asked Mr Vecera, his voice raspy and coarse.

"Shh," Anouma scolded. "or I'll have to start over."

Mr Vecera smiled at her, his patchy white beard a sharp accent to the gaps in his teeth, brown and black. His hospital gown hung on him loosely, dried blood down the front. An IV hung behind him, dripping saline slowly.

Anouma flung the stethoscope round her neck, jotted on his chart with a too-short pencil. She scratched underneath her surgeon's mask with the bunched-up wrist of her glove, sighing.

"Bad news?" Mr Vecera asked, half-serious.

"No worse than before," Anouma replied. "continuing this way, you will live forever."

Mr Vecera laughed loudly, and two of the patients nearest him grunted and tried to roll themselves so they'd be facing away from him. He patted Anouma's hand kindly.

"You lie badly," he said. "but thank you."

Anouma didn't answer, kept her expression the same. She looked down at his chart, and he squeezed her hand to get her attention back.

"Miss home?" he asked sincerely.

Anouma shrugged.

"I am liking it here," she said.

"Your language is better. Give it another month and we won't even know you're not Czech."

Anouma laughed this time, patted his arm and put his chart back at the end of his bed.

"What's it like where you come from?" he asked her.

"The place I lived in Côte d'Ivoire, they call it the hot country," she said, her eyes alive, remembering. "We in the north are teased for poor constitution, how we cannot survive in but a peaceful, sunny clime. But you know, after all these years up here, in your city, Mr Vecera… well, my friends in the south, near the ocean, they have no idea what cold really is. Having a nice breeze off the water is nothing like a day such as today."

"Ah! So you like it here, then?"

She smiled, her mask tipping to the side.

"How could I not like a place that gives me patients like you."

He beamed happily, waved her off with a shaky hand.

"I'm glad you've stayed with us, doctor," he said. "You're tougher than those southerners could ever hope to be."

"Thank you," she said with a nod. "I will be back to check you again. Soon." She pulled the curtain round his bed back, letting in the full sound and sight of four hundred sick and dying patients.

They were grouped and partitioned by type and severity of disease, and though there were signs up to help pinpoint whichever strain you were after, anyone with a passing familiarity of modern plagues could get their bearings at a glance by the particular skin tones or the stains on the bed sheets. From the middle of the floor, the sounds of different species of moans swept past Anouma as she stood alone, the tallest thing in the rows of beds.

She felt a calm breeze blow her hair across her forehead, and for a moment she swayed, smiling at the sensation, calming, quiet. But then her eyes opened and she stared up at the ceiling, at the large fans up there, swirling slowly, picking up speed, and her breath left her.

She turned quickly to the far end of the room, down by the generators, and saw a nurse playing with a long row of switches, trying to see which one powered the old X-ray machine. Anouma started to call out, but clipped herself off, clenched her fists and made a quickly dash to the nurse.

She slammed all the switches down, with a furious hand, grabbed the nurse by the collar.

"What do you think you are doing?" she hissed.

"I can't figure which one turns on the—"

"Take a look at the ceilings!" Anouma whispered. "You've been running the fans! How long have you been at the switches?"

"I… I don't know," fumbled the nurse. "A minute? Maybe more?"

Anouma shook her head, squeezed back a head ache.

"Air flow *must* be restricted in this room," she said. "Our partitioning is not good enough to stop cross-contamination."

"I know, I—"

"You must be more careful," Anouma said, her tone softening. "If Dr Bastien noticed this, you would be—"

"Help!" came the call from the old foyer, across the sea of white linen. Anouma glanced back, then abandoned her warning and started running, stethoscope slung into her ears in mid-stride. Across the hall, Dr Bastien was running too, tearing his gloves off urgently.

A man in a work suit was leaning against the wall, a small child in his arms, wrapped in a blanket and drenched with rain. The man was panting, wheezy breaths, and looked like he'd been crying. The girl coughed loudly, and he nearly dropped her onto the ground.

"Help her... I don't know what's wrong..." he gasped, then collapsed down in a heap, barely keeping her frail body from slamming into the floor. Anouma slipped on a new pair of gloves, crouched down and pulled the blanket away from the girl's face. It stuck, glued with dried pus to the face, and the girl cried out, then coughed again... a terrible, hacking cough.

"Kiev-5," Bastien muttered grimly from behind, blasting his stethoscope with disinfectant and pushing it against the girl's pocked chest. "How long has she been sick?" he asked the man.

"I... I think three days," he muttered, his eyes rolling back in his head.

"Catch him," Bastien said, snatching the girl as Anouma gently lowered the father's head to the ground. She pried open his jacket and shirt, saw the smallest of blisters on his chest.

"Cover his face with a mask and help me get the girl outside," Bastien said, pushing his white hair from his eyes.

"Outside?"

"We need open air," he said sternly.

"She needs a bed!" Anouma whispered urgently. Bastien stared at her seriously, spoke in hushed French, darting quick glances back to the sick room.

"Kiev-5 is airborne at this stage. Half the people in this room would die tonight if they caught it. Even with the fans off, we cannot take that chance."

"She will die out there," Anouma replied, unfazed.

"She'll die in here too. Don't let her take the rest with her."

A loud cry came from inside the room, weak but hysterical.

"I can't die!" a woman cried in French. "I can't die here!"

"Shit," Bastien muttered, then called out to her: "If you say one word of Czech about this to anyone, I'll make this girl your bed mate, do you understand me?"

There was a long silence.

"Y-y-yes," came the reply.

Bastien nodded to Anouma.

"Grab the ultrasound and meet me on the steps."

Anouma quickly draped a blanket over the girl's father, a mask securely over his face, and ran back into the treatment room, to the cupboards near the crash station, and pulled a small, stained ultrasound out. She pushed the battery check as she ran, slowed when she saw it had half power. She stopped by the drawers at the door, rummaged around for some gel and a spare battery. All she found was a half-used bottle and an empty battery package.

Bastien had the girl on her back on the steps to the hospital, checking her airway. He motioned for the ultrasound, and Anouma handed it over, squirted gel on the girl's stomach, the greenish colour mixing with thick yellow. Bastien pushed the sensor down, and she lurched up, gasping.

"Hold her," he commanded, squinting at the screen.

Anouma angled down on the girl's shoulders, watching the poor swollen eyes twitching in a pained sleep. She looked away, to the monitor, squinted at it, then glanced at where Bastien was pointing.

"Her liver…" she said tentatively.

"Kidneys too," he muttered. "Her lungs are going now."

"Should we…?"

"No," he said, snapping the machine off, wiping it clean. "once the liver's gone, so is the patient. Her father got her here too late."

Anouma blinked, looked down at the beautiful blonde hair round the distorted face, brushed it with a gloved hand. When she looked back up, Bastien was preparing a shot.

"What is…"

"For the pain," he said, pushing it through her veins. "whatever good it might do her."

Anouma nodded, watched the girl calm suddenly, her breathing watery and slow. Bastien handed the ultrasound over, checking the rain that was blowing onto their temporary operating room.

"Get that inside," he said. "we'll have to move her to the back until it's over."

Anouma nodded, pushed the heavy wooden doors in and paced back to the crash station, setting the machine atop the counter absent-mindedly.

"Are we dying?" asked the lone voice, in French, nervously.

Anouma turned back to the room, curtains and beds and drip bags everywhere, and had no idea whose voice it was.

"You are fine," she lied. "The girl was fine. It was just a cold, nothing more."

No one answered.

As she made her way to the front, she heard the sound of Dr Bastien shouting. She ran to the door, pushed into the cold, wet air, and saw the old man yelling into the rain. There, in the middle of the ambulance bay, was a dark figure wrapped tight in leather and metal, and Anouma gasped.

A Healer.

"You will not pass this door!" Bastien growled. "Go back east, you monster!"

The Healer carefully raised a hand and tapped his right temple with a finger. Anouma glanced over as Bastien mirrored the action, a faded tattoo etched on his face, four short bars. He touched them gingerly, as if they stung.

"Yes, I remember," Bastien spat. "And it won't be repeated! This is my redemption! Go kill somewhere else!"

Bastien picked up the girl with some effort, glanced over at Anouma.

"I'll be in the back. Lock the doors behind us."

"But—" she started.

"Do it, Fanta," he grunted. "He cannot be allowed inside."

She nodded solemnly, opened the door for the old man, then crept in herself, locking the dead bolt in the middle of the panelling. The doors were thick and old, but something about the seal said they couldn't *really* be closed against someone who wanted in badly enough. She nervously glanced outside, through the tall window in the door.

The bay was empty. Rain poured freely down, rushing off the faded 'Ambulance' sign like a waterfall, the backed-up drain in the centre of the pavement unable to keep up with demand. The thing had gone. She leaned closer, trying to see around the corner—

A mask shot into view, right against the window, meeting her gaze, and she yelped. Warm, processed breath hissed out of the ventilation ducts by his neck, fogging the glass in irregular bursts. Anouma recoiled, but was too scared to run.

The Healer stared at her dispassionately, then looked over, carefully and deliberately, to the dead bolt. Then he looked at her again. She shivered, shook her head 'no'. She darted her eyes over, checked that she had really locked it.

There was no movement for some time.

He stepped back one pace, not breaking eye contact, and without warning, slammed his hand against the glass. She jumped back in shock, pushed a fist against the lock, held her breath.

He was taping a paper to the window, in short, almost mechanical motions. She backed up further from the door, bumping into a gurney left on the far wall, draped with sheets to cover the bloodstains the doctors had been unable to clean off. She gripped the cold metal bars for support.

Once the paper was fully fastened, the Healer turned and began walking away without a pause; down the steps, through the growing puddle, past the waterfall sign, and around the corner. Anouma waited another minute or two before moving forward, checking more closely.

She exhaled for the first time in what seemed like hours, and pressed her forehead against the door, trying to get back her nerves.

"He is gone," she said to herself. "You did fine. You did fine."

She looked up, saw the poster he'd left. An information sheet in French, in clear and clinical grammar: symptoms of a strain called 'LS-411'. How to diagnose it. How *not* to treat it. It was always fatal. She lightly touched her fingers against the window, her mouth falling open, and gasped at the photo of the lesions to take care for.

She ran to the stairwell without a word.

* * *

Franz stripped the plastic wrap from a stale hospital sandwich at the bottom of a dark green dumpster, trembling hands nearly losing the cheese and ham. He shoved it into his mouth, chewing furiously, and licked off his grimy fingers, darting nervous glances out past the bags above him.

"Franz!" hissed Luka, half-peering over the edge inside.

"Still nothing!" Franz replied, trying to conceal his chewing. "Looking!"

Luka lifted his head a bit higher, leaned over the edge, but kept his eyes elsewhere.

"Not that," he whispered urgently. "You have to see this."

Franz frowned, got to his feet, and stood on a crushed plastic bin for a better view. Out in the clearing, slowly pacing around the west side of Building A was something he'd never seen before.

"A Healer?" Luka asked cautiously.

"Looks like it," said Franz. "Quick, help me out."

He landed on the wet pavement, pulling his worn hood over his hair against the rain, and joined his friend back behind the dumpster, out of sight, as the figure walked past. They watched him from the dank shadows, white eyes wide in fear, or anger.

"Come on," Franz nudged, and they followed, hands in pockets, as if on a casual stroll.

The Healer turned a corner, into an alley, and the two of them paused at the entrance, looked around. The street was deserted. Behind them, the forest was awash in orange leaves dissolving in the rain. Franz checked a pile of garbage, found a heavy wood plank and an old rusted pipe in the mix. He handed the wood to Luka, motioned to head in.

The Healer was staring at an open window on the third floor, its fire escape too high to reach. He ran his finger along the handleless metal door before him, the only break in the ominous concrete structure. He backed away carefully, then he lowered his head, paused, and turned around to see Franz and Luka, inching toward him, closing in on their prey.

"Fuckin' killer," Franz spat, swinging the pipe from side to side. "Come to finish what you started, eh?"

He lashed out with the pipe at a distance, and the Healer stepped back, held his hands up, cautiously, as if he were asking for peace. Still, no words. No expression to read.

"Not so smug, are ya?" Luka said, circling the Healer menacingly. "Couldn't kill us *all* with your germs, so now y'have to fight like a man!"

"He's not a man," Franz sneered. "A man has a soul. This is a baby-killer!"

Luka's eyes started to water, his face twisting, and Franz gaped at the sight. Luka wiped his eyes with his sleeve furiously, choking back tears, and his face turned red as anger rushed through him.

"My son!" he screamed, and charged, swinging the board straight at the Healer's head. Its hand moved fast, bracing up to deflect the blow, and the board snapped in two. The loose side flew against the wall in a shower of splinters. Luka skidded straight into the Healer, who caught him by the throat with the other metallic hand, held him tight.

Luka's passion drained fast, so close to the mask, and he gasped for desperate breaths, dropping the rest of the board at his feet.

The Healer spoke in a raspy, processed voice. Words neither of them understood. Tears kept running down Luka's cheeks, but he never stopped staring into the empty goggles.

Then, the Healer cocked his head slightly, and ducked out of the way as Franz's pipe swung past. It missed him, smashed into the side of Luka's face, a loud crunch echoing out. The Healer dropped the body and stepped aside, facing his next opponent.

Franz gasped at the sight of his friend in a pool of blood, his pipe smeared red too. He re-gripped the metal, inhaled slowly, letting his fury boil over.

"You fucking murderer!" he screamed, and charged again, swinging madly. The Healer side-stepped the attack, grabbed the pipe and twisted. Franz felt his wrist pop, and he lost his grip, his footing. A rough hand grabbed the back of his coat, shoving him into the hospital wall. He stumbled back, nose bleeding, then was dragged by his hair, crying out in pain.

The Healer held the pipe up as if to strike, but then tossed it away, across the alley, never taking his gaze of Franz. He spoke, again in a tongue Franz didn't understand.

"Fuck you," Franz said through the blood and pain. "Fuck you and fuck your Chinese whore mother."

No reaction. Franz spat blood onto the mask.

Then he noticed it… the handle of a blade on the belt. A machete. He made a mad grab for it, snatching the tip with his fingers. The hand pulled his hair tighter, and he looked up. The Healer shook his head 'no'. Very slowly. Very solidly.

Rain poured down, running across his battered face, drips pounding into the hand on the blade. He felt the strain of the grip on his hair, but saw no emotion in the mask, and it unnerved him.

He pulled, heard the blade come free, and in a moment of elation, pulled it back to thrust… his face betraying a smile…

But just as quickly, the Healer planted a calculated blow to his chest, felt his ribs crack, and the machete fell from his hand, straight into the enemy's. He desperately gasped for breath, but none came. And then in an instant, he felt a hand on his chin, a quick crack, and then nothing at all.

The Healer carefully lowered the body to the ground, laying the arms across the chest respectfully. He glanced back at Luka, the pool of blood growing and diluting in the rain, running down the slight incline towards the sewers.

A woman screamed hysterically, and he stood quickly, machete ready. She stood at the entrance to the alley, hand to her mouth, her soaked clothes dripping dirty water in streams at her feet. She stumbled back, eyes darting between Franz, Luka and the Healer, terrified.

She yelled for help, called for the police, and ran off, out of view, leaving him alone, isolated. He quickly looked around himself, machete loose in his hand, backed himself into the corner with enough room to fight. He heard the sounds of angry men yelling, of metal and wood and other would-be weapons being pulled out of trash bins. The sounds of an angry mob forming.

"You!" called a French voice from behind, and he turned, saw the metal door, now open. Anouma leaned out carefully, anxiously. "This way! Hurry!" she hissed.

10

The end of the hall was shut off with misty plastic taped to the walls, ceiling and floor. A biohazard sticker was peeling off in the middle. Eva slowed her pace as she approached it, but the cops shoved her forward, then jerked her to a stop at a door to her right. A paper hung over the 'Janitor' sign.

"Interrogation Room B," Eva muttered.

"Someone sneezed in A," the female cop grunted, opening the door to a tiny room, a table improbably wedged inside a closet space. "Lucky you."

Eva was thrown into the chair at the back of the table, landing with a whimper. The two cops sidled around to the far side, sat down casually, and leaned back in silence.

The woman was thickly built, with a strong jaw and short hair, cut in a five-year-too-late style. The man was gruff, large and balding, his brow deep; when he clenched his jaw, it almost changed the shape of his face as the bones clicked into a new arrangement.

"Ms Kolikov," began the woman, not making eye contact. "My name is Inspector Sobotka. This is Inspector Crew."

"You're… you're Foreign Police?" Eva ventured.

Crew chortled, stroked his stubbly chin.

"Why? Not an immigrant, are you?"

Eva met his eyes nervously.

"No…" she answered.

"Good thing. Shouldn't be any immigrants any more, yeah?"

"No, Ms Kolikov," smirked Sobotka. "We're just your average cops, taking care of average business."

Eva watched them watching her, said nothing.

"Of course," mused Crew, "my papa was with the Foreign Police. Must have some of it in my blood, yeah? 'Cause when I saw your file going by, I said to myself: that's someone we ought to have a chat with."

"I thought so too," nodded Sobotka.

"Pff, maybe just common sense then," smirked Crew, leaning forward on the table so it creaked under his immense weight. "We hear you had some trouble on the train."

"It was a big misunderstanding," Eva stammered. "I was just talking to this officer when someone came out of nowhere and beat him up, and…"

"Killed two guards?"

"Really, I had nothing to do with that. I swear."

They stared at her seriously for a moment, then Crew yawned noisily.

"Let's move on. Tell us about Paris."

Eva blinked.

"I… uh… well, I went to school there. University."

"Studying what?" Sobotka queried, clicking a pen open, and flipping through a few papers in a folder.

"Fine arts," Eva replied.

"What about computer science? I have you enrolled in that, but nothing about fine arts. That's pretty strange, now isn't it?"

"I switched majors."

"Interesting. What was your minor? Biology, maybe?"

Eva paused, swallowed slowly.

"No," she said softly.

"I'm sorry, hearing's going; what did you say?" Crew asked, cupping his hand to his ear.

"I didn't study biology," Eva said clearly, then sat up a bit straighter, squinted at them like she was preparing for a storm.

"How long have you been making viruses?" Sobotka asked.

Eva didn't flinch.

"I don't make viruses," she replied. "I'm a painter. I make—"

"Yeah, yeah, yeah," interrupted Crew, waving his hand at her. "and the hitman's not a hitman, he's a plumber. You're not the first to dream up a cover, kid."

"It's not a cover. I don't make viruses. I wouldn't even know where to start."

Crew grunted, stood up roughly.

"I've gotta piss," he said, slapping his partner on the shoulder. "Call me when she stops lying."

Sobotka eyed Eva carefully as Crew strode out of the room. She folded her hands together, leaned forward slightly.

"What's up with your mum?"

Eva looked up like she'd been run over by a car.

"I don't know," she said.

"You two were close?"

"Y-yes."

"All that time you were roaming around Europe, she found a way to get you care packages every month. Not many parents would do that kind of thing."

"I… I guess."

Eva exhaled deeply, sunk a bit lower in her chair. Sobotka leaned back, crossed her arms, stared at the wall past Eva.

"We heard you watching the news this morning. Did you happen to catch the story about the kid with the breakfast cereal?"

Eva's eyes shifted left and right.

"Um. Yeah."

"That was us. I mean, we found the kid. Used to be, we'd be chasing murderers and thugs and thieves and such. Now we call it a victory if we find a kid who kept himself alive without our help."

"It's good he's alive."

"He's got Bonn-22. A week to live, tops."

Eva said nothing.

"But you can see how, after living and breathing *that* shit for the last few years, when we see someone like *you* in our fair city, it brings a certain… *liveliness* to our day."

A grunting from the hall signalled Crew's return, and the door swung open as he lurched in, a large machine in tow. He lifted it with two hands, creaking its handle, and dropped it on the table in front of Eva. It was browned and burnt, cracked in places and looked to be barely functional. Its large, square screen was warped, and the clear glass canister in its core was growing mould at the edges. Still, it was clear to Eva what it was.

"An incubator?" she asked.

"Oh, so you *do* know about making viruses!"

"No, I—"

"What was your mum doing with a pack of refill capsules?" Sobotka asked, a smirk on her face. Crew dropped himself into his seat, put a foot on the table.

"I don't know," Eva said quietly.

"You don't know?" Sobotka continued. "Okay, let me try this again. You mother was in possession of some highly illegal materials, as well as numerous documents relating to the manufacture of viruses. Why do you think that is?"

"She's an expert at epidemiology. It's probably part of her research."

"Sure. I get it. Yeah. So… switching gears… let's talk about travel. Where've you been since you left Paris?"

Eva shifted in her seat.

"A bunch of places," Eva said, willing her face not to flush. "Spain, Italy, Austria, Germany. I passed through others on the way, but it's tricky to get past borders because of the outbreaks."

Sobotka nodded.

"Must have been hard," she said, almost kindly. "But you seem to have made it through all right. Did you travel alone?"

Eva paused.

"No," she said.

"Our records show you were with someone named, one second..." Sobotka flipped open a folder, skimmed a few pages. Crew leaned over, pointed down to a spot low on the page, and she nodded to him. "Right, Rhodri Tenant. British national. Is that right?"

Eva nodded: "Yes."

"Boyfriend?"

"Was."

"Bad break-up?"

Eva looked at her hands, fidgeted her thumbs.

"I'd rather not talk about him," she said quietly.

Sobotka paused, nodded.

"Fair enough," she said. "We're here for *you* anyway."

Crew grinned.

"So when did you *start* making viruses?" he asked.

"I *told* you, I don't make viruses! I don't know how!"

"But you're pretty good at computers, right?"

"I don't know. Just average, I guess."

Crew scratched his cheek absentmindedly.

"You got into the University of Paris' computer science graduate program. As a foreign student. At nineteen. That's gotta say *something* about your skills, right?"

She didn't reply. He put his other foot on the table, waved his muddy boots from side to side.

"See, my question is this: why *wouldn't* you look at making viruses? Someone like you, having a doctor for a mum, and this computer science education, and that stint in prison—"

"Excuse me?" Eva gasped, her face turning bright red.

"The year in prison? What, you *forgot*?"

"I... how did *you*..."

"Oh, it's all right here. Hacked a bank when you were fifteen, left behind enough crumbs that the cops up in Sweden found you, and spent a year in jail for it."

Eva's eyes were starting to water. Sobotka continued.

"And what's shocking to me is that it says here that your *father* was the one that requested you be tried as an adult. Your own father! That must have stung."

"Her dad's a dick," Crew nodded.

"Those files were supposed to be sealed," Eva muttered.

"It's funny," Crew said, cracking his knuckles. "Things have a way of *unsealing* themselves, when they meet the right criteria."

"What kind of criteria?" Eva asked.

"A pattern of using technology for criminal acts. Hacking banks, making viruses. It's a bit of an evolution of technique, but it sounds the same to me."

"I *don't* make *viruses!*" Eva shouted, tears in her eyes.

"Let's come back to that," Sobotka said, leaning forward as Crew looked away. "See, looking at your travel history these last few years… what strikes me is that you seem to have been in a variety of cities around Europe just before they got shut down with major outbreaks."

"We left when things were looking bad."

"I'll say."

"A *lot* of people left when things were looking bad. Wouldn't you?"

"I dunno," mused Crew. "I think I'd stick it out and fight for my city. How 'bout you, Sobotka?"

Sobotka nodded slowly.

"How'd your mother take being fired, Ms Kolikov?" she asked.

"Excuse me?"

"Your mother was fired from the World Health Organization three weeks ago. Dereliction of duty. After twenty years of service. She got chewed out pretty bad in public. That must have hurt her."

"I… I didn't know."

"When did you talk to her last?"

"About two months ago. I haven't been able to reach her since."

"Not even last night?"

Eva blinked. The two inspectors were stone-faced, but their tone spoke volumes about their confidence. She was headed into a trap, and she had no idea what it was.

"What *about* last night?"

"You're entitled to a lawyer, of course, but it's not easy getting one here in person anymore. Especially to defend foreigners. Foreigners who just arrived."

"I don't understand —"

"Modena, Italy. Graz, Austria. *Linz*, Austria. Nuremberg, Germany. It seems pretty odd that every time you and your boyfriend leave a town, a massive outbreak hits and wipes out half the population. Doesn't it?"

Eva said nothing, clasped her hands together.

"You can imagine how excited we are that you stopped by," she said darkly. "Especially given the little warning you sent us."

Eva looked back and forth to them, eyes wide.

"What warning?"

Crew snorted, flipped out his phone and tapped a few buttons. He handed it over to her, screen sideways, and she saw a video playing…

Time-lapse clouds rolled through grey skies, distorted at the edges by flickering compression. There was audio to it, faint on the tiny speaker, but she thought it might be German. Then, atop the clouds, letter in cold, stark black letters: *"January 8: Modena-1".*

"That was sent to the Mayor's office three weeks ago," Sobotka said. "The voice is computer-generated, totally fake. Speaking German. Took us a while to translate, but this is the gist…"

"March 2: Graz-3," the screen said now.

"Let's see," Sobotka said, flipping through her notes, then read dryly: "The greed and hypocrisy of society is a cancer on humanity which must be removed at all costs before the blah, blah, blah. You get the point."

"I don't… I don't understand…" Eva said. "What does this have to do with me?"

"April 21: Linz-1," said the text.

"The video arrived through a proxied mail server in Russia, but since the Russians have become so touchy about communications lately, they were able to tell us where it came from *before* it hit their borders. And you'll never guess what we found."

"*July 6: Nuremberg-5,*" said the text.

"The originating account was registered to your mother," Sobotka said, leaning in. "But apparently, there was a *secondary* account on the file. *Your* account. And forensics is pretty sure it's a match."

Eva blinked, looked from Sobotka to Crew and back again, felt her stomach turn inside out. She looked down at the video, saw the words changing again, and gasped when she read them:

"*December 1: Prague-1.*"

She looked up at the inspectors, panic swelling over her.

"So tell me, Ms Kolikov," said Crew. "How're we gonna die on December 1?"

11

Eva was trembling, tears in her eyes.

"This isn't me. I didn't… I don't know anything about this!"

"Your history of criminal behaviour indicates otherwise," said Sobotka. "So what did you do? Come home with a new brew ready to strike, found out your mother'd had a change of heart? Killed her to keep her quiet? Is that it?"

"Killed her? She's dead?" she cried. "No, that's not… What's going on? Where *is* she?"

Crew chortled.

"You tell us."

Sobotka slammed her fist down on the table, jolting Eva into silence.

"Ms Kolikov, you're going to want to be a bit more forthcoming with us. The courts being what they are these days, it can take months to get you to trial. And honestly, a lot of prisoners come in with the sniffles—"

"Hold up," Crew interrupted. "We don't have time for—"

"Give me a minute," Sobotka warned, then turned back to Eva. "I'm going to *highly* recommend you tell us what we want to know, or we'll have no reason to keep you in isolation. Do you understand me?"

"Oh *come on*," Crew vented. "Give me five minutes alone with her, that's all we'll—"

Sobotka held a calming hand out to her partner and he paused, looked away, barely keeping his frustration in check. Sobotka leaned close to Eva, squinting.

"I don't think you're going to tell us anything," she said. "I think you'll stonewall to the end. And every minute I spend in here with you is another minute I'm not *out there*, hunting the damn virus. So if you're not going to come clean, tell me now so I can stop wasting my time."

"But I honestly don't know what this is all about... you have to believe me... please..."

Crew clenched his fists, looked like he was on the verge of boiling over with fury.

"Listen, you spoiled brat," he seethed. "It may not look it to you, but this city ain't dead yet. This is my *home*. Even if I have to boil and sterilize every drop of water I use in the shower, it's still better than packing up and giving up. That's what you and your kind don't get, and it makes me sick. It's no great loss if Prague is wiped off the map, right? Well you're *wrong*!"

He got to his feet, shoving the chair against the wall. It toppled over behind him. Eva jerked back, but he caught her by the hair, held her tight, leaned in furiously.

"Tell us where the virus is!" he yelled. "We don't have time to watch you play innocent here! Tell us where it is or I'm sending you to the most crowded cell I can find, I swear to god!"

Eva was crying, trying to get free of his grip, pleading.

"Please..." she sobbed. "please, I don't know... I don't know anything about it... please..."

"Crew, come on," said Sobotka, stepping into the hall. "It's not going to work. Leave it."

"Fuck it!" Crew growled, and slammed her head down into the table with such force her nose started to tingle. She tasted blood in the back of her throat, her eyes swirled with light. Crew stormed to the door, put his head in his hands, trying to regain his composure.

"You're going into lockup," he growled. "and you're not getting out."

"Wait…" Eva sputtered, reaching out to him feebly.

"Too bad mama can't help you now, hmm?" he smirked, and left the room, slammed the door so powerfully it sounded like cracking wood. A thin shaft of light beamed in along the bottom. Outside, shadows moved across the doorway, and she heard the inspectors talking again.

"Forgot my keys," called Crew. "Lock it for me."

Footsteps came closer, a jingling, a sorting of keys, and Eva tensed.

"How much do you think she knows?" asked Sobotka.

"Who gives a shit. We've got to keep working the angles. We got any leads yet?" Crew said, hushed.

"A few hits. It'll take us a while to cover them all. You got time?"

"Apparently just a few days. Any ideas on where to start looking?"

"None, really. It's complicated by her… you know…"

"Yeah."

"So let's print out a list and pick a place at random."

Just then, Eva heard the faint ring of a cell phone, Crew answered, his voice quiet and more distant as he walked away from the door. Then a click as the phone shut, and he called to his partner: "We've gotta go. Something big in the west end. Captain says Sestak's asking for us directly."

Hurried footsteps disappeared into echoes, and Eva was left in awful silence, the wedge of light cutting straight across her ankles. She breathed slowly, shakily, waiting.

"Hello?" she asked the darkness. "Anyone coming to get me?"

She couldn't hear a thing beyond her own breathing.

Carefully, quietly, she got out from her seat and edged towards the door. No sounds at all. She touched the doorknob tentatively, listened for a sound, a voice, anything to make her pause.

She turned the knob gently, and it clicked, popping the door open slightly. She creaked it out further and peeked outside.

The hallway was yellowing like old paper; filthy water streaked the floor, no people in sight. Eva leaned her head further out, checked both ways, and saw nothing. Nothing to stop her. She shivered.

"I'm leaving the room now..." she whispered.

Less than a metre from the room, Eva heard a scuffle up ahead, like a paper shifting. She froze, eyes wide. She heard a loud sigh, and a grunt. She searched the hallway for someplace to hide.

There, a few steps ahead, another door off to her right, half-closed, lights off. She waited, listened. The air filters in the ceiling hummed and hissed, and the fan somewhere nearby ground its gears with a grating rumble. Then, another scuffle, footsteps.

Eva held her breath and made a dash for the room, slipped inside and back behind the door, the darkness piercing after the light of the hallway. She let the breath out slowly, evenly, tried to hear outside again.

Footsteps now, closer, and she could see through the back of the door, black boots outside the room, paused. Breathing, she heard breathing. A long pause.

The boots slid back a bit, then turned, and she could hear muttering as the footsteps got further away. A calm, even pace. Eva exhaled again, her lungs loosening a bit. She leaned closer to the hinges now, saw into the hall, empty as before.

She turned round to leave when she noticed, back against the wall next to her, a computer workstation. The screen was off, but its power light was on, casting a pale green light across the room.

A police workstation.

She carefully and quietly slid over to the chair, sat down. It creaked a bit, and she strained not to move anymore. She turned the brightness on the screen all the way down with the dial on the front, and then powered it on. She could make out the words, but took a moment to take in all the information.

There was a search box in the corner, cursor flashing on and off, inviting input. Checking over her shoulder, Eva typed: 'Kolikov', and hit 'enter'.

The screen refreshed in a second, showed two entries. Eva's file, and Dasa Kolikov, her mother. She hovered the cursor over her mother's name, then clicked her own, bringing up a file that included her passport photo and a few stills from the security cameras on the train. She skimmed the file quickly, pausing only to try and discern the meaning of '17-5'. No luck there, so she tore through the data, deleting and fabricating information as fast as possible. By the time she finished, they'd know nothing about her at all.

She smiled at a job well done and hit the 'back' button, diving into her mother's file. What she found was worse than she'd expected:

ARREST WARRANT #058833153

CONSPIRACY TO COMMIT MURDER

BIO-WEAPONS ACT VIOLATIONS

Eva involuntarily put a hand to her mouth, gasped quietly.

"Oh, mama…" she said. "What happened?"

She heard a crackle in the room, but no time to react. A hand wrapped round Eva's mouth, pushing down, and she couldn't breathe. She flailed, cracking her wrist against a desk, and wasting the last of her breath on a scream no one could hear.

12

"I didn't expect to see you here so soon, Will," said the Director as Carey shuffled in the door, a pack of papers under his arm. He smiled weakly, made his way to the chair opposite his boss' giant throne of a seat, and almost fell into it. Janice trailed him like an impressive shadow; the kind that outshines its owner.

The room was like a photo gallery, a shrine to people the Director knew (or had been photographed with). Carey could see former Prime Ministers, rock stars, athletes and famous scientists. One picture of the current Prime Minister had a message scrawled across the front in silver ink: 'We'll beat this together!' — the slogan he'd won on.

Everything about the room was 'old school.' The desk looked to be over a hundred years old, the lamps and general decor smelled of Victorian spit and polish. There was a large map on the back wall — the biggest single space in the room not yet turned into a mosaic of tiny frames — showing the British Empire sometime before the First World War.

The Director was a man who loved glory, who killed and mounted it on his walls to show his dominion over it.

"Sorry to barge in like this, sir," Carey said, trying to gather some of the papers back into something resembling a pile. He knocked an ink blotter off the edge of the desk and ducked down after it, smacking his head against the desk on the way. He came back up holding his head and the blotter, and his papers drifted out of his hands and onto the floor. Janice sighed loudly.

"Sorry, sorry…" Carey said again.

"Not at all, Will, not at all!" boomed the Director, apparently enjoying how his office intimidated people. "Listen, would you like a drink? And you, miss?"

"No, sir. Thank you, sir," said Janice flawlessly.

"Um, if you don't—" Carey began, before Janice kicked his shin so subtly she nearly didn't move. "I mean no sir, I'm good, thanks."

The Director nodded at this, leaned back in his chair, started spinning an ornate letter opener on his desk in a way that made Carey sweat. He grabbed the top paper from his pile and nervously, shakily, handed it over.

"We've found something, sir," he said, and tapped the paper lightly. "Something that could be quite bad."

The Director took the paper lightly, nudged his reading glasses on his long pointed nose and sniffed loudly, like he was jarring his brain into gear. He smacked his lips once or twice, squinted, and then started to read it, because his face hardened abruptly. He looked up, and Carey immediately looked away.

"What is this?" the Director asked, his voice low.

"Um… Janice?" Carey invited.

Janice cleared her throat to speak, but the Director leaned forward suddenly, with a low growl to his voice.

"This is a senior level meeting, my dear. You're excused."

"But sir," protested Carey. "Janice is—"

"Not a part of this conversation, Will. You are excused, miss."

Janice blinked, confused, but then put on her more composed face, and carefully backed out of the room without a word. Carey was left alone with the stone-faced man with the old colonial empire at his back, and he felt horribly alone.

"You were stationed in Madrid, weren't you, Will?" the Director said, creaking back in his chair.

"Yes. Yes sir. Eight years."

"So you're a team player. You know what's at stake here. I don't need to go over how a little information can do a lot of wrong."

Carey shook his head slowly.

"No, sir."

"Excellent. So tell me about these papers, Will."

"It's… it's… well, it's the transmission logs for Zemus Pharmaceuticals, sir. It seems that they're… uh… they seem to be integrating vaccines into their booster shot programme without… er… testing them."

"Are we sure about this?" said the Director, his voice dispassionate but somehow accusing.

"Yes, sir, we are. And we… we think we've found out why."

Carey handed over the next set of papers in the stack, a listing of communications in excruciating detail, complete with timestamps and origin addresses.

"It… at first we thought Zemus had been… well, maybe compromised by some malicious persons. Trying to… you know… well…"

"Spread a virus through a booster shot," said the Director, obviously quicker than Carey had been.

"But… well… as you can see, sir, the bypass orders all came from a single person, a registered person, and we have good reason to believe he was the one making the inputs himself."

The Director looked up from the paper, bore into Carey.

"Is this who I think it is?"

"Yes, sir, I'm afraid so."

The Director laid the paper down on his desk, folded his hands above it, closed his eyes. His jowls trembled as he breathed, and he looked like a beast from a nature video, so unreal you wouldn't have believed it existed. The Director's brow furrowed slightly. He was thinking, and Carey felt like he was intruding on a private moment.

"Will," the Director said, opening his eyes, staring coldly at Carey. "Thank you for bringing this to my attention."

He paused again, seemed to be thinking, sniffed, his face twitched. He licked his lips slowly, then leaned forward, his suit's worn elbows pushing down on the scattered papers around the desk.

"Can I ask... what made you leave Madrid? Was it stress? Family?"

Carey looked at his hands.

"I was recalled, sir. The... uh... the Dominguez case, if you know it."

"I don't think I do."

Carey continued to avoid eye contact.

"To be brief, sir: there was a woman named Rosa Dominguez who hadn't made it back before the Containment Order went into force, and had since tested positive for P-150."

"So the boys in Brighton would have refused to quarantine her, even if you let her back in."

"Exactly. I was tasked with delivering her Notice of Exile, but her name made it extremely hard to pin her down. I eventually did, down in Alicante, at a spa there. She'd apparently saved for years for a vacation, and had decided to go through with it despite the border closing."

"Foolish," the Director said with a grunt. "Foolish and tragic."

"Ms Dominguez was a rather stubborn woman, I'm afraid. She refused to come out of her full body mud pack session to meet me, so I was forced to go in and deliver her Notice against her wishes."

"It was the right thing to do, Will. Absolutely the only call."

"Yes sir. Well... Ms Dominguez didn't see it that way. She filed suit against the Ministry for sexual harassment. Given the... uh... *full-body* nature of the mud pack."

"Ah. I see."

"They settled rather than suffer the publicity, and I was put behind a desk in your fine department, sir."

"And what of Ms Dominguez?"

"She used the settlement money to buy the spa."

"Good on everyone, then."

Carey nodded unhappily.

"Yes, sir."

"Well then," the Director said, puffing up again. "How do you feel about working behind a desk?"

Carey was automatic and severely mechanical:

"Very good, sir. Most rewarding."

"I don't think you believe that, Will. I think you're hating it. Papers and spreadsheets and kissing the right ass in the right way… it's not who you are, is it?"

Carey honestly did not know what to say.

The Director took the papers he'd received, held them under his desk, and Carey heard the sound of a paper shredder eating the evidence. The Director didn't take his eyes off Carey, just sat there as the sounds whirred below, like he *wasn't* doing what he was doing, and anyone that indicated otherwise was mad.

The last of the papers disappeared and the Director put his hands back on his desk, interlocking his calloused fingers lightly.

"I am removing you from your position in the Department."

"But sir—"

"You are now working as my chief investigator. You report to me, and me alone. I want you to use your experience on the Continent to keep things at home under better control. Starting with this Zemus mess. It must be dealt with quickly and *quietly*. No one but the two of us should hear of it, do you understand me?"

"Yes sir," nodded Carey, then shuddered. "But sir! Janice knows! What should we—"

"Janice is replacing you as department head, of course. She's got a good head on her shoulders, I can tell. But even still, what she knows — without the backing evidence — that's inconsequential. From here on out, these secrets stay between us."

"Yes sir."

"Zemus have a new booster coming out in three weeks, and I don't think anyone could stand the financial or political fallout if it were to be pulled over a scandal."

"Sir...?"

The Director leaned in close, eyes narrow, his voice so quiet, Carey found himself leaning forward to hear.

"I've known this man my entire life. He is a good soul, Will, a very good fellow. And yet..." his gaze shifted, he was looking past Carey, but at nothing, "... yet, I can see this being true. I can see him doing this because he thinks it's the best way to protect the public."

Carey nodded.

"But it's against the law," said the Director, and Carey stopped nodding abruptly, frowned. "And he has to learn to accept it. So I need you to talk to him, Will, and let him know that we know, and unless he quits now, it'll only be a matter of time before it gets out. You tell him — not for me, you understand — you tell him that he needs to submit those vaccines for proper testing, and to follow normal procedure from now on."

Carey nodded weakly, understanding.

"He means well. But one mistake could..." he met Carey's eyes, and he was sad, sad for his friend and the trouble this would be. "One mistake could gut our country, Will. You have to make him understand."

13

The rear stairwell to the hospital was dark and dank, littered with junk that had accumulated over years of disuse. Down on the ground level, masses of biohazard canisters littered the floor, scratched and worn by staff that had left long ago. No one had been in this shaft for some time; the only lighting was the thin strip of red emergency beacons along the edge of the steps.

Anouma faced the Healer, his cold visage made demonic by the surroundings. She was exposed here, alone in a place where no one would find her body for weeks — if ever. Alone with a murderer. She grabbed the railing with a slippery hand, her handheld flashlight dangling from the lanyard around her neck.

"Why are you here?" she asked, her voice cracking, her French precise, tentative.

The Healer observed her for a moment.

"You know why I am here," he replied, rough and distorted through his mask. "You have information about LS-411. You will tell me now."

He took a step forward, and Anouma held out a warning hand, her jaw setting.

"I want to know what you will do if you find this strain. What are your orders?"

"My orders are to diagnose and contain."

"Contain *how?*" she asked, lowering her arm but not breaking her eye lock.

The Healer didn't move for a moment, except to twitch his head to the side.

"Containment requires the destruction of the host, usually by lethal injection. Sometimes incineration is deemed necessary, as well."

Anouma nodded slowly, her eye twitching with fury.

"So you find the sick and kill them? They did not do this to themselves! The ones that infected them are still out there, and you let *them* go?"

The Healer was shaking his head at her.

"Euthanizing the general population is inefficient. It is not my commission. I contain only the vectors."

"The vectors…"

"The hosts that infect the rest. The closer to the source, the better. These diseases tend to be built poorly. They lose virulent qualities as they pass each generation. The closer to the source, the greater the effectiveness of containment."

"So if my patient is the vector for LS-411…"

"I will perform my duty."

Anouma crossed her arms, shook her head.

"That is unacceptable. I cannot let you do that."

The Healer stared up the stairwell, back at Anouma.

"You have confirmed the patient is here. Your permission is irrelevant."

He turned and started up the stairs, a soft metal *clang* at every footfall. Anouma called after him as he reached the first landing.

"This is one of the biggest hospitals in Europe!" she said, her voice cracking with anger. "In this wing alone, we have seven usable floors, with a thousand patients per floor."

The Healer turned around, stepped a few steps down, stared at her ominously in the red light. She kept her arms crossed, stood her ground.

"And I have not said if the patient is in *this* wing at all."

There was a brief pause. A liquid dripped in the shadows, hit a pool amongst the biohazard containers. It sounded thick.

"What do you want?" the Healer said.

"You must promise you will not kill him."

"That is not in my power to promise," he said, shaking his head.

"Then I wish you good luck up there. Especially once I tell the police you broke in."

The Healer made its way down the stairs again, moved quickly and silently towards Anouma, until he had her pinned against the railing. His mask hissed spent carbon dioxide into her face.

"I can get the information from you however I choose," he breathed angrily. "I am not bound by your doctors' ethics."

Her expression didn't change.

"But *I am*, so I will never tell you. Never, unless you swear to leave him alive."

Without warning, the Healer grabbed Anouma by the throat, pushed her back against the concrete wall. His fingers tightened around her, but didn't finish the job. Anouma held her breath, terrified, but didn't betray any emotion.

They stayed frozen, neither one budging.

The Healer let her go.

"I will not euthanize your patient," he said, stepping away. "But you must show him to me now. No more delays."

Anouma rubbed her neck for a moment, then nodded and took her flashlight in her hand again.

"This way," she said, starting up the stairs. He followed close behind.

There was a general grit to the steps that was slippery, yet rough. She couldn't see what it was, nor did she see the glass that crunched harshly underfoot along the way. They moved slowly, cautiously, careful to avoid stepping on used needles. Mouldy pillows, shredded gowns, and a bloodstained sink lay cracked along the way.

"What is your name?" she asked as they passed the third floor.

The Healer thought a moment.

"We have no names," it said, simply.

"Your French is better than I thought."

There was a pause as they walked. The Healer sounded hesitant.

"We are trained to communicate with medical personnel."

"You handle it well."

"I… I have had time to practice."

Another half-floor later, it spoke again:

"What is *your* name?"

"Dr Anouma," she replied. "Fanta Anouma. Médecins Sans Frontières."

"I know your colleagues."

"And they know you, too. Here… wait here."

She left him standing there on the steps and creaked open the fourth-floor fire door. She leaned into the hallway beyond, the pale light casting a soft shadow in the shaft next to him. He walked up behind the door, watched her carefully.

"Dr Anouma!" came a voice, a man, from the hall. Anouma jumped at the sound. She drifted further out, let the door slide closed behind her, held open just enough for her hand to peek through.

"Dr Laroche!" she said, failing to sound as calm as she wanted to be. "Is everything okay?"

Dr Laroche was close now. The Healer could see his shadow mixed with Anouma's underneath the door.

"Fine, fine," he said. "Just grabbing some supplies for the floor. Why are you using the back stairwell? It's not safe there, is it? There are discarded needles everywhere."

The Healer tensed, lay a hand on his machete.

"Oh, no. I was just… I heard a young patient on the fifth floor talking about a special fort he had built back here, and I thought I should check it out."

"Really! The things kids dream up!"

"I know… it seemed silly to me, but—"

The door pushed open more, and Dr Laroche's voice was near. The Healer unsheathed his weapon, held it ready.

"Did you find anything?" Laroche asked.

"No!" Anouma gasped. "No, nothing. Many discarded needles, as you said. I would not risk going in there. Who knows what people discarded."

Dr Laroche chuckled to himself, but the door stayed open. The Healer did not move.

"Might want to get the boy checked for dementia if he's coming up with imaginary forts in the darkness. Could be Waterloo or London-9. Wouldn't want him cross-contaminating his roommates."

"Certainly not, I agree. I will order the tests."

A brief pause, and then the door swung shut.

"I'll be down in the pit if you need anything!" Dr Laroche called, his voice getting fainter as he walked away. "Say hello to Adjobi for me!"

"I will!" Anouma replied, then waited quietly for a minute, not moving at all. She began to push the door open again. The Healer caught it with an impatient grab, shoved it all the way open, and pushed past her into the hall.

"You lie well," he said, taking stock of the surroundings. "Which one is it?"

"This one," Anouma said, leading the way into a room halfway down the hall. She came to a stop at the bedside of a sickly-looking African man, wired with a dozen monitors and IVs, breathing weakly under the pressure of his yellowed hospital blankets. His eyes were closed; they fluttered wildly in his sleep.

His skin sat on him strangely, like a man who was once full of life, round and happy, and whose joy had been chiselled away until he was nearly a living corpse. A shadow of better times ghosted in his face.

"This is the patient," Anouma said solemnly. "My brother, Dr Adjobi Anouma."

14

Anouma took Adjobi's hand and rubbed his fingers gently, and he opened his eyes. At first he didn't notice his visitor, but when he caught a glimpse of the mask, he panicked, tried to climb up the back of his bed as if it were an escape route.

"Shhh, quiet, brother," Anouma said, and put a hand on his shoulder, gently pushing him back down. His heart monitor rang louder and louder, a red light flashing more urgently on the console above the bed. An emergency call button. The Healer put a hand on his machete.

"Quiet, quiet now," Anouma said with a soft voice. "He is here to help you."

She turned her gaze to the Healer, hopeful. After a brief moment, he put his hands out, palms up, and bowed as a gesture of goodwill. It worked well enough: Adjobi's heart rate was calming fast. Anouma stroked her brother's head, and though he was much less agitated, his eyes were wide with fear.

"Adjobi and I came from Ferké three years ago—" she began.

"What is Ferké?" interrupted the Healer, "Where is this place?"

"What is it to you?" Adjobi said, then coughed a hoarse, dry cough.

"If your infection began in another town, I must travel. I have no information that LS-411 is anywhere but Prague."

"Ferkessédougou is in Côte d'Ivoire," Anouma said. "In Africa."

The Healer nodded slightly.

"There are no synthetic diseases down there," Adjobi said, wincing at a sudden pain. "Whatever it is I have, I got it right here."

"Besides," said Anouma, "they do not let sick doctors help in the relief."

The Healer tilted his head.

"*Relief*," he echoed.

"Six weeks ago," Anouma continued. "these lesions appeared on Adjobi's neck and chest..." she held out his arm and showed a purplish patch no more than a few centimetres across, shiny even in the dim light.

"At first we thought he had contracted something from one of the patients here, so we started him on Pathenex and kept him in isolation. Unfortunately, the other symptoms he developed do not fit with any disease we have encountered before. We have compared it to every entry in the WHO Pandemic Database. No one has made a virus this way before."

The Healer leaned a bit closer to Adjobi, mask hissing at regular intervals.

"What other symptoms?" he asked.

Anouma held the LS-411 card, blocking his view; her voice grew stronger. A bit more resolve.

"These," she said simply, and dropped the card onto the bed. The Healer stood up straight and looked towards the sealed window, the drawn curtains blocking the faint light from outside.

"Your brother did not die within days. He must be a carrier, not a victim. Most of your diseases... they make longer the life of the vector. To infect more. You have done... done good in isolating him. You have slowed the spread.

"It is usual for a vector to show symptoms. I have only seen this once before, where the host was bed-ridden."

"How did it turn out?" Anouma asked.

"Badly."

"So what, then?" Adjobi asked. "I'm not the vector? There was someone else before me?"

The Healer nodded, removed a black pouch from his belt. The two doctors became noticeably tense. He paused, hand over it, not opening it up.

"I will require a blood sample to verify... but in my experience, you do not look like a first-degree vector."

Anouma's face betrayed a smile.

"Then you will leave him alone? You are only interested in the vector, yes?"

The Healer stared at the black pouch for a moment.

"I have given you my word," he said quietly. "But my directives are to eliminate hosts. I should euthanize him now."

"But... but you won't..." Anouma said, uncertain.

The Healer only looked at her.

"No, he won't," Adjobi said weakly. "And he won't draw any blood either—"

"That is not what I said—" the Healer said.

"Because if he does, I won't tell him who infected me."

Both Anouma and the Healer looked at Adjobi, Anouma's mouth hanging open slightly. She took his hand in hers, squeezed it gently.

"Adjobi, what are you..."

"There was a man. An American. His name was Lewis. I never learned his last name. He was a junkie, a sickly old thing. I was working the pit alone when his girlfriend — a prostitute I think — came and begged me to check on him. He'd passed out, possibly from an overdose. She couldn't wake him, couldn't move him, but she'd brought her car, so she drove me to his house.

"When I got there, he was barely alive. I performed CPR and flushed his system with the tools I had, and he seemed to be recovering well enough. But when he came to, he was delirious, probably spooked by my hospital uniform. He... he stabbed me. With a needle."

Anouma covered her mouth in shock, sunk lower onto the bed.

"It didn't hurt. I didn't think much of it at the time. I flushed the wound, took the standard stopper dose of Pathenex, and moved on."

"You think he was your vector," the Healer said.

"It would make sense. I got sick a few weeks after that. What else could it be?"

The Healer looked at the black pouch for a moment.

"Where does 'Lewis' live?"

"Michalská, house number 21, I think. It had a green door. That much I remember."

The Healer took hold of the pouch, put it back into his belt, did not look at either Anouma or Adjobi. He turned away, heading to the door, dust swirling in his wake.

"Will you come back?" Anouma asked him. He stopped, looked at her, framed by banks of monitors and equipment flowing wires onto the floor.

"Pray I do not," he said, and left.

*   *   *

"That was… dangerous, Fanta," said Adjobi, when they were sure the Healer had gone. Anouma backed away from the door, returning to his side. Her eyes glistened with fear.

"I am sorry, Adjobi. I thought the lesions matched yours… I thought he might help you."

"You *know* Healers don't help anyone but their own. He might have killed me."

Fanta lowered her head, contained her crying. Adjobi patted her hand with his, weak, faltering.

"But it will be fine," he said softly. "If he finds my vector, we might have hope. They have some of the best minds in the world working there. If anyone can crack it, they can. It's a long shot, but we can't lose hope."

She smiled at him, but it was clear she didn't share his optimism anymore.

"How do you feel today?" she asked.

"A bit better. I haven't got much left to vomit, and the sedatives help with the rest. No new lesions this week, either. It's as close to 'progress' as I can manage, I think."

"That is good. That is very good. Dr Bastien will be happy to hear it. He does not get much happy news these days."

"Oh?" asked Adjobi, straining to sit up a bit in bed.

"The Director of Public Safety is causing problems again," Anouma explained. "He has summoned Dr Bastien five times this week already, always without notice. I have heard he is trying to implement a new policy to screen all aid workers."

"We're subject to that already…"

"Not like this. He is looking for anyone whose vaccines are not up to date, to have them deported. A doctor in Ostrava contracted measles and passed it on to his patients, and it has everyone scared. He wants to force every doctor in Prague to be fully protected. From everything."

"So are they going to provide us with the vaccines they withheld before, then?" Adjobi said, his voice weak but increasingly angry.

"They say they still do not have the resources."

"So they'd give up some of their best minds to satisfy some knee-jerk reaction…"

"Bastien is fighting it. He says they have no right to meddle with MSF affairs."

"I doubt that," Adjobi sighed. "But they're still fools for trying. You have to refuse, Fanta. I can't be stuck in this hell hole alone. You have to stay hidden. At least until Bastien gets word from Geneva…"

"I do not think we will hear from them soon," Anouma said gravely. "He said not to expect anything for many days, at least. The mail servers have been shutting down often, too. No one knows what got out and what got lost."

"You've got to be careful, then. You should be switching masks every few hours. Carry extra gloves. Don't take any chances, Fanta. All they need is for you to show signs of a fever, and you'll be caught."

She lowered her eyes.

"Adjobi... why did you not tell me about your accident? It changes so much..."

Adjobi sighed, put a hand to his forehead, and the cables tugged gently at the movement.

"Bastien would have left me for dead for disobeying his orders. He'd be mad as hell if he knew I'd been galavanting around the city, Stall Kit in hand. No, it was too risky. Better he think I got it from someone *here* than someone *out there*."

Anouma nodded, quiet.

"He is wracked with guilt, though," she said. "He thinks it is his fault."

"Don't read too much into Bastien's guilt. He's been wearing it round his shoulders since before we got here. I'm not worried about adding to his sorrows. I'm scared to death of disappointing him."

Anouma smiled at this, patted his hand. Adjobi winced at pain somewhere in his frail body, half-rolled to his side. His heart monitor beeped faster and faster, and then slowed to a normal crawl.

"I will get more morphine," she said, moving off the bed, but he caught her arm, held her back.

"It's okay," he swallowed. "I'm fine. Don't waste it on me. With any luck, that monster you found will have a cure for me, and all of this will be a faint memory."

"I would rather never see him again," Anouma confided.

"Neither would I," said Adjobi quietly. "but somehow I think we will."

15

The corpse tipped into a black body bag, joining errant rainwater that was skirting off the roof into the alley. The workers, heavy masks strapped tight to their faces, tossed it around callously, their shoulder-long black gloves squeaking from the effort. Two of them stood impatiently above the other victim, blood long since drained.

Sobotka took one last look, stood up, and they moved in for disposal, this time with yellow plastic. A sticker was glued to the head and toe, detailing the type and strength of the virus found in the body.

The body bags were lazily added to a pile of other corpses, all colour-coded, waist-high and exposed to the elements. Further down, the pile of yellow bags was being loaded into a flatbed truck. It would take several trips to clear that stack, as tall as it was.

Sobotka walked down towards the mouth of the alley and joined Crew, who was interviewing a bruised old woman in bloodied clothes. Her eyes darted between them, but never *at* them, like she was talking to ghosts and not people.

"A brown cloak?" Crew asked, tapping his pen on his notepad. "Anything else?"

The old woman nodded furiously.

"Yes! Yes, a dark face! Like a fly! He had no eyes! No eyes and no soul!"

Crew smiled a bit, jotted notes. Sobotka checked his scribblings, put a hand to the woman's shoulder.

"Did he hurt you, ma'am?"

"No. No no no, not me. Only Franz and whashisname. The one with the kids. They're upstairs, you know. He talks about them all the time."

"I'm sure. So this dark-faced man… did he say anything to you?"

"No, no words, not to me. Though I heard a woman's voice. She spoke something… I can't say what. It was foreign."

"Have you heard it before?" Sobotka asked, checking back at the crime scene.

"Yes. Yes, I have. I'm sure I have."

Crew stood a bit straighter, frowned at the woman.

"*Where?*"

"In my nightmares. It was the devil. The devil! I'm sure of it!"

Sobotka rubbed the woman's grimy shoulder, and kindly lead her back to her campsite off the side of the hospital.

"That's good, ma'am. Thank you. You've been a big help."

Crew was kicking over a bottle of antiseptic into the bloodstains when she got to him. She looked at the large metal doors against the concrete facade, the piles of trash everywhere.

"What do you think?" she asked, not making eye contact.

"Same thing you do. It's gotta be."

Sobotka's phone buzzed quietly, and she flipped it out, put it to her ear, taking a step back out of the rain.

"Sobotka," she grunted. "Yes sir. I think it is, sir, yes. A Healer. It matches the description perfectly. No face, the cloak, the bloodbath."

Crew's jaw set tightly.

"Yes sir," Sobotka nodded. "We understand. Completely, yes. Not a problem. We're on it."

"So the Cap' agrees?" Crew asked as she shut the phone, "We're good to go?"

"It wasn't the Captain, it was Director Sestak. And we're not good to go, he's telling us to leave it alone."

"*Alone?* We've got two dead bodies here, and who knows how many more coming! We can't just ignore it!"

"Are you kidding me? It was an *order*, Crew! And he's right. Healers are untouchable. If anyone found out we were even *looking* at investigating a Healer, the bunch of us would be called up on charges by sundown. The rules come from too high up. Higher than us, higher than Sestak—"

"What, God himself?" Crew smirked. "Look at you. All for defending the peasants, until the peasants meet some Chinese butcher, and then you're *fine with it*?"

"Of course I'm not fine with it!" shouted Sobotka, and the nearby crowds turned to stare. She lowered her voice, growling. "But this is a fight you can't win, Crew. Without the law on our side, at best we're on even footing with a Healer. At best. And everything I've heard says he's got almost supernatural powers. You really want to go up against that?"

Crew grinned.

"I do. I really do."

"Look, I hate being pulled in a thousand directions as much as you do, but that's what we get for not retiring with everyone else. We have to cover extra ground… ground we don't want to cover. But what we *don't* do is go *looking* for trouble where there isn't any!"

"This *is* trouble!"

"You know that's not true!"

"You heard that woman! The Healer was talking to someone… some woman. Here in the hospital. That means he's got an accomplice. The President himself might be watching the Healer's back, but there's nothing that says we have to let a Czech citizen call him in! To me, that's betraying your own. That's treason."

"You're insane. We'll never find a woman in a hospital of thousands, and we'll damn sure never be able to arrest her for *talking* to someone who is technically doing *nothing wrong*."

"You have no faith in the power of the badge, Sobotka."

She growled, turned away, staring into the rain. The flatbed truck's gates clanged shut, its cargo full.

"Know what I'm thinking?" Crew called to her. "This isn't a coincidence. This joker shows up in the last days of November, right after we get that note."

"You can't be serious."

"What? It's *beyond* them? After this? After Russia? After what they did in their own backyard?"

"It's the wrong MO. It doesn't fit, and you know it. We can't waste time on something like this when there is a *real* threat out there that needs our attention."

"Listen. He's already put two more in the pile. I'm not letting him add any more." Crew motioned to the pile of yellow body bags. The truck chugged to life and started away, off to the incinerator. There were still hundreds of yellow body bags stacked in the road. Sobotka shook her head, slumping her shoulders.

"You're a fool."

Crew shrugged.

"You with me, or do I do this alone?"

Sobotka shook her head, annoyed.

"We've got enough on our plates with the girl. *That's* our job. That's what we're paid to do. Sestak is waiting for results there. And it's a real public safety issue, Crew. This? This is just glory-hunting."

"So I do it alone, then."

"Damn right," she said, burying her fists in her jacket pockets. A cold wind blew across the alley, whipped her hair in her face. She clenched her teeth to keep the shivers at bay. Crew stared at the ground, kicked at the dirt.

"You can't take the car if it's not official business," Sobotka grumbled. "You're on foot. You're going to be out in the snow, looking for a ghost. You sure you want that?"

"It's not going to snow," he said, pacing away from her, arms folded and chin out. "It's only November. It'll slush a bit. I'll survive."

Sobotka watched him go, shaking her head to herself.

"I'm not so sure," she said.

16

Via Rainusso 108, Modena, Italy
April 22, one year earlier

The lead snapped off the pencil mid-stroke, ripping a hole in the page. Eva brushed the fragments away, smudging the lines all around. It looked like a hole in the sky, a tear in space. She checked the actual sky outside her window, pale blue with a few clouds drifting. Very different worlds.

Her hands were shaking, but she tried to ignore it. Her legs were like sticks these days, so thin. The roundness she'd been teased for in university had all melted away, leaving a lean, almost sick-looking girl, wrapped in a light jacket and jeans.

She had just laid down the first lines on a new page when the door to the hotel room opened and Rhodri entered, hands behind his back. His smile was contagious. She shut the sketchbook and hopped off the wicker chair, meeting him before he could kick his shoes off.

"Guess what I found?" he asked with a sly grin, turning this way and that, keeping her from seeing behind him.

"Magic beans," Eva teased, reaching around, meeting empty air as he dodged her.

"Magic beans won't fill our bellies. Try again."

Eva bit her lip, her stomach rumbling angrily. There was *food* in the room. This was no time for games.

"If it's stale bread again, you're making *way* too much of a fuss about it."

"It's not stale, and it's not bread. It's…" he held out a pair of red, shiny apples. "A treat!"

Eva could barely contain herself. She leapt at him, giving him a hug that made his back crack. He blew her bobbed hair off his face and laughed.

"If you make me drop them, you're homeless, got it?"

"How did you find them?" Eva gasped, pulling back, taking an apple in her hands. "Last time I was down in the market, they were like ten euros each!"

"Eleven, actually. Inflation. Got the two for twenty, though."

Eva's face dropped slightly. She took a step back.

"Twenty? How did… how did you get that much money? I thought we were saving that for emergencies. Things are tight, Rhodri, and I don't know how much we can—"

"It's not our emergency fund. That's the second bit of news."

Eva crossed her arms.

"Do tell."

Rhodri took a large bite out of his apple, chewed noisily, a smile betraying how much he was enjoying it. After a few chomps, he explained, words slurring from the juice.

"I got a job."

Eva leapt at him again, knocking him back a bit, wrapped her arms around him and kissed him hard on the mouth. Sweetness from the apple juice. He started laughing, kissed her back.

"So you're happy for me, then?"

"How did you do it? There's a company in town? Where? I thought we'd checked everywhere, and—"

"You want to keep asking, or you want me to tell you?" he teased.

She unwrapped herself from him, threw herself on the bed, legs crossed, and started eating her own apple. It was magnificently sweet, made her warm in the brisk spring air. Rhodri kept standing, foot tapping madly on the ground. He was full of excited energy, and it was infectious to watch.

"It's not the kind of work you're thinking. It's for a restaurant."

"You're cleaning dishes?"

"No, not dishes. The owner wants to shut down his dining area for good. He lost a pair of waiters last month, and he's sick of it. So he put up this ad, says he needs couriers to deliver food to customers around this and a few other towns."

"Nice racket. All the money, none of the risk."

"Can't blame him. But yeah, I saw he was running it purely by phone-in, and I saw an opening. How many people have proper, working mobile coverage these days? Right? Not many. But how many people can still squeak out a data connection to their laptops?"

"Clever," Eva said, her face bright with admiration. She started fidgeting as the apple was bitten down to the core.

"I talked him into letting me build him a website, complete with online ordering. Nothing too fancy, but it saves him having to hire a full-time receptionist."

"Pretty smart there, science boy!"

Rhodri finished his apple, tossed the core from a distance into the garbage can. His eye were twinkling.

"Eight hundred euros, and I've got two weeks to work."

"Eight hundred! Just think of all the—"

"Hold on, Eva," he said, sitting next to her, taking her hands in his. "It's a lot right now, but I don't want to go through another year of starving like we have. I don't want an apple to be the highlight of my month. Hell, my year. We've got to be careful with this money."

Eva nodded, avoiding his stare. She shrugged.

"I should probably get a job too, then. Help out more."

"You could be a courier for the restaurant! Just think! Running around town, delivering cold food to angry customers! Who needs a car when you've got spunk!"

She shoved him playfully.

"You're such a bastard," she grumbled. "Actually, I was thinking I could find some paint and see about selling some more work downtown. I sold one this morning, straight out of my sketchbook, totally by chance. This middle-aged guy from out of town, just wouldn't take no for an answer."

"Congrats! Which one?"

"The one of Maselle by the river," Eva beamed.

"Ah, yeah, I could see that one being popular. She had that seductive look about her."

Eva frowned at him.

"What seductive look?"

"Oh come on, *you* drew it. It was her whole 'come hither' thing."

Eva pushed him over by his face, crossed her arms in mock anger. He laughed.

"All I'm saying is that when you're living in a world like this, sometimes you want a little bit of the world the way it was," he said. "These days, how many times are you going to be able to hook up with a sultry college girl with a body like that?"

"Digging yourself deeper," Eva warned.

"I think hope sells, is what I mean."

"Or sex," said Eva.

"The hope of sex, then. Either way, it's a powerful thing. You should embrace it. Sell more work, spread a little joy, even if it *is* by proxy. Give the people what they want."

Eva leaned over him, her nose touching his. Her hair made a bridge between them. His breath was sweet and warm, his eyes dancing across her face.

"People should give *me* what *I* want first," she breathed.

"What do you want?" he asked, softly.

"You know damn well," she said, and they kissed, long and slow, in front of the open window, the pale blue sky filled with the sounds of passing ambulances.

17

"Eva! Eva, wake up!"

Her vision was blurry, and she coughed violently as if she'd nearly drowned. Blinking, she forced her eyes to focus, could barely make out the shape of a face above her, the green glow from the computer lighting his haggard appearance. She gasped, squeezed her eyes shut, tried to shake herself back awake.

"Pyotr...?" she wheezed, voice weak.

Pyotr smiled nervously, nodded, brushed her cheek with rough hands. His hair was cut short, patchy, like he'd done it himself. His eyes were ringed with creases, dark circles, tiny scars and the wear and tear of a living hell. They were still brilliantly blue, but the rest of him made the colour feel tired, not vibrant anymore. He wasn't the wiry kid she'd known at school. He was lean and muscular, tougher.

"I'm sorry, Eva," he whispered. "I didn't know it was you. Are you okay? Can you breathe?"

"You... you choked me..."

"I'm so sorry, I didn't know. You look a lot different. I thought you were one of them. You might've found me."

"Where are we?"

"The police station," he said, checking over his shoulder nervously. "We've got to get moving. Can you walk?"

Eva got to her knees, her legs wobbling beneath her. She put a hand on the wall, and yelped at a pain in her wrist. She held it close, tight, felt it was swelling slightly.

"You hit it when you were fighting me," Pyotr said, voice wavering with remorse. "Can you bear it for now?"

Eva nodded, cradled the arm and got to her feet. Pyotr stood next to her, supported her with a well-toned arm, craning his neck to see out into the hallway.

"It's good timing, you stopping by," he said softly. "Guess I'll have some company for Christmas after all."

Mention of the holidays dragged Eva back to reality, and she backed up suddenly, face blanching.

"Oh my god, Pyotr!" she gasped. "we have to get out of here! There's a virus… an outbreak hitting here December first!"

"Shh! Eva, quiet or they'll hear us!"

Eva lowered her voice, but her eyes were wide with fear.

"We can't stay here. We need to get out before it starts. Please, you have to help me!"

"I will, but—"

"— we have to find my mother and escape before—"

Pyotr put a hand over her mouth, kept her quiet while he checked down the hall.

"I will. I promise. But for right now: shut up and move fast, or we'll be rotting in jail when the city explodes. Got it? Now move!"

*　　*　　*

The windows were broken, shards strewn all over the weather-worn carpet. It smelled of smoke in the third floor bedroom, though it was uniquely untouched by the fire that had gutted the rest of the building. The floor creaked when Eva stepped on it, so she walked gingerly, followed Pyotr precisely.

"We don't have time, Pyotr," she called. "We need to start looking for my mother and finding food to travel and—"

"First things first," he interrupted, reaching a solid portion of the room and kneeling down on a mattress, pressed up against the wall. "We need to check your arm and get you fixed up. The way things are out there, you wouldn't last long like that."

Eva didn't respond, so he grabbed her arm and rolled up her sleeve. She bit back a yelp at the pain. Her wrist was purpling and noticeably swollen. He sighed.

"Looks nasty. Sorry about that."

She shrugged, then cried out loudly as he tried bending her hand up and down. He let her go, started rummaging through his pockets, pulling out food packets, half a dozen marbles, a pair of pliers, and a bundle of beige elastic wrap.

"You come prepared," Eva smiled.

"This isn't what I usually use it for. But I think it'll do…"

He reached out to the nearby window ledge and grabbed a handful of snow, and carefully put it on her arm. She was already so cold it barely registered, but as it melted it made her skin tingle, like tiny fiery pinpricks.

Eva looked up at him as he applied the second round of snow, shook her head.

"You look so different, Pyotr. Your hair is… it used to be beautiful."

He shrugged, cocked his head.

"Don't rub it in. It was getting too hard to manage without a bath. Took me days to get up the nerve to do it all in. With the edge of a tin can, no less."

"It shows," Eva smiled. "The beard is new, too. You were always the clean one. It's just kind of strange to see you like this."

"You look awfully new yourself," he said. "But long hair suits you, I think."

"Thanks," she said. "I think it's awful."

"Goes with the wrist."

"Yeah," she said, and caught some of the water dripping off her arm with the palm of her hand.

Pyotr put another handful of snow on her, wiped his hands on his jacket, and picked up the food packet he'd removed earlier.

"You keep that up until the ledge is clear, and I'll get us some dinner. A quick dinner. Yes?"

Eva nodded hesitantly. Pyotr tried to rip open the package, but it wouldn't give.

"Stupid things never open right…" he grumbled.

"It's so good to see you," Eva said softly. "It's good to know *someone* here."

"Someone alive from the old days."

"Yeah," was all she said.

Pyotr did a mock roar and pulled furiously at the package, but it still wouldn't budge. He stomped an angry foot on the ground and leaned into it with all his strength, the wrapper foiling his every move. Eva laughed, shook her head, and watched him a moment.

"You know, I used to have the biggest crush on you in first year," she said.

This caught Pyotr off guard, and just at that moment, the package burst open and half the ration skidded across the floor, right to Eva's feet. Pyotr stood there, stunned. Then upset, then shocked. He looked at the other half in his hand, sighed.

"That was sudden," he said, then handed her the safe half of the ration. "Here you go. Eat."

Eva took the food with her good hand, and gave a weak smile, which dissolved as Pyotr snatched the other part from the ground, dusted the dirt off its bottom. Eva reached out to him.

"Don't." she said seriously. "It's not worth the risk."

His blue eyes caught hers, he shrugged slightly.

"I'll live," he replied, but she grabbed his arm with her swollen hand, wincing.

"Don't be stupid. You can't know that. You can't risk that."

Their eyes stayed locked, and Pyotr dropped the food on the ground and flicked it away, under a chest of drawers. Eva handed him her own ration, and he snapped it in half for her, giving her a part back.

"Be careful with it this time," she warned.

He smiled at her. She bit into the wafer, winced at the taste, how it sucked the moisture out of her mouth.

"Yum," she sighed. "Stale strawberries."

Pyotr laughed a big booming laugh.

"Stale strawberries would be a step up. This is old cardboard sprinkled with strawberry extract. I'd throw up, if I had anything in my stomach."

Eva smiled, then almost gagged on her second mouthful.

"What are you doing here anyway?" Pyotr asked, swallowing the rest of his share. "Last I heard, you were going to stick it out in Paris. Where's Rhodri? You two are still together, right?"

Eva clenched a fist round the wafer, but it refused to crumble.

"No," she said, not looking up. "Not right now, no."

"But you will be again? There's hope for you two, right?"

She said nothing, closed her eyes.

"Maselle and I took some time off, after I left school," he said, trying to fill the gap. "Thought we were done, but you know, after a few months, it worked out okay."

Eva smiled, flicked a glance up at Pyotr, whose face had changed from hopeful to distant somehow. He was staring at the ceiling. Then he jerked out of it, took the elastic wrap and started bundling up her arm in slow, careful movements. She did her best not to show how much it hurt.

"You two were great together," Eva said. "I don't think I ever saw you apart, the whole time I was in Paris. Rhodri and I used to joke that we'd have to be surgically joined at the hip to even come close to your level of commitment."

"Heh," said Pyotr absent-mindedly. "Probably right."

"How is Maselle?" Eva asked, and Pyotr shifted his stare to the window.

"She died a few months ago," he said, with a dead expression. "Nuremberg syndrome. Out of nowhere."

Eva blinked, looked down at the wafer in her hands. At Pyotr's hands. At his sad expression.

"Pyotr... Nuremberg is... that's highly contagious... and air-borne..."

He didn't face her, just stared at his hands.

"Yeah," he said. "they warned me about that when they put me in quarantine."

18

Eva gasped, moved away from Pyotr urgently. She had no mask, no protection… she covered her mouth with the sleeve of her sweater, taking shallow breaths. Slow, shallow breaths. The elastic started unravelling onto the floor.

Pyotr didn't even notice her.

"I spent six weeks in quarantine," he said. "Couldn't see another living person for six weeks. They shoved food in under the door, and all I had to do was knock twice a day to tell them I was still alive. Lived in my own shit. They torch each cell after you die, so why bother cleaning?

"After five weeks, I'm sure I'm near death. I'm losing my mind, I've lost so much weight. I'm on the verge of a massive breakdown. This doctor in a full biohazard suit comes in, takes some blood, and tells me… he tells me Maselle died a week earlier. I can't see her. I can't see her at all. She's already being carted off to be incinerated, and all I get from her is the ring I got her when we… we got engaged."

Eva didn't move her arm, but tears were in her eyes, and she blinked them back.

"A week later the doctor comes back, tells me they've re-run my blood, and I'm clear for Nuremberg. It was a lab error the first time. I was fine. I could have... I could have been with her at the end, but they made a mistake. So she died alone, starving, drowning in her own shit. It's just wrong, Eva. It's so wrong."

Eva carefully, gently, lowered her sleeve from her face, reached out towards Pyotr. He was still staring out the window, watching something that wasn't there. They sat in silence, the snow making no sound as it drifted onto the window ledge.

Eva offered the last of the wafer to Pyotr.

"Are... are you hungry?" she asked quietly.

Pyotr looked at the wafer, his eyes narrow, then carefully plucked it from her hand, perched it in his fingers, but didn't move to eat it.

"What were you doing at the police station? Was it business or pleasure?"

She laughed at this.

"Very much business," she said, leaning back on the mattress, the dampness making her shiver. "They think I'm some master virus-maker."

"*You?*" he laughed. "Our little Eva? You're joking, right?"

"Wish you'd tell *them* that," she said, shaking her head. "they don't believe me."

Pyotr patted her knee, held his hand there a bit longer than necessary.

"They don't believe anyone," he said.

"I've noticed. But listen... we need to get moving... I have no idea where my mother is, and there isn't much time before the virus hits, whatever it is."

"You really trust cops? About this virus theory of theirs?"

Eva's eyes darted to the ground.

"I do. I wish I didn't, but I do."

He nodded, started on her wrist again, wrapping faster this time. She gritted her teeth.

"Sit tight. I'm not a doctor or anything, but I'll make you useful again."

Eva looked outside, the snow falling, then back to Pyotr.

"Thanks for this. I'd be lost here without a friend."

A gust of wind outside blew drops of water into the room. Pyotr wiped it off his face.

"Don't worry about it. Thank *you* for warning me about the impending doom and all."

Eva laughed.

"Sorry about the accommodations, by the way," he said, frowning. "You interrupted my apartment hunting. The police keep the best list of vacant buildings in town, so I like to plan a little raid every so often to find some new digs."

"Why do you live like this anyway?" she asked.

"My folks died two years ago. Battinger's D. I wasn't there, but y'know… when the bank account stops getting filled, you kinda figure."

"God, I'm so sorry, Pyotr."

"It's okay," he said, but his expression said otherwise. "Part of the package, right? Anyway… I made it this far home, ran out of money just east of Prague and had to turn back. Been living the life of adventure ever since."

"For how long?"

"Almost a year and a half, I guess. Can't afford a watch battery," he said, smiling again, showing her his stopped watch. Eva frowned at it, then pulled the wad of papers and cards out of her pocket, fished through them until she found a hundred-euro note. She handed it over to him.

"Here you go," she said. "Get yourself hooked up. It's on me."

He took the money, waved it a bit, smirking.

"Now all I've got to do is find someplace that sells batteries, that's still open for business. And accepts cash. Yay!"

"So it's really that bad here? They were still taking paper money in Stuttgart when I left a few days ago. What're you supposed to do then? How does anyone survive?"

"They don't, mostly," said Pyotr seriously. "But when you need food, there's a government stockroom across the Charles that's open most days. A lot of the packages are ripped open or otherwise trashed, but it's better than nothing. But for the rest... yeah, it's not too good in Prague. Pockets of civilization next door to splashes of apocalypse. It's surreal sometimes. The only fully-functioning facility left in town is the Motol, and even that's not what it used to be."

"You got sick?"

"Broke my arm. They set it in the parking lot and sent me home without pain meds, just in case. No x-rays, no follow-up. Too dangerous to go inside. Kind of like how I'm treating you, but I think they had medical degrees."

"Jesus, that's brutal," Eva whispered, glanced outside and noticed the snow was falling harder now. Pyotr put the final touches on the bandage and turned her arm around back and forth.

"How's it feel?" he asked.

"Like utter crap, but well contained."

"That's what I'm going for!" he smiled, then his expression changed. Worry. "Eva, is this your passport?"

"Yeah, why?"

Pyotr got to his feet with a start, looked around himself, then ran to the window, crunching glass as he went, leaned out. Eva stood up too, the room colder without the blanket, and watched as Pyotr threw the passport into the empty fireplace, kicked ashes onto it.

"What's going on?" Eva asked as Pyotr started picking up his things, shoving stuff into his pockets.

"You're 17-5, right?" he asked, and she flinched.

"Yes. I mean, they keep saying—"

"It means tag and trace," he said seriously, looking out the door to the landing. It had taken some work to make it up the fire-ravaged steps on the way here. Rushing down was not an option. "They put a chip in your passport so they can find you if they lose you."

Eva looked back at the fireplace, at the ashes kicked around, then back at Pyotr, who suddenly shifted back into the room. A flashlight beam shining up from the floors below.

"Ms Kolikov!" came a voice, calm and determined. "we're not done our chat yet!"

"Sobotka," growled Pyotr, backing up till window glass broke under his feet. He turned round, looked out the window. Eva was by his side in an instant, saw the fire escape, checked his expression.

"We've got to get out of here," she said, swinging one leg over the window ledge and planting a foot on the rusted metal outside. She grabbed hold of the railing with her good hand and pulled herself out. The metal was slippery from the snow, and before she could stop it, she slipped sideways, landed on the window sill on her right shoulder, the fragments of glass cutting into her skin, and she called out in pain.

Pyotr put his hand over her mouth before she could do much damage, a panicked look in his eyes. He climbed out, too, helped Eva to her feet, and without a word, nudged her down the stairs.

After one storey, Eva got her footing, and picked up speed. She skidded round the last bend, grabbed hold of the railing, but with her bandaged hand, and the pain was so terrible she shrieked and let go. She slipped onto her back and fell off the edge of the gate, only catching hold of the metal at the last second, holding on so tight it felt like her fingertips had fused into her palm.

Pyotr was on his chest, wrapping his strong hands around her forearm, his teeth gritting audibly.

"Hold on," he whispered through the strain, trying to pull her back up, the sidewalk cold and icy below them.

"Ms Kolikov *and friend!*" shouted Sobotka from the window above. "Bonus for me!"

Eva heard the sound of heavy feet on metal. Pyotr wasn't making any progress getting her back up… their eyes met quickly, urgently, and for a second neither said a thing. Then Pyotr knew what she was going to do, and he shook his head as much as he could manage.

"You can't," he grunted.

"I can't go back," she said, and pulled herself free.

19

Eva's heel hit the ground, and for a moment she thought she had dropped two storeys unscathed.

But then her weight shifted, her foot slipped on slick ice, and before she could react, her head hit the pavement. Pain shot pink and bright blue streaks across her vision; she blinked rapidly to regain her sight. She gasped at the pain, closed her eyes again and held them shut so tight it felt like her brains might collapse from the pressure.

When she opened them again, she was floating, her arm wrapped over Pyotr's shoulders, her feet grazing the ground like they were pretending to walk.

Shock set in, and she gripped into Pyotr's neck and gasped. He pulled her against a cold wall in the darkness, pushed her back and looked at her with a panicked face.

"Don't make a sound," he whispered so quietly she almost didn't hear. She tried to calm herself, but her head was swimming and something about it didn't seem real to her, and she shuddered, her head aching so intensely she had trouble seeing past it.

To her right, a street. She was in an alley she didn't recognize, off a wide street without tire marks on it. Snow was melting from the buildings above, dripping down next to her, on her, and the *tap, tap, tap* of drops hitting puddles was mesmerizing. She almost didn't hear the footsteps in the street, cautious and careful.

Pyotr put a hand down onto her stomach, pushed her back, and she fought against her delirium, kept herself still.

She saw the figure through the pain: Sobotka, silhouetted by streetlights, standing at the edge of the alley, peering in. She checked over her shoulder, then back towards them. Eva didn't even breathe, heard her heartbeat in her ears, the sound of her head rubbing against brick.

Sobotka pointed a light into the alley... too far left, too far right, then she settled on a spot just ahead of them, so close the beam was blinding...

Water tapped, and Eva could hear Pyotr's slow breathing beside her, and his hand was pressing so strong into her stomach it hurt. The light wavered slightly, darted quickly toward them, and then swung back, away, and Sobotka was gone.

Neither of them moved for a minute or more, and Eva put her hand on Pyotr's, took hold and tried to move it so she could breathe again. The pain came flooding back to her head in the absence of fear, and she nearly collapsed. She looked to Pyotr, who was still watching the street nervously. He reluctantly pulled his gaze away, saw her, smiled.

"Are you okay?" he asked.

Eva nodded, willing a calm facade.

"Thank you," she said quietly. "you saved me."

They moved deeper into the alley, took a turn to the right, then a few turns more that Eva only noticed in the corners of her mind; the pain kept coming in waves up her neck and into her eyes.

They paused in a small deserted courtyard, a bench bolted to giant slabs of concrete. Empty, broken, wooden crates strewn everywhere. Eva smiled weakly at it, the refuge, and then promptly fell to her knees and vomited all over the slushy snow.

Pyotr ran to her side, rubbing her back and carefully leading her to the bench, helping her down. She felt another wave coming on, but swallowed, tried to see past the pain in her head.

"Concussion…" she wheezed, spitting bile into the snow.

Pyotr ran a hand across her cheek, looked nervous.

"You're pale," he said, uncertain, probing for answers beyond his reach. She squeezed her eyes shut and tried holding her breath.

"It's going… to get… worse…" she gasped, and he gripped her hands tighter.

"Wait a second," he said, rattling urgent fingers through his pockets. Eva doubled over and tried not to vomit again. She was counting to ten for the third time when he found them: two large, blue pills, dusted with lint.

"Take these," he said gently.

She squinted, looked up at him, her vision laced with light and pain.

"W-w-what are they?"

He put the pills in her hand, and she squeezed them tight as another shot of nausea stunned her.

"It's called Tezocet, I think. Painkillers. Um, anti-inflammatory something."

She nodded slightly, the motion causing unbearable pain. With a quick motion, she shoved the pills into her mouth, swallowed, then pushed the heels of her hands into her eyes, trying to focus past the agony so she wouldn't throw up again.

Pyotr was rubbing her back, gentle circles counter-clockwise, over and over… she felt the pain slide back, and she turned her head to him, opened her eyes, groggy.

"Working," she said quietly.

He nodded, smiled.

"Where did you get those pills?" Eva asked, her vision not clearing but the pain almost a shadow of what it was.

Pyotr looked down at the snow, guilty.

"Maselle," he said simply.

Somehow the cold was less frightening than it had been before, and Eva almost thought the sound of the wind on the rooftops above sounded muffled. Somehow off. She took a deep breath and her vision rippled with light.

"Painkillers working," she slurred. "and *strong*..."

She fell into his arms, and he held her tight.

"Listen, Eva," he said softly. "I know you and Rhodri had your differences, but..."

Eva's vision was so blurry suddenly she couldn't see her own legs beneath her, and the fuzzy shapes around her were shifting and turning, and she felt so dizzy and sleepy it was hard to listen ...

"Sometimes you don't appreciate what you had till it's too late," she heard Pyotr say, but she didn't really know what it meant anymore.

"I need to find my mama," she sighed, and he caught her head as it fell backwards.

"Eva? Eva, can you hear me?"

Eva felt her eyes roll back in her head, and fell as if she were sinking into a snowy field, with Pyotr somewhere out in the sky, calling her back to him.

The cough was ragged, so grating it was surprising no blood came out with the mucus. Anouma held the plastic bowl close to his mouth and leaned him forward so it was all out. He gasped for air and fell back, lying on the sweaty mattress he called his home. His arms moved helplessly at his sides, waving back and forth as if he were drowning.

The pit nurse checked her clipboard, glanced at the man's tag number.

"So he had no ID on him?" she asked, checking through papers quickly.

"None," said Anouma softly. "He was dumped outside in a hospital gown."

"Cast-offs from Františku Hospital again?"

"It could be. I have heard they are closing soon."

The nurse sighed, flipped a few more pages, looked at the patient.

"So what's his diagnosis? We need to find a place to move him. He's end-stage, isn't he?"

Anouma urgently motioned for the nurse to follow her away from the bed, down a short distance to a spot where most of the patients were still asleep.

"Be careful what you say," she whispered angrily. "He can hear you."

"But he—"

"He is fully conscious. He knows what is happening to him, but he cannot control his body enough to tell us. His motor control is gone, his lungs are failing, and he is living with endless pain we cannot treat. Do not add to his misery."

The nurse looked sufficiently chastised, met Anouma's eyes.

"Fine. I'm sorry," she grumbled. "But what I want to know is if he's going to die soon, we'll leave him here. Otherwise, he's going upstairs."

Anouma sighed, looked out over the floor.

"He will survive indefinitely. It is how it works."

"Upstairs, then," said the nurse, and started to leave, before Anouma caught her arm. She pulled a nearby IV bag towards her, twisted it. The side of the bag was wet, and a tiny drop fell off the edge when it moved. The nurse looked closer, too, mouth hanging open.

"How did this happen? Are these being re-used?" Anouma asked squinting at it.

"Can't be. Those are fresh from upstairs. Must be a defect."

Anouma let it go, frowned down the row of beds, their own bags dangling above patients like bulbous flowers in a field of white.

"Double-check the supply room. We will lose a great deal of volume if there are others like this."

The nurse gave Anouma a withering look that went unnoticed.

"Yes, doctor," she glowered, then walked back to her muted patient, clipboard in hand. She kicked the brakes on the bed and began navigating it out of the room, clanging against other patients as she went.

Anouma rubbed her eyes with weary hands, slow and agonizing.

"Long day, doctor?" asked a voice from behind her. She turned, saw an old man laying in bed, his face covered with boils so big he almost didn't look human anymore. Still, somewhere in the mass of distorted flesh were brown eyes, dancing.

"Every day is a long day," Anouma said to him, picking up his chart and glancing over it. "How are you feeling today?"

"As well as I should, I think."

She checked his meds, eyed him cautiously.

"You are not depressed? Fatigued? Thoughts of suicide?"

The man laughed — or at least, laughed as much as he could without being able to move his face to smile.

"Because I won't be on the cover of a fashion magazine? No, I'll live."

Anouma laughed, clipped the chart back to his bed.

"Perhaps not a fashion magazine, but you should qualify for a medical journal write-up soon. It is widely assumed that Lumberger's causes depression as one of its symptoms. Apparently that is not the case."

"No, they're all just sad they look like burnt mozzarella," he replied. "Me, I'm used to being called ugly. I've been married for fifty years."

Anouma smiled, patted him on a clear shoulder, and he patted her gloved hand back. Then she saw it… another drop falling off the edge of his IV bag. She squeezed it gently, and saw a tiny trickle from the side of the bag, running saline down onto her glove.

"Odd," she whispered. "Another one…"

The patient tried to turn his head to see what she was looking at, but was prevented by his ailment.

"What's what? What's wrong?"

Anouma let go of the bag, shook her head.

"Nothing. We have to get you another bag. Some seem to be leaking for some reason. I will fetch a new one now, I think. Just wait a moment while I—"

"Help!" came a shout from the far end of the room, and two paramedics in heavy masks burst in the doors dragging a wretchedly battered woman in their arms, her chest all bloodied and her head hanging limp, bouncing lifelessly as they pulled her onto a stretcher. Anouma made a dash for them, saw Dr Bastien hang up a chart and start running too.

"What happened?" Anouma asked, swapping gloves and swinging her stethoscope around, checking vitals.

"White female, mid-twenties, looks like a knife attack. Three lacerations to the abdomen, one to the neck."

They lifted some gauze off her neck and blood sprayed out, making them both flinch.

"Hold it steady," she ordered.

"But—"

"If you are scared of blood, you are in the wrong job! Vitals?"

The paramedics scrambled to answer. Anouma ignored them, checked the wounds, probing with gentle fingers.

"Very deep. Liver, maybe. Vitals! Now!"

"We couldn't check," said one of the paramedics, backing up again at the sight of blood. Anouma glared at him.

"Bag him or get out," she said coldly.

"How many?" Dr Bastien asked, arriving at her side, pulling on fresh gloves.

"Three at the chest, one at the neck."

"Blood pressure?"

"We do not know yet," she said, glaring at the paramedics.

Dr Bastien snuffed, knocked the brakes off the stretcher and wheeled the patient over to the makeshift trauma area. Anouma kicked a pedal up and down near the bed, priming the generator. A short cough later, the lights came on, beaming bright white onto the blood.

One of the paramedics had already disappeared.

"Do a blood test on her, for god's sake," Anouma hissed to the other. He nodded, pushed a portable testing unit against the woman's arm and backed away as Dr Bastien pushed his way in, feeling the chest wounds.

"Decreased lung function on the left," he said to Anouma, squinting as he listened, looked. Blood bubbled up and out of the cuts. The woman's eyes suddenly shot open and the shock of what was happening to her made her convulse violently. She jerked upwards, trying to escape, gasped and coughed, spitting blood across herself and onto the doctors.

"Blood pressure dropping," Anouma called out, watching the monitor she'd hooked up herself. Dr Bastien grabbed a scalpel off a tray, began work on the highest of the wounds. Anouma grabbed the suction tube and was about to hand it over when she noticed it was already bloody. She threw it to the ground.

"Suction contaminated," she growled. "I will find another."

"I'm losing her pulse," Bastien said as the monitors wailed. "Skip the suction. We need to stop the bleeding!"

Anouma nodded, passed him a new package of scalpels and gauze, and then swung back for a pack of clamps. The cart with supplies was too far away... she reached for it, but the monitors whined loudly, warning the patient was crashing.

"Twenty cc's of Entophin!" Bastien called, starting compressions. Anouma snatched a vial off the cart, punched a syringe into the needle dispenser and drew serum. She aimed for a bulging vein on the patient's arm.

The woman convulsed again, and Anouma's hand was hit so suddenly the needle missed its target and slid across the back of her right glove, ripping latex and hitting her skin.

The paramedic gasped, but Anouma didn't flinch, tried again and pushed the meds. The woman's heart rate started coming back up, and the monitor calmed, but the blood was still pouring from her wounds.

"I need suction," Bastien called, already cutting and probing without the aid of the clamps Anouma had missed. She pulled off her gloves, opened a drawer with her fingertips, removed a packaged suction head and swapped out the old one. She handed it over to Bastien, who took it without looking.

The back of her hand was bleeding slightly, but she ignored it, threw on a new set of gloves and re-joined the crisis. The paramedic eyed her anxiously.

"You will need a packer," she said, checking the stats. She started to go back to the cupboard, but Bastien caught her hand, letting the suction drop out and away, and twisted it so he could see the blood beneath her glove.

"When did this happen?" he said gravely.

"Just now," she offered, tried to pull away.

"Fanta," he said, holding tight. "*when?*"

She met his eyes, cold and unforgiving.

"Yes, I came in contact," she admitted.

Bastien pushed down on the wound he was working on to stop the bleeding, waved a bloodied hand out to the paramedic.

"Give me the test results!" he shouted. The paramedic was startled, jumped up and almost tossed the device towards Bastien, who caught it deftly and quickly paged through screens.

"TB-G 14," he sighed, threw the device at the side of the bed, then looked at Anouma. "Go clean that, and stay away from the patient, Fanta."

Anouma shook her head, grabbed the suction, started back. Bastien caught her wrist, squeezed.

"Dr Anouma, *leave the room.*"

"You need me."

"Find Dr Laroche!" Bastien barked at the paramedic. "Now!"

Anouma tried to break free, but she wasn't nearly as strong as the old man. His eyes were cold and menacing.

"It is a tiny scratch," she tried. "*you need me now.*"

"TB-G 14 could kill you!" he boomed. "You don't have the antibodies. Someone else will take your place. That's final. Now back away so I can save this patient!"

The ferocity of it make her flinch, and she reluctantly stepped back, held her hand gingerly, watched him work on his own.

"TB-G is not the same as Tuberculosis," she said quietly. "I am in virtually no danger of contracting it from her."

"'Virtually' is not 'absolutely', Fanta. There's a very large gulf between them. One I've lost many colleagues to."

She didn't want to leave, hesitated, but saw he wouldn't hear any more objections. She nodded. Slightly. Turned halfway.

"I will go clean this out. And… find Dr Laroche."

He didn't reply, just kept working.

She stormed into the side room and hit the water on harder than she needed to. She started scrubbing disinfectant onto her hands, her teeth clenched shut and her eyes not watching what she was doing. She heard the sound of the monitors coding again, and though Dr Laroche ran past her as she stood there, by the sounds and shouts and panic in the air, she knew it was too late.

She gripped the edge of the sink, her head bowed, and refused to cry.

OUTSIDE PRAGUE, CZECH REPUBLIC
NOVEMBER 28

It was close to eleven o'clock before the Healer escaped the old city limits. Behind him, Prague was a faint glow, patches of lights coming from fireplaces and not electricity, dark spots where civilization had retreated. Like a medieval town again.

He passed a man with a bucket, trying to steal some water from a public drinking fountain; all that came out was dark sewage. The man took it anyway. Nearby, a manhole bubbled up, pushed by foam and dirt as the old underground infrastructure crumbled. A pair of bodies lay in a ditch, decomposing in the frigid air. They were being submerged by the sewage leak, would stay frozen until spring. It was a long time away.

An armoured car driven by two men in hazmat suits rumbled down the country road. On the side of the truck was a picture of a young woman smiling, a crystal glass in her hand, the vibrant logo of her company teasing the grey, decrepit world she passed by.

The proud stadium, once a great and majestic thing, had been turned into a sorting area for the dead. A large billboard along the road had advertised a EuroCup match there from years before, the larger-than-life players faded and blue. There were no games there now, only massive furnaces turning the sky red with heat.

Large trucks covered in snow and mud paced through, in endless shifts, dropping off their grim cargo. The colour-coded body bags were deposited in heaps at the entrances, and workers moved with uneasy speed to get them cleared away, to the incinerators, as the cold set in. In the centre of the stadium, four pillars of smoke reached into the sky and faded into the clouds. Ash covered the snow on the ground.

Across the way in a soccer pitch, a large group had gathered, all dressed in black, watching the stadium's fires. Some were praying, others weeping, and the rest just staring in uncertain disbelief. The Healer saw one cough openly, no masks in sight. He looked away in disgust.

He found a small patch of unused land at the edge of town, near a brook, and set up his tent. He lay there in the darkness, the mask pressing against his skin and the cold seeping past his armour. He listened to the sound of his breathing.

The radio crackled to life.

"Home to Green Four," came the familiar voice. He sat up, flipped up the antenna, stared up into the sky.

"Green Four here. Go ahead."

"You are outside Prague city limits," Home said. "Please advise on timetable."

He pushed open the door to his tent, looked at the pitch black sky.

"I have a credible lead. Will investigate tomorrow."

Static.

"Understood, Green Four. However…" the voice trailed off, tentative. "Your schedule may not allow for delay."

The Healer looked at the ground, let the tent close again.

"Approaching a target in the dark risks unnecessary violent confrontations," he said, devoid of emotion. "It is best to make contact in the morning, in my experience."

"Such tactics are not standard practices," came the answer. It was meant to be the final word.

"Standard practices," the Healer said coldly, "do not reflect the reality of the mission."

There was a long silence. The wind blew the tent and it angled slightly, fluttering.

"Green Four, your experience is noted. You are the last of the first wave. There had been talk of relieving you as well, to give you the hero's welcome you deserve. But you, above all others, were able to bring satisfactory results for us."

The Healer put his head in his hands, said nothing.

"However, your rate of progress has slowed in recent months. We are re-evaluating our earlier decision."

Static again. The Healer didn't move. The wind gusted again, twigs hitting the tent and flying away.

"How long do I have?" the Healer asked.

Static.

"You must leave Prague within forty-eight hours. One way or another."

The Healer said nothing for some time.

"Good luck, Green Four. We will monitor your progress carefully."

He turned down the antenna once more, and sat there in the dark, unmoving.

*   *   *

In his dream, he felt the warmth of a summer's day in the fields of Tacheng. The grass was brushing against his palms as he ran toward the piercing blue sky, chasing his brother, and he felt lightness in his chest in a way he had forgotten long ago.

And then the warmth grew stronger and redder until it was a sudden fire, lashing at his face, and he was aware he was wearing his mask, and he heard the sound of his voice (though he wasn't speaking) in his native tongue, calling for rear guards, to hold the line. Hold the line.

And he saw the eyes of a girl in the eastern provinces, not angry, not sad, just bewildered as the smoke choked her and her black hair burned so brightly.

He never heard her scream, not this time, but he was so overcome with his own voice calling out orders that he woke with a start, gasping, his suit whining in his ears, warning him to pace himself, to calm himself, to stay on target.

*   *   *

Carey sat on a wire-mesh chair beneath the giant logo for Zemus Pharmaceuticals, a blue glow shining from behind its spotless silvery lettering. He paged through the magazine one more time, not pausing at the articles or photos; just going through the motions, his eyes on the clock above the receptionist's desk.

He put the magazine aside, straightened out his trousers, and got up. Once he was at standing height, the receptionist gave him an evil stare, a carrot stick hanging out of her mouth, pinched between manicured fingers.

Carey leaned on the edge of her desk, smiled as best he could.

"I don't suppose you have any further information about Mr Daniels, do you?" he asked.

The receptionist chewed her carrot at him.

"Mr Daniels is not in the office at the moment," she replied. "If you'd like to leave a message, I can be sure he calls you as soon as he gets in."

Carey sighed, played with a set of business cards on the counter, which were promptly taken away from him.

"Actually, I did that yesterday. All day yesterday, in fact, and he never did call back."

"He's a very busy man, Mr Daniels is."

"I appreciate that, but I'm here on government business."

She rolled her eyes, cracked off another piece of carrot, chewed noisily.

"*Everyone* calling Mr Daniels is on government business," she sighed. "But if you want to leave another message, I can be sure he —"

"Okay, listen, I don't believe you anymore. He's in his office right now, isn't he? I just can't believe that a vice president at a major pharmaceutical company isn't in the office at… at a half past ten on a Tuesday. It's just beyond belief."

She said nothing, but made it clear it was because he bored her.

"I demand to be taken to see Mr Daniels immediately!" Carey said, his voice rising.

This got her attention. She scowled at him, waved a menacing carrot.

"Mr Daniels got in a half hour ago," she said.

"And you're just telling me this *now?*"

"He's gone straight into a board meeting. All-day type of thing. You could come back tomorrow, or leave a message, which I assure you he will reply to as soon as he can."

Carey pressed his forehead against the counter, whimpered, then started to laugh quietly. He propped his head up on one hand, and let out a loud moan, much to the receptionist's displeasure.

"Miss, this is not the situation I wanted to be in."

"No, sir," she said, inching away from him.

"My boss — he's the Director of the Containment Office, mind you — he's very strict about these kinds of things. Has rules. Follow the rules. Goose-stepping sort of fellow, if you know what I mean."

By the way she slowed her chewing, it was clear she did not.

"Now my boss, he told me very clearly: if they give you any lip, *any lip at all*, I want you to declare a D-22 right there, on the spot."

The receptionist blinked twice, refused to betray confusion.

"I said to him: sir, I think that's counter-productive. A D-22 would just… just… it would be totally out of proportion to the crime, honestly. And I—"

"Fine, I'll bite. What's a D-22?"

Carey sprung to life. He pulled a small handheld out of his pocket, hit a few screens, turned it to show her briefly.

"Strictly speaking, a D-22 is when I say our scanners have picked up a foreign substance in the air, and you all have to be quarantined until further notice."

She stopped chewing altogether.

"See, it's completely unethical in these circumstances, because first of all, I don't actually have a scanner on me most of the time. And they take, literally, *an hour* to process the air for a sample. So the suggestion that I'd be able to say for certain that you were all infected with something like Kiev-7... it's absurd, really."

The receptionist swallowed slowly.

"And in the end, it really gets us no closer to whatever we're after in the first place. Sure, they'd lock down the whole building, strip every worker naked and spray them with six batches of disinfectant. And sort you by function and rank, then clothe you in standard issue government jumpsuits — good God do those chafe, let me tell you — and send you to Brighton for quarantine."

"B-B-B-Brighton?"

"Oh certainly, for at least twenty-six weeks. By which point they'd have ascertained that my original reading was probably incorrect, and they'd replace my scanner and shrug and say 'Oh well! Better luck next time!'"

The receptionist smiled weakly.

"But as I said to my boss... it won't really help me have a sit-down with Mr Daniels."

"Mr Daniels hasn't been in the office for weeks," blurted out the girl, blanching horribly. "Nobody's seen him for so long. The president is in a tizzy, everyone is after him. I honestly, truly, don't know where he is!"

Carey leaned over the counter, close to the receptionist, squinted at her.

"Are you sure about that? No idea at all?"

She darted nervous glances left and right. Leaned closer to him.

"He... he's been accessing the mainframe here, through a secure connection," she whispered.

"Do you know where from?"

"It's never clear, but one time I saw his address resolving to something to do with 'Praha.'"

Carey frowned.

"Prague?"

"That's what I thought, too. But I can't be sure."

Carey nodded, stood back from the desk, checking his handheld again.

"Well," he said loudly, jovially. "No readings here. Must be clean. Thank you!"

He turned to leave, hit the button at the lift, and his phone buzzed in his pocket. He slid it out, flipped it open, and was greeted with the sound of the Director clearing his throat.

"Good God, Carey, it's been a full day. You're supposed to have told me you took care of things."

Carey smiled a fake smile, nodded to the receptionist, who was eyeing him cautiously.

"Took longer than expected, sir. Ran into a bit of interference, but I pulled the old D-22 card, and things worked out fine."

"The what? Listen, Carey, there's no time for prattling around. Have you given him the message, or not?"

Carey nodded to the receptionist, got into the empty elevator, and the doors closed. His composure melted instantly.

"No, sir. He's not here."

"Then go to his home, blast you. Show some initiative!"

"It's not that, sir. He's not in the country. I have reason to suspect he's in the Czech Republic at the moment. Although I'd like to get our boys here to check server logs to be sure if—"

"No time for that, and no politics about it. Listen here, Carey... if anyone but you or me thinks he's outside the country, there'll be hell to pay. Absolute hell."

"Yes sir."

"I need you to get on a plane, get to whatever backward shithole he's stuck in, and bring him back."

"S-s-sir, we're talking about a black zone... there are... there are protocols about quarantine and such, and I'm not sure—"

The Director cleared his throat.

"You've done this before, haven't you, Will?"

Carey rested his head against the wall of the elevator, closed his eyes.

"Oh, uh, yes sir, but I... well, yes. Yes I have."

"Good. I'll requisition the plane. Get back here as fast as you can."

Carey shook his head slowly, as if trying to jostle a good excuse to the fore. His hand pressed against his forehead, he whimpered a reply.

"Sir," he said. "Sir... if... if I find him, there are only two ways this can turn out. Prison, or... or —"

The Director interrupted him.

"Or exile," he said, his voice almost angry, but eerily calm.

In the oppressive dark of the night, snow still glowed impossibly as it drifted into the street by the hospital. Anouma leaned against the wall, her mask hanging loose around her neck, breathing in the clear cold air.

The scrape on the back of her hand was wrapped in a thick bandage meant for purging wounds. She absent-mindedly rubbed it, the peach colour stark against her brown skin.

A woman pushed a baby carriage down the side street, the wheels catching and spinning in the thickening snow. There was no baby inside: it rattled and clanked as the random junk and food shook on the uneven ground.

Anouma heard the crunch of snow underfoot behind her, didn't turn, waited for Dr Bastien to stop next to her, looking out into the winter.

"I didn't mean to be harsh," he said. "I hope you understand."

She nodded, looked over at him.

"I just wish I could have helped more."

"I do, too," he said, his tired eyes meeting hers. "I think we all do. I wish to god they'd immunized you before you got on that plane. It's unfair, leaving you with that handicap. You've been so brave, coming here."

Anouma shrugged, watched the woman with the carriage.

"It is what they would have done for us," she said.

Bastien snorted, she felt him watching her.

"Not most of them," he said, angrily. "And that you think that... it's what makes you a good doctor, I suppose."

"People are not as callous as you think, Bastien," she said, meeting his gaze again.

"Not callous, no," he said. "Myopic. Dangerously myopic."

"I cannot forget what they did for my people," she said.

"And you shouldn't. Those doctors, the scientists and their companies, they saved the world. Once upon a time. But you can't forget what they *didn't do*."

Anouma nodded slightly.

"It is not their fault. There are only so many resources they can —"

Bastien coughed loudly, waved her to silence.

"Don't buy their bullshit so willingly," he grumbled. "You embarrass yourself."

"They saved my country when we were on the brink of extinction. They may be only human, but they are good people."

"You've got your history confused," he said simply.

Anouma put a hand on his shoulder and he winced, refused to look back. The scars on his face, around his neck... signs of battles he'd fought with diseases that would have crushed anyone else where they stood. He was not easily bowed by anything anymore.

"What happened in Russia, that is not your fault," she ventured. "The odds were against you. Against all of you. And you did the best you could. But it is *different* here! This is not the same situation. You cannot go on carrying the chains they forced on you back then."

He looked round at her suddenly, his eyes narrow.

"The chains aren't gone," he growled. "they'll tug them when they're threatened."

Anouma tried to object, but he cut her off.

"The only difference between then and now," he said bitterly, "is that they've become better at wrapping the truth in dangerous hopes."

"Hope is not dangerous. Hope is how we survive."

"Hope is how you *think* you'd survive. But you won't." He seemed lost in a flash of a painful memory, squinted at her. "Hope helps nothing. And in a painful majority of cases, neither can you. Sometimes it almost seems better to do it like the Healers did it. Clean it all out, start fresh. The battle here just... it just never ends."

The wind blew, knocked Anouma's mask about her neck, and she pushed some hair from her face. They stood there in the cold as the snow fell.

"How is Adjobi?" Bastien asked, his tone back to his normal, battle weary self.

"He is brave. His white count is very low, but he has not worsened."

"That's good," was the reply, empty.

"What is wrong?" she asked. He avoided her eyes.

"Word came in from Paris," he said. "They say there isn't sufficient demand yet to produce another run of vaccines."

Anouma's face went blank, she could feel it.

"Did they say..."

He shook his head grimly.

"Twelve months."

She nodded solemnly.

"At the earliest," he added, then shook his head. "And I'm not sure I can keep the health director at bay to the end of the week, let alone a year. He's demanding all blood samples be delivered tomorrow, so they can start issuing deportation orders on December the first."

Anouma said nothing.

"I'll cover for you as best I can, Fanta, but I can't hide you forever. Too many people know where you and Adjobi came from, and they'll make the connection."

"If only they had kept a little of the vaccine. Just two doses, and we would be fine..."

"Fanta," Bastien said gravely. "nearly two million Africans died from AIDS last year alone. Two doses doesn't begin to cover it. It's an untreated epidemic of dead diseases, and it makes me sick every time I talk to Geneva."

Anouma bowed her head, stared at the snow in silence.

"It's not what they do," he said flatly. "it's what they ignore. And they'll punish you for their faults, believe me. It's the proud chains they'll use to hang us all."

NOVEMBER 29

23

In his backpack were the instruments needed for a sustainable incursion into a foreign land, all carefully wrapped and positioned in layers of tough bullet-proof cloth; never easily accessible, most of it rarely touched. It weighed as much as a second person on his back, and despite the metal rails built to alleviate the strain on his spine, the Healer had built a formidable set of muscles along his shoulders and torso because of it.

Before the sun rose that morning, he was perched in the darkness of the tent, carefully sorting and shifting the things he needed to set out.

The outer layer of the pack was the easiest to reach, but it contained mostly armour plating and bandages, never anything breakable or important. He removed the topmost covering on his gloves and used the latex layer to grab a pair of lifting tabs on the pack, slowly and patiently shifted the entire platform over onto a clean space on the tent floor.

In the next layer was a red plastic device meant for blood analysis. He removed it from its holding brace and connected it to a small battery wire that peeked through the middle of his pack. He left it on the ground, its battery indicator slowly animating upwards.

Another device, this one grey and half-metal, connected to a socket along his left biceps, and his suit contracted slightly along his arm like a mechanical tourniquet. A faint beep close to his ear announced the end of the test, and his suit relieved the pressure gradually, the feeling coming back to his clenched hand. He replaced the device in the pack, exactly as before, and dismissed the results readout on a small screen below; he did not pause to read. The radio lay silent on the ground beside him; that was all he needed to know.

The blood analysis device finished charging, and a faint blue light pulsed to life on its head. The Healer slipped his hand back into its outer glove, unlatched a piece of armour on his left forearm. He folded it back and peeled open a portal in the suit, rimmed with bright yellow, clean white rubber beneath.

Sliding his glove off again, he carefully placed his index finger and thumb on two depressions along the yellow rim, twisted counter-clockwise twice, and then pushed down. It clicked open, and he pinched his fingers together to remove it, placing it next to the blood analysis device in his pack. A disinfectant spray doused it immediately on contact.

The grey device connected seamlessly with the new socket he'd uncovered, and he rotated it clockwise, a quarter-turn, until he heard it latch. He pushed the blue button at the head, and a quiet beep played in his ears; he felt a tug and hiss as the device sucked the air out of the connection, creating a miniature vacuum. A small LCD readout showed the airlock was confirmed, and a second beep preceded a thirty-second spray of strong disinfectant. His skin stayed carefully isolated from this routine, covered by two further layers of protection.

After a moment of calibration, the device connected itself to his static IV and pumped five millilitres of blood into a small vial, closed the connection and began processing. He unlatched it, replaced all the covers in a careful repetition of his earlier routine, and glanced at the device's small screen. No warnings.

He checked his second pack, the smaller one that carried his food and tools, saw the edge of a wafer package, beckoning him. He looked away immediately, back at the task at hand. The sun was rising.

* * *

It was an hour before he made it back to the main road north into Prague, his pace methodical, yet faster than usual.

The neighbourhood he was tracking was made up of low-rise buildings, blankets hung from open windows. In the early morning light, he heard the sounds of children waking their parents, almost-quiet clanging dishes, yawns travelling far in the thin cold air. An old man in a housecoat stood on his front step, smoking a cigarette, his eyes locked on the Healer, his hands frozen.

The Healer checked the street sign again: Michalská. This was the right place, but not yet at the right house. He turned his head away from the old man, looked down the street. A thin coating of snow lay on the ground, and more was falling. He kept moving, checking back a few steps later. The old man's eyes narrowed, frozen, his head turned but his body unmoved. *You are not welcome here.*

Number 21 was a two-storey apartment complex with a small chimney off to the right, puffing out smoke in a lazy drizzle. The front door had a large oval window in it, though the glass was badly cracked, the shiny metal handle dented and warped inward. There were no lights inside the foyer.

A shift in light to his left caught his eye, and he twitched his head slightly to see. Three men, just out of bed it seemed, watching him from a distance. The street was suddenly silent. Children were quiet.

He turned his head straight again, as if to show he would ignore them all. He listened carefully for the sound of feet in snow. There was silence for a minute. No sounds, no movement, no hint of intention. The Healer carefully walked up the steps to the front door, wrapped his fingers round the handle, and opened it.

Still, silence.

He stepped inside, his foot gravelled and rough, grinding into the dirty wood floor, a piercing noise. The door slowly eased to a close behind him, but he did not turn his head to look out. They were watching him with gaping mouths.

The door at the end of the hall was shut tight, but in the dark he could clearly see the hint of shadows right under the door. The peep hole flickered light. Nervous movements. He stopped to the left of the door, his back to the wall, and listened.

Outside, faces at the base of the steps, watching him through the shattered glass. No sounds.

He reached a hand out, saw the faces outside tense, and knocked on the door three times. The faces at the door creeped ever closer, desperate to see what would happen. After a short period of silence, he reached over, knocked again, three times.

He heard a quiet shuffle from inside, fading as it went, a floorboard creaking. Escape! He quickly unsheathed his machete, wedged its blade against the doorknob and slammed down the handle until the brass orb hit the ground with a bang.

There was a yelp from inside as the blade pounded into the locking mechanism. The door swung open. He pushed it, but a chain at the top stopped him. He glanced back at the front door, the faces right against the glass now, their expressions tense, angry, vengeful. He kicked the door open and quickly stormed in.

He was straight into the living room, a single rug covering the abused oak floor. To the right, a grimy kitchen, the refrigerator door slightly ajar, feeble light lighting the cupboards; no one there. He turned and saw, in the corner, a woman and a child huddled in the corner, behind a chair. The woman didn't make eye contact, but the boy watched the Healer with wide open eyes. Not afraid, just... in awe.

The Healer carefully walked over, knelt down in front of the woman, but did not speak. The boy's mouth was crusted over with scabs, his skin yellowing, and he was thinner than he ought to be, even malnourished. The Healer reached out a careful hand, pushed the boy's long hair off his forehead, saw the pox there. The woman could tell, pulled the boy closer, tighter, started whimpering.

Behind him, a creak, the floor giving the rescue party away, and the Healer got to his feet quickly, put his hand out to them as a warning. There were five of them, all large men, all groggy, but intensely awake. He stared them down, one by one, and then shook his head.

They started to spread out, trying to encircle him. Their stances were brave, but inexperienced; spurred on by a sense of nobility, protecting their own. The one further to his left put his arms out, his fists ready, and made quick eye contact with the others.

The Healer lowered his hand, kept his palms out, passive. The men all shifted themselves, nervous. The Healer — hands out and visible — slowly bowed to them... but as he held the bow he heard the swish from the left, and caught a man's leg before it hit his face.

With a quick twist, the man was flipped off his feet. He landed on his back, and the Healer threw his leg away, stood straight, and blocked a wild punch from another attacker. He grabbed the wrist, hit the elbow to disable him, and then slammed his knee into the man's right side, knocking him down and away. He turned to the last three assailants, each backing up, looking oddly exposed with the numbers in their favour.

The Healer again reached out a hand, shook his head 'no', but the boy was crying now, and it added fire to their cause. The two downed men were groaning and rolling back to their feet. He darted a look to them, and shook his head again.

The man in the middle was whispering something to himself, and the other two reacted, became calm. The Healer didn't understand the language, but grasped the meaning by the pauses made at the last second...

One... two... *three!*

They charged him at once, a primal scream filling the room, but he was too fast. He slammed the middle man's head into the attacker on the right, and then pounded the left-most face with a sharp plated elbow, sending them all sprawling, but none to the floor. He kicked the middle man in the small of the back with so much force the poor wretch lost his footing and landed on his back, his head crashing into the wood.

The one with the bloodied face was stumbling forward, not able to fight in his state of shock, but valiantly wanting more. The Healer hit him in the stomach as hard as he could, winded him so badly he collapsed onto the ground, probably glad he had an excuse to stop.

The last man was dazed and unhurt, but the Healer passed up an easy kick to the head. Instead, he grabbed him by the throat, lifted him off the ground, and pinned him against the wall, the muscles in his arm twitching madly under the strain.

The Healer shook his head again, and the man's eyes said he finally understood. He sputtered something in gasps, and at the last, the Healer recognized a fragment of German. He barely understood, but there was enough to follow…

He let the man go, let him drop to the ground, slumping into a pile. The Healer knelt down before him, hand on his machete, warning.

"This boy sick," he said, only able to piece together slivers of German to make his case. "I must look… look for blood of Lewis."

The man stared up, his eyes narrow, scared, his lip trembling.

"Boy?" he asked, speaking quietly but slowly. "Lewis is not here."

The Healer looked at the boy, huddled in his mother's arms, tears in his eyes, and pointed.

"Lewis is not?" he asked.

The mother made eye contact, shivering, face wet, and urgently looked at the man at the Healer's feet, shook her head, didn't speak, but shook her head.

"Lewis is not here," the Healer understood from the tired man. "Not here… large."

The word was wrong, but the context made sense. Lewis had not been there for some time. The men behind him started getting their strength back, creaked back to their feet.

"Where did Lewis go?" he asked, his voice deep with rage.

The man and woman traded looks, and she quickly glanced at the Healer nervously, then back down, then seemed to think. She spoke quickly in Czech to the man, her voice wavering, fearful, desperate. The man looked solemn, took a shaky breath himself.

"We not know," he answered cautiously. "Not here large."

The Healer nodded, checked out the window at the distant skyline beyond the snow. A massive city, with no leads.

The woman was talking again, and it sounded like an argument. The Healer looked down at her and she quieted immediately, her eyes continuing the conflict silently. The Healer glanced at the man, who was looking away, trying to avoid saying something. He looked back up.

"Lewis —" … something new, difficult to understand … "— with. I know where."

The Healer repeated the word he had missed, but the man seemed at a loss. The Healer repeated it again, his voice sounding angrier than he intended, and the man's face fixed in fear.

"Lewis with wife. But not."

"Wife," he repeated.

"Not."

The Healer nodded.

"Where is his wife?" he asked. The man looked sheepish now, glanced to his comrades anxiously.

"Home of fire work," the man said.

"Fire?"

"Big fire. With… people?"

Pause. He heard the breathing of the other men, but they were not moving.

Then, he understood.

"Home of big fire… old home of… games?"

The man looked at him blankly.

"Home of big fire, is also for games?" the Healer repeated, urgent.

The man nodded slowly.

"Games not large," he said solemnly. "Not large. Fire now. Big fire."

The Healer nodded, stepped back.

"Yes," was all he could think to say.

The man touched his hand before he could leave, and he looked down again. The eyes were red, pained, wrestling with a guilt he would never defeat. After a pause, a raspy breath, he spoke:

"Wife… Marta. Lewis Kwong."

Kwong. He bowed to the man, who retreated at the motion, straightened and said a simple: "Thank you."

The man didn't answer. None of them spoke a word until he was gone from sight.

24

Rhodri rolled off Eva and collapsed on the bed, arms over his head and breathing heavily. She curled around him, rested her head on his chest, kissed it.

"Don't go back to work," she murmured, holding him tight. "Take the afternoon off."

He brushed her bare back with a dancing fingertip, smiled at her.

"What about you? Nothing to sell today?"

She rolled her eyes at him.

"I've got to paint more to sell more. And I'm definitely not inspired these days."

"What do you need for inspiration? Tell me and I'll get it for you."

She stretched out and kissed him, his beard scratching her chin, and rested her face against his neck.

"You don't need to buy me things. I'm fine the way I am. And we should be saving, not spending. Who knows when your luck will run out with the web jobs?"

Rhodri shrugged, stared at the ceiling.

"I'm pretty confident I've got it all taken care of."

"Yeah, you say that a lot. But I seem to remember being overjoyed about eating an apple a few months ago. I know how fast things can change."

He bent his face down, looked her straight in the eyes, spoke softly.

"Things are going to be good now, Eva. I promise you that. Things are under control, and getting better. I'm finally happy, and I'm going to make you happy too."

She grinned at him, then swung a leg across him, crouching among the sheets, and kissed his chin.

"Make me happy. Take the day off."

He tried to protest, but she moved her body down gently and took away his argument.

It was only minutes later that the peace was interrupted by the phone ringing loudly, shattering the moment. Rhodri turned an anxious face to the bedside table, and Eva caught his cheek with desperate hands.

"Ignore it," she pleaded. "They'll call back."

He did, and they did. A minute later. This time, she couldn't stop him from snatching the handset off the cradle and holding it to his ear, his other hand pressing a gentle finger to her lips to keep her quiet. She gave up the sounds, but not the motions. He bit back a moan himself.

"Rhodri here," he said, wavering.

He listened as Eva continued to make love, kissing his neck and his other ear, so immersed in the act that she didn't notice he was starting to sit up in bed, his brow tight with concern.

"Right now?" he asked. "Do I have time to—"

Eva saw his expression, held back a bit, and tried in vain to hear the other end of the conversation.

"All right," Rhodri said. "Got it. I'll call you when we get there."

He hung up the phone, tossed it to the end of the bed. Eva, pausing herself, tried to catch his gaze.

"When we get *where?*" she asked.

He was distracted, looking around the room.

"Graz. Austria."

"*Austria?* What's in Austria?"

"A great new opportunity, apparently," he said, sliding out from under her and throwing on his clothes. She sat there, nonplussed, and made no move to prepare.

"That was Dmitri again?" she asked, coldness in her voice.

"Yeah. He just heard there's a big demand for web designers in Graz right now. Money to be made. He's already got us train tickets, but we've got to be at the station by six."

"And you trust him? You think this is a good idea?"

Rhodri smiled at her, but it was a weak smile. He shrugged.

"Dmitri's always come through for me. If it weren't for him, we'd be out on the street right now. So if he wants us to go to Austria, I think we ought to give it a try."

"What if we don't *like* it there. What if there's an outbreak, or the only place to stay is worse than this?"

"The trains run both ways, Eva. Now come on, we've got to get ready. I need to pack up the office and tell the landlord I'm leaving."

Eva slipped into a pair of pyjama pants and a top, reached Rhodri as he was tying his shoes. She crouched down next to him, brushed the side of his face with her fingers and he looked at her. She rested her forehead against his.

"Are you sure we need this? I like it here. I thought we could just stay. You know. Like forever."

"Eva, I'm sorry. I like it here, too. But this is important to me. I wouldn't even entertain this idea if it weren't important. We can make things better in Austria. Just give it a try, okay?"

Eva looked at the ground for a minute, frowning. Then she met his eyes, nodded slightly.

"Will you get any afternoons off in Graz?" she asked, and he grinned.

"I'll make sure I do," he replied.

*   *   *

Beyond the blue haze, Eva could see shapes. White and brown, grey and black… they swirled ever so slightly, then began to solidify, became clear. She closed her eyes for a moment, and when she opened them again, she was on the ground in the snow, staring at a broken crate.

She rolled over, arm numb, and hit her head on the underside of the bench. Her vision flooded again, but she fought it and crawled out into the square. The snow had slowed to a trickle, though the sky was clear, light blue with only a few clouds. The air was colder than before, and she pulled her jacket tight.

She was alone; Pyotr had left in the night. The only footprints were her own.

Just then, a shuffle from the alley sent her racing for the nearest wall. She pressed herself against it tightly, grabbed a piece of broken wood from the ground and held it ready. She heard the sound of feet crunching in the snow, and then, at the entrance…

"Eva?" asked Pyotr from a distance. She dropped the wood and rushed to him, and he wrapped her in a blanket, rubbing her back. "Are you okay? When did you wake up?"

"Just now," she wheezed, her teeth chattering. "Where *were* you?"

"I had to go check on some—"

"You *left* me here, *alone?*" she said furiously.

"Listen, nobody'd come near you, lying on the ground like that. You were safer here than most places."

"So you say. I could've frozen to death."

He nodded solemnly, met her eyes.

"I'm sorry, okay? I just wanted to see what I could find out."

"About *what?*" she spat.

"Your mother," he said, staring at his feet.

Eva closed her mouth, bit her lip. She was still woozy, but she had enough wits to know what to do. She wrapped an arm around Pyotr, holding him tight.

"I'm sorry," she whispered. "I'm sorry, and thank you."

She let go and he shrugged, unhappily.

"It's not all good news," he said. "All I've got is an address from three weeks ago. If she's moved since then — and given the neighbourhood, she would — we're out of luck."

Eva nodded, her determined air returning.

"How far is it?" she asked.

"Not far. A few blocks, actually. But... Eva, listen. You said this new plague hits in December, right?"

"That's what the police said."

"That's in two days, Eva. I don't know if we have enough time to... I mean, if she's really lost out there, I don't know if we'll be able to find her before—"

"I know. I know what you're saying," said Eva. "But we have to try. She's all I've got left."

"You've got Rhodri..."

"Not anymore," she said, and started down the alley without him.

"Eva! Eva, what's going on? What *happened* to you?"

She ignored him, kept walking, swaying side to side from the Tezocet, and he caught her by the arm, turned her around.

"What happened with Rhodri, Eva?"

She didn't meet his eyes, took shaky breaths.

"I can't talk about it, Pyotr. I'm sorry. All I can say is that... that we're not together anymore, and you have to leave it at that."

He stared at her, then nodded solemnly.

"Got it. Sorry. Forget I said anything."

She managed a weak smile.

"So let's go find your mum, and get out of this hellhole before the end of the month, all right?"

*   *   *

Three blocks away, they stopped across the street from low-rise building, torn apart by fire, looting and general decay. The top floors were missing entirely and she could see the pale clouds and snow falling through the windows.

"This is it," he said.

"Doesn't look like the kind of place my mother would live," Eva said.

"You'd be surprised," he said. "Come on, let's go see."

The ground floor of the building was mostly boarded up, spray painted and abused. There was trash piled up so thick it was like a horrible wall of filth blocking their way. Pyotr pushed his way in and reached back for Eva, who had a hard time managing the uneven footing to get to the windows. She thought she saw a human arm sticking from one of the bags there. The air was ripe like sour grape jelly.

Pyotr brought them through to an old wooden window that thankfully slid up without much trouble. He climbed inside, then and lifted her over the ledge, putting her feet down carefully on an old wood floor.

It smelled of urine and cinnamon, which was an odd and sickening combination. Eva fumbled trying to cover her mouth and nose with her hand. Pyotr just screwed up his face, persevered.

The room was mostly empty, a broken chair lying sideways in the corner. A door at the far end that was waving slightly in a breeze Eva couldn't feel, a sliver of light easing in and out along the floor like a faint heartbeat. An odd tension, the starkness of it, and it made Eva's haze lift even more. She swallowed slowly.

Pyotr opened the door halfway and they sneaked through, found another empty room on the other side. It didn't smell nearly as bad here, but again there was no sign of Eva's mother. A cool breeze drifted through.

Then they heard it: a scuffling, a thud and scuffling, and the creak of a floorboard above. It stopped suddenly, and the room got so quiet Eva tried not to breathe, as if there were something to hear her. She cocked her head to Pyotr, motioned to the door.

He nodded to her, continued on. She followed through the doorless exit and into a narrow hallway, a row of nails in the wall where frames had once hung. At the end of the stretch was the source of the light: a stairwell leading up, the head of the bannister missing and a coat draped over the railing.

Eva grabbed Pyotr's arm before he could walk further.

"It's not my mother, I can tell," she whispered as quietly as she could.

He nodded to her, reassuring, and she felt her fear starting to ease away just by the motion.

"We'll see," he whispered back. "You can never be sure."

He took her hands in his, and tugging her along, they walked as gingerly as they could to avoid making noise.

She heard another scuffle, another thump, then more silence. They stopped, within reach of the bannister, and Pyotr leaned forward to peek around the corner, up the stairs. Eva moved with him, and she eased closer, closer, trying to see…

A crazed man's face stared her down intensely.

"You!" he roared.

"I said *quiet!*" shouted the man in a deranged voice. He reached between the bars and grabbed Pyotr's jacket, pulling him into the chipped wood banister with a jerk.

"They've found me!" hissed the man, let Pyotr loose a bit, and then slammed him back into the columns, and then again, and again. Eva tried to get a hold on the man's fists, but he was moving too much ... Pyotr started twisting, trying to get free.

"You can't have me!" shouted the man. "The lions can't have me anymore!" And he suddenly bared his teeth and lunged at Eva's neck. She flinched, but the railings were too close together. The man hit his forehead and grabbed his face in pain, cursing loud, uneven words to himself. Pyotr stumbled backwards against the wall and put his arms up, ready to defend himself.

"Pyotr, let's *go!*" Eva implored, backing towards the door.

Pyotr watched the man, his face cocky and sure.

"If your mum's here, we can't leave her," Pyotr said, not taking his eyes off the man. "I think we should fight for it."

The man peered from between his fingers, blood dripping down his forehead where he seemed to be clawing himself raw. He stared at

Pyotr for a moment, as if something connected, as if he remembered...

"Fight?" he said, his voice quiet. "Fight..."

"Pyotr!" Eva whispered, edging away. "This is a bad idea."

Pyotr waved her off, started sliding around the stairs, his fists out, ready for anything. When he got around the side of the steps, the bleeding man turned savagely, shuddering. They stared at each other, neither moving, like a showdown between hopeless fools.

"Get out now," Pyotr growled to the man, his face so solid and imposing.

Eva was just about to say something when the man leapt off the stairs and slammed Pyotr into the wall, both of them landing on the ground with a crunch. Eva stumbled back and fell too, the world still not steady enough through the painkillers.

Pyotr held onto the man's wrists with steady grips, but the beast was too determined ... three long gashes of red along Pyotr's cheek made Eva cringe. She yelped for him, but he didn't react. He swung the beast away, then slammed his head into the wall.

The man screamed out in pain, rolled on his back, scratched at his own face again. Pyotr quickly got to his knees, tried to stand, but the man grabbed his leg and pulled, knocked him down onto the steps, starting clawing up him ferociously. Pyotr was reduced to smacking the advance away with his fists, grunting as he was scraped along the belly.

Eva pulled herself up the wall, stumbling forward down the hall toward them. She had the determination, but her body wasn't playing along: her elbow landed weakly on his spine, and he quickly changed his gaze to her instead. She skidded back, narrowly avoided a red hand swinging out at her.

The movement gave Pyotr his chance: he planted a hand on the man's neck and crushed his head into the bannister so viciously it creaked. Then, not taking any chances, he grabbed the tattered shirt with both hands and threw him sideways into the far wall, and the man crumpled to the ground in a murmuring mess.

Eva pulled herself off the ground and came to Pyotr's side, gripped his arms tightly and pulled him to his feet. She put her hands in his shoulders and caught her own breath a moment.

"That was stupid," she said, her mind clearing faster after the adrenaline rush.

He nodded weakly, closed his eyes and winced at the cuts to his cheek.

"It'll be worth it," he said quietly. "If she's here."

The motion was so fast, Eva didn't have time to react. The bloody man slammed a gnarled elbow into Pyotr's neck, and he collapsed down instantly onto the floor, and Eva found herself face-to-face with a dripping red nightmare.

"Eva…" Pytor murmured from below, "Run for it. Run…"

The man snickered at her, at her being cornered. She glanced left, saw the door they'd come through. The man was daring her to do it, to run, to give him some sport. She returned her gaze to him, defeated. Sighed.

And punched him so hard in the face his nose broke.

As he stumbled back in pain, Eva made a run for it. She skidded down the hallway and around the corner, back into the far room, where she lost her footing briefly and bounced into a wall. She grabbed hold on the door frame and pulled herself into the outer room, and slammed the door, pushing against it for a second before it shuddered violently as the madman threw himself at it. Her bandaged arm seared with pain, but she couldn't let up.

Eva knew her position was tenuous at best, and the pained screaming from the other side of the door made her push harder, keeping her safe, but also trapped in this horrible little room. At least Pyotr was safe while she was being chased.

Then, a pause, a break in all the noise.

No pressure on the door, no sound at all. Eva pushed her ear against the wood, trying to hear something on the other side.

It was quiet. Her own breathing was slow and shaky, and she tried to filter it out as she searched for some sign from the other side. She heard nothing but silence.

Then she heard a scuffle, a thump, and scuffle, and more nothingness. She exhaled, trembling now, and swallowed down some of the fear she'd been holding on to.

"Pyotr?" she called through the door.

Bang! the door shook, and the screaming returned, and Eva's feet slid on the damp wood floor and she scrambled to regain her footing before the man charged the door again, pounding it violently.

She leaned into it with all her weight, turning to the side and shoving her shoulder against the side of the door, gripping the doorknob so tightly her fingers were numb. The man rammed the door again, again, and again, and then suddenly the hinges blew off and the door flew in, pinning Eva against the wall and letting the madman surge through.

She was so shocked by the door breaking that it took her a moment to get back up, to push the wrecked wood off herself. The man had collided with the far wall and was stumbling to his feet, too, but he was closer to the window, her only escape. Impossibly far away. The man slowly straightened up, blood pouring out of the scrapes in his forehead and his nose, and stared at Eva with irrational hatred.

"Lions!" he snarled, and lunged, shoving Eva back into the wall, fingers trying to claw and scrape at whatever they could. She was overwhelmed, but swung her knee up into the man's groin with as much force as she could muster. It had little effect but to throw them both off-balance, so they fell back onto the floor, the man atop Eva, still trying to kill.

Behind her, Eva could feel the edge of the broken chair, and she tried to pull herself up enough to get hold on it. She succeeded, but at the cost of a deep gash to the side of her face. She inhaled at the pain, got a mouthful of the smell of the room again, and gagged.

Her fingers slipped off the chair leg and the man put his filthy red hand over her whole face, squeezed, and smacked her head back onto the ground, cackling, dripping all over her.

Eva's thumb pushed the chair leg in a bit, and her hand wrapped around it. She swung it forward with such force it broke free from the rest of the chair. The wood hit the man in the side of the head, and he screamed out in pain. He rolled away from Eva, clutching his ear, snarling loudly and scuttling away into the corner.

Eva gasped for air, but her body didn't like what it was getting. She felt light-headed, groggy, but intensely alive. She managed to get to her feet, started towards the door, back to see if Pyotr was alive. Just as she reached the door, she heard a noise from behind, and swung around with the chair leg, hitting the charging man in the side of the head; the wood and his skull cracked, and he flew sideways and onto the floor, skidding to a stop in a pile, blood pulsing out from so many places she didn't know what she'd done.

He took a shallow breath, bubbling, and Eva dropped to the man's side, tried to feel for a pulse. She was crying, her head aching, her cheek stinging, and blood everywhere.

"Eva," came a voice from behind, and she jerked, looked round at Pyotr, hand on the back of his head, groggy. His eyes were narrow and pained.

"He… he wouldn't stop…" Eva stammered, her arms wrapping round herself, tears still flowing.

"It's okay, Eva," Pyotr said, coming closer, offering her his arms. "You had to."

From behind, the man exhaled a long breath, and then the bubbling stopped. Eva didn't look back, pushed her face into Pyotr's chest and cried.

"Come on," Pyotr said, lifting her up. "Let's see. Let's see if she's here."

Eva nodded, got to her feet, and paced up the stairs to the second floor, slow and careful, watching her feet as she went. When they got to the landing, she hesitated, kept from looking up. Pyotr nudged her forward, then took off and checked the various rooms off the main area.

Eva looked around, saw the space, the half-normal living room that had been picked apart over the years. A table and chairs, a potted plant that had withered to nothing. A large painting of blotchy patterns on the wall. A simple rug, frayed at the edges and rippled so it fit into a smaller space than it should have. A long red jacket, black embroidered flowers at its base, was draped over a leather sofa at the far end of the room.

"She's not here," said Pyotr glumly, kicking around.

"No," said Eva, her eyes locked on the jacket. "But she was."

The fence around the stadium was tall, chain link, rusted but un-broken. The parking lot was covered with ashes and large metal containers, several workers milling about in hazmat suits, pushing sealed carts around, ferrying the dead to their final resting place. No one spoke.

At the entrance there was a guard with a machine gun, and he stared at the Healer passively. He wasn't there to keep people out, didn't care if some fool wandered in. The Healer watched him as he entered, studying the gun carefully.

Right next to the stadium doors was a small shack, the head office, and from the gates to the office was a wide boulevard where the collection trucks rode. The Healer made his way down the centre of that street, looking at the crates to his left and right, and the workers around him froze and stared, anxious.

He stopped at the office and stared at the fogged windows, the steps leading up to the thin wooden door. He took a step towards them when he heard the faint static of his phone in his ear, and froze, looked around, and then up at the sky.

"Green Four, this is Home. What is your status?"

He started away from the shack, back the way he came. He spoke quietly, backing against the concrete wall of the stadium.

"All is well," he said.

Static.

"You are outside the city core," Home said. "What is your status?"

"I am following a lead," he replied.

Pause.

"You were following a lead last night, Green Four. What was the result of that action?"

"The target was not at that location," he said. "but I have solid information about his whereabouts."

"Your schedule does not allow for errors, Green Four. If you are encountering difficulties—"

"I will meet my target before—"

"— we can have another agent at your location—"

"No." said the Healer loudly, and the workers nearby checked him warily. "LS-411 will be resolved today. I will have results soon."

Static, silence. Out of the corner of his eye, he saw a man dressed in a half-mask heading toward him, directly at him, his stride aggressive. The Healer turned away, waited on the reply. When it came, it was distorted and fragmented by the clouds above.

"We... review... will recall," they said before the radio cut out. The Healer tightened his fists, trembling with anger. The man who had been approaching was close now, confident and imposing; the Healer spun around, hit him in the chest, knocking him flat on his back. He knelt down on the man, foot on a flailing wrist, and leaned in, using his mask and inhuman voice to their fullest potential.

"Marta," he growled, and the man twitched, terrified. "Marta!" he shouted again

The man nodded urgently, spoke in Czech, voice high and whining. The Healer let go his hand and he pointed up, up at the stadium. He spoke more, but the Healer ignored him, threw him to his feet, and shoved him towards the massive entrance doors.

Inside were the furnaces. Giant corroded metal beasts sprawled across the turf, their large vaulted doors lit at the sides by fire so hot it left no trace of their fuel at all. Ashes landed heavily around them, covering the aisles in centimetres-thick horror. Workers in heavy masks pushed wide shovels down walkways, clearing the mess, the last hint of their friends and neighbours dumped into dustbins and carted away.

The Healer paused briefly before a large orange furnace, different than the others. Older. On the side, beneath a Czech ID number, he saw the traces of a word he understood, in characters so familiar they seemed foreign:

SHANGHAI

He trembled, turned away, and his hostage paused too as the other workers slowly backed into the shadows and ran away. The Healer took heavy breaths as his suit whined urgently in his ears, then forced himself to be calm, standing up tall, his grip on the man's arm re-tightening to the point of agony.

They continued forward, around another corner, until the man paused slightly, pointed with a hesitant finger. There, in the distance, was a woman with a flimsy cloth mask and a scarf tied round her hair, pushing a shovel down the aisle.

The woman noticed them, looked up slowly, then her eyes widened, fear, terror, and she ran, back and to the right, disappearing behind a set of furnaces.

The Healer let go his captive and took off after her, his pack slamming against him with every stride, but his pace quick and precise. He ran down the near side of the furnaces until he came to a corner, peered around carefully and caught sight of Marta dashing away. He tore off, his feet skidding a bit in the ashes, awkwardly dodging the red-hot furnaces.

At the end of the aisle was a crossroads, a few pale shafts of light making it into the clearing past the smoke and machinery, and he paused to check around him. No signs of anyone, no hints of where Marta had gone. The ashes on the ground blew around in a whirlwind, and soon even his own footprints had disappeared. He turned in circles, watching, listening beyond the roar of the fires.

Nothing moved but the embers, dancing up and out of the stadium.

With a start, he ran back towards the doors as fast as he could, cloak flapping behind him as he mastered his environment, picking up speed with every step. As he looked to his right, he saw Marta across the way, running the same direction.

She caught sight of him and screamed, started running faster. The Healer fell around a corner, slid in the ashes and landed on his knees. He skidded, putting out a hand at the last second, involuntarily, and touched a furnace. His fingertips seared with pain, and he bit back a curse.

He got back to his feet and started running fast again, came round the far corner and turned left, saw Marta clearing the doors, out into the sunlight, quick but faltering, wheezing in the impure air. The Healer closed the gap, came close enough, and then slid along the ground beneath her, tripping her up, and she crashed to the ground.

His suit whined at his exertion levels and he struggled to calm his breathing, but he kept moving, crawling up and over her, pushed his hand into her neck, holding her hostage. Her eyes, dizzy and dazed, opened wide again, and she struggled, tried to get free.

She screamed out for help, but he ignored her, pulled the mask off her mouth; the falling ashes landed on her tongue, and she gagged, spat them out.

"Lewis Kwong," he said.

She just stared, shook her head, terrified by the mask, he could tell. He gripped her neck, squeezed, and she whimpered.

"*Lewis Kwong!*" he roared.

She started to cry, nodded to him over and over again. He eased up on her, placed his burnt hand against her forehead and leaned in close. She met his goggled eyes, hysterical and terrified.

"Lewis," he said. "Kwong."

And she nodded again.

He got to his feet, grabbed her by the front of her jacket and pulled her up too, tossed her back onto her feet. He pointed back, out the gates, into the city. She nodded weakly.

"Lewis Kwong," he said simply.

"P-P-Panská," she stuttered, holding up ten, then two fingers. "Panská dvanáct."

He repeated the words back to her, his pronunciation imperfect, but she nodded a terrified 'yes' to him, eyes wide with fear. He was so intent on the address that he very nearly missed the man to his right, swinging a fist at his head. He stepped back quickly, caught the arm and twisted it back and around, and the man fell to his knees quickly. The Healer hit him on the back of the head with his arm, and he fell unconscious. Marta yelped, backed away.

Three other men were closing in, ready to tackle him. He unsheathed his machete and lunged forward, grabbed Marta by the hair and flung himself around behind her, the blade to her neck. He pulled her head back and slid the weapon a bit to the side, cut her slightly, and her friends stopped.

He shook his head to them, slowly, carefully, and watched them. The two of them backed away towards the gate, encircled closely by the collection of workers, angling and shifting, waiting for the right moment to strike.

The Healer saw the chain link next to him, the fields beyond, knew he was nearly there. But then… the guard, the gun! He ducked quickly as the machine gun blasted Marta in the neck and head, sending her flailing forward. Without pause, the Healer spun round and embedded his machete in the guard's neck so fast his dead body bounced off the gate before falling.

The Healer caught the gun and reared about, aiming at Marta's friends, who were in shock at the sight of her lying on the ground, their own faces splattered with red. He backed up carefully, gun never wavering, and passed the gate, out onto the road, shaking his head slowly to those that would try and follow. None moved.

"Green Four to Home," he said as his pace quickened along the main road. "I need directions."

"Green Four, what—"

"Panská dvanáct," he interrupted savagely. "Make sense of it and tell me how to find it. This ends now."

MOTOL HOSPITAL, PRAGUE, CZECH REPUBLIC
NOVEMBER 29

Crew put his hand over the heater vent on the dashboard, tried to feel the warm air as the engine purred. The snow on the windshield was falling, sliding on slick ice. He cursed, stomped his foot on the ground, and turned the air flow up to the highest setting.

"Come on… work faster…" he grumbled.

His phone rang and he screwed up his face, holding it to his numb ear.

"Crew," he said.

"Any luck?" came Sobotka's voice.

"None yet. Just got back from the square, turned up nothing. Did you know the clocksmith died?"

"No kidding. I bet the mayor's having a fit. What happened to his security detail?"

Crew cricked his neck.

"I heard they were out drinking last week. Haven't heard anything since. How much you want to bet they get charged with criminal negligence over it? The son's sick, the daughter's clueless… pretty soon, there's no one left that can keep that thing running anymore."

"What's it been, 500 years?"

"Something like that."

Sobotka grunted something similar to disapproval, despair.

"What're you doing now?"

"Just taking a break," he sighed. "How bout you?"

"Interesting development," she said. "I'll tell you later."

"Sure," Crew said, felt for the heat again, still couldn't tell.

"What's that noise?" Sobotka pried. "Do you hear that?"

"Don't know. Don't hear anything."

"Crew, you moron, did you break into another car?"

Crew rolled his eyes, turned the heat dial down, then all the way back up.

"I ran the plates, the owner's been dead a year."

"It's still against the law. If a cleaning crew finds you you're going to get in trouble."

"Listen," Crew said, looking out the window at the empty street, "those lazy cleaning bastards haven't been down this way for a long time. And I *need* this break."

"Right," said Sobotka, and the word was wonderfully loaded. Crew stretched his legs, shifted in his seat and felt a spark against his knee. Two dangling wires underneath the steering wheel dropped loose and the car went dead.

"Shit, hold on," he said, threw the phone on the passenger seat and bent down, tapped the wires back together and twisted them a bit to keep them joined. He grabbed the phone, perched it between his shoulder and his ear, and felt for the heat again. "Made me knock the car off."

"Can you feel my regret?" Sobotka deadpanned.

"Oh yeah," Crew grumbled.

"So you ready to come help me fix the Kolikov problem now?" she asked. "Or are you still wasting time?"

Crew's eyelids drooped halfway and his jaw clenched.

"I'm still wastin' time," he replied.

Then he saw something, out of the clearing windshield, through a space in the snow... a figure in the distance... a head, dark brown, bobbing behind a snow-covered van. Crew froze, watched carefully. The head ducked down out of sight for a second, and then came back up, checking away from him, and then turning back again. Crew clenched his teeth: a full mask wrapped round the head, no skin in sight.

"I'll call you back," he said, closed the phone, and quietly opened the door. He drew his gun as he crossed the street with light-footed caution, came round the van in a rush.

"You! Don't move!" Crew shouted savagely, gun darting forcefully towards the stranger.

The man reacted immediately, dropped the metal case he had been carrying and placed his hands up above his head. Crew moved in behind him, ready to fire into the back of his skull, and kicked the case away. The man twitched at the sound, glanced back at him, like he was sizing up his opposition.

Crew kept a safe distance, motioned downward with his gun.

"Get down on the ground! Hands behind your head!"

The man complied, got to his knees, put his hands to the back of his mask. He didn't seem to be armed. At least not obviously.

"Down! Down!" Crew repeated as the man paused on his knees.

"Don't shoot!" the man yelled, his Czech heavily accented. "Don't shoot!"

Crew walked closer to the man and kicked his shoulder, and he fell over into the snow, but kept his hands over his head, obviously taking Crew seriously.

"I'm with the British government," the man called as Crew circled closer. "I'm not armed."

"What's in the case?" Crew challenged, keeping his gun very visible.

"Equipment," the man pleaded. "for blood tests. Just for testing."

"Where did you get that mask?" Crew asked, edging closer.

"It's standard issue for—"

"Looks Chinese to me."

"It is! We buy them from Beijing, but I'm British, I swear!"

Crew grunted, re-gripped his gun, nudged the man in the shoulder with his foot.

"So why the Healer get-up if you're not Chinese?"

"Healers are guaranteed safe passage. It's… it's considered a safe cover—"

Crew laughed maniacally.

"*Safe*? You've never been this far east, have you? Any able-bodied Czech with a sense of honour would kick a Healer's ass in a heartbeat if he got the chance. Really, *really* poor choice of costumes on your part."

"It's standard issue," he pleaded, "in all black zone areas."

Crew's gun faltered a bit, he stepped back.

"Black?"

The man turned his head slightly, not moving his hands at all, checked Crew nervously.

"Ev… everything east of central Germany is considered a black zone now."

"When is *that* supposed to have happened?"

"T-two months ago," the man stuttered. "At a meeting in Geneva."

"So why'm I just hearing about it now, from you?"

The faux-Healer put his head down onto the sidewalk.

"They're still trying to think how best to inform the public. They're… they're afraid of civil unrest."

Crew snorted, turned away briefly and put his hands atop his head, sighing loudly.

"Why? Just because they're leaving us here to rot, so they can come in later and 'start fresh'? Why'd *that* lead to civil unrest? That sounds like a *great* plan!"

"I can understand you're upset, but—"

"What're you doing here?" Crew said, re-training his gun. "Who are you?"

The man turned his head slightly to look at Crew.

"My name is William Carey. I work for the Containment Office in London. I'm… I'm tracking a British national who was last seen living in Prague."

"Who is he?" Crew said, his tone a civil sort of demand.

"I'm sorry, it's… it's classified," Carey muttered.

Crew half-lowered his gun, took a tentative step forward. Carey didn't move, stayed still. Crew's voice was quiet, angry.

"You're here illegally. Tell me why I shouldn't shoot you now. Give me one reason."

"I'm here legally!" pleaded Carey. "Ask your Director of Public Safety! I'm due for a meeting there in an hour, I swear!"

Crew shifted his weight.

"Sestak? Knows you're here?"

"Call him. We're co-ordinating efforts."

Neither man moved for a moment.

"What will you do when you find this fugitive?"

Carey motioned to his case, looked back up.

"Test him, make sure he's clean, and... then... then bring him home for trial."

"And if he's not clean?"

Carey paused.

"I have... I have an order of exile for him. He'll be banished from Britain forever."

Crew snorted a laugh.

"So he's *our* problem?"

"We have a directive! It's out of my hands! A directive to protect our citizens from any dangers... even themselves."

Crew nodded at this, put his gun away too, grunted angrily.

"Funny," he said to no one in particular. "so do we."

He delivered a swift kick to the back of Carey's head, and could see he was out cold. Crew nudged the metal case with his foot. It had a complex lock on it, which he spun the numbers on casually, then picked it up, slammed it against a nearby wall, and threw it down the sidewalk as far as he could. He lifted his mask long enough to spit on Carey's unconscious head.

He turned, took his phone from his jacket and rang Sobotka.

"Sorry. Thought I had something there," he said, pacing away from the scene.

"Dead end?"

Crew glanced back at Carey, lying in the snow.

"Might be later."

He kept walking, stopped in front of the car, the beautiful abandoned car. He looked around the street, didn't see anyone.

"You don't suppose..." he began, but Sobotka cut him off.

"You can't steal the car."

"It's more like borrowing."

"You *can't* take it."

"It's an Aston Martin, though."

Pause.

"Silver?"

"In-dash GPS too. And it *works.*"

Pause.

"Park it away from the station, and don't leave fingerprints."

Crew smiled, snapped the phone shut and got into the car, gripped the steering wheel longingly. The heat had kicked in.

28

Eva turned the coat over in her hands, the smell of her mother still strong. Pyotr stood beside her, frowning.

"I got her this coat the winter before I went to school," Eva said quietly. "She said the red and the black flowers made it look like she was the angel of death."

"Nice," Pyotr smiled.

"She wore it anyway. I think she liked being the angel of death sometimes."

She felt around it, in the pockets, found nothing but tissues and fluff. Then, on the inside breast pocket, she pulled out a folded fragment of a paper. It was filled with numbers, split by dashes, spilling off the edge. She grinned at it, then flipped it over and gasped. Pyotr caught the paper before it dropped out of her hand.

It read: 'Rhodri,' and a phone number.

"Is that…?" Pyotr asked

"Our old number, yeah."

"Did your mother know Rhodri?"

Eva shook her head, sat down on the sofa.

"No, they never met. I don't know how she'd have this number. We never called each other or…"

Pyotr sat down next to her, took her hands in his.

"Maybe she was contacting him, trying to find out where you were? You said you've been travelling a lot… maybe she got worried and was checking up on you."

Pyotr sprang from the sofa, across the room to a small rotary phone, sitting in the corner, dusty and cracked. He brushed it off, carried it over to Eva, set it on her lap.

"Maybe she went after you. Maybe she's already out of town."

"What's the phone for, Pyotr?"

"If she went to Rhodri, the two of them might be looking for you."

Eva took the phone, gripped it tight.

"That didn't happen," she said seriously, and put it on the ground beside her. She flipped the paper over, looked at the string of numbers.

"What's all that? Some kind of address?"

"It's a note to herself. She writes in code to keep people from snooping."

"What people?"

"Me, mostly," Eva said with a smile, "Lists for birthday presents, stuff like that. Letters-to-numbers, shifted on a rolling cipher. It's complicated, but she really has it down."

"She's pretty good with patterns, I guess."

"Yeah," nodded Eva, squinting at the paper, "Took me until I was seven to catch on myself. Learned about my first laptop three weeks early, and I've been keeping my codebreaking skills secret ever since."

"So wait, you can read this?"

"Oh yeah, definitely," she smiled, "It's a bit tricky with the edge of the page ripped off, but I'm pretty sure it says something like 'Wednesday, five o'clock, Sestak'…"

"Dobroslav Sestak?" Pyotr hissed.

"It doesn't say. Who's that?"

"Director of Public Safety. Real hard ass. He's the one who shut down all the city squares, made the police his personal germ-killing army. He's got more power than the mayor, and he knows it."

"So my mother went to him for what? As an advisor?"

"Couldn't be. She was fired. Why would he meet with her?"

Eva nodded, rubbed her temple gently. The leftovers of the Tezocet were making her so tired…

"There's only one way to find out," she said. "We'll have to go ask him ourselves."

Pyotr barely got in front of her, pushing her back with a pleading hand.

"Eva, wait, hold on! His office is like a fortress over there. There's no way we'd get in to see him, even if we weren't *on the run from the police!*"

"He might know what happened to my mother, Pyotr!"

"All you have connecting them is this… this scribbled note that means nothing! Eva, listen! I want to find your mum as much as anyone, but this is *not* the best use of our time right now!"

She grabbed his shoulder tightly, looked into his eyes.

"I'm going," she said simply. "With or without you."

She started down the stairs again, holding her breath for fear of losing her resolve. Pyotr stayed still a moment, then let out a deep sigh and followed her outside.

*   *   *

The gear they'd stolen from the storehouse at the park on Rašínovo nábřeží smelled clean and crisp, like antiseptic and lemons. Eva fidgeted with the latch on the back of her mask, pulling it tighter around her face until she could no longer feel the cold air on the skin below her cheekbones.

Pyotr rifled through a plastic bag, frustrated.

"There's only one glove in here. They forgot to pair them, the bastards."

"You should go back and complain," Eva smiled.

They paused at a corner near the old apartment building Sestak had claimed as his office. They glanced around in turns, checking out the trio of armed guards by the front doors, floodlights blasting onto the sidewalk like a fortress.

"See what I mean?" Pyotr whispered, "It's not like they're offering tours of the place."

"Maybe there's a side entrance or something," Eva said, "We've got to get closer. Come on—"

Pyotr grabbed her arm, pulled her back.

"Not a chance," he warned, "You're waiting here. *I'll* go see if there's another way in."

"Is this chivalry?"

"No, it's you looking so dazed that they're going to know something's up at the sight of you. I can still pull off 'casual' if I have to."

Eva nodded, patted him on the back.

"Keep the mask on tight, and don't stare, okay?"

"What am I, an idiot?" he smiled back, then strode around the corner as if on a midday stroll. In any other circumstances, it would have seemed natural.

Eva peered around the corner, watching as Pyotr closed the gap towards Sestak's building, hands deep in his pockets. He skipped off the sidewalk, down onto the street, and started crossing closer to the floodlights.

"Hey!" shouted one of the guards, taking aim with a machine gun, "Other side, kid!"

Pyotr skidded to a stop, held his hands up to show compliance, and moved back to the far side of the street, eyes carefully away from the guards, who were watching him cautiously.

Eva tracked him until he turned the corner a block away, then started walking back to meet him halfway, breath streaming out of her mask in tense bursts.

Just as she spotted Pyotr rounding the corner ahead, the air filled with the sound of bells… clumsy at first, then a slow, mournful tolling that echoed off the buildings, drawing Eva deeper into despair.

"What's going on?" she said to Pyotr when they met halfway down the block.

"The clocksmith's son just died. People are freaking out."

Eva glanced up as more bells rang out, the distant sound of weeping from untold homes nestled away from this frozen hell she was living.

"They were really that loved?" she asked.

"The clock's a symbol of hope to the city," Pyotr said. "It's irrational, but people really care about that family. Nuts as he is, Sestak understands that pulse."

Eva squinted, looked to Pyotr.

"Sestak knows them?"

"*Knows* them? They're like his pet project. He's going to have a hell of a time finding a way to spin this mess. He must be in agony right now."

Eva checked back the way she'd come.

"You said there was a daughter, right?"

Pyotr glared at her.

"Yes. Why?"

"How old is she?"

"I don't know."

"How old was the son?"

"I don't know that either. Listen—"

"You know all the ins and outs of this entire city, but when it comes to the most beloved family of all, you're drawing blanks?"

"Yeah, right after I eat my stale wafer rations off the floor, I put on my tux for a night out with Prague's social elite. *Nobody* gets to see these people anymore. They don't leave home *at all.*"

Eva smiled to him, patted his cheek.

"Not usually, no."

*　　*　　*

The guards outside Sestak's building had their guns on her the second she started towards them. They were not taking any chances, especially with a lone woman weepy and stumbling, wearing no jacket in this weather.

"Other side!" the close one called, but she didn't turn or slow down. He stepped out onto the street, adjusted his mask and took careful aim at her head.

"Ma'am! Stay on the other side of the street!"

Eva looked up at him with horrible, teary eyes, her mask pulled tight around her face, and choked down as loud a sob as she could manage.

"They're all dead!" she wept, treading a fine line between melodrama and authenticity.

"Ma'am, you need to back up right now," the guard warned, taking a step back himself. Eva slowed, stood there in the street, shivering from the cold.

"My... my father was the clocksmith," she said staring into the sky. "My brother just died. I need to see Dobroslav. I need to tell him... my brother, he left a message for him."

The guard squinted at Eva a moment.

"You're the clocksmith's daughter?"

Eva met his eyes, pushed as many tears as she could to the surface.

"Y-y-yes," she nodded.

The bells in the air were stifling. Inescapable. The guard kept his gun on her, but touched his earpiece, tilting his head away.

"I've got the clocksmith's daughter here to see the Director. Says she has a message from her brother."

He heard something over the radio, glanced up at Eva.

"She said that too," he nodded, easing his gun a bit.

Eva tried to bide her time with as authentic a way as possible, staring into the clouds and praying for the soul of her lost family. It wasn't as hard to do.

"Hold on," said the guard to the radio, then looked at Eva sternly. "You're Ana?"

Eva realized she had no idea what the daughter's name really was. The guard looked suspicious, untrusting. If it were a trap, she'd have no way to talk him out of it. She wavered, let out a long, sad breath, met the guard's stare head-on.

"Yes," she said.

He watched her seriously as the wind bit cold across them both. His left eye twitched.

She let her breath go, inhaled sharply, let her gaze wander down, down to the snow, and started to cry again.

The guard watched her, wincing, then lowered his gun.

"Give me the message," he said.

"I… I need to see—"

"Nobody sees the Director, ma'am. I'm sorry. Give me the message and I'll let him know as soon as he's free."

Eva shook her head sadly, inhaled deeply.

"It's… it's personal. I don't think Dobroslav would want anyone else to—"

"Ma'am, I appreciate your concerns, but I'm afraid there's no way you can see him. No disrespect, but you've just come from your brother's deathbed. I can't take the risk that the Director will catch whatever it is that killed your family."

It was the perfect cue. Eva began crying loudly, fell to her knees, cupping her face in her hands.

"Please!" she wept. "Please, it was his last request! I can't ignore his last request! Please!"

The guard grit his teeth, looked back at the building and put his hand to his ear again.

"You're getting this?" he asked quietly. "Yes. All right."

He reached a hand down to Eva, touching her shoulder lightly.

"The best I can do is the clean room," he said. "You'll be separated by two sheets of plastic, but you'll be able to talk. I know it's not what you want, but it's private, and it's as personal as you're going to get."

Eva looked up with teary eyes.

"Thank you!" she gasped. "Thank you! That will be perfect. Absolutely perfect."

"Are you sure I can't offer you something to drink, Mr Carey?" asked Sestak, pouring himself a glass of scotch behind his large, ornate desk.

"No sir. Thank you, sir," said Carey, bowing politely, the stiff leather of his suit creaking with every movement. "I'm afraid I can't take the mask off to enjoy it."

"Ah," nodded Sestak. "Quite right. I apologize. But do you mind if I…?"

"Not at all, Director. It's your home."

Sestak smiled serenely, putting the glass to his lips, pausing to watch the absurdity of the scene: this almost inhuman monster standing in the middle of a classic Prague drawing room. Buckles and air filters met plush velvet curtains, and the result was unpredictably obscene to his sensibilities.

"Shall we get straight to business? I have a call I must tend to soon, unfortunately tight due to your late arrival."

"Ah yes," Carey nodded, rubbing the back of his head absentmindedly. "Again, I apologize for the delay."

"Not at all. But if you please, time is tight."

Carey quickly brought his dented and scraped metal case around to his lap, unlatched it with a few quick turns of the dial, and pulled out a mid-sized envelope with both hands. It sounded like metal inside. Heavy pieces of metal. He carefully placed it on Sestak's desk.

The Director stared at it a moment, but did not move.

"What is it you're after here, Mr Carey?" he asked.

"A British national living in Prague. Mr Daniels."

"The Zemus fellow," Sestak said ominously. "Yes, what of him? What's he done now?"

"Now, sir?"

Sestak grunted unhappily, swirled his drink.

"He's an insufferable fool, that one," he said. "Constantly second-guessing city policies, sticking his nose where it didn't belong. Why, once he tried to convince me to keep the opera house open, despite all indications that it was a major infection point for the city. He tried to bribe me to keep it open, the fool. Bribes are beneath me. Offends me to no end when fools think they can buy away my sense of duty."

Carey nervously glanced at the envelope on the desk.

"So Mr Carey," Sestak said, leaning back in his chair. "What *has* he done this time?"

"I'm… not at liberty to discuss the details of his case, sir, as you know. But I can assure you that his behaviour poses no risk to the city of Prague. Or its citizens."

Sestak sipped at his scotch again, scratched the tip of his nose with a carefully-manicured nail.

"I've already granted you free reign of the city. What more do you need?"

"Well, sir… first of all, I would appreciate if you could convey my status here with your local police. I had a small mishap earlier which has greatly… um… impeded my ability to operate."

"I'm sorry to hear that."

"Nothing a good night's sleep and some painkillers won't help, I'm sure. But if you could…"

"I will pass along the warning," Sestak said, jotting down a note on a pad of paper.

"Thank you, Director," said Carey, genuinely appreciative. "And also, if I may ask… do you have an address for Mr Daniels on hand? The house we suspected him of occupying is empty, and I'm afraid I'm running out of leads."

"You've tried the place across the Charles, then?"

Carey sat up straighter.

"No, sir. Do you happen to know the—"

"Indeed I do," Sestak said, scribbling an address on the bottom of a sheet of paper and ripping it off for Carey. "Since my secretary passed last year, I've found I've a better memory than I knew. Send enough bottles of wine to someone, and you remember their address forever, I suppose."

Carey got to his feet, hand out to shake, happiness showing through the mask. Sestak accepted the hand, if hesitantly.

"Thank you, sir," said Carey. "You have been a very great help to me."

"It's my pleasure, Mr Carey," said Sestak, glancing down at the envelope again. "Don't forget your package, please."

Carey quickly slid the envelope back into his case, snapped it shut and backed towards the door, bowing like a fool in the presence of royalty. Sestak replaced his glass on his desk and walked Carey out, patting him on the back jovially.

"One last word of advice, Mr Carey, if I may," he said as they reached the exit out into the hall.

"Yes, sir," said Carey obediently. "Absolutely."

"I would leave your trip across the Charles until tomorrow. It's late in the day now, and with the cold and the summer we endured here… and with your suit looking so much like…" he trailed off, then smiled. "Well, I can't imagine you'll want to be seen out in the dark dressed like that. For your own safety, naturally."

Carey barely responded. His voice was small and weak.

"No, sir. Thank you."

As soon as they opened the door, Sestak's assistant rushed forward, notepad in hand, clicking and unclicking his pen as if to punctuate his displeasure at the schedule being thrown off-kilter. He bowed politely to Carey.

"Sir, if you please… one of our men will help you back to your accommodations."

Carey was led by the arm down the hall and away. As soon as he was out of earshot, the assistant began speaking in hushed tones to Sestak as they made their way back down the hall.

"Was it a good meeting, Director?" he asked.

"Fine enough," grunted Sestak. "Any news from the Golden Tree apartments? Any more cases?"

"None reported, sir. I am still getting hourly reports, but it seems limited to the fourth and tenth floors."

"Excellent. That's good news. Keep the ventilation shut down, and tell the army to keep its position until I give the word."

"And what of the press, sir? They're asking about the barricade."

"Tell them nothing for now. I don't owe them anything. If we start torching — and that's *if* — release a statement detailing the facts. Otherwise, this is just a routine quarantine. If anyone knew it was Nuremberg, we'd have a riot on our hands, and I can't handle one of those right now."

"Yes, sir."

"Any further word on the Healer?"

"Scattered reports, sir. Housing complexes in the south, Stadium Eden just recently. A few deaths, but nothing actionable."

Sestak growled, checked his hair in the glass of a painting along the wall.

"Call the Chinese ambassador and express my displeasure at civilian deaths in my city."

"Yes, sir. Certainly. Should I demand they recall the agent?"

"Gods no, man! Whatever you do, don't upset them over this. I won't have Prague mentioned in the same breath as Kiev, not over a few fools with an inflated sense of their ability. Nobody burns this city to the ground but me."

"No, sir. Understood, sir."

"Oh, and can you please remind the police that they're to leave the damn Healers alone. I thought it was well-established, but apparently not. I can't control the populace, but law enforcement is supposed to understand the law, at least."

The assistant touched a hand to his ear, eyes darting left and right. Sestak began adjusting his jacket sleeves impatiently.

"Is Sobotka on the line yet?" he asked.

The assistant blinked to attention.

"Yes, sir, but if I may... it's confirmed that both Mr Kopecky and his son have died."

Sestak stopped dead in his tracks, stared at the floor.

"Damn," he breathed. "God keep their souls. Who else knows about this?"

"The city bells are tolling, sir. It can't be long before it's everywhere."

"Damn and damn again. Prepare a press conference. We have to get ahead of this. Have Dr Mueller check Ana Kopecky's blood and get her over here for the cameras. We need to show the city there's hope in the face of tragedy."

"Sir, that's the other thing," said the assistant haltingly, "Ana Kopecky... she's already here."

Sestak paused, turned urgently.

"Here? Why?"

"She says she has a message from her brother. A personal message. For you, sir."

Sestak nodded, loosened his tie and removed his jacket, immediately taking on the air of a concerned grandfather: caring, compassionate, mourning with the people he loved.

"She's in the library?"

"Yes sir," the assistant said.

Sestak rushed down the hall, dropping his jacket on a chair, and paused outside the library door.

"Call the Mayor, have him declare it a day of mourning. Help him with the details if need be. And tell Sobotka I need a progress report when I'm done here. If I'm not out in ten minutes, remind me of the time."

"Yes, sir."

Sestak clicked open the door, stepping into a the dark library, windows sealed shut and the only lights set to a dim glow, disappearing into the rich stained wood at all sides. A sheet of clear plastic hung through the middle of the room, sealed to all sides with thick tape. On the other side of the room, beyond the plastic, was a young woman, standing facing away from him, breathing softly.

"My dear, I'm so sorry to hear about your brother…"

The woman turned slowly, mask dangling from her face, letter opener gripped tightly. Sestak jerked back.

"You're not Ana…" he gasped.

"No," said Eva gravely. "But you and I still need to talk."

Sestak took a step back towards the door, eyes wide with fear. Eva pointed the tip of the letter opener against the plastic sheet between them, pushing slightly, but not breaking the seal.

"Don't even think about calling for help," Eva said.

Sestak eyed the plastic carefully.

"You're here to kill me?" he asked, defiant.

"I'm here to talk," Eva said. "But if you give me one hint of trouble, and I'll cut the seal and spit in your face."

He watched the tip, then Eva.

"What are you infected with?"

Her face didn't twitch.

"Wait and see."

Sestak exhaled slowly, then nodded and walked to the edge of the room, grabbed the arm of an old wooden dining chair, and pulled it in front of the plastic. He sat down carefully, his expression calm, serene almost. He thought a moment, then looked Eva straight in the eye.

"I suppose you're Ms Kolikov," he said.

Eva fought back a twitch in her face, grit her teeth.

"You met my mother," she said.

"I was under the impression Inspector Sobokta had you contained."

"I'm not easy to pin down," Eva replied.

"I'd think not, or they'd have stopped your little killing spree in
Germany."

Eva pushed the blade tighter against the plastic. Sestak's facade
faltered, and he nodded with a controlled anxiety.

"I met your mother, yes."

"About what?"

He lowered his gaze, licked his lips.

"It's a complicated subject."

"Then get talking. Why are the police after her?"

"You should know as well as anyone."

Eva pushed the letter opener through the first sheet of plastic, and
Sestak's eyes jumped up. Now the second sheet was being pressured,
and Eva's face was dark with determination.

"What did you meet about?"

"The last time I saw her was three weeks ago. A routine status
update about recent outbreaks and how to stop them."

"You… you worked together?"

His eyes narrowed.

"Certainly you know this already."

"Indulge me."

"Yes, we worked together," Sestak said, leaning back in the chair.
"Your mother was our WHO liaison, overseeing the classification
and treatment of strains found—"

"Stop stalling. What happened three weeks ago?"

Sestak thought a moment.

"We were discussing a smallpox outbreak in Pardubice," he said.
"A minor affair. She was reading the report, and her face went white,
and she excused herself."

"What was in the report?"

"Nothing of note. Two hundred casualties, well-contained, and
there was no threat to the city here."

"You've followed up on it?"

"My dear, Pardubice is over one hundred kilometres away. I have enough on my plate already. I don't need to be adopting someone else's troubles."

"So that's it? She just left? Then why did you send the police after her?"

"The police found their evidence quite independent of me, I'm afraid. If I'd had an inkling of what she was involved in, I never would have given her access to our containment practices. My biggest fear is that she can use my own strategies against me now."

"She's not a terrorist."

"You *would* say that, wouldn't you?"

Eva nearly punctured the second sheet. Her grip on the handle was making her hand shake.

"You think she was behind the outbreak in Pardubice?"

"By the way she reacted, no. She seemed genuinely concerned about it. Which frankly makes it all the more stunning, knowing what she'd been up to all this—"

"Save your whining for someone who cares. If she didn't make the virus, who *did?*"

Sestak folded his hands on his lap, paused a long while.

"When we deconstructed the strain, we saw it was signed by the authors."

"What, *actually* signed?"

"In the code, yes. Incidental protein strands. Crude, but effective. They call themselves 'ex-facto', I believe."

"Are they local?"

"It's impossible to say. I think your mother suspected they were Russian. She rambled off something when she read the report."

"What did she say?"

"I'm afraid I don't speak the language. All I caught was 'repa', but still—"

"Where would she have gone?"

Sestak sat forward, brow wrinkled with bemusement.

"I would think you would know better than anyone," he said. "Didn't you have a plan in case either of you was caught?"

"I keep telling you people! We have *nothing* to do with this out-break! I'm an artist and my mother is a *hero*! She saves people, she doesn't kill them!"

He smiled serenely.

"We all have our tipping point," he said.

Eva set her jaw, tightened her grip on the opener, and pushed it through the second sheet of plastic. Sestak's body went rigid, pressed back into the chair, and he met her eyes again. She took a long, slow breath.

"Call off your dogs," she said. "You're wasting time hunting us. You're going to lose the city, and it will be on your head, not mine."

He said nothing.

A knock at the door drew both of their gazes. Sestak turned back to Eva, anxious. Her face betrayed no fear.

"Director?" called the assistant feebly. "Sir, it's getting to be that time."

Sestak opened his mouth to speak, but Eva shook her head slowly, twisted the blade in the plastic so it made a perfect hole. Sweet air rushed from one side to the other, and the sheets rippled from the change in pressure.

Sestak held his breath, his face twisting in an effort to stay calm.

The assistant knocked again, more urgently this time.

"Director? Is everything okay in there?"

Eva nodded towards the door, a slight smile creeping across her face. Sestak's teeth rattled, but his lips stayed sealed, his lungs tightening with pressure.

He doubled over, fighting to control himself, but it was too much. Panic gripped him, and he bolted from the chair, toppling it, stumbling back towards the door. The assistant fell back at the sight of his Director collapsing into the hallway on his hands and knees, sweat pouring down his face. The old man gasped for air, wheezing with every breath.

"Sir? Sir, what happened?" asked the assistant, peering back into the room. It took him a moment to see the hole in the plastic, and the absence of the clocksmith's daughter.

"It was… Kolikov," Sestak gasped. "Seal this hallway, quarantine everyone inside. I want that air tested for everything we know."

"She… she was infected?" the assistant asked, blanching.

"She said she was. I can't trust a word she said, but I'm not taking any chances."

"No sir. Should I have the men detain her before she—"

"Leave her. Inform Sobotka, and let her follow the trail. And warn her not to give the leash so much slack next time."

* * *

Eva met Pyotr back at the corner a few minutes later, eyes gleaming and a smile so wide and frantic that he couldn't help but look worried.

"You made it?" he said in disbelief.

"Not only that, I know where to go next."

"Wait… you actually saw Sestak? And he told you what you wanted to know?"

"Not intentionally, no. But he mentioned she said the word 'repa' last time she was there."

"She was talking about Russian turnips? I don't get it."

"It's not turnips. It's Stepan. Stepan Krejci. An old friend of my parents, back when I was a toddler. I couldn't pronounce his name, so I called him Repa, and it stuck. He must know something about what happened to my mother."

Pyotr shook his head.

"But even if that were true, how would we find him? We don't know where he lives, and there's no way to find out!"

Eva's smile got even bigger.

"We'll look the same place my mother would have: his office in the biology department at Charles University. He was the head of their epidemiology department."

31

The smooth carpet ran down the length of the main foyer, the floor so shiny the Healer could almost see his reflection in it. Untouched, as if no one passed the threshold anymore. Glimmering chandeliers hung on domed ceilings above, the brightest lights he had seen in many months.

It had been a hotel once, this place, but the front desk was empty, left in pristine condition by the last employee to leave. There was no building directory, no guest list, nothing to go by. He started up the polished wooden stairwell, watching his surroundings closely.

In the corners of some steps were white and yellow flakes, like a strong antiseptic that wasn't properly washed away. There were pots of flowers on every fifth step, as if the smell of daisies could drown out the industrial-strength cleansing. The flowers were new, so someone had been there recently.

At each door was a camera encased in a dark glass dome. At one room, a brown paper bag sat outside the door, its bottom stained with some kind of grease. A room at the far end of the hall had at least two dozen newspapers stacked before it.

By the third floor, the walls were decorated in fine wood panelling, accented with classic-looking murals. The lighting was all finer, the bulbs all aimed at the ceiling for a calm, subdued feel. He passed by a large mirror, and paused there, seeing how foreign he looked.

On the fifth floor, the final change. Down the hallway and on the left was a simple wooden stool, straddled by a large squarish man in a green military uniform. The man was already watching the Healer as he reached the floor, but he made no move. He just watched.

The Healer walked slowly down the hallway, but there were no other doors to check. He stopped a safe distance away from the man, who was still watching him passively. He had bright orange hair, and his uniform bore no stars, no commendations, just two simple "U.S." pins on each lapel, and the name "Shaw" on his chest.

The two of them stared at each other for quite a while, no movements, as if in the midst of a duel that neither would admit to.

The Healer slowly, deliberately, reached out a hand and knocked on the door.

Shaw placed a firm grip on the Healer's forearm and squeezed. His green eyes were not angry, just professional, and he shook his head slightly, as if his say-so would let the Healer concede defeat.

The Healer kept his stare at the larger man, and with some strain, knocked on the door again: one, two, three.

Shaw seemed to grit his teeth at this, maybe amused. Suddenly, he swung the Healer's arm down and away, and with the other hand pinned him against the far side of the enclave, fingers wrapped tightly around the armoured casing on his neck.

The Healer moved fast, grabbing hold of Shaw's arm, twisting it. The sudden pressure made Shaw lose his grip, and the Healer pushed the arm down and backwards, up behind his back.

The man barely reacted to the move, and with his other arm reached back and grabbed the Healer's chest. With a bit of a crack in his twisted arm, he heaved strongly enough to break the Healer's grip, and threw him across the hall and into one of the murals that hung there.

The Healer regained his footing quickly, and Shaw cricked his shoulder, grimacing at the sensation. The Healer made a point to not make any sudden moves, but his opponent had no such concern: his right hand slid to his side and pulled his pistol from its holster, swinging it up towards the Healer's mask.

The Healer was prepared. He side-stepped, grabbed Shaw's wrist and twisted until her heard a crack, and then with his other hand caught the falling gun and threw it down the hall. When he looked back up, it was too late to stop Shaw's fist from hitting him in the side of the head, and was spun round by the impact.

His suit whined a warning, his heart rate increasing, and he heard a constant ringing in his ears. He backed up instinctively to give himself room to think. Shaw took the time to diagnose his wrist, and seemed to write it off, letting that arm hang loose by his side.

They watched each other for another moment, and then Shaw lunged forward, his punch missing, and was caught with an armoured elbow to the neck, and then a swift low kick to the legs that sent him sprawling.

Shaw landed on the crimson carpet and rolled to his back with some difficulty. The Healer was already turned, ready for more, his cloak swung back and his machete now clearly visible at his side.

The Healer held out his hand in a warning, and shook his head slowly, but Shaw was too stubborn or honour-bound to give up. He got to his feet, his knees smarting from the kick, and pulled himself straight, though his body looked ragged.

The Healer shook his head slowly one more time, keeping his hand out, but adjusting his stance to be ready for the next move.

Then it came: Shaw grabbed the Healer's outstretched hand and twisted, pulling back. It would have worked, but it was predictable, and the Healer spun round, his elbow finding its mark on Shaw's nose. There was a loud crack and Shaw gasped, his grip gave way, and the Healer kicked his feet out from under him again, grabbing his wrist on the way down and pinning him on the floor with his arm twisted up behind his back.

Shaw's nose was bleeding on the carpet, red on red, his breathing rough and bubbly, but he turned his head enough to see his attacker through bruised eyes. He said something in a tired but vengeful voice that the Healer didn't understand — his English was worse than his German — and then started jerking about, trying to get loose.

The Healer held him there for a minute, watching him fight uselessly.

With his other hand, the Healer grabbed Shaw by the back of the neck and pulled him upright, then let go of his arm and let him turn around, limping and wrecked, his face a swollen bloody mess. The Healer stood a safe distance away, machete in his hand, ready. He pointed down the hall to the stairwell, then his weapon, and left it at that.

Shaw watched silently; then, after spitting out a pair of teeth, turned around and slowly creaked down the hall, his stride a sad imitation of pride. The Healer waited until he was on the stairwell and out of sight before turning his attention to the door.

It took him only a minute to dislodge the handle and push the door open. The room inside was unlike the rest of the building. It was grey, the blinds drawn with all the lamps off, and the walls were stark and bare, like a home waiting to be lived in.

There were blankets across all the floors, and a large white sofa oddly-placed in the middle of the main room, pointed at the windows as if the dirty shafts of light that shot through were somehow worth watching. At the end of the sofa, the Healer noticed a pair of socked feet lazily waving from side to side. Dancing to music no one else could hear.

The Healer took another step forward, and heard a scraping, a metallic grind under his foot, looked down. It was a spoon, rough and beaten, stained in the middle with a dark substance, like a makeshift boiler. And there, another spoon. And another, and mixed in between were used needles. Thin ones at that. The Healer navigated his way to the sofa, careful to avoid stepping on anything dangerous. There he stopped, looking down on poor Lewis Kwong.

He was old and exhausted, so thin he almost didn't look human, and his skin hung loose on his body, scarred and wrinkled from years of abuse. He was wrapped in a military jacket, highly decorated, high rank, resting heavy on his frail chest. His left arm was out of the sleeve, instead resting loose by his side, a tourniquet tied around the middle, purple pocked veins bulging, waiting for more.

The Healer picked a small packet of white powder off the back of the sofa, squeezing it gently between gloved fingers. Heroin, probably. He dropped the bag and rubbed his fingers along the white upholstery.

Kwong opened his eyes slowly, blinking at the weak light to his left, and turned his gaze to the Healer, pupils flushed wide. He didn't react, but was watching carefully.

The Healer removed his black pouch and placed it on the back of the seat, removed a vial and put it towards Kwong. With abrupt dexterity, Kwong moved his arm away and into his jacket, and his eyes narrowed, judging.

He said something in English, and the Healer shook his head to it. He motioned with his needle, but Kwong rolled himself to his side, and then sat up, wobbling, his back to the Healer, and exhaled.

"Why you here?" he said in Mandarin, the voice weak and tortured. His accent was heavy and his words very simple, like a very old child fumbling through the language.

"I not with... use... any illness," Kwong said.

The Healer paused, seemed to think.

"You may be sick," he said. "With a deadly disease. I must sample your blood now."

Kwong shook his head, curled up a bit.

"My sick, all me. My fault."

"That may be," said the Healer.

Kwong turned around part-way, eyes narrow and pained, lips trembling with fear or hurt or self-pity. "Then let me die," he said, and he meant 'alone'.

The Healer shook his head gravely, and Kwong winced. The Healer showed him the needle, the grey display, what must be done.

"I must sample your blood, because you have infected others," he said slowly, hoping the meaning would get across. "We cannot cure them without this sample."

They sat there in silence for a moment.

Kwong turned on the sofa, and put out his arm towards the Healer, and closed his eyes tightly, as if he'd never had a needle before, and the thought of blood scared him. The Healer filled a first vial easily, and as he was attaching the second, Kwong spoke, his eyes still closed.

"Grandfather taught me language," he said. "I never study big. Wish now I did. So much to say."

The Healer waited until the second vial was full and then switched to the third. He didn't speak.

"I am alone here, this city," continued Kwong after a time. "I cannot go home. My family... I cannot see. Too sick in Europe. All safe at home in America."

The Healer nodded to show he understood.

"I am waiting to die," Kwong said. "Can you know when?"

The Healer met his imploring eyes as the last of the blood was drawn. He slid it into his device and let the tests run. As the characters flashed by, he lowered it to his side, nodding slightly to the old man.

"I sorry for my faults," he said, on the verge of tears now. "Can you... tell family about me?"

The Healer didn't respond, but looked away, then down at his diagnosis. He paged to the next screen, then back.

"What is it?" Kwong asked, as the Healer was reaching for his blue pouch. Kwong stood up quickly, spun round to face the Healer, defiant. "What is it?" he said again.

The Healer left his pouch where it was, lowered his hands to his side, bowed.

"You carry a deadly virus," he said. "If you live, you will kill anyone you see."

Kwong closed his mouth, gritted his teeth and the Healer could see the muscles in his jaw clench beneath the sagging skin. He closed his eyes and nodded ever so slightly.

"It is over," he said.

The Healer nodded, though Kwong did not see it.

The old soldier put his arm out again, a small trickle of blood wrapped round his elbow from the earlier pricks. He took a long, deep breath, and opened his eyes, squarely at the Healer.

Then, in an instant, his eyes twitched to the left and back, and the Healer heard the faint sound of metal grinding behind him; he spun to the side as a loud crack rang out. Kwong's chest popped with a gushing red wound, and he stumbled backwards, onto his knees.

Shaw was standing in the doorway, pistol out, a quick look of shock and regret in his eyes as he realized what he'd done. The Healer was off-balance, but saw the gun veer towards him, and ducked down towards the kitchenette behind him.

A searing pain ripped through his shoulder, and he felt the horrible sting of antiseptic as his suit reacted to a bullet wound. He collapsed back around the corner, sliding against the wall.

Behind the sofa, the life had drained out of Kwong, his eyes glazed over with shock and confusion, and his mouth swung open and closed a few times before he toppled backwards onto the floor. Shaw cursed loudly in a stuffed, nasally voice, and the Healer could hear heavy footsteps as he marched forwards over the spoons and needles. When the gun peeked beyond the corner, the Healer was gone, a streak of blood against the wall heading into the kitchen.

Shaw turned himself with his back to the wall, the gun leading him, and slowly edged towards the opening, following the trail. His breaths were slow and quiet as the nose of the pistol edged a bit beyond the entranceway…

Before he could make his move, a crunch erupted beside him and his elbow was crushed by a powerful blow, making his hand spasm and the gun fall from his fingers.

The Healer caught it ably, coming around the corner, right arm loose and useless, his cloak dark and shiny where the bullet had passed. He left his machete punctured through both the wall and Shaw's elbow, holding him hostage.

He paused a moment, watching his prey.

Then, almost cruelly, he shook his head from side to side, and tossed the gun across the room. The two of them stayed there another moment, the sound of Shaw's blood dripping in a pool below him. His breathing was getting ragged and urgent, and he fought back a scream.

The Healer turned slightly, leaned around the corner into the kitchen, and Shaw felt a sharp pain as the machete shifted in the wall. He scowled at the Healer, his cheek twitching involuntarily.

Then, with a jerk, the machete came free from his arm, from the wall, and he had a moment of levity before the blade swung back around and tore through his bare neck, and he felt nothing at all.

The Healer paced back from the scene, reaching over the sofa, grabbing his grey device from beside Kwong's body. With shaky hands, he paged the screens, back and forth, pausing at the last: "xFacto Emaciator 1.0", it read. "3rd Generation Infection".

He squeezed the device until the plastic creaked in his grip.

32

Eva and Pyotr walked down the final stretch of road, the stately old building off to their left casting a weak shadow over the snow. There were tire tracks in the street, but no other hint of life for as far as they could see. The lights in the building were all off, the pale facade ominous in the dim wintry afternoon.

They stopped in front, looking up.

"You sure about this?" Pyotr asked, weary.

"We're close," Eva said, shivering but calm. "I can feel it."

They climbed the four steps up to the entrance, a simple set of doors framed in weathered ochre paint. They were covered by heavy planks, hammered in tight. A series of warning stickers were plastered across black paint, announcing the facility was closed until further notice. Another paper, half-ripped away, warned the premises was quarantined due to an outbreak of Battinger's.

"This way," Pyotr called from the right of the doors, where one of the tall windows had been smashed in, giving them access.

Inside, it was as if the foyer had been spun upside-down somehow. Large, heavy desks were upturned, chunks of plaster and rock were smashed on the coarse wood floor. The walls were thick with black mould; most of the old yellow paint was chipped or simply dissolved. A window somewhere at the back was letting in sunlight, but it wasn't nearly enough. The air had the texture of rotting vegetables, even through their masks.

"You know where his office was?" Pyotr asked.

"No," admitted Eva. "I didn't see a building directory either. How should we look?"

Pyotr pulled open a door off to the right, nudging some debris out of the way.

"Door by door?" he offered, then lead the way in.

The room was empty. What furniture had been there was stacked in a messy pile in the far corner, away from the windows. The floor was spotless, despite the dusty atmosphere, but for that pile. Eva could make out a faintness in the wood floor around it, like an entire layer of finish had been worn off by something.

"Look at this," Pyotr said, rubbing a gloved finger down the wall. It was stripped down to a thin layer of plaster, ripped apart by raw streaks, like thick claws had worked it away. It was only up near the ceiling that the thickness returned, and with it, the black mould.

"Somebody hates mould," Eva said quietly, adjusting her mask. "Let's keep moving."

Down a quiet hallway, past a bulletin board that still had notices about flats for rent in town, they found a large auditorium, its modern desks ripped and beaten from their bases, up and to the back of the room. To their right, a drinking fountain lay on the ceramic floor, a small trickle of water pouring into a neat pool. Again, no sign of life.

"This is going to take a while," said Pyotr, surveying the wreckage.

Just then, a shuffle, and some wood fell over, far at the back of the room. Pyotr moved closer to Eva, shielding her.

"Who's there?" he called.

Eva's heart beat loudly in her ears. She reached down to her left, grabbed up the arm of a destroyed overhead projector, felt its weight. Her sprained wrist screamed out at her, but she grit her teeth and kept a careful eye on the room.

"Hello?" Pyotr yelled, stood ready.

Then, near the middle of the room, up and away from them, came a waifish girl, no more than twenty, her eyes dark with exhaustion, hair in filthy streaks down her face. Her bare arms looked almost blue in the frigid air, and she hugged herself, twitching.

"Are you okay?" Eva asked, starting forward before Pyotr caught her.

The girl didn't seem to see them, started climbing and sliding down and across desks. She ducked her head underneath one, then reached her arms under, lowered herself down, out of sight. They heard shifting debris, broken glass.

"What's going on?" Pyotr called, moving himself and Eva further away from where the girl had disappeared. "Are you the only one here?"

The girl reached a hand up on top of the desk, put her head half-above the wood, shifted her gaze left and right, never looking at them. Her lower lip was chewed on and scabbed, sharp teeth marks red and trickling.

"I can't find it. Can't find it," she said, though not to them. "Can't find it anywhere."

"Can't find what?" Eva asked, looking around.

"My eraser. I had an eraser. I brought it to class. I can't find it. I swear I brought it, I know I did!"

Eva and Pyotr exchanged wary glances. Pyotr held a pausing finger up to Eva, then reached down and began pushing bits of broken wood around as if searching. Eva gave him a warning look.

"Don't…" Eva whispered.

"She might talk to us if we're nice to her…"

"I don't think—"

"Hey!" interrupted Pyotr with a loud call, "I think I see an eraser here!"

The girl's eyes shot at them, wide and delirious. Her mouth snarled open, showing browned and bloody teeth.

"*Mine!*" she screamed, and leapt, animal-like, down the desks, straight at the scrambling Pyotr. She threw him against the wall, grabbed at his wrist and started slamming it against the stonework savagely.

"Let it go! *Let it go!*" she howled, pushing his other hand away from her, snapping at it with her wretched mouth. He grunted in pain, trying to force her off, but she was too wild to stop.

"Hey!" Eva called from behind. "I've got your eraser right here!"

The girl turned viciously, throwing Pyotr's battered hand away. She crept around, hunched like an animal, trying to circle Eva, who held the projector arm loose by her side. The girl wiped her mouth with her bare arm, leaving a trail of red to her elbow.

"Give me the eraser," the girl said. "I lost it. It's mine."

Eva nodded slowly.

"I'll give it to you. I will. Just tell me… where is Dr Krejci? Dr Stepan Krejci."

The girl's eyes opened wide, then narrowed quickly. She started looking left and right again, like the prey and not the hunter. She seemed to see Eva again for the first time, shot through emotions from happy to scared to angry in a second.

"Have you seen my eraser?" she asked, tensing her hands back and forth and back and forth.

Eva re-gripped the projector arm.

"I've got it—" she began, and the girl leapt at her. She was ready: she stepped to the side, swung the metal underhanded, catching the girl in the stomach. She collapsed to the ground, coughing wildly, grasping at herself, her chest, wheezing.

"I need to find Dr Krejci," Eva repeated, colder this time.

The girl looked up at her, eyes narrow and insane.

"I want my eraser!"

She spun around, trying to attack, but Eva hit her across the side of the head, sending her sliding into the first row of desks. Blood trickled out of her temple as her eyes rolled back in her head.

"Eva…" Pyotr gasped, running to her side.

"It's always the same," Eva growled, throwing the projector arm against the wall. "Wherever you go, they chip away at your soul, bit by bit. I can't stand it, Pyotr. I can't take it any more…"

Pyotr rubbed her back gently, then picked the discarded metal off the ground. Eva shook her head at the girl, turned and left the room. Pyotr followed close behind, checking ahead nervously now.

They came to another room, large and cold, its windows all broken, a thin layer of snow spread halfway across the floor. All around, atop desks and thrown across chairs, were the pieces of bodies of five terrorized souls. Their faces were scraped with deep gashes, their eyes merely bloodied sockets. Arms torn from torsos, some seeming to have died trying to crawl away as their legs were shredded behind them.

Eva choked back vomit, turned to Pyotr, who braced himself against the wall.

"Jesus…" he gasped. "Do you think… *she* did this?"

Eva couldn't look back, just shook her head.

"I don't know. I can't look. Can you see… is my… my mother in there?"

Pyotr tensed, looked left, right.

"No," he said. "The two women are too young."

Eva took a deep breath of processed air.

"Good. Then let's get out of here. This was a bad mistake. We've got to go."

They were just past the threshold when the banging started: furious, mad pounding. They paused, half-turned back, and heard it, faintly:

"Hey! Don't go! Please, you have to help me! *Please!*"

Eva and Pyotr rushed back into the room, and saw a refrigerated locker, off to the side… a desperate face calling out to them from a narrow window at the side. They ran to him, started pulling the door handle, but were stopped by a fierce slam against the glass.

"No!" shouted the man inside, his cheeks hollow, lips blue. "Please, no. It's airborne. I need a mask first. Please tell me you have one."

Eva looked to Pyotr, who shook his head.

"We only got two," he said weakly.

The man inside pressed his forehead against the glass, seemed to be weeping. His fist pounded the glass again, thin and wretched. Eva grabbed the projector arm from Pyotr, nodded.

"Go back to the storeroom and get another," she said.

"What?" Pyotr gasped. "Eva, even running that's going to take me at least ten minutes! And whatever did *that*—" he motioned to the shredded bodies, "might come back and find you!"

Eva swung the projector arm back and forth lightly, smirked.

"I'll manage."

"Eva, please… this is insane."

Eva pointed at the carnage of the room angrily.

"No, *that* is insane. This here, this is me putting some sanity back into the world. Go get the mask. I'll be fine."

Pyotr shook his head at her, but took off into a sprint. She waited until she couldn't hear his footsteps anymore, then turned back to the man in the refrigerator. He had tears in his eyes, was choking back sobs.

"Thank you," he said loudly, his voice barely passing through the thickness of the door. "I... I don't know how long I've been in here. I'm so hungry, I can't even..."

He trailed off, disappeared from view. Eva leaned closer to the glass, tried to see in.

"Hey! What happened here? How did this happen?"

The man appeared back at the window, looking away from Eva, trembling.

"We made it," he whimpered. "We all made it, and it killed us."

"Made what? Who's 'us'?"

"The xFacto team," he said, with an odd mixture of sorrow and pride.

Eva's mouth dropped open beneath her mask.

"Wait, you're a virus crew? The same one that made the Pardubice smallpox?"

He nodded.

"Yes, but that was a mistake. We don't target Czechs."

"You... *what?*"

"We... we're the only ones standing between Russia and the complete genocide of the Czech race."

The words were thick with self-important propaganda, and it made her sick. Eva put a gloved hand to her forehead, turned around.

"*This* is all you? These people, that girl next door... you made a virus that... that..."

"It breaks down the wall between reality and paranoia," he said, proud. "It makes you see things your subconscious dreads. It's like a living nightmare you can't wake up from."

Eva slammed an angry hand against the glass, and the man recoiled back.

"What kind of idiots are you?"

"We were trying to keep the Russians at bay! If they're tearing themselves apart, they'd have to leave us alone! It would save us all!"

"Yeah, until one of them finds out it was you, and launches a counter-attack into Prague!"

"We wouldn't let that happen!" he boomed defiantly, then collapsed out of view again, and she heard sobbing. She sat at the other side of the door, her back to the cold steel, watching the entrance where Pyotr had left.

There was a faint thump from inside the locker.

"It wasn't supposed to work like that," he cried. "It wasn't made to be airborne."

Eva frowned, looked up at the window. The man was staring out at the room, hand dragging down the glass slowly.

"The vector was going to be a hospital in St Petersburg. Untraceable, but direct. Aerosolizing it was never part of the plan. It's too messy that way."

"So what, you built it wrong?"

"No," he sobbed. "There's no way. Our incubator was broken, didn't have the aerosol option in the first place. Believe me, we tried to use it. If it's airborne, it was someone else, like that woman."

"What woman?" Eva asked, getting to her feet quickly and leaning into the door.

"She came here… two days before Siman showed symptoms. She must have done something… modified the code."

"What was her name?" Eva asked urgently.

"I don't know. Some doctor. I don't know how she knew about us. Kept saying she was looking for Dr Krejci."

"Where is he? Dr Krejci, where is he now?"

"He died in the Battinger's outbreak, before we claimed the building. Did… did you know him?"

"Used to," Eva sighed, distant.

"He was a great man. Taught me everything I know. I mean, to a point. I don't know how he'd feel about… you know… all this…"

Eva said nothing.

"We put a little tribute to him in all our viruses. A quote, buried with our name: 'And he stood between the dead and the living; and the plague was stayed.' He… he used to write it on the blackboard at the start of each semester."

Eva pressed her forehead against the door, felt her temples surge with pain.

"That woman, the doctor… what did you do to her?"

"Do? Nothing! Rayna was looking to infect her with something, but she took off before we could. Probably because she'd hacked our code and didn't want to be near when things went wrong."

Eva looked through the window, narrow eyes furious above her mask.

"I wish to god I hadn't sent Pyotr off to save your life," she seethed.

"You don't know me," he said, eyes darting down to see if the door was opening. "You don't have the right to judge me."

Eva controlled her breathing, kept quiet.

"Once I get out of here," he seethed. "I'm going to find that fucking bitch and dose her with everything we ever made. She'll die so many ways at once they'll never know what got her."

Eva met his eyes, dead and empty.

She unlocked the door with a hiss.

"*No!*" screamed the man, trying desperately to pull it closed again, but Eva yanked harder, swinging it all the way out until he collapsed on the ground, covering his mouth with too-thin hands.

"Go on, hold your breath," she growled. "I've got all the time in the world."

He flailed about, trying to avoid the air, but it was no use. He dropped to his hands and knees, squeezing his face up, trying so hard… He reached a frail hand towards her, trying to grab her shin, but she kicked it away. It was too much, and he gasped a long, slow breath, and broke into tears, bowing his head against the floor.

Eva watched him, cold eyes blazing, without a word.

Then he started to laugh. He slammed a fist against the ground, staggered to his feet.

"Fine," he spat. "Fine, whatever. You got me. Good for you. But I've got at least twelve hours before I'm symptomatic, and that's plenty of time to find you and slice you all to pieces."

Eva cocked her head, then took a swing at his left knee with the metal piping. She heard a soft crack, and he collapsed sideways, back onto the floor, screaming madly, clutching his leg as it bent the wrong way. Eva nodded to him.

"Good luck with that."

He roared, flipped to his stomach, buried his face in his hand, panting.

"You're fucking dead!" he cried.

"No," she said coldly. "You're dead. You and your xFacto buddies. You all die here. That's the end of it. I've had enough of this shit from you people, you and your kind. Your nightmare virus won't ever see the light of day, do you hear me?"

He looked up at her with wet, terrible eyes, half-laughing, half-crying.

"It's too late for that," he cackled. "The buyer's already *got* the package. It's on its way to be deployed right now."

"*What?*"

"Hell, it might be out there already."

Eva held the projector arm up like a bat, threatening, adjusting her stance to dominate him. He didn't seem to notice; he rolled himself onto his back, staring at the ceiling, laughing at nothing.

"Who is the buyer?" she demanded.

"Fuck you."

She swung the bar down onto his shoulder, cracking bone, and he screamed, kept laughing.

"*Who is the buyer?*" she yelled.

"Fine... fine, whatever..." he cried. "Have it your way. You'll never find him. He's probably—"

But before he could say another word, a huge menacing form leapt down onto him, shoving a blood-dried hand around his neck and slamming it down onto the ground so suddenly it snapped, killing him instantly. Eva backed up quickly, weapon at the ready, as the monstrous man tore his victim's eyes out, squeezing them into his pocket, then stroking the savaged face gently.

"Shh…" he said softly. "Quiet, I found them. They're safe now."

His face had a heavy beard, marked with dark red scratches along his cheeks, down his neck, and all over his bare torso. His cargo pants were so thick with dried blood they were almost black, and his bare feet were scarred with scabs and open wounds from all the broken glass around the building.

"What?" he said suddenly, to the air around him. "Again? Where?"

He looked down at the body below him, traced a careful line down the shoulder, to the left arm, and stopped at the elbow.

"No, that won't do," he mumbled, then pulled a worn scalpel from his back pocket. Eva moved back even further, edging towards the door.

"This won't take a minute," he said, jabbing at the arm wildly with the scalpel, and then began screaming as if he were the one being attacked. Eva was nearly at the door, eyes never leaving the scene, when her heel cracked a bit of glass.

The monster looked up at her suddenly, eyes wide.

She made no move.

"Yes," he said to the air, but looking straight at her. "Yes, she has ants in her too."

Eva stumbled further back, ready to fight. He made no move to follow her, just stared.

"Just stay back," she warned. "Stay there and everything will be fine."

His eyes shifted slightly, and it was clear he now saw her fully.

"I'll get the ants out, and she'll feel better," he said, then bounded towards her like a demonic gorilla, screaming as he made the final approach. It was so terrifying, Eva nearly missed her chance: she swung at him, hitting his shoulder instead of his head, sending him back onto the ground, and sending her to her knees from the momentum. Her wrist burned angrily, and she lost her grip with that hand.

The monster quickly skittered to his feet and ran at her again, and she took off towards the door, slipping on the glass on the floor, and only just reaching it before he grabbed at her heel. He pulled, and she flipped over onto her back, dropping the projector arm. He yanked her back in one, two, three painful lurches. She tried to kick him off, but he was just too strong.

He straddled her, eyes utterly mad, and licked his lips.

"Those ants must go," he said serenely, and reached back a bloodied hand.

Then his chest popped open. Once, twice, and the third time he collapsed backwards into the glass, and Eva covered her ears, ringing from the boom of the gunshots. She rolled to her chest, looked back, and there at the door was Pyotr, smoking pistol in his trembling hand.

"I guess you don't need the mask after all, huh?" he asked.

34

Anouma stopped by Mr Vecera's bed sometime after ten that night, checked his chart, and the quantity of Pathenex he had left in his IV. He watched her weakly, a smile flickering on and off, as if he were confused about his state of mind. She patted him gently, nodding.

"You are still up, Mr Vecera?" she asked quietly, as most of the other patients in the hall were asleep now.

He didn't answer, looked away from her suddenly, then closed his eyes. Anouma frowned, took out her penlight, turned his head back her way, and checked his pupils. Fixed and dilated.

"Mr Vecera?" she asked again, calling louder this time. "Mr Vecera, can you hear me?"

His eyes suddenly fixed on her, and he took a ragged breath.

"My… my granddaughter is drowning…" he gasped.

Anouma checked around herself, and he grabbed her wrist, held it tight.

"You have to help me, doctor. My granddaughter is drowning!"

She rubbed his chest roughly tilted his head, and saw he wasn't looking at her anymore. He looked as if he was about to cry, and then his heart monitor started to whine below the bed.

"Blood pressure rising…" she said to herself. "Mr Vecera! Wake up! Wake up please!"

He suddenly threw his arms back, sat up fast in bed, and began screaming a loud, blood-curdling scream, and the other patients began to wake too, whimpering or crying out in fear. Anouma leaned into him with her shoulder, held him down on the bed.

"I need a sedative!" she yelled as the frail man fought her. "Sedatives and restraints! Now!"

Two of the nurses on the floor took off, one towards the medicine locker and the other to help Anouma. She pushed down on Vecera's right arm with all her strength, and his body shook up and down, flailing like a fish, as they fought to keep him still.

"Mr Vecera!" Anouma called. "Mr Vecera, everything is all right! You are safe! Please calm down!"

But he didn't hear her at all, he kept gasping, rocking up and down, back and forth, trying to break free.

"Someone save my granddaughter!" he screamed. "What's wrong with you people? Hurry!"

The other nurse arrived with a long needle and a pair of long, blue straps. Anouma tossed one to the nurse, and began to wrap hers around Mr Vecera's legs. The nurse did the same for his arms, but he broke free suddenly, clawed out at her, scraping at her neck. She clutched it quickly, staggering back.

Anouma checked behind her, at the second nurse. She was pushing the meds already. Mr Vecera started to falter, his motions becoming subdued, and he slowly fell into a state of muttering semiconsciousness.

"You! Take her and clean out that wound. I want you both on high doses of Pathenex now. You are off the floor until I say so. Do you understand?"

Both nurses nodded solemnly, headed out, past Dr Bastien, who was rushing down the aisle towards Anouma. Behind him paced a man in a business suit, heavy mask over half his head, arms gloved to the elbows. He wore a city badge in his breast pocket. A bureaucrat.

Bastien checked the heart monitor quickly, the pupils.

"He is altered," Anouma said. "and I have no idea why."

"It's not in the spec for his condition," Bastien said grimly.

"Dr Bastien," the bureaucrat interrupted. "Is this Dr Anouma?"

"Not now!" Bastien barked.

"Dr Bastien, if you're trying to interfere with state business, I don't care *how* senior you are in this place, you will be—"

"I said *quiet!*" Bastien yelled, not turning around. He looked to Anouma, eyes dead serious.

"What else could it be?" he asked.

"Maybe the Pathenex is having a delayed reaction?" she said.

"Unlikely," Bastien said. "Has he had any visitors? Someone that might have upset him?"

Anouma shook her head, thought.

"I do not think he has had any visitors since he arrived here. Maybe it is just… cabin fever?"

Bastien nodded, looked around the room.

"We should get him upstairs somewhere, so he doesn't scare the others. Find Laroche and see what zone he can accommodate a new bed. I'll—"

Then, several rows away, another patient began convulsing madly, his bed rattling.

"It's too hot!" came a desperate voice. "Please open the windows, it's too hot!"

Anouma and Bastien exchanged worried glances, and took off towards the woman who was shielding her face with her arms. Bastien restrained her while Anouma checked her pupils.

"Hello?" Anouma called directly into her face. "Hello, can you hear me?"

"It's so hot! Help me! Help me please!"

Anouma looked to Bastien, who strained against the wild movements.

"What's going on here?" squeaked the bureaucrat, backing away from them. "Dr Bastien, I need to know what's going on!"

"A new infection," he growled.

"We need more sedatives!" Anouma shouted across the room. "Bring as many as you can carry!"

The woman was sweating heavily, jerking this way and that, trying to get free. Bastien risked a hand on her forehead, neck.

"She's not feverish. She's hallucinating. What could cause this?"

"I don't know," Anouma said, searching her memory. "sometimes Battinger's B causes sleepwalking, but—"

"This isn't Battinger's. God help us, I hope it's not airborne."

The bureaucrat took off, scrambling out of the room.

"We need to start everyone on aggressive Pathenex routines," Anouma said, checking around. "We must slow it down if we can."

Bastien swore angrily.

"We'll run out before we cover the room once over! Dammit, we should have partitioned the floor better!"

Another nurse arrived with a handful of heavy needles, quickly pushed the sedative into the woman's IV. Bastien kept her down until she was safely subdued, when he heard the gasp of another patient, a few beds over, starting to become aware of a waking nightmare. He looked to the nurse, Anouma.

"Sedate anyone that shows even the slightest signs," he said. "Mark the time and repeat the dosage every hour. I want this controlled until we know what we're dealing with."

The nurse nodded and took off, but Anouma was interrupted by her pager beeping. She checked it, her face dropping.

"Adjobi…" she gasped. Bastien grabbed the needles from her, nodded.

"Go," he said sternly. "We've got this for now."

She smiled behind her mask, then ran fast, through the room, to the front stairwell, and up to Adjobi's floor. She tore down the hall till she came to his room, skidded around the corner and stopped cold, eyes wide at the sight of the Healer looming over her brother. At the sound of her, the Healer swung around, bloodied machete at the ready, prepared to strike.

"What's going on?" she gasped.

The Healer put his weapon away, staggered a bit. She saw blood on the back of his cloak; he tipped to the right as he stood. He held out a vial in a trembling hand, and shoved Adjobi's head back against the pillow savagely.

"What *is* this?" he snarled. "It is not your vector!"

Adjobi shook, terrified, darted pleading eyes between the Healer and Anouma.

"I… I don't know… I thought it—"

"This is a third-generation infection!" the Healer boomed. "You said this man infected you, and you lied!"

Anouma started forward.

"Please, maybe Adjobi just—"

"Give me one good reason why I should not kill you right now," he seethed, ignoring Anouma entirely.

"I… I assumed he was the one," said Adjobi, a bit of life coming back into him as he pleaded. "We… we'd shared needles, and…"

Anouma gasped, stepping away from her brother, shocked.

"Adjobi, no…"

"I'm sorry, Fanta. I don't know what I was thinking, I just…"

The Healer unrolled his blue pouch, pulled out a needle and tested it. Flawless. He grabbed Adjobi's arm with his thick bloodstained glove, and turned the veins outward.

"No!" shouted Anouma, and covered the arm, weeping.

"There's another," Adjobi said urgently. "There's another. I didn't think of it before, but there's another."

The Healer looked at the needle, then seemed to fight with himself, and pulled away, letting Anouma fall on the bed. Adjobi pulled up, sitting in stunned silence. The Healer took another step back and gripped the syringe tightly.

"I have no more time for games," he said to them, and the syringe dropped to the floor out of weak fingers. He paced forward, Adjobi and Anouma both cowering on the far side of the bed.

"You will give me the name now," he said gravely. "Or I will burn you alive."

They stared at him in shock, at the coldness in his voice, and Adjobi nodded. He searched about the bed, then started nodding again, feeling up and down his sheets, the wires attached to his arms swinging up and down like spiny wings on a spry bird.

He found a small scrap of paper and, with trembling hands, held it out for the Healer.

On it was another name, another address. The Healer slipped it into a pocket, and with his vision blurring slightly, shook his head.

"When you see me next," he said darkly, "it will be *your* time to die."

35

Eva collapsed on the sofa, pressed her hands to her face. The mask was so tight on her, and she itched at the edge, groaning. Pyotr rummaged through the pack of supplies he'd stolen from the depot, took out a half-litre aerosol can.

"Better stand up," he said, shaking it. "We've got to sterilize everything before we take off these masks. I'm not taking any chances with whatever those nut jobs had."

Eva sighed, got to her feet, and spread her arms and legs so Pyotr could coat her with the spray. It tingled as it hit her skin, gave her a second chill, on top of the cold. When he finished, she sprayed him, careful around his eyes, shut tight.

They stood there, looking at each other.

"Do the room," he said. "I want to try sleeping without this thing on my face."

She nodded, proceeded to dose the entire room with antiseptic. He took out a second can, shook it vigourously, and joined her, doing the undersides and ceilings where she had trouble reaching. They finished, sweating and out of breath, and unlatched their masks to breathe in the vile lemony air.

"Home sweet home," Pyotr smirked.

Eva coughed at the taste. She sat down on the floor, legs crossed, then lay back, staring out the window, at the stars. The clouds were disappearing, the deep blue sky shimmering gently.

"So we're done for the night," Pyotr said, laying down next to her.

"Where'd you get that gun from anyway?" she asked suddenly. "They give those out at the food depot?"

"No," he sighed. "Saw a guard leave it at his station when I was heading out, figured it'd be a good thing to have, given the atmosphere at the university."

"Good call," Eva said.

Pyotr yawned loudly.

"So where do we go tomorrow morning? Another insane asylum? Or do you want to branch out a bit?"

Eva slapped his arm with a friendly hand, laughed.

"I don't know," she said, becoming sombre. "That was our only lead. I have no idea where else to look."

Pyotr sighed.

"Well, like I said: maybe she's already left town. If that guy was telling the truth, maybe she went looking for... whoever that buyer is. Maybe she's in Russia or something."

"Not too likely. She might run into my dad."

"They're not close, eh?"

"Let's put it this way... his sending me to jail wasn't even close to the biggest reason they got a divorce."

"Ouch," Pyotr nodded appreciatively. "So, if you don't mind me asking... why'd you hack a bank anyway? You didn't get rich off it, I'm guessing."

Eva winced, turned her head slightly away.

"It wasn't about the money. Not really, anyway. I mean, I could have moved billions while I was in there, but that's not what it was about."

Pyotr thought a moment.

"So if not money, then what?"

Eva sighed, propped her head up on her arm and faced Pyotr. She was distant, reminiscing.

"My dad had a bit of a gambling problem. Nothing dramatic, not what you'd expect. A little here and there, but it was always under control.

"One day, my mother comes home absolutely furious, because the bank had given her a call, saying they were overdrawn on their joint account. He'd lost a mountain of money on the wrong bet, and even with everything they had, it wasn't enough to pay it all off. All he had was this stock in a second-best security firm that was on its way out. He was scared shitless."

"So you... you what, you stole the money back or something?"

Eva closed her eyes, shook her head.

"I thought I could fix it. I worked at it and I researched and I found a way into the bank's systems through a stupid back door software glitch. Unpatched for years, it turns out... if they'd looked at things, they would have seen it.

"I got in one night, thought I should just steal a little bit from every account in the system. Just a tiny bit, and maybe nobody would notice."

"Not likely. They'd see the pattern right away."

"Exactly. Even a string of five transfers would probably get traced before I'd logged off. But that got me thinking... I didn't need the money, really. I just needed to set things right. So I wrote a script that did a mad sweep through the accounts, moving money around. A hundred dollars from one person to another, back and forth, all over the map. I wasn't doing anything they couldn't undo, but when people checked their balances the next morning, they'd be in for a surprise, one way or another."

"Mayhem. Got it."

"The bank had to issue a warning, take massive write-downs after the 'gifted' customers spent money they shouldn't have had. It was all over the news, an unstoppable scandal. Lawsuits filed, lots of firings. And the company that provided their security, they got canned right away."

"Oh hell, you mean—"

"Yeah, the company my dad invested in picked up the pieces, and their stock surged."

Pyotr whistled.

"Now *that's* some fancy footwork."

Eva lay back again, covered her face with her crossed arms.

"Not fancy enough. The cops traced me across ten proxy servers, figured out which internet cafe I'd been in at the time, got a bunch of CCTV footage and nailed me a week later. I didn't even get a chance to deny it, they were so sure.

"And so I'm sitting there in jail, a fifteen year old girl, desperate for some kind of news. Anything I can get. And my dad comes in — first time I've seen him in weeks — and I ask him if everything's okay with money. And he says everything's fine. And then... then he says he wants me to confess to the police, because it's worse for me if I don't. And I believed him. I mean, why wouldn't I?"

Pyotr said nothing, watching Eva speak, her voice trembling.

"He told them to try me as an adult. He basically *forced* them to try me as an adult. He took the money I made him, and he took his girlfriend and he moved back to Russia, and left me to rot in prison."

"That must have hurt..."

"First six months I was there, it's all I could think about. I wanted to get out, to find him and ruin his life. Like completely. I knew I could... there's so much you know about your parents you can use if you try. I could have got him in such deep shit with the wrong people, they never would have found his body."

She took a long, rattling breath, stared out at the stars again.

"But then he sent me a letter, and it changed things."

"Changed how?" Pyotr asked gently.

"He told why he'd had them punish me. It wasn't vindictive or petty or anything like that. He was afraid for me. He thought, 'here is this girl I raised, and she's become some kind of monster who breaks the law like it means nothing', and it freaked him out. He wanted me to be better than I was, and he thought the best way to show me the right path was to punish me like that. Show me the consequences for breaking the rules."

"Mean-fucking-spirited and messed up, Eva," said Pyotr. "What a bastard. And *wrong*."

Eva shrugged.

"He *was* wrong," she said. "But he was right, in a way. Or at least, I think he showed me something I hadn't seen. When I'd heard about his money troubles, I thought a good and reasonable way to deal with that badness was to break the rules, to even the playing field. It was justified to me. It made sense.

"And to him, putting me in prison seemed like a justifiable way to fix a problem. It was evil, and I know it ruined whatever chance he had of making up with my mother… but it *made sense*, you know? He thought it through, and that's what he felt needed to be done."

"That doesn't make it right," Pyotr said.

"No, it doesn't. But it taught me something I hadn't really seen before: nothing makes a wrong become right. These viruses, all the suffering they bring, it's all just some fool thinking what they're doing makes sense. And it doesn't. They took something good and pure and fantastic and they used it to shit all over humanity."

They lay there in the dark. Pyotr shrugged.

"See, if you told *that* to the cops, they might believe you're not a virus-maker."

She laughed, wiped a tear from her eye with her sleeve, sniffled.

"The fewer people that know that story, the better, I think," she said.

"I think you're wrong," he said, propping himself up, closer to her. "I think you hiding that side of yourself, it's just dumb. I knew you how long in university? And never once did you mention you had an inkling about computers. I thought you were all about the painting. Could never figure out why you wanted to hang around with us geeks."

She sniffled, smiled.

"I was trying to steal you away from Maselle," she admitted.

He laughed loudly.

"Are you saying you settled for Rhodri?"

She shrugged, avoided eye contact.

"Sometimes I like to think that was it, yeah."

They lay there, their faces close, neither saying a word. Pyotr seemed to be thinking something, took a tentative breath, then smiled.

"We should take Pathenex boosters," he said, getting to his knees, digging through the bag from the depot. He pulled out a pair of pill bottles, popped the tops open. He handed a pair of pills to Eva, and a small bottle of water. His went down quickly.

"What's the second one for?" she asked, shaking the pair around in her palm.

"It's some kind of emergency immuno-booster, plus the regular Pathenex. Should fight off whatever random crap may have made it into our systems this afternoon."

Eva cracked open the water, swallowed both pills ably. She re-capped the bottle and put it on the floor next to her.

"We should leave first thing tomorrow," she said, avoiding his eyes. "You're right. My mom is probably gone already, and we're just risking our lives by staying here. We've got to get moving."

Pyotr nodded.

"I'll go steal some more supplies tomorrow morning," he said.

She looked at him, shy, smiled.

"Thank you for everything," she said. "I wouldn't have made it this far without you."

He shrugged it off, knelt down next to her, rubbed her shoulder gently. She felt so warm, she closed her eyes and breathed into a sudden wash of tranquility.

"It's nothing, Eva. Really. And Rhodri—"

"Not Rhodri again..." she warned, pushing his hand away. "I'm so sick of Rhodri..."

He put his hand on her cheek, brushed the hair out of her face, spoke softly.

"I'm not telling you to call Rhodri," he said. "I was going to say... having spent this time with you... he was a fool to let you go. You're worth fighting for."

She smiled, but it was cut short by a kiss, and she found herself kissing back, harder and stronger, her arms wrapping round him. She shuddered as he nuzzled her neck, gripping his back with grasping fingers; and when her shirt came off, his lips on her flesh, she didn't feel the cold, but disappeared into a swarm of colours that flowed into the night.

A capsule sat at the side of the road, perched on three short legs like a metal grapefruit on a pedestal, a red beacon flashing intermittently on its top. From every angle, a reflective biohazard symbol warned the curious away. But there were none to see it this night.

The Healer sat shivering in the cold night-time air. A strap on his shoulder, re-adjusted round his arm, had stemmed the blood loss, but his arm was numb, hanging weakly at his side. He kept his other hand over the wound, feebly protecting it from the elements.

A crisp wind blew across the field beyond, and a swirling mist of snow kicked up and flew into the moonlight. It was a desolate, evil place, but it was beautiful. The shades of blue and purple in the sky pulled him up, into sleep, but he shook himself awake when he felt himself fading.

The phone came alive, but it took a moment before he picked up the handset, awkwardly pushing the antenna up once more, then let it drop by his side.

"Home to Green Four, what is your status?"

He took a slow, shaky breath before replying, his voice a forced kind of calm.

"Mission is in progress," he said.

There was another pause. Longer than usual. Longer than necessary.

"Your armour is reporting a breach, Green Four," came the reply, the tone somehow sharper.

"A small cut," he lied. "It has been contained."

He heard the echo of his own voice in the silence and he looked into the sky.

"We are tracking your package," Home said, then another break, like they were trying to approach the obvious question with some kind of tact: "LS-411 has been contained?"

The Healer's good arm started to tremble.

"The sample is not LS-411," he said. "A false lead gave me access to a new virus. It is not part of my current mission, but—"

"Green Four, you must evacuate Prague as soon as possible. If LS-411 cannot be—"

"I will handle it," he interrupted, sitting taller. "I have enough time."

Static. Then, silence.

"You must be out of Prague within twenty-four hours, Green Four."

"I will be," he said, slumping a bit.

Static again, and he heard some distant clicking, like typing or a pen tapping or... he was falling asleep again, woke up with a start.

"Green Four," Home said. "Your heart rate is quite low."

He was having trouble keeping his eyes pointed in the same direction, tried blinking slowly to keep himself in the present, but he was drifting to the right.

"It is cold in Czechia," he said simply. He tipped over, his elbow catching him on an angle, and the pain from his shoulder erupted again, making his blurred vision wash blue, meshing perfectly with the blue in the sky.

"Indeed," said Home, somewhere in his ears, in between white noise. "You... mission not... recall... recall..."

"No..."

And then he landed softly in the snow, and the static over-whelmed him.

*   *   *

He was standing on the banks of the river in the days when a light mask would do, and the water seemed very clean somehow, and he couldn't remember if it had ever been that way. Though he knew all that followed, he still had a sense of wonder, being so far from home.

"Xiao Li!" called a voice, and it seemed constantly behind him.

It was her, that woman. He knew her name, but he couldn't find it, and as he turned round he was standing in a dirt field, the metal risers beyond him, his captain high above them, and he was explaining their commission, their fates. Xiao Li couldn't understand the words, but he knew what they meant, and a part of him — a future part — recoiled in disgust.

And then with a jolt, there he was, assembling the fence with his comrades, in the dark of night, locking in a city that never knew why. And the fences seemed impossibly tall to him, and the metal sharp as knives, and he thought he remembered it was so cruel what they were doing, but that also felt insincere.

And now, again, at the fence, the survivors rushed, their faces so white with fear when they saw the barricades, the guards, their masks, their horrible lifeless masks, and Xiao Li was calling out to the others to stay close, hold the line, and he knew he was firing into the crowd, and he willed his arms to stop, but they were beyond his control now, and he wished he could die rather than see what came next, but he knew he must see it again.

And there she was, the girl, the beautiful young girl with the wavy black hair, watching him, asking him why. And though he tried to look away, he could see her, see her hair burning, her poor brown eyes asking him why.

But then somehow it was different, and he was still warm, but there were no more sounds, he heard only breathing. Soft, intense breathing, and he saw her eyes, that woman; who was she? And she looked at him so closely he almost disappeared into her, and her lips bit together so wonderfully. He felt her hands on his back, like a thousand caresses brushing past as one, and dove into her completely, and the sensation was swirling and wonderful and so wonderful he almost… almost couldn't…

Couldn't what? Couldn't do this, no. He was standing on the border to Russia, his cloak new and brisk in the spring air, the fresh flowers never penetrating his mask. And though the sky was a glorious pink, yellow and blue, he never enjoyed it, remembering how he'd come to be here.

He hadn't told her he was leaving, had he?

What was her name?

And then, from the hospital, that poor wretch and his sister, begging him like the girl in the fire, their eyes wide with fear. Fearing him, and he feared himself too.

Over and over, Xiao Li couldn't help but stare, and he felt the coldness overtake him again, and he wished he could remember the name before he awoke… But he knew it was too late, that his job was not done, that he still had work to do.

NOVEMBER 30

It was so hot the mask was slipping off her face, slick with sweat, as she sat in the bedroom, sketching the quiet little house across the street, a massive tree throwing shadows across the lawn. There was a breeze making the light yellow curtains flutter, but the summer was impossibly dry and stifling, and the wind carried no relief.

She checked the clock again, waited until she saw a digit change. Two o'clock in the afternoon, and she was sitting in bed, wearing a tank top and underwear, waiting. The clock jumped another minute and she put down the sketchbook and the pencil, lumbered over to the window and peered out over the lazy street below. A bead of sweat fell off her nose and onto her arm.

Just then, a knock at the door made her jump. She ran to the bed, threw her artwork to the floor, and sauntered over to the door, placing an inviting hand up the frame, and creaking it open gradually to give Rhodri a warm welcome.

"Well hello there," she said in her best sultry voice.

But it wasn't Rhodri.

"Oh shit!" she spat, and ran back into the room, snatching a thin blanket off the bed and wrapping herself quickly. The door swung open at the hand of a large and wide man, heavy muscles bulging through his drenched short-sleeved business shirt.

"Hi," he said in Russian, smiling in a way that he meant to be embarrassment, but was something less. "Lookin' for Rhodri."

Eva shrugged, moved back around the bed, covering herself more.

"He's not home yet. But. But he'll be here any minute, so—"

"So I'll just take a break, thanks," said the man, and he reached outside and slid a large cardboard box into the room, closing the door quietly. He pulled a folded magazine from his back pocket and waved non-existent cool air onto himself.

"You got any lemonade?" he asked, cricking his neck. "Or just water? Anything cold-like?"

Eva darted a look to the small mini-fridge they had by the window. She smiled weakly.

"Cold bottled water?"

"Fucking awesome," he exclaimed.

She made her way over to the fridge, carefully holding the blanket around her, and pulled open the door. There were two bottles left, and she took the one with the dent in the side, handed it to the stranger carefully.

"Thanks. You want any?"

She shook her head no.

"Suits me," he said, and downed the bottle in one go. "I'm Dmitri, by the way."

Eva was so shocked, she dropped the blanket, had to rush to catch it before it hit the ground.

"*You're* Dmitri? Wow! Oh, sorry, I didn't know what you... I mean you never..."

"I'm the silent partner, yeah," he said with a grin. "You oughta get some shorts on Eva. Gotta be hotter in that blanket than anythin' else."

She nodded, backed away, snatched her shorts off the end of the bed, and slipped into the bathroom. She heard Dmitri tromping around the room, the sound of him shoving things around on their table, and the cardboard box sliding on.

"So no idea when your boy gets home?" he called to her.

She finished changing, came out into the room, pacing anxiously.

"None at all," she said. "he's usually home by twelve-thirty."

"For your 'afternoons off'?" Dmitri said with a grin.

"Uh…"

"Yeah, he told me you wanted those. Refused to say why." He observed her appreciatively. "But I've figured it out, just now."

She blushed, backed into the other side of the room.

"I guess I should thank you for all the help you've given us for the last few months," she said. "I know Rhodri always says we'd have died of starvation if it weren't for you."

"Oh, I don't know about that," Dmitri said. "Rhodri's a pretty smart kid. I'm sure, between the two of you, you'd have found a way to make ends meet."

There was something about the last part of the sentence that hung in the air, and so neither one spoke for a moment.

"So what's in the box?" Eva asked, trying to lighten things again.

"The usual equipment. Refills."

"Refills? For websites?"

"Something like that," he said, tossing the empty bottle to the garbage, a perfect shot. "You keep in touch with anyone from Italy? Austria?"

Eva shook her head sadly.

"No, I didn't get to go out much except to sell my art. Didn't have many clients, and fewer friends."

"Read the news much?"

Eva frowned.

"I can't read German. Can I… why do you ask?"

Dmitri shrugged.

"Things in the news, is all. Don't worry about it."

Eva was unsure. Dmitri checked his watch suddenly, wincing.

"Listen, I've gotta catch a train soon. Can you make sure Rhodri gets this box as soon as he gets in?"

"Absolutely," Eva said, the imminent departure releasing her tension. "I'll tell him you stopped by."

Dmitri nodded.

"Do that. And can you tell him to call me? We need to chat, I think."

"Of course," she said.

Dmitri strode to the door, put a hand on the knob, then paused, turned back.

"Say, Eva," he began, then lay silent for a moment, thinking. "You… you don't help ol' Rhodri out with his work, do you? I mean, when you're not paintin' and such?"

"No," Eva said, shaking her head slowly. "Rhodri keeps the work stuff at work, so I don't hear much about it. Why?"

Dmitri shrugged, scratched his chin.

"It's nothing," he said, his good humour returning. "Just didn't want him dragging you into the nuts and bolts, if you know what I mean. Work is work, and home is home, as you say. I'm just thinkin' ahead of myself here. Pay no attention."

He smiled, waved, opened the door.

"See ya later, kid," he said, then let himself out.

Eva stood there in the empty room, chilled despite the heat, and stared at the cardboard box on the table. A thin layer of tape held the flaps shut, but it was already re-sealed once, Eva could tell. She stood over, fingers dancing across the rough brown surface, thinking.

The door was closed, no sounds from outside. She checked the clock again, then back to the box.

Carefully, very carefully, she pulled the tape loose.

The first thing she saw was a stack of long and thin boxes, wrapped in words in all languages, but one leapt out at her: "Incubator Refill". She took it out, opened it, slid out one of three long plastic tubes, filled with a milky gelatin, its cap a smooth brass disc. She ran her finger down the side; it was cold, sterile, vicious.

She dropped it back into the package, closed it carefully, hands shaking. Next to it was a folder, and inside was a data disc, marked with pen, scratchy and sloppy:

NUREMBERG-A1
CODE AND INSTRUCTIONS

Her mind in a haze, Eva put the disc down on the table, flipped through the papers in the folder: reams of hex code, instructions in a syntax she didn't understand... ten thousand lines of them. She closed them, replaced them in the box gently, and accidentally toppled over a small container with a bright orange lid.

She picked it up, and saw it was filled with a clear liquid. It had the same writing on it as the disc: Nuremberg-A1.

"You fucker," she gasped. "What have you *done?*"

She put the container back into the box, rifled through the rest and came to a red folder which she tore open, and then staggered back at what she saw. Newspaper articles, a huge array of them, printed badly, detailing death at the hands of viruses that had killed thousands. She shivered as she saw the places, the dates... Modena, Italy; Graz, Austria, Linz...

She turned round, saw the door behind her, saw the clock, saw the bed, and just stood there, unmoving.

Outside, the first breeze in weeks blew by, and she heard the distant laughter of children, a dog barking. She looked back at the box, at the orange container, the disc. She grabbed them up, ran to the dresser, threw it open and pulled out random clothes, scattershot, throwing them into her old backpack, shoving it full.

She found a framed photo of her and Rhodri, just after Italy, intertwined happily in the countryside. She threw it against the wall, the glass shattering all over the bed.

At the door, she felt the weight of the orange-topped container in her hand, and she looked at the bed, the shards there, and down at the poison she held. She wound up, ready to throw... but then, then she squeezed it, shoved it into her backpack, and ran out the door and away; never once looking back.

Eva came back to life as the pale light came through the windows and crept across her face. She rolled to her side, the blankets soft against her skin, the room still warm as the heaters clicked off. Slowly, her head started to ache, a dull pain right behind her eyes, and with it, the cold got to her. She slipped on her clothes, let the mask hang loose around her neck, and ripped open a food packet from the depot the night before.

"Pyotr? You gone to get the stuff?" she asked the open air.

No one replied.

The sky outside was clear for a change, a soulless white and grey, and she wiped the sleep from her eyes, trying to think straight. She thought she heard water running, but the kitchen was empty. She shook her head, went back to the living room, stared out the windows at the street below.

There were no footprints in the snow today, no trace how she and Pyotr had arrived. A gust of wind blew some trash from the long pile in front of the building. A yellow plastic biohazard bag, emptied of its deadly burden, floated ominously down the street.

"Eva," said a voice, and it wasn't Pyotr's. She got to her feet, turned around quickly, backed to the empty window.

"Who's there?" she called.

Still, no one replied.

She edged to the kitchen, found a knife in a drawer, and moved back to the window, keeping her back to the wall at all times. She swore she heard scratching from the far end of the room, but it was impossible... there was no one there. She could *see* no one was there.

She checked out the window, back to the clean snow, shuddering.

"Pyotr... please come back... please..."

When she turned back, Rhodri was standing before her.

"Eva," he said, his eyes raw, skin pale. "You left me..."

She shrieked, held the knife out at him, backed further, but there was nowhere to go.

"Stay back!" she shouted. "Don't come any closer!"

He didn't move his feet, but he reached a poor, wretched hand out to her.

"Why did you leave me, Eva? Why would you leave me there?"

"You're a monster!" she shouted.

"But we're in love! You love me!"

"No!" she shouted, swinging the knife at the open air between them, covering her eyes. "You're a monster! Just leave me alone!"

When she looked back, the room was empty. Her heart skipped a beat, and she lowered the knife, eyes darting left and right. The wind blew snow into the room, cold blades on her face, and she flinched.

"Eva," said Rhodri from right beside her.

She screamed, swung the knife out, missing by an inch, and scuttled backwards, into the wall, and then ran full-tilt back to the stairs, slipping and tumbling down them until she crashed to the floor, the knife sliding away. She made a mad scramble towards it, grabbing it with her sprained hand, quickly scraping to her knees, and up, down the hall.

She heard a thump from above, and a scrape, and the light down the stairs was blocked by a tottering form.

"Eva..." called Rhodri, ghostly. "Eva, we need to talk..."

She raced around the corner, into a back part of the house, and slipped onto her face at something slick on the floor. Blood. She got to her feet, bracing against the walls, ran faster, down to a small closet at the end of the hall, pushed inside and curled into the corner, knife pointing up and out, trembling, fighting off hysteria.

"Go away… go away…" she cursed. "Leave me alone, please leave me alone…"

The only light came from a crack in the door, pale yellow, right across her eye. She reached back into the darkness, found a blanket on the ground, covered herself, trying to make herself invisible. While she struggled, something fell out of the blanket, hit the ground with a *thump*.

She froze, knife pointed at the crack in the door, looked down, up, and down again. It was a small laptop, lying on the floor, its soft blue sleep light pulsing. She reached a nervous hand out, turned it over right side up, and lifted the lid.

No sound from the hallway as the computer resumed its previous state. It took a moment, hummed to itself, and then began showing a flickering video feed, distorted and grainy. She stared at it a full minute before she realized what she saw…

The room upstairs.

The window, the snow-covered streets, the sofa, the sheets where she'd made love, the wrapper she dropped on the floor…

Into the shot, stiff and awkward, walked Rhodri. He looked round the room, to the window, then back to the stairs. And then, very deliberately, he looked straight at her. She shuddered, threw the computer back against the wall, covered her eyes. When she looked back, he was gone, but the computer had switched programs, bringing another to the front.

A browser window, showing a discussion forum. She recognized the colours instantly, read the banner with a gaping mouth: The University of Paris Alumni Association. She reached out, pulled the computer closer, touched the trackpad and scrolled down the page, up again. Notices of births, weddings, so many deaths. "Have you seen Fréderick?" or "Remembering my dear sweet Anabelle".

She clicked on one, saw a photo of a girl she'd never known, smiling in her school colours, with an accounting of her death at the hands of the one of the western plagues. The smile didn't fit the words, and Eva closed it quickly to avoid the sight.

And there, at the top of the page, she saw something that tore at her eyes.

RHODRI TENANT READ THIS NOW!

Checking the crack in the door, she clicked through, read the short message: "Rhodri: Loving your girl for you. Love Pytor @ Prague XOXO". Below was a video clip on a loop, and she bit back a gasp as she saw herself, naked on the sheets upstairs, Pyotr over her, moving back and forth in the dim light. She began to shake, tears in her eyes, hand covering her mouth.

"I'm sorry you had to find out like this," said Pyotr from the doorway, hands in his pockets and his face solemn and cold.

"I... I don't understand..." Eva gasped. "W-why?"

He pushed the door open, further, and she re-gripped the knife, the tip aimed straight at his heart.

"They're after Rhodri, Eva. Not you. It was never you. You were just—"

"Bait? You used me as bait?"

"I had to," he said, not pleading.

"Bullshit," she spat.

"They gave me no choice! They said if I didn't get Rhodri to Prague, they'd send me back!"

"Send you back *where?*"

"Prison," he said, dodging her glare. She pulled further back into the closet, kept darting looks to the hall beside him. "I've been locked up since Maselle died. I almost beat her doctor to death."

Eva blinked, stunned.

"So all that about... about finding new places to live... you being at the police station... that was all lies?"

Pyotr nodded meekly, ashamed.

"It was a set-up. They left the door unlocked so we could run into each other, escape together. Sobotka's been taking care of us. The pills were her idea."

"Like throwing me onto my head?"

"Listen, we both freaked out about that. The last thing either of us wanted to do is have you die over this. Hell, she gave me the gun when she found out about the university. Hurting you is not what we're about, Eva."

"Yeah, not until you get what you want."

He shook his head, sighed.

"I know this won't count for much, but I… I'm ready to run away with you for real. They can trace me, but I bet they won't if we move fast. I got the stuff ready. I was coming back to get you, to take you away. I was going to get out of here. With you. And you'd never have to know about any of this."

She aimed the knife at him, breathing deeply.

"You lied to me. You're lying to me now. All you want is Rhodri. I'm bait, and that's it."

"Eva, that's not true! I'd *take care* of you! Not like Rhodri did. From what I hear, he's done some twisted shit, and he's put you in the middle of it. I'd never risk you. I wouldn't launch a major virus strike into my girlfriend's hometown."

She narrowed her eyes, got to her feet, back against the wall. Pyotr did the same.

"Rhodri's behind Prague-1?" she asked, weak.

Pyotr nodded, solemn.

"They think if they can get him here, he won't launch the strike, and they can arrest him."

"So why not just ask me? Ask me to lure him? Why all this?"

He shrugged.

"Frankly, Eva, they're not sure you're not working *with* him. They couldn't risk it."

"And you? What do you think?"

He smiled at her, and it was almost like his old self was back again.

"I heard you last night. I know how you feel about all this. I know you'd never kill innocent people."

The knife lowered gently, then shot back up. Pyotr kept a safe distance, eyeing her carefully.

"I just want my mother back," Eva cried. "I want my mom and I want to get out of this town and never come back!" Her eyes cleared suddenly, and she stepped forward, jutting. "What did they do to my mother? Where is she?"

"They don't know, Eva, I swear. They planted her coat upstairs with Rhodri's number to make you call, but they are as much in the dark about that as you. I swear, none of us know where she is.

"Now listen, please. Your plan to escape was a good one. I'm ready to go, and I know it'll take time before you really trust me again. But we have to go *now*, before Sobotka catches on…"

She didn't lower the knife, kept checking for Rhodri around the corner. Pyotr sighed.

"But Eva, really, if you're not on board for this, I'm still going," he said, and pulled the gun from his belt, aiming it squarely at her chest. "So you're going to have to make a pretty big choice right now."

He flicked the safety, shook his head slightly at her. She watched the weapon anxiously, the knife swaying downward, but not out.

"What's it going to be?" he said.

Just then, a second gun slid in, pointed at Pyotr's temple, turned a bit to the side. Eva gasped when she saw the face beside Pyotr, grim and unflinching.

"Put the gun down," said Dmitri. "or I paint that wall a nice shade of fucked-up."

39

When he awoke, the Healer felt cold; much colder than he should have. He had trouble seeing in the darkness, but he noticed the brown spines of his tent above him, and eased back, calm again. There were voices next to him, laughing, happy, speaking in a language he didn't understand. He turned his head stiffly towards them, pain shooting from his shoulder.

Anouma sat close by, smiling and putting beads and jewels in the girl's hair, which shone a fiery orange and yellow, but black at the same time. The girl noticed him first, her expression changing from joy to anxious observation.

Then Anouma looked over, kept her smile, and nodded to him slowly, reassuring. She reached out to him, but he stopped her, catching her hand in his. Her skin was so soft, and he caressed her fingertips with his thumb... gentle... gentle...

He felt a sudden panic, jerked upright when he realized: he wasn't wearing his gloves! He grasped at his chest, his arms... they were bare... his skin exposed, his body in the open air... he threw his head back, gasped madly, but the oxygen was tight, and he flailed against it, fought against it... but then... then the darkness swarmed over him again.

*   *   *

Anouma was checking his wound the next time he opened his eyes, her face so close to his, he had trouble telling if it was another dream. He moved his head slightly, and she recoiled, scared of him, but not running yet.

His shoulder ached with a strange dull pain he couldn't pinpoint. He tried moving his arm to feel it, but realized his arms were strapped down... several straps around his forearms, his thighs and calves. He was trapped. He panicked, started to struggle against them.

"What are you doing?" he said, his mask making it hard to breathe. "Let me go!"

"You were flailing in your sleep," she said, pushing a firm hand down on his bare chest, and it calmed him somewhat. "You had nightmares."

"They're done now. Let me go!"

"You said the same thing an hour ago," she warned, pushing him back. "Lie still or you will tear the stitches."

He obeyed, slowing his breathing, laying back again. The straps were tight and thin, cutting into his skin, but when he relaxed they were much less obtrusive. He stared up at the tent, the wind blowing it softly, and said nothing.

"You have lost a lot of blood" Anouma said, sliding closer again. "It was a gunshot?"

He nodded slightly.

"Your brother's fault," he said. "How did you find me?"

"I followed you as you left the hospital. You did not look well. I was not sure what I... what I would..."

"I did not see you," he said, worry strong in his voice.

"I do not think you saw much. You should not be alive, with all that blood loss. The bullet did not do any major damage, but you will have to stay here for several days."

"No," he groaned. "There is no time. I must go by morning..." He checked the sides of the tent suddenly, back and forth, looking for a crack, for a hint… "What time is it?" he gasped. "How long have I slept?"

She pushed his chest again, and he stopped fighting, lay back again.

"The sun is still down," she said. "But it would be foolish to go out there too soon. You do not know what might—"

"I have a schedule. It cannot wait."

She nodded, said nothing for a moment.

"Whose mission is it?" she asked. "Are you helping my brother, or yourself?"

He looked away, his arms tensing against the straps.

"Neither," he said, bitterly.

She sighed, reached over and pulled the gauze off his wound, checking it carefully. He groaned at the contact, but didn't resist it.

"It does not hurt," he said.

"That is the morphine. I found it in your pack."

He stared at her, eyes wide behind his mask.

"What did you touch? What did you *touch?*"

"As little as possible. And I will keep the morphine, just in case."

She sat back, pulled a needle from her pocket, stared at it guiltily. It seemed to weigh more to her than it should have.

"Why are you saving me?" he asked, voice flat.

"I… I do not know if I am, yet," she whispered.

They sat in silence again, both staring at the needle.

"You must be shot at often," Anouma muttered.

"People fear me," he said, his voice stale.

She nodded.

"That is your nature. You bring fear and pain."

His eyes couldn't leave the needle. He strained against the straps again, getting nowhere.

"I do not bring pain," he said, his temper rising. "The pain came before me."

She looked at him again, her eyes were narrow, cold.

"Suffering comes before you," she said, her voice filling with venom. "Death and agony come too. But *you* bring pain. You kill their hope when you enter the room."

"They should not use rooms!" he spat, and her face twitched. "It is cruel and unfair."

"Unfair? Unfair to whom?" she snapped. "The patient? or your sacred social order?"

"Both!" he hissed. "Neither deserve that fate!" He would have grabbed her if he could, but he was stuck there, a captive, awaiting his execution. His frustration boiled over: "We warned them. We told them to outlaw the machines before the damage was too great. They ignored us, and they are paying for their mistakes."

"Those machines did so much good!" she argued. "The cure for AIDS—"

"They denied it to you! You defend them?"

"—many other great things as well! If it had not been for the incubators, where would humanity be now?"

"Alive!" yelled the Healer. "We would find the same cures, without the damage done! But their decisions left us with none! All my work, all my sacrifice, undone in a moment. All because of weak resolve. I will not let that happen. If they will not take care of themselves, *we will do it for them!*"

She stared at him, her mouth clenched shut.

"You cannot believe what you have done is right," she said, and he focused hard to block the image of fire. "You cannot believe you are not guilty of murder."

He paused, tried to control himself.

"I am not answerable to you," he said, and she gripped the syringe tighter, looked away.

"No…" she said quietly.

He sighed loudly.

"And you? Are you a murderer?"

She met his eyes, then held the needle up before her, turned it slightly, as if contemplating.

"I cannot tell. Is there such a thing as a necessary evil?"

He rolled his head back, slammed it against the ground, agonizing.

"Stop trying to be a hero! We are all killers, here!"

She shook her head slowly.

"I am not. Not yet. And I cannot tell… if taking one life to save another—"

"The hundredth is the same as the second. Or the first. Be done with it! Whatever you wish, do it!"

She lowered the needle, but didn't put it away.

"You are wrong. There is a difference between the one and the many. You are guilty of far worse, and you know it."

He barely flinched.

"Our hospitals," he began, quietly at first, "they help broken bones and pregnant women. Yours are like funeral parlours staffed by doctors. Our children wear masks for colds, not to survive. You live in a pandemic day after day. To us, it is a distant nightmare."

She sneered at him.

"A nightmare black with ashes," she intoned.

"We made sacrifices. We saw the future and stopped it before it killed us. It hurt us far more than it hurt you to watch. It was *the only way to survive*. In eight months, we were safe; yet you have worked for five years with no progress, no victories. Society rotting from all sides. We contained our tragedy. You wallow in it."

She looked at her hands on her lap for a few moments, her fingers unmoving, curled slightly, and he said nothing, let her be. Her weapon rolled between her palm and her fingers, gently.

"Society is not the sum of its people," she said, talking more to herself than to him. "It is not something you protect at the expense of its parts. You see a man with a diseased leg, you do not kill him because the effort to save him is too great. You treat him, you fight for him, you save him and if you cannot, you give him hope in his last days."

"Hope is a luxury you cannot afford," he replied.

"You sound like someone I know," she sighed.

"The older man? The doctor?"

She nodded.

"He thinks hope is dangerous, too," she said. "Hope and trust."

"He has seen things you cannot comprehend."

"And what about you? How did you deal with those things he saw? You were there, were you not? You saw what happened there—"

"An entire generation of medical genius, destroyed," he interrupted.

"By a set of plagues so much simpler than the ones we fight now."

"He learned from his mistakes," he said. "Some of them, anyway. We did our best to contain it. But without the social structures being enforced, it means nothing. Your doctor saw that. Noble intentions count for nothing if you fight a blaze by spitting at smoke."

"This is not your battle—"

"It's not *your* battle! You are not even *from* here! What did they say to convince you to risk your life for them?"

"I could not let them die like this—"

"No? They had no trouble leaving you at the mercy of Tuberculosis, Meningitis, AIDS… We would never abandon our allies. If we did, we would be alone in the world."

"You *are*. You lost the last of your friends the day you set those towns on fire."

He said nothing, turned his head away.

"You dream of them," she said, guilty almost. "They haunt you."

He looked back, tired.

"You know nothing about it."

She nodded, turned the needle over in her hand again.

"There is enough morphine here to stop your heart," she said, morose. "And I cannot think of a reason not to use it."

She met his eyes — or his goggles — with a sad stare.

"And it is wrong, is it not?" she asked.

He said nothing.

"You would kill my brother," she said. "You would kill him and anyone else you choose, all to keep a schedule. A *schedule!* These are *people* you are hurting, but they are just names on a page to you. Another job to finish before the time is up."

"I have no choice. It is my duty."

"And what if you fail? What happens if you just refuse? What if you say: 'Enough is enough. I will not do it anymore'?"

"That is not my choice," he sighed. "I cannot stop."

"Why not?"

"I cannot fail them."

"*Why not?*" she yelled.

"Because they would send me back home!" he boomed, fighting against the straps and sending pain shooting down his arm. "They would send me back and I *cannot go back there!*"

Neither spoke for a moment.

Finally, she nodded, carefully held the needle to his arm, and he felt the prick, a warm sensation creeping up and through his body, and he gasped, closing his eyes, letting it carry him. He felt the straps come loose around his arms, falling to his sides. The pain slipped away, and he realized... slowly... that he was not dying.

He looked over at her, slow, uncertain, and she shot the rest of the morphine onto the ground, threw the needle there.

"You *do* have a choice," she said to him solemnly.

He said nothing, stayed still, watching her pull her knees up, hugging them gently, resting her head there, quietly distraught.

"You will save my brother, and you will wipe his disease from the face of the Earth. And then, when you place another check mark next to your list of accomplishments, you can make your choice."

She wiped a tear from her eye with her sleeve, took a shaky breath. Then, he found himself reaching a hand out, touched her arm, and she didn't recoil.

"This nightmare," he said softly, "it ruins your soul."

She choked on a sob, shook her head.

"My soul is broken already," she said. "I have blood on my hands. Each one of the lives you will take today, those are all my fault. I could have stopped you here, tonight, but I refused."

She looked at him, eyes full.

"I am not scared of hell," she said. "I am terrified of the company I will have to keep there."

40

Eva landed on the floor next to Pyotr as Dmitri paced in behind them, cracking his knuckles. He stood in front of the door, feet apart, ready to keep the peace inside the small, white-tiled room. A simple metal desk and two chairs sat along one wall, three drops of red beneath them, stark against the overwhelming white.

"Now then," Dmitri said, twitching his mask side to side. "Let's get you two sorted. Eva, I know. Hi, Eva."

She said nothing, pulled herself into a ball and watched him.

"But this joker, all I know about him is that he was pointin' a gun when I first saw him. Which, at least in my books, isn't the proper way to treat a lady."

Dmitri winked at Eva, but she ignored it.

"I'm her b-b-boyfriend..." Pytor said, and Eva just laughed.

"I can think of at least two people who'd say otherwise," chuckled Dmitri.

Eva's mouth dropped open and she remembered...

"Where's Rhodri?" she demanded, getting to her knees now. "What's going on?"

Dmitri shrugged at her, scratched his cheek.

"You tell me," he said. "I haven't seen Rhodri in… well, longer than you, I think. You passed along my message that time?"

"Not exactly."

"Figures. Well whatever happened, he ain't here."

"But I *saw* him! Back at the building! He was chasing me!"

Dmitri cocked an eyebrow at her, glanced to Pyotr for confirmation, but Pyotr seemed just as confused. Eva was running her hands through her hair, trembling.

"Eva, kid, if he'd been there, I would've seen him, believe me."

She shook her head anxiously.

"I saw him. I know I did. He's here, in Prague. He's looking for me."

Just then, there was a quick knock at the door, and it opened, slow and creaking. The light from the hallway was musty and almost grey, but the silhouette there was unmistakable. Eva screamed, backed behind Pytor, pointing madly.

"Liar! Liar! He's here!"

Rhodri stood in the doorway, arms crossed, head shaking sadly. He was wearing a black suit, no tie, but his hair was a mess as always, his beard looking sickly and crusted.

"Eva," he said solemnly. "You shouldn't have run…"

She wailed, backed into the corner, covering her head with her arms. She felt strong hands pulling at her, and she fought and kicked, trying to keep them off, keep the smell of him away…

Suddenly, she was thrown onto the ground, on her back, hands holding her arms at her sides, someone else pinning her legs down. She heard them talking, but she refused to open her eyes for them, weaving her head from side to side, as if she could escape by sheer force of thought.

"Eva, look at me," said Rhodri.

"Eva, look at me," said Dmitri.

"She's… too… strong…" grunted Pyotr.

She pushed with all her strength, kicked Pyotr off her legs, and he slammed into the wall. She twisted and fought, wrestling against impossible odds… but then she felt a tight, strong hand around her neck, squeezing slightly, and she lay still, refusing to open her eyes.

"Kill her, Dmitri," Rhodri said. "She betrayed me."

She cried, tried to swat him away, but he tightened his hold.

"I'm sorry, Rhodri…" she stammered. "I'm so sorry, I didn't mean it…"

The hand on her neck eased up slightly, and she took a ragged breath.

"What the hell is she…?" Dmitri said, his voice distant.

"Shit…" gasped Pytor. "She's infected. She must be infected!"

"With *what*?" growled Dmitri.

"I… I don't know. It drives you insane, whatever it is, and—"

"Eva," whispered Rhodri in her ear. "Eva, why won't you kiss me anymore?"

She felt a cold hand run down her neck, her chest, and slip against her bare waist, sending a chill up her spine. She kicked out, missing him, and he ran his fingers up along her side, gentle, probing.

"Stop it!" she screamed. "Stop touching me! I hate you!"

"Did you give her a Pathenex stopper?" Dmitri said, fading into the distance, while his hand was still on her neck.

"H-h-half of it," Pyotr admitted. "I used Tezocet for the second pill."

"Are you a fucking moron? That's a hallucinogen on its own, not to mention the immuno-suppression she must have going on!"

"I… I needed her asleep… I didn't mean to…"

"Oh Eva," whispered Rhodri in her ear. "What did you do? Did you fuck him? Did you betray me?"

"No," Eva gasped. "No, I'd never…"

"I *saw you*," he breathed. "I saw it all. And I think you liked it."

The hand around her neck loosened again, and she flailed her arms around, hitting Dmitri, his stubbled cheek, but missing Rhodri every time. Dmitri knelt on her hurt wrist, and she cried in pain, pushing her other hand against her forehead, weeping uncontrollably.

She heard the sounds of the door opening, quick footsteps, the clink of plastic on the ground. A light prick on her arm, just about the elastic brace, and then a cold, metallic sensation flooding her veins.

"You'll like this," Rhodri whispered to her, his hand brushing the side of her breast. "I made it specially for you."

"Murderer!" she screamed, and had her head pushed back against the floor, smelled onions, cologne.

"Eva," said Dmitri, loud and clear. "Eva, it's all in your head. I know you know that, and I need you to focus. It's all in your head. Rhodri isn't here. It's just me and the fucktard. Nobody else is here, I promise you."

Eva slowed her breathing, felt the depth come back to the room, the sounds less threatening, and her heart rate slow. She didn't open her eyes, but stopped crying.

"Y-y-you promise?" she whimpered.

"I do, Eva. Open your eyes. It'll be okay."

"I can't..." she pleaded. "I can't, I can't..."

"You can," Dmitri told her.

"I can't. He'll be there. I can't see him. Please."

"He's not here, Eva. You know that. You know this disease. You know how it works. Think past it, kid. It makes sense if you think past it."

Eva stopped breathing, listened. She heard two sets of breaths, two sets of clothes moving, two souls around her. She exhaled slowly, cautiously.

And she opened her eyes.

"All good?" Dmitri asked her gently.

It was him, and only him. No one else. No Rhodri.

She nodded, faintly, and he let her go. She sat herself up, rubbing her neck, taking stuttering breaths. Pyotr lay against the far wall, white as a ghost, and the rest of the room was empty. There was no Rhodri.

Dmitri patted her knee, got to his feet.

"That shot should keep you stable for an hour or two," he said, dusting off his trousers. "But if you start to see anything else odd in the room, let me know, okay?"

"Okay," Eva nodded, catching her breath. "What did you give me?"

"A little cocktail we made that seems to suppress the symptoms," Dmitri replied. "Temporarily. And never as far as we'd like."

"What do you—"

"I'm at a loss about what to do with your boy toy here," Dmitri interrupted, darting a mean glare at Pyotr. "Cause as I see it, he's lied to you, he's denied you vital drugs at a critical time, he's given you what might charitably be called a date rape drug—"

"It was for her head! She was in pain!"

"Yeah, and my gun's primarily for pistol-whipping. Shut your hole. It's not your turn to talk."

He turned back to Eva, then pulled his gun from within his jacket, dropped the safety, and pointed it at Pyotr.

"Eva," Dmitri said, business-like. "I don't know what happened after he gave you that pill, and I don't wanna know. But since you and Rhodri were like family, I'm gonna give you this choice. How's he going to leave the room? Cause I'm fine with either way."

Eva saw Pyotr, cowering in the corner, looking at her with pleading, desperate eyes. She rubbed her bandaged hand across her head, tried to think through the pain, the confusion. Pyotr said nothing, but mouthed words to her that she couldn't understand. Things she didn't care to understand.

She shook her head, turned away.

"No more killing," she sighed. "Just get him out of here."

Dmitri looked to Eva, paused. Pyotr was trembling. Dmitri put his gun away, paced to Pyotr and yanked him to his feet, dragged him to the door.

"Eva, wait!" Pyotr cried as he was forced against the wall as the door opened and two large men in black suits came in. "Please! They'll put me back in! Please don't do this! We can still get away! It wasn't all an act! *It wasn't all fake—*"

The door closed and Dmitri turned to Eva, his hands in his pockets, sighed.

"'Wasn't all fake', he says," Dmitri mused. "'s what my ex wife used to say."

He smirked at his own joke, coughed and pulled a chair from the table, offering it to Eva. She sat, tentative, and he hopped up on the table itself, lounging comfortably in the cold, sterile room.

"So you feeling okay?" he asked her. "Just you and me in here now?"

She nodded, checked around just to be sure.

"Good. Cause what I need you to do, I need you to focus on."

Eva frowned.

"What do you need me to do?"

"What you've got, Eva, we know it. It's called Nuremberg-6. It's nastier than you know. And the kicker is, it's infected some of our people. We didn't see the signs until it was pretty far advanced, and we've been fighting to contain it ever since."

Eva scowled at him.

"How's this my problem?"

"It's your problem because the same things that're happening to them, they're happening to you too. We don't know what its endstage is, but we're not keen to find out. We want it fixed, and we want it fixed *now*."

"So what, you want to test the cures on me? I'm your guinea pig?"

He laughed, patted her shoulder, but she swatted him away.

"Hell no, Eva. See, our regular programmer has gone missing. I think you know him."

She scowled.

"Yeah," Dmitri continued. "And without him, we're kinda screwed. Or we *were* screwed, until you showed up."

"I keep telling people: I don't know how to make viruses. And even if I did, I wouldn't help you."

Dmitri gave her a dead look, scratched his chin under his mask.

"Even if it means you go bat shit crazy?"

Eva shuddered, remembering the sound of Rhodri in her ear. But she shook her head.

"I won't lift a finger to help you. You're all murderers."

Dmitri sighed, slapped his knees and got up off the table, leaving Eva sitting there, alone.

"Fine," he said. "I kinda thought you'd say that."

He opened the door, leaned out and motioned, then looked back to Eva, shaking his head.

"I get that you don't want to help me. You don't know me. If I asked myself for this kind of help, I'd probably have trouble resolving to pitch in, too. But you don't need to do it for me. Or for you. On the other hand, you may want to do it for somebody else."

"You can all fucking die for all I care," she spat.

"Even her?" Dmitri asked, as a stretcher wheeled in, carrying Eva's mother.

41

MUSÍLKOVA 27, PRAGUE, CZECH REPUBLIC
NOVEMBER 30

"Mama!" Eva gasped, running. She grabbed her mother's shoulders tightly, brushed her hair back, held back tears.

Her mother stared blankly at the ceiling, her face aged, worn, and two long cuts on her cheeks half-healed. An IV strung up and out of her arm, saline dripping in like a heartbeat. She was restrained, but she made no move to escape, and at once, Eva started fighting with the straps, trying to undo them, let her free.

A large hand wrapped around hers.

"You don't want to do that," Dmitri said. "She doesn't do well when she's free."

Eva held her mother's hand gently, stroked it.

"What did you do to her?" she whispered.

"She's got what you've got, but it's much worse. We gave her one of those cocktails about twenty minutes ago, and this... this is as good as it gets with her. She's not really conscious unless she's full-on sick, and that's not a pleasant place for her to be.

"I know you don't trust us, that you don't want to help us... but Eva, babe, if you don't fix this thing for us, *this* is going to be *you* in three weeks. This, or worse."

Eva saw two suited men carrying in an incubator, setting it on the table and plugging it in. She looked back to her mother, rested her head against the blank, scarred face.

"I don't know how to do it," she cried softly.

"You keep sayin' that, and it sounds just like Rhodri, back at the start. But he picked it up real fast. And from what I hear, he wasn't half the bright one that you are."

"Don't these incubators have some kind of… automated system? Something more reliable than human trial-and-error? *Anything else?*"

"Could be," sniffed Dmitri. "Might be a software patch somewhere I don't know about since *the manufacturers have all been out of business for years!*"

Eva looked to the incubator, eyes shot with tears.

"What if I screw it up? You really want to take that chance?"

Dmitri punched the incubator on, the screen flickering to life. He dusted off her chair, turned it.

"Give it a go, let me know what you think."

He nodded to her, and she reluctantly sat on the chair, touched the trackpad and began investigating the incubator's software. A large, simple window opened, happily showing a stylized molecule, and welcomed her to the world of personalized bio-engineering. A small alert flashed before her, giving her the "Tip of the Day":

THE RESULTS PANE AT THE BOTTOM OF THE SCREEN SHOWS YOU THE OUTCOME OF YOUR WORK AGAINST THE MOST COMMON BLOOD SAMPLES FOR YOUR GEOGRAPHIC LOCATION. TO TEST AGAINST OTHER LOCALES, PLEASE CHOOSE "EDIT LOCALE…" UNDER THE "PROFILES" MENU.

She clicked "dismiss", got a lay of the land. Dmitri reached a finger in, pushed the screen as he talked.

"I'm no genius, but what Rhodri told me is this: You load in a blood sample here, and it does up a nice doodle of what the virus looks like. So let's give this a go, load up one of the samples we've got."

He swatted her hands off the trackpad, navigated a few menus until a complex string of different-coloured rectangles filled the middle pane of the screen, faux-glossy and inviting, like a children's puzzle game and not a matter of life or death.

"You seem pretty good at this," Eva remarked. "Why don't *you* find the cure yourself?"

Dmitri smirked.

"Just cause I can print, don't mean I can write. Look here... left side, this is your toolset. There are, what, about a hundred different things you can drag around and slap together. Me, I don't know shit about this, so I just make the prettiest little chain I can figure. So let's try the red square, the blue diamond, and the... yellow whatsit-called."

"Trapezoid."

"Bless you. Now see..."

Dmitri demonstrated his new creation in the top pane, the background a calm sea blue with animated bubbles creeping up. Almost pleasant. Eva sighed at it all.

"Now we hit this button here... 'test'... and..."

Dmitri's structure melded itself together, grew stems connecting some elements, and then a set of arrows appeared between the top and middle panes, suggesting the application of the first to the second. After a moment or two, new shapes and colours fell from the middle pane into the bottom, and the window's frame turned red. A warning flashed on the side of the screen:

4 ALERTS REPORTED:

PATIENT DIES OF MASSIVE INTERNAL HAEMORRHAGING;

PATIENT SUFFERS SEVERE STROKE;

PATIENT MAY EXPERIENCE VISION LOSS;

PATIENT MAY EXHIBIT RASH.

Eva cocked an eyebrow, and Dmitri sighed.

"Believe it or not, this is better than usual. Last time it told me I'd successfully constructed Ebola. That was a good day, let me tell you."

Eva shook her head, hit the 'clear' button and Dmitri's creation disappeared. She pointed at the toolset, scrolling down the list, incredulous.

"I don't know why you thought I'd be good at this," she said. "This is a stupidly complex program to figure out. Look at all these things… I don't know what even a fraction of these mean!"

"The incubators were made for pharmacists, I think. They kind of assume you know a bit about medicine or something."

"Which I don't."

"But neither did Rhodri. And what he told me… he said the only things you really need to worry about are the first twenty shapes. The rest are compounds, and you can live without 'em. He said that when you really get down to it, this is like any other program. Forget about the molecules or the blood samples or any of that crap, and just treat it like what you know."

Eva shook her head sadly.

"I'll screw it up," she said.

"Then it'll tell you. And you start over. It doesn't require skill, it just requires a brain that can think a certain way. And yours does that."

Eva sighed, moved a red square over to the compound in the middle, and watched part of the structure crumble.

"Hey cool, real-time," exclaimed Dmitri. "Didn't know you could do that! See? You're a natural!"

Eva slammed her fist down on the desk, turned on Dmitri.

"What happened with Rhodri?" she demanded. "He was good! He was good, and somehow you corrupted him, made him do *this*! What in the hell did you do to him?"

Dmitri placed a heavy hand on Eva's shoulder.

"Less chatter. More working. We don't have all day here. You're due to start flaking out in ninety-some minutes, and I don't have an infinite supply of that cocktail if I'm feeding three people at once."

Eva hesitated, as if she might refuse, but then slowly turned back to the incubator, put her hands on the trackpad, and began to work.

Dmitri leaned back in his chair, staring at the ceiling, arms behind his head.

Eva began by figuring out the effect of each shape in her palette. The red squares chipped away at certain parts of Nuremberg-6, but left other by-products behind. The yellow circles helped with others, but again, let dangerous elements fall. She tried pairing a red square with a yellow circle, and it *did* eat up most of the usual suspects, but then it left a shower of purple squares that did more damage than anything before.

After some work, she found a way to embed a trio of shapes inside a container, which was attached as a subset of another element. This one lead to no fall-out, but it made Nuremberg-6 split in two, each piece much more immediately dangerous than mere delirium. She made a more complex compound, creating depths and depths of embedded elements, trying to catch every bit, stop them from falling into the bottom of the screen.

Dmitri watched her work, held his breath every time the machine processed results, sighed quietly every time it returned a death sentence. He didn't speak a word, just sat beside her, observing.

Eventually the compound was too big to fit on the screen, and she scrapped it all, starting with a single purple circle, and built more streamlined functions around the core. The results were discouraging, but after a while, she started to see a pattern emerging... she clasped her hands together, leaned back from the table.

"What?" Dmitri asked, waking from a stupor. "What's wrong? What happened?"

"I'm close, I think," Eva said, eyes fixed on the shapes. "I think this is close."

"You've got four big chunks of it that kill the patient more ways than I can count," he complained. "I think you and me have different definitions of 'close.'"

"Ignore that. Look at how it works... I'm breaking it up so this red, this blue... see? They don't stay together. They were causing the strokes. I'm splitting it up so the worst parts don't survive. Then all I need to do is beat those four compounds, and... and..."

"And we've got a cure?" Dmitri said, hopeful.

"I don't know. But it's the best I've got right now."

"Eva!" called her mother suddenly, seizing up, trying to escape her restraints. Dmitri and Eva ran to her side; he tightened the straps while Eva stroked her hair.

"Mama? Mama, can you hear me?"

"Eva! Someone find Eva! She's all alone in the bath!"

Her mother wasn't looking at her at all, she was in her own world, and it made Eva shiver to remember the feeling. Dmitri checked her IV, shook his head.

"She's coming out of it early. We need another cocktail."

"Somebody help me! She might have drowned! Someone please give me a ride home before she drowns!"

Eva turned away, back to the incubator. Dmitri opened the door, leaned out, frowning. The hall was empty. He took his phone from his jacket, hit a button.

"Where is everyone?" he barked in heavily-accented English. "We need another..."

He trailed off, listening, then nodded.

"Be right there. Somebody get a new cocktail down to Kolikov. I'm locking them in."

He looked back to Eva, the door half-closed. She darted nervous glances between him and her mother, who was starting to fight harder against her restraints, crying at the imagined fear of losing a child.

"Sit tight," Dmitri said. "I'll be back as soon as I can. Just concentrate on the virus and ignore her, got it?"

He didn't wait for an answer, just ran out the door, locking it behind him.

Eva took her mother's strapped hand in hers, stroked it warmly.

"Mama, I'm here. It's Eva."

"Eva, my baby!" her mother screamed. "She's drowning, my baby! Why did he leave her alone like that?"

"It'll be okay, mama. I'm going to take care of it."

Eva threw herself back at the incubator, dragging shapes in and out of the structure, breaking bits, shattering structures, cutting away at the most deadly bits. Six warnings, five warnings, four, and three... she had the thing on the ropes, but it kept tossing out surprises, things she couldn't decipher. She slammed her hand against the desk, furious, and her mother whimpered.

"Die, damn you. Just die..." she sighed, lowering her head. Warm hands wrapped over her shoulders, began to massage her tense muscles. She sighed happily, nodded.

"Feels good," she said, looking back at the screen as the hands kept working.

She drew down another compound, tried it, and it worked. She gasped, elated, and began to fight off the last two survivors of Nuremberg-6: fatal stroke and fatal fever. She tossed shapes across the screen with amazing dexterity, the stress melting from her body, her hands feeling warm for the first time in days...

"I've got you now," she growled to the virus.

Strong arms wrapped around her shoulders, but she kept working, taking their energy and using it. She felt breath on her neck, then the brush of beard, and a kiss on her ear. She shivered, closed her eyes a moment, just a moment, let the kiss linger.

"You miss me," whispered Rhodri softly.

"I miss you," Eva replied.

A hand slid up, up around her neck, caressing her, fingers touching her lips. She held her breath, her hands falling away from the trackpad, touched the arms, held them there, turning her head to him, desperate, desperate...

"You need me," Rhodri whispered.

"I do. I need you," she answered.

"Then why," he breathed, his mouth close to hers. "Why did you *leave me?*"

The hand at her neck tightened suddenly, fingers digging sharp into her skin, and she convulsed, but he held her tight in his arms, keeping her there, locked in a killing embrace, and he dug his nails into her skin, dragging up and down, then moved gently to her ear, beard rough and scratching.

"You should have stayed," he growled.

Eva trembled, her head up and her neck exposed, and she tried to see behind her, tried to see him.

"You're not real," she cried. "You're not here. Dmitri locked the door."

"I have a key," he hissed. "You can't keep me out."

"You don't have a key. This is the virus. You're not here."

He laughed at her, moved around to her other side, still holding her tight, and bit the edge of her ear.

"If I weren't real," he said. "Then how could I do *this*?"

She felt her neck released, and a sharp burn shot across her cheek. She grabbed at it, felt the sting, checked her fingertips and saw blood. She gasped, squeezed her hand into a fist.

"Why would you leave me?" Rhodri asked, moving back to her other side, his hand tracing down her face, her neck, like a lover's caress, but evil.

"You know why," she spat. "It's this. This and all those other viruses you made."

He laughed, nuzzled close to her neck.

"You know I made them because of you," he whispered. "I dreamed them up while we made love."

She shook her head, but he grabbed it, held it steady.

"You were my greatest inspiration," he sang almost. "My muse. You made these viruses. They're yours."

Eva's hands hit the table, the trackpad, and then her eyes opened, but narrow.

"I didn't make them," she said cooly. "But I *will* destroy them. Just try and stop me."

She looked forward, despite his hands, reached hers to the trackpad and moved the blocks around, shifting at a furious pace; breaking compounds, catching fall-out... Rhodri couldn't stop her, his arms unable to shift her determination, his hands stroking her body top to bottom, trying to dislodge her concentration... She fought past it, fixing errors and finally, finally, leaving the cure with only one side-effect.

"Fatal stroke," Rhodri laughed, kissing her neck. "You'll never beat me, Eva. You never could."

"You never saw what I can do," she said, and drew a yellow rectangle over the last compound, hanging it over, pausing. Her mother sang a quiet lullaby, Rhodri licked her jaw sweetly, and she... she let the last piece fall.

The bottom pane glowed green, ran a notice saying: "Minor side-effects: raised blood pressure". Eva gasped, shoved back from the table, hands in the air.

"I did it!" she exclaimed, and her mother laughed out at the same time, but for unknown reasons. She hit the 'save' button, then another marked 'process', and she saw a vial of serum in the incubator's central chamber slide into place and start to churn slowly. She pressed her palms to her eyes, holding back a laugh of joy, listening as the cure was made.

When she opened her eyes again, Rhodri was right before her, scowling.

"You *bitch!*" he screamed, and grabbed her head with both hands, scraping at her. She kicked and pushed and fell back off the chair, scrambling back to the wall, and Rhodri stormed her, grabbing at her legs, pulling her towards him, psychotic and maniacal and so unfamiliar all she could was scream.

The door burst open suddenly, and Dmitri was there, flanked by two guards. He looked to Eva's mother, crying in her stretcher, and then down to Eva, and in a flash he shot across the room, needle at the ready, and pushed her down onto her side, jabbing the point into her arm, and she felt it, felt the rush again...

"He came back," she gasped, face ground into the tile. "He came back. You said I had hours. What... what happened?"

Dmitri kept her there, but his lock was almost gentle.

"I don't know," he said. "Might be the Tezocet again, or the damn thing might be mutating as it spreads."

Eva nodded as best she could, looked forward and saw Rhodri there, lying on the ground with her, his hand stroking her cheek.

"Shh," he said, smiling. "Don't worry. It'll be okay."

Eva looked away from him, grunted.

"I did it," she said. "I broke the virus. Check the machine."

Dmitri shook, looked back, then leaned in to Eva.

"You still see him?" he asked.

Eva looked across the room. Rhodri licked his lips at her.

"No," she lied. "No, he's gone."

Dmitri got up quickly, moved to the incubator and checked the progress bar as it crept across the screen. It chimed happily, and the serum tube rotated around, then emptied itself into a small container at the base of the machine. An orange cap attached, and with a hiss, the work was done. Dmitri picked it up as if it were the most valuable thing in the world.

"I've got to go use this," he said to Eva, pocketing it. "You stay put."

"Go? Wait, I thought this was for my mother! You said I was helping my mother!"

Dmitri shrugged, the door half-closed.

"You are," he said. "But she don't pay my bills. So she can wait a bit. The *both* of you can."

And he closed the door, leaving her alone with her comatose mother and the ghostly Rhodri, who watched her hungrily from the corner.

42

Crew was on his way in to the hospital when a pair of nurses, masks clutched to their faces, ran out past him, screaming. He watched them go, curious, then shrugged and continued inside.

To his left, the large heavy doors to the treatment area were being locked shut, an old man in a blue hospital uniform wrapping yellow tape across the handles and to the frame. The echoes of hundreds of screams seeped through the cracks. Crew motioned to the tape, cleared his throat.

"What's up with the panic?" he called, and the old man turned with a start, his mask too tight on his face.

"Outbreak," he gasped. "Something terrible. The whole floor has it, and two of the nurses. We're quarantining everyone. City is bringing in the army."

Crew crossed his arms, made a face.

"Who started it?"

The old man tried to run past, but Crew caught him by the sleeve, swung him around.

"Please!" cried the man. "Please, I have a family… I can't stay here, it's not safe!"

"I'll tell you what's not safe," said Crew calmly. "Pissing me off, that's what. *Who started the outbreak?*"

"Nobody knows. They're all delirious… they're having waking nightmares, terrible nightmares, and they scream day and night. We were sedating them at first, but there wasn't enough to last. We don't know what else to—"

"Yeah yeah, not my problem," Crew cut in. "There's been a Healer around here, right? Could it have been him? Did he come into contact with any of the patients?"

The old man tried to run again, but Crew re-gripped him, slammed him into the wall.

"I *said*," said Crew, "did the Healer see any patients?"

"No… no, Dr Bastien kept him out of the hospital. He never got in. He… he couldn't have been involved."

Crew gritted his teeth, checked over his shoulder, grim.

"Who treated the first patient?" he asked. "Which doctor?"

"Dr Anouma," the man stuttered. "But she's been missing since last night. Nobody can find her, and she won't answer her pages."

"Any idea where she lives?"

"Here at the hospital, but she's not here, I swear. She had an emergency with her brother, and she was just… gone…"

Crew reared on the man, leaning in close.

"Her brother?" he breathed.

*   *   *

The room was so dark that Crew got antsy, pulled his gun. He nudged his way forward, checking every angle with quick sweeps, until he arrived at the back of the room, dim light shining through thick plastic covers over the window.

A single bed was propped on the side, and there, sheets askew, was a frail black man who seemed to be on the verge of complete disintegration. He was watching as Crew approached, eyes bloodshot and fearful.

"You're Dr Anouma's brother?" Crew asked, rough from the start.

Adjobi nodded, weak but anxious.

"She saw you last night? Late last night?"

"Yes…" whispered Adjobi.

"Did she say where she was going?"

Adjobi sat higher in the bed, pupils opening wide.

"She's not downstairs?"

Crew shook his head.

"She took off after seeing you. Any idea why?"

"I… I don't—"

"What do you know about the outbreak down there? Did she mention it?"

Adjobi sat up, thin arms bracing on the rails beside him, gasping for breath.

"Outbreak? What outbreak?"

"Something about screaming, I don't know. She treated the first patient, so I need to find her. So really: anything you've got rolling around in that head of yours would be very useful right now."

Adjobi blinked, seemed lost in thought, shook his head.

"I don't know. She didn't mention anything, didn't say she was going *anywhere*. But I…" he strained, unlatched the rail at his right side and swung his legs over the edge. "I've got to go help. They're understaffed enough as it is…"

Crew did a double-take, put a hand on Adjobi's shoulder, holding him back.

"Hold a second there. I don't think that's a good idea…"

"I'm a doctor, I know what I'm—"

"I don't think you do!" Crew interrupted, motioning to the dozen wires that strung from machines around the room, taped and deep-set into Adjobi's arms. "Are you going to bring all this crap with you when you go? No! So sit down and let somebody else deal with it!"

Adjobi eyed him sadly.

"I just… I just want to help."

"You can help by telling me where your sister might be. She might be the only person that has a chance of finding out who did this."

Adjobi sighed, sitting at the side of the bed, thinking.

"I don't know. We have cots here in the hospital, and I... wait, there's something. There's a place we used to go when we first arrived... it's a sports field, out on Bruslařská. She used to go there to think. She might be there, I suppose, if anything."

Crew nodded, tapped Adjobi on the shoulder as he backed away.

"Thanks, that's great. Now get back in bed. I've got to go catch a monster."

"You think he's behind this?" Adjobi asked, and Crew paused suddenly, by the door.

"What did you say?" he asked.

"Do you think the Healer started the outbreak?" Adjobi said, perched at the side of his bed.

Crew turned around, stormed back into the room, and shoved the frail man back onto the mattress, pinning him down with a hand to the forehead.

"Who said anything about a Healer?" he sneered.

Adjobi's eyes were wide with pain and fear. He couldn't move, with all the IVs and probes in his arms, and they strained viciously, making him whimper in agony.

"I... I just assumed because..."

"Ha! You lie like my mother," he cackled. "What do you know about the Healer?"

Adjobi shook his head frantically as Crew leaned in.

"Nothing! I swear, I don't know anything at all!"

Crew grunted, reached out and grabbed the mass of wires that strung into Adjobi's arm and twisted them, and the poor man screamed hoarsely at the metal under his skin pulling, tearing. Crew held the wires in a swirl and did not let go, leaned in a bit so he was close to Adjobi's pained face.

"We've got an outbreak down there, and you're playing games with me?"

Adjobi sputtered, tears in his eyes, begging or mouthing a prayer or something to make the pain stop.

"He was here," he gasped. "he's hunting a virus."

"The one downstairs?" Crew demanded.

"No! No, not that. It's me. He was hunting me."

Crew eased up a bit, sized up the confession.

"So why's he out there and not here?" he asked, uncertain. "They don't leave the victims alive."

"He's looking for the one who infected me. We... we made a bargain..."

"What *kind* of bargain?"

"I... I told him what I knew, and he let me live."

Crew leaned in close, breathed foul breath through his mask into Adjobi's face.

"Don't lie to me. I'm having a bad day."

"It's not a lie! He let me live! All I had to do was give him a name, and he let me go!"

"Then that makes you an accessory to murder. As many murders as he commits."

Adjobi cried, but couldn't reach his hands to his face for the wires.

"I'm sorry. I'm so sorry," he wept.

Crew grunted, stood back up, letting go of the wires, pressed a hand into his forehead. He looked around the room, back at the door, back at Adjobi.

"Will he be back?"

"I hope not," Adjobi said weakly, and Crew nodded.

"Where is he?" he asked, avoiding eye contact.

Adjobi looked away, almost ashamed, winced. He said nothing. Crew turned to him, fists on his hips, tilted his head unhappily.

"I said *where is he?*"

Adjobi sighed a long sigh.

"I... I promised I wouldn't..."

Crew grabbed the wires again, twisted them, and pulled back. Two of the IVs pulled free from Adjobi's arm, pouring antibiotics and blood out onto the bed and floor. He shrieked in pain, but his head was held tight by his interrogator, and he just twitched helplessly on the bed. He gasped for air, the pain blinding him, and tears poured down his cheeks.

"Where is he?" seethed Crew, each word accented with a light pull at the tangled cords.

Adjobi swallowed, almost crying, and spoke softly: "I don't know."

Crew shook his head with grim disappointment, reared back to pull the wires clean out of the frail man's body, but felt Adjobi's other hand hold his wrist, pleading. After a pained pause, he spoke:

"But I know where he's going."

43

Halfway down the stairs, Eva heard the familiar thump of the street door, and the *shuffle, shuffle* of feet on the steps. She froze, bag over her shoulder, hand on the wall, dead silent as she waited. The footsteps got closer, closer, and then she saw him: Rhodri came pacing upwards, caught sight of her, and paused.

"Eva!" he panted. "What's… what's going on?"

She adjusted the backpack, took a deep breath, tried to stay calm.

"I'm going out," she said quietly.

"Out?" he asked, stepping towards her. "With all *that*? Where are you going?"

He smiled, happy, seemingly innocent. She returned the smile, but artificially.

"Just out. Nowhere special. I'll… I'll be back in a bit."

Rhodri frowned at her.

"What about my afternoon off?" he said, touching her hand, and she flinched, very slightly.

"Can it wait?" she asked, sliding past him, but he caught her round the waist, leaned her against the wall, leaned in to kiss her. She kept her mouth away, and he brushed up against her cheek, once, twice, checking to be sure.

He moved back.

"What's wrong?" he asked, his tone hardening. "What aren't you telling me?"

Eva pushed him back suddenly, and he fell into the railing.

"Not telling *you*? What are *you* not telling *me!*"

She started down the stairs, but he caught her arm, turned her around. He looked desperate, confused, flustered. Angry.

"Eva, listen, I don't understand. What are you talking about? What happened?"

She pulled herself away from him, but didn't run. She stood there, eyes shooting left and right, thinking, fighting with herself. She threw her backpack off, reached in the side pocket, and pulled it out: the container with the orange lid.

"What's this supposed to be?"

His mouth dropped open, but he didn't move. Then he closed his mouth, jaw clenched tight. He met her eyes reluctantly.

"It's complicated," he said.

"I'll bet. So try me."

"Eva, not out here—"

"Yes out here! Come on! Let me have it! What have you really been doing all these months? It's not web design, is it? Is it?"

He shook his head slowly, sat on the steps, head low.

"No, it's not," he admitted. "But it's not what you think—"

"Oh spare me the sob story! You've been lying to me, pretending to do good, and all this time, you've been messing around with *this*, killing innocent people! People we know! my clients! our friends! You've been killing them!"

"What are you *talking* about, Eva? I'm not—"

"Save it! I saw the news clippings! Modena, Graz and Linz were all eaten up by major outbreaks just days after we left! It's not a coincidence, Rhodri! Nobody could think that's a coincidence! That's just murder, plain and simple!"

"Eva, I swear, if you just—"

"No!" she shouted, gripping the vial tight in her hand. "No more lies! That's it! I'm done! Burn in hell, Rhodri…"

She grabbed her bag up off the steps, turned to leave, but Rhodri reached for her, grabbed her elbow. She turned fast, slammed her fists into him, and he stumbled back, trying to hold her arms. He reached forward, trying to wrap his hands around her head, trying to bring her to him. She kicked out, hit his shin, and they both fell down the steps, crashing into the landing below.

Eva scrambled to her knees, reaching for her backpack, slid her mask onto her face, as Rhodri lay there against the wall, bleeding out of his temple, head turned strangely, eyes half-open, twitching with his heartbeat.

She backed up, hit the wall, and then saw it: the container lay beside him, lid nearby, his shirt and face wet with its serum.

Eva checked herself quickly, patting herself down, feeling everywhere, the mask, her hair, her clothes... she was dry... she was dry, but Rhodri was... he was...

His chest was still, but she was too scared to reach in and check for a pulse. She slid further away, eyes never leaving him, slid further down the hall, and away. Rhodri made no move to stop her. No move at all.

44

Eva sat in one corner of the room, knees up, while Rhodri sat in the other, biting his lower lip like he was containing a thought best left unsaid. She shivered through her sweater, pulled herself tighter, refusing to take her eyes off him. Her mother sang lullabies softly between them.

"You're not real," she told him, spat the words across the room. "You're not real and we both know it."

Rhodri said nothing in return.

"The cocktail is working, so you can't speak, you can't touch me. If you were real, you wouldn't sit there so quietly. You and I both know that."

He shrugged, noncommittal.

Eva got up, moved to the stretcher, took her mother's hand, but kept a careful watch on Rhodri, who stayed in his place, silent.

"Mama, I don't know if you can hear me in there. I hope you can. I just want you to know… just know that I'm going to make you better. Soon. I promise you. You just have to hold on there a little bit longer."

"Shh, dear, shh," said her mother softly, her hands brushing hair that wasn't there, in a reality long since gone. "No more nightmares for you, dear. It's all right."

Eva smiled weakly, nodded.

The door opened, and Eva made a quick check to the corner to make sure Rhodri hadn't moved, that it wasn't him. He hadn't moved an inch; he sat there, nonplussed, watched Dmitri come in.

"So?" said Eva urgently. "Did it work? Did it do anything?"

Dmitri tried to hide a smile, but failed.

"Like magic," he said happily. "It cut through the delusions like nobody's business. I can't tell how much he remembers, but he's definitely back to his normal self. The virus wasn't destructive, whatever it did. It just messed with brain chemistry."

Eva smiled, nodded.

"So we can make up two more doses then? We can fix my mother next?"

He winced, scratched at his cheek.

"Actually, the boss wants to see you first."

"But I—"

"He says it's important, and honestly, I kind of agree with him. You'll want to hear this."

Eva shook her head, holding on to her mother's hand tightly.

"I'm not leaving until she's cured. Leave me if you like, but you have to let me fix her before anything else. It's hell, the place she's trapped. I can't leave her there any longer."

"I get you, kid. So listen, I'll start the incubator working, and we can see the boss while it works. Sound fair?"

Eva eyed the machine, checked Dmitri's expression of pure sincerity. She nodded slowly, and he made his way over, tapped the trackpad and started the process to create another container of serum. Then he took her by the arm and led her gently to the door. She turned back to her mother, touched her shoulder lightly.

"I'll be back, mama. I'll be right back."

Dmitri brought her out, down a narrow hallway to an antechamber, built like it was an entirely different building. The walls were a dark crimson, gold patterns accenting the design. A pair of antique chairs sat at either side of a set of large, heavy double-doors. The floor was layered in opaque plastic covering, the kind used to contain spills; it ran up the edges of the walls slightly, roughly laid; out of place.

The doors opened as they approached, and Eva found herself in the most magnificent bedroom she had ever seen: intricate wood panelling and murals all around the room, like a Renaissance exhibit where you slept. The ceiling was high and was laced with pinpoints of light in columns up to a single spot at the top of an arch, where a skylight gave an almost unlikely view of the heavens.

To the right was a large window, an arched stain glass portion at the top, giving a frosted view of Prague that did a wonderful job of hiding the truth. There were dressers and a desk, a large reading chair and a dozen antique lamps, and in the centre of the room was an expansive plush bed.

Like the floors, the bed was like an anachronism, layered with plastic and synthetic fabric, machines framing it coldly, all whirring and beeping the status of their patient. Dmitri deposited her at the bedside, backed away quietly, and the man on the bed opened his eyes weakly, smiled at her.

"Eva," he said weakly. "welcome. It's good to see you at last. I'm Richard, an acquaintance of your mother's."

Eva said nothing, tried to find the right expression for the situation.

"I hear that I have you to thank for my life," he continued, then tweaked to something, motioned to the side. "Dmitri, could you make sure Eva's cure is uploaded with the rest of them? I don't want to miss the deadline."

"Already taken care of, boss."

"Excellent," Richard said, nodding happily. "Yes, the cure seems to be brilliantly made, Eva. But I must say, it's not that much of a shock to me. I've been trying to convince your mother to let me invite you into our little club for some time. I wonder if things would have turned out differently if we'd had your help instead of Rhodri's…"

On the other side of the room, in the corner again, Rhodri rolled his eyes in silence. Eva ignored it.

"What does my mother have to do with this? She was a *doctor*. She helped people! How did you make her have *anything* to do with the kinds of atrocities—"

"Eva, dear, I think you misunderstand us."

"Oh, I understand you pretty well. You kill people for kicks. It's pretty easy to grasp."

He shook his head, reached a weak arm out to her, but she pushed it away. Dmitri made a subtle step forward behind her.

"Eva, we don't make viruses. We make the *cures*."

Eva blinked, backed up.

"You... what? What cures?"

He sat up, pained, leaned forward in bed, his arms across his folded legs, like a sickly skeleton wrapped in sheets. He thought a moment, avoided looking at her.

"For the last two years, we have been working here, in Prague, and elsewhere, to discover, isolate and treat strains of viruses that are largely ignored by the major corporations. They're not as glamorous, not as profitable, I dare say, but they're vital. If left untreated, they grow and spread and mutate and then one day, they take down a city, kill millions, and it's only *then* that people wonder what went wrong. 'How could this happen?' they ask, 'I thought the worst of it was over.' It's a cycle that never ends, and I've seen it far too many times to bear.

"My goal — our little group's goal — was to eliminate those strains before they took over Europe. We had our hands full with the eastern plagues that passed through Prague. The ones the Chinese didn't catch. But we also wanted to tackle the western ones as well, and ideally before they got this far east. We tried making alliances with doctors across Europe, offering bounties, but there are only so many incubators left outside government hands, and the risks of using them is not for the weak of heart. So it was decided we had to find an agent who could sample and treat the viruses no one else had seen..."

"Wait, are you saying…"

"We hired Rhodri to handle that role."

At the side of the room, Rhodri seemed close to tears, hurt by the revelation, lowered his face into his hands. Eva nearly threw up.

"He was *saving* people?" she gasped.

The frail man said nothing for a moment, and Eva noticed Dmitri shake his head to himself.

"Rhodri saved thousands, I'm sure. We sent him an incubator, and he used it to do the initial diagnoses, and build the cure compounds. By the time you left Italy, he'd found the treatments to nearly two dozen diseases. Diseases that, because of his work, will never harm another soul again."

Rhodri stared headlong into Eva, accusing.

"I… I didn't know…"

"Your mother didn't want you to know. She thought you weren't able to cope with it. She was afraid of what it might do to you, after you'd worked so hard to get your life back together. She outright refused to let me offer you the job, and I admit, when I heard about Rhodri and his apparent skills, I went behind her back to recruit him. When she found out, she was furious; she was certain that bringing your boyfriend into our team would put an unbearable strain on your relationship. I think he agreed with her, vowed to keep it secret."

"If I'd known… I *blamed* him…"

Dmitri coughed from behind, and Richard reached out, held Eva's hand.

"It's not as simple as it seemed, my dear," he said. "Not by a long shot. It missed our attention, too, at first… but after watching the situation closely, Dmitri realized that every time the two of you left a city, a massive plague ravaged the population. Almost like clockwork. Right after he finished deploying the antivirus, the reports began to trickle in from sources around the region; within days, it was a flood no one could overcome."

"I don't understand," Eva said blankly. "Deployed *how*? He worked hard, but never long enough to vaccinate dozens, let alone hundreds of people. How can you be sure it was him?"

"Oh, it was more than *possible* it was him. So much so, it was unlikely to be anyone else. We weren't inoculating in the traditional sense, given how limited our resources were. We created a series of aerosolized payloads, left them in key locations around town, and let the contagious nature of our compounds do the rest."

"Just like a typical terrorist strike—" Eva began.

"But with an anti-virus instead, yes," smiled Richard. "Traditional treatment vectors like booster shots are still part of the plan, but those methods are delayed, wrought with red tape and political infighting. We thought of all the lives we could save by pushing the cures straight to the people at risk, right when they needed them, and we decided it was worth the risk."

"Except if something went wrong," Eva noted.

"Indeed. We were shocked to discover things *had* gone wrong, and put countless hours into deciphering the cause."

Eva frowned.

"So you were treating multiple viruses in a single treatment, right?"

"Yes, it was the most efficient way to operate."

"But if you mixed that many compounds, maybe they were interacting with each other, making something new, something dangerous you didn't expect. I saw that a bunch of times... you might have been making a poison with all your cures."

"We thought of that, too," he said sadly. "So in Linz, we were careful to test that angle. Our agent here, he tested the compound endlessly, checked it from every angle, and he was *certain* there was no chance of side-effects from that set. And yet, somehow, once deployed by Rhodri in Linz, we had the same results. Massive casualties."

Eva looked to Rhodri. He seemed as confused about all this as she was. She shook it off, kept from looking at him. Dmitri's phone purred softly, and he flipped it open, backing out of the room.

"We checked and double-checked everything," Richard continued. "You can imagine our emotions at the time: we were mortified that we were somehow making things worse, and we were desperate to figure out how it had gone all wrong. We'd been working nearly a year in advance of Rhodri's involvement without any issues whatsoever, and now suddenly it was all falling apart? It made no sense; we started second-guessing ourselves, thinking maybe it was a difference between eastern and western coding techniques… anything that might help it make sense.

"But in the end, it was clear it wasn't on our end. It wasn't the individual cures. It was something added to the mix right before deployment. It had to be. Somewhere along the way, Rhodri had decided to *use* us to release new viruses into the wild. We had enabled him, and so many lost their lives because of it."

"Wait, hold on," Eva said, her voice cracking with emotion, Rhodri in the corner looking hopeful and yet tired, weak. "How do you know it was him? Maybe it was one of your other people. You had someone reviewing stuff, maybe *that* person did it, and you're just blaming—"

"That man is in the hospital, fighting for his life, after falling prey to one of Rhodri's booby traps."

Eva blinked. She glanced over to Rhodri, briefly, and in that second, his expression changed. A slow, sly grin.

"What are you talking about?"

"This virus, the one that infected me, your mother… it was put into a package we received from Rhodri. He's trying to kill us, Eva, because we know what he's done…"

Eva sighed loudly, overcome, lowered her head in shame, regret, something.

"Don't worry," she said softly. "It's over now."

"What do you mean? What's over?"

"He's not going to hurt anyone anymore. He's dead. Rhodri's dead."

Richard sat up in bed, mouth hanging open, reached out and touched Eva's shoulder gently, squeezing.

"What do you mean, he's dead?"

"I killed him. It was… it was an accident, but it happened. I haven't been able to tell how I should feel about it, all this time. But now I think… I think it was for the best. It's horrible to say that, but I do. I'm glad he's dead, that he can't hurt anyone else."

Rhodri scowled at her, got to his feet, and her heart jerked in her chest.

"Eva," Richard said carefully, deliberate. "When did this happen? When did he die?"

Eva frowned.

"Months ago. Early July. He—"

"He's not dead," Richard said, ominously. "He can't be dead. We were poisoned three weeks ago, Eva. He's been threatening us, the whole city, for weeks."

"Wait, you mean Prague-1—"

"Rhodri is alive," he said, weak. "And I fear he's come to finish what he started."

45

Sobotka stepped around the blood on the floor, the streaks leading to the corner where the body of a badly beaten man lay, propped up against the wall, eyes open and manic. It stunk horribly, and she pulled the strap on her mask tighter, kept from gagging. She moved silently into the hallway beyond, checked up the stairs, the wood scraped and raw.

As she slipped into the living room on the second floor, she loosed her gun from its holster, kept it trained at the floor, but ready, eyes wide open. She paused there, by the entrance, saw the sheets on the ground, the broken window, the spent clothes. A large, open duffel bag, stuffed with food packets, gadgets and blankets.

Just then, Pyotr came shuffling into the room, his beard shaved, clothes fresh, carrying a selection of toiletries in a large biohazard bag. He threw them into the duffel bag, began to turn back, then saw her, froze.

"Hello, Pyotr," she grinned, aimed at his heart. "Where are you off to?"

His eyes darted, trying to imagine an excuse. She stormed towards him, used a bloodied boot to kick him onto the floor, kept the gun at him.

"Please," Pyotr pleaded, "I was going to tell you—"

"I'm sure," Sobotka sneered, and kicked him in the knee. "Where's your girlfriend, Pyotr? I don't see her, and I seem to recall telling you *not to let her out of your sight.*"

"We were kidnapped!" he explained, desperate, and she rolled her eyes. "Well, I mean, *she* was kidnapped. They let me go."

"How convenient for you."

"It's the truth, I swear! She made them let me go!"

"If she knows about your little scam, why would she cut you any slack? You helped her escape, didn't you?"

"No! She let me go! She said she's sick of people dying, told them to kick me out alone!"

Sobotka perfected her aim on his forehead, scowled.

"Too bad for you, I'm still good with the dying."

He covered his head with his arms, ready for the shot, but just then, Sobotka's phone rang. She kept the gun at him, reached into her pocket and flipped it open.

"Hold that thought," she said to Pyotr, then barked into the phone: "I'm busy. What?"

"Did you hear yet?" Crew wheezed. "You know what's going on?"

"No. What's going on?"

"There's an outbreak at the hospital. They've shut down the main floor, locked everyone in. They're already calling it Prague-1, whatever it is."

Sobotka's mouth fell open, then curled into a smile.

"Rhodri Tenant's come to town," she said.

"Tenant? Hell no! The Healer!"

"Oh for the love of god, Crew. It's obviously not the Healer. Give it up!"

"That's what you say, but I've got a witness that puts him tight with a doctor at the source of the outbreak."

"So what, a doctor is working with a Healer to kill us? It kind of goes against both their philosophies, don't you think?"

"People do stupid things," Crew said ominously.

"Case in point," Sobotka cracked.

"So I'm going it alone? You're not going to give me backup when I take this joker down?"

Sobotka checked Pyotr, the snow-covered city outside, thought a moment.

"No," she said. "I've got enough to cut through here. Waste time if you need to. Let me know how it goes."

Crew harumphed and hung up on her. She slid the phone back into her pocket, cricked her neck and refocused on Pyotr, who hadn't found a good alternative to cowering yet.

"So it seems you did your job half-well," she sighed. "Tenant's here."

"*He came?*" gasped Pyotr. "How do you know?"

"Kicked off a new outbreak. *The* outbreak. And god knows, he's probably looking for you now, after what you did to his girlfriend."

"But she isn't—"

"I'm pretty sure a homicidal maniac isn't going to care," she interrupted, stowing her gun, offering him a hand. He looked at it, apprehensive, then reached out and let himself be pulled to his feet. He watched her, cautious.

"The ones who kidnapped Kolikov, did they seem friend-like, or enemy-like?"

Pyotr thought a moment, tense and spastic.

"I think they knew her. I never found out from where, but—"

"They're probably friends of Tenant's then," she grumbled, grabbed him by the collar and dragged him to the stairs roughly.

"Where are we going?" he squeaked as he was thrown down the first few steps.

"You're going to show me *exactly* where they brought you," she called down. "And we're going to turn Mr Tenant's head into a sieve."

*   *   *

Carey put the magazine down atop the pile of seven others, his gloves creaking from the effort, and adjusted the mask on his face to alleviate the pinching on his nose. The goggles fogged briefly, but then a quick hiss later, things went back to normal. He checked his watch again, shook his head.

"I don't suppose you have any more information…" he began asking one of the dark-suited guards who stood by the door, hands folded neatly, staring at nothing.

The guard continued to ignore him.

Carey picked up another magazine, flipped the first few pages, then checked the date.

"This one is ten years old," he sighed to no one, certainly not the guard. "Don't you people recycle anything here?"

He checked his watch yet again, then threw the magazine down, got to his feet. The guard turned slightly, hands ready, stared down and down and down at Carey's impressively bundled figure.

"I'm sorry," Carey said, angry but still apologetic. "This just won't do. I have been waiting here for nearly two hours, and there's been no indication that anyone even knows I'm here. I am an agent of the British government, and I *insist* on seeing Mr Daniels right n—"

Mid-word, the doors opened and a thickly-set man with a stubbly jaw and a crisp white mask strode in, hand out; Carey shook it, apprehensive.

"Mr Carey, is it?" the man asked, accent thick. Eastern European.

"Y-y-yes. I've been waiting—"

"Yeah, I should apologize for that. My staff ain't the brightest, got the lines of communication tangled, as it were. I didn't hear you'd arrived until just a few minutes ago. Did anyone get you something to eat or…" he smiled at the full-head mask, shrugged. "Or not."

"It's quite all right. Are you… Mr Daniels?"

The man guffawed loudly, slapped Carey on the back.

"Me? No, I'm his executive assistant, Dmitri."

"Just 'Dmitri'?"

"Unless you're buyin' drinks," he smirked, leading Carey into a hallway. A guard stood every few metres, hands posed like the one Carey'd seen, staring past them. Expertly trained.

"I have a warrant here to take Mr Daniels into custody immediately and—"

"Yeah, he's aware. He wants me to show you in right away. But…"

Dmitri paused them, leaned closer to Carey, confidential, eyes darting around.

"He's been a bit under the weather lately. Had a bad cold. Prague winters, y'know. So whatever you do, don't go rushing to conclusions, okay? He's pretty sensitive to people treating him like he's diseased and such. Just try and act natural. Pretend he looks fine. Got it?"

Carey nodded tentatively. His body suit made it somewhat difficult, however.

He was led into an ornate bedroom just as a young woman, pale and trembling, shuffled out. She watched him carefully, keeping a broad distance, in complete silence. Carey arrived at the bedside of a frail-looking man, various life-saving machines slid into dark corners of the room, but strikingly present.

Carey cleared his throat, reached out a cordial hand.

"Mr Daniels," he said, noticing three of the guards in the room stepping forward, ready. "So good to finally meet you."

Daniels took the hand, nodded as if he were at a dinner party, meeting a random guest.

"Likewise," he said. "I'm afraid I didn't catch your name."

"Oh, William Carey, sir. Special agent for the Containment Office. My Director—"

"I know your Director well, Mr Carey. I trust he's well?"

"Yes, sir. Actually, he made me promise I would ask how you're doing, too."

There was an uncomfortable pause. Even the guards looked like they wanted to leave.

"I'm doing fine, thank you," said Daniels, smiling at the stiffness of the moment. "Tending to business, all that."

Carey nodded in agreement, big long bobs of his head, and clasped his hands around the heavy metal case that was pulling him downward.

"I don't mean to impose, sir," said Carey, jovially. "But I'm afraid I will need to gather a quick blood sample from you, if it's convenient."

"Please do," Daniels smiled, gesturing to his bed. Carey heaved the case up onto the sheets with some effort and popped it open. He worked fast, hands shaking, clicking the syringe together and attaching it to the base of the extraction instrument.

After a moment of work, he had gathered a decent sample of blood from Daniels' arm, slid the vial into the case's built-in processor. He pushed the 'test' button, sighed a self-satisfied sigh, and nodded to Daniels.

"Won't be long," he said, as if he were waiting for dinner to reheat in the microwave.

Daniels put a hand on Carey's shoulder, causing instant tension. He shifted slightly.

"We are at war, Mr Carey," came the voice, quiet and confidential.

"Indeed, sir," he said, not knowing what else to say.

"If these viruses make it into Britain somehow and we could have stopped them…" Daniels said, his voice filling with anger. "I found these diseases, I cured them, and I did it for my country. And I cannot accept that that is somehow wrong."

Carey nodded.

"I understand, sir. But… one thing at a time, I suppose."

He motioned down to the computer, still chugging away. Daniels' eyes were cold.

"You think I'm dying."

"Well I mean… er…" Carey said, catching a mean glare from Dmitri, who stood to the side with his arms crossed unhappily. "In all honesty, sir, you don't look healthy, and you've been living in a black zone for… well… quite a long time, we think. Certainly a long time to not have picked up *something*."

Daniels smiled, and the computer purred softly as it finished its work. Carey looked down at the read-out and frowned. He looked back up at Daniels, cocked his head.

"It… you're… you're *clean*."

Daniels' smile seemed relieved at the same time as vindicated. He patted Carey on the shoulder.

"It's okay, Mr Carey, I know I must not look it."

Carey nodded blankly, then snapped out of his stupor, shoulders straightening, and he clasped his hands together tightly.

"In that case, sir," he said, nearly regaining his authoritative footing. "I'm going to have to place you under arrest for violating the National Containment Order."

Daniels nodded again, this time less happily, but still with confidence. Carey removed a pair of handcuffs from his pack, and the guards in the room began to move again, until Daniels held up a pausing hand. To them, but also to Carey.

"If you would be kind enough to wait a moment, Mr Carey," said Daniels kindly, stopping Carey dead in his tracks. "I have a favour to ask of you."

46

When Eva arrived back in the room, Rhodri was already there. She shut the door behind her, eyed him carefully.

"I should have made sure you were dead," she told him, cold and dispassionate.

He didn't reply, just smirked at her.

"Still in my head," she sighed. "But I guess that's better than the alternative."

She checked the incubator, and pulled the finished container out, the lid fastened tight. She pushed it into her pocket, hit the button to create another batch, but the machine flashed a warning: "Please insert serum refill tube". She checked inside, and sure enough, it was empty. She looked back at her mother, heard a soft lullaby, squeezed the container in her pocket.

"I'll be right back, mama," she whispered, and opened the door a crack.

Outside, another guard stood with his back to her, watching the hallway carefully. He turned his head slightly at the door opening, then looked back ahead.

"Go back inside," he told her.

"I need some needles," she said, "so I can help my mother."

He didn't move a muscle.

"Stay inside," he repeated sternly. "Until I say otherwise."

Eva stepped into the hall, tense and angry, looked left and right, trying to find a medical station somewhere. The guard turned to her, grabbed her by the arm, tried to push her back into the room.

"I said stay inside!" he growled. She fought back, gripping the door frame. The guard was clearly not prepared for such an occasion, let go over her arm, and planted his palm on her face, pushing her. She ducked away from the movement, slipped outside, and he stumbled in.

She was halfway down the hall when she was caught again, dragged back off-balance, and slammed against the wall.

"Don't mess with me, girlie," he said, angrily. "Just get in the room and shut up."

She kneed him in the groin, and he fell over at once.

"Don't mess with *me*," she seethed, stepping over him and checking down the hall. But then she heard it: the clear click of a gun ready to shoot. She looked over her shoulder, saw the guard there, carefully aiming at her, eyes narrow with pain.

"That's it!" he said, vein bulging in his forehead. "On your knees!"

Eva's face was blank with fear. She'd overstepped, and now this... she was halfway to complying when she heard angry shouts from behind, and Dmitri rushed in, snatching the gun away from the guard and slamming him against the wall.

"What the hell do you think you're doing?" he yelled into the guard's face. "I told you to *watch her*, not shoot her!"

"She was trying to leave the—"

"I don't care what she was doing! There's no excuse for this!"

"But—"

Dmitri ripped the man's mask off his face, threw it to the ground. He grabbed him on the collar, shoved him towards Eva, onto the floor.

"Get out of my sight. You're fired. If I see you again, I'll have you shot. By someone *competent*."

The guard scrambled away, rushing down the hall, through a door and out of sight. Dmitri helped Eva to her feet, turned meekly to the others who'd come with him.

"Sorry about that, Mr Carey," he said apologetically. "Hard to find good help round here."

The masked man — whom Eva thought looked horribly like the Healers she'd heard about all these years — nodded. Richard looked rattled, kept checking Eva, making sure she was okay.

"It's hard to find good help pretty much everywhere," Carey agreed. "Now if you don't mind…"

He held out a small device with a needle at its point, started towards Eva. She backed up, hitting the wall.

"What's going on?" she gasped.

Richard put a hand on Carey's arm, held him back.

"I'm sorry, Mr Carey, I thought I made it clear I was seeking asylum for my wife and step-daughter."

Eva's head swam suddenly, and she slid to the ground, looking from Richard to Carey to Dmitri, trying to see… trying to make sense of it. It was impossible to read Carey, but by the change in his stance, he was preparing to be tough.

"You made it perfectly clear, Mr Daniels, but I'm afraid regulations require me to check their health status before I can process them, even as refugees. They can't be admitted, even to Brighton, if they're actively infected."

"Listen, I have a personal facility outside London I can sequester them in if that—"

"I'm afraid not, sir. It would be nearly impossible under normal circumstances, but given the particulars of the trial you'll be subject to, we wouldn't stand a chance of sneaking something like *that* under the rug. No chance at all. We can only mask scrutiny so far."

Eva had her head in her hands, trembling.

"You're *married*?" she said, staring at the floor. "And nobody thought to tell me?"

Carey looked to Richard, cocked his head.

"Mr Daniels…?" he asked.

Richard waved it off, a hint of a politic smile, but drowning in concern.

"She's been gone for many years. Travel. I don't think she got the wedding announcement."

Eva glared at Richard, cold. Dmitri, behind Carey, gave her a very slow shake of the head. She frowned briefly, and he returned it with a wordless urgent appeal.

"If she's been travelling, I've double the reason to check her blood," Carey said. "Now if you don't mind, I've a schedule to keep."

Eva looked to Richard, to Dmitri, desperate for advice, guidance. They both nodded to her solemnly.

"Fine," she sighed, rolling up her sleeve and letting him draw the blood. When he was done, she slid her arm close to herself, backed against the wall, waited. Carey stared at his device intently, seemingly oblivious to the rest of the tension in the cramped hallway.

He looked up, to Eva, then settled on Richard.

"She's infected," he said, double-checking the results. "I'm afraid I can't take her with us."

"You'll leave me here alone? What about my mother! She'd never agree to that if she were—"

"If she were *what?*" Carey asked, checking between Richard and Dmitri. "Is she infected as well?"

"Mr Carey, if you could just…" Richard began, but he was cut off by Carey swinging a pair of handcuffs up.

"I'm sorry, Mr Daniels. We've no more time for these games. You've got to come with me."

He pushed Richard against the wall, pulled one arm back, then the other. And then a gun pointed carefully at the side of his head; he almost didn't see it through the goggles.

"Mr Carey," Richard said darkly. "I'm afraid this won't work out after all."

Dmitri motioned with his gun, and Carey obediently backed away from the rest of them, hands in the air, cuffs hanging from his fingers. Eva got to her feet behind Dmitri. Richard smiled weakly.

"And now we will have to reconsider our plan of action," he said without a hint of frustration. "If you'll come with me, then."

Dmitri kept the gun on the prisoner, and the three men walked down the hall and out of sight, leaving Eva alone again, only Rhodri keeping her company. He heard him chuckle quietly. She scowled at him.

She went back into the room and found her mother crying softly, shaking her head side to side as if trying to wake up. Tears streamed down her face, and her arms tensed violently; if she'd been free, she might have done something horrible with her clawing hands. Eva brushed her hair gently, leaned in and kissed her on the forehead.

"Just another minute, mama. I promise," she said, then snuck back into the hall. Down, away from Richard's room, she found a small walk-in-closet filled with shelves and drawers and a large needle dispenser in the back. She ducked in, took a syringe from the counter and clipped on a head. She pulled the container from her pocket, undid the lid, and gently placed the needle into the serum.

Just then, she heard loud footsteps in the hall, shouting. It startled her, and she dropped the container... she tried to catch it before it hit the ground, but it bounced off the countertop and crashed on the floor, upside-down. The cure flowed quickly onto the tile.

She bit back a curse as she heard the quick pause of footsteps outside.

"Hey, should this be open?" called a gruff voice, a guard, in Russian.

Eva reached down, snatched the fallen container off the ground, and quickly slid back to the side of the door, the unused needle in her hands as her only weapon. She stayed there in the dark, the door open a crack, waiting.

She heard the sound of heavy boots stepping into the room, and the door swung wider. Breathing, panting almost, and the shadow on the wall told her he was alone. She held the needle backhand, evened her breathing. She waited for him to move.

But instead, he ducked back out, closing the door behind him, and she stood in the darkness.

"All clear!" he called out, and took off down the hall.

Eva released her breath, felt shaky. She reached over, turned on the lights, and checked the spilled antivirus. The container was empty, and what was left on the floor was so dispersed, it was unusable. Eva stood up, ran her hands through her hair, trying to think. She felt the warm breath of Rhodri on her neck, but ignored it.

She started rushing through drawers, cupboards, anything, until she found a tray labelled "Incubator Refills". It was empty. She slammed it back into place, swearing.

"If I can't make any more…" she whispered to herself.

It came to her suddenly: the refills at her mother's apartment! She smiled broadly, and turned, hearing Rhodri clapping at her, sarcastic applause. He didn't speak, but he was getting clearer in her mind. She grimaced.

"I need to slow it down," she muttered.

She rummaged again, quickly coming to a small refrigerated compartment labelled "Cocktails". She threw it open, and stumbled back at what she saw: there was only one vial of cocktail left. She darted eyes to Rhodri, then to the door, and she grabbed it out of the fridge, another needle, and rushed back down the hall.

Her mother was starting to scream again, convulsing angrily. Eva filled the needle, pushed it into her mother's IV, then paused.

"I need you to stay calm until we get home, all right, mama?"

There was no response. Eva inhaled slowly, then injected the last of the cocktail. She rested her head on the panicked chest, hearing the heartbeat, hearing it slow, becoming calmer, and then she carefully undid the restraints, pulled her mother out of bed, and with the incubator in one hand, stumbled her way home.

Rhodri trailed behind, nearly stepping on her heels, grinning all the way.

47

The Healer's suit was humming softly as the snow melted on his shoulders. He watched the building across the street, a stark white structure almost trying to blend into the cold wintry afternoon. The lights were all on, but there was no motion from inside.

Beside him, Anouma was shivering, her winter jacket atop her white coat, but neither warm enough to fight off the breeze.

"You will stay here," he said to her, blunt and brief.

She looked at him, squinted. She seemed to see right into him, and he looked away as if to stop her. She shook her head.

"No," she said firmly. "I've got to go with you. I need to stop you from killing any more innocent people."

"It could be dangerous," he countered.

"Not if I do the talking," she said. "If it were up to you, everything would be a bloodbath. Let me try."

Silence. He stood beside her and the snow continued to fall.

"Fine," he said bitterly, and started across the street, aware of her following close behind.

They reached the main door and he reached to knock, but she moved him aside, out of sight, and knocked on the door herself. He stared at her, warning, but she kept her arms tightly locked behind herself, watching the snow, waiting.

He heard the dead bolt unlock. A tentative noise. And then, a pause, a quiet scraping of metal on the door. Anouma didn't notice it, kept a pleasant, hopeful smile on her face. But the Healer knew. He threw his cloak over his shoulder, shoved her to the side, and as the door opened, he grabbed the gun that peeked through the opening. With a solid pull, he found his mark: he pinched a gloved hand so hard it spasmed and dropped the weapon.

Anouma fell to the ground just as the Healer spun around, letting go the door and giving it a swift kick, straight into the face of a guard, who fell backwards into the hallway, his nose broken and gushing blood.

The man, stunned and disoriented, reached feebly for his second weapon as the Healer marched forward, stepping on his right arm, and then punching him squarely in the face. The man's head hit the ground with a thud, and his eyes rolled back into unconsciousness.

The Healer looked back to Anouma, scowled beneath his mask.

"Wait outside. I must deal with innocent people."

He walked past his first target, flexing his hurt shoulder as he made his way down the hall. It hurt, but burned in a way that pushed him forward.

As he came to the first door, on his left, he saw on the frame the quick movement of a shadow. Without losing his pace, he leapt forward into a roll, fast and low, and his machete swung out in time to catch another guard's arm in the middle as they reached out to fire. The arm wasn't cut clean off, but it hung uselessly, and the guard screamed loudly, fell down into the doorway.

The Healer noticed, just in time, the accomplice inside the room; another roll helped him dodge a wide shotgun blast. He spun his weapon around in his hand, his back to the wall, out of view.

The first guard, on the floor, was choking now, having cried himself into a daze. The Healer heard a quick inhalation, and the second man leapt out of the room, gun firing blindly, hoping for a hit. The Healer ducked down, pushed into the attack; he collided with the man, shoving him into the wall, and then hit him with his elbow, knocking some teeth out and sending the enemy sprawling.

The gun skidded down the hall, out of reach, and the Healer kicked the side of his head with a heavy boot. He hit the wall, left a mark of blood.

The Healer had just enough time to duck into the side room before a round of automatic weapons fire sprayed where he'd been standing. Inside, two large tables stood against the far wall, a collection of metal chairs, some beverages scattered around. He noticed the light switch next to him and flicked it downward, disappearing into the darkness.

The shadows of the new assailants slid towards him, becoming sharper and sharper as they closed in. He darted across the room, upended one of the tables, and slid it towards the door, covering the opening. In a second, the table shattered in a dozen places, wood chips tossed wildly by bullets. The Healer ducked around the other side of the door, out of view, silent.

The light from the hallway shone through the holes in the table, streaks through the dusty air, and for a moment, all the Healer could hear were the pained gasps of the bleeding guard outside. Then a hit, a crunch, another hit, and the table started to move. Another pause, and the Healer turned his machete around again, backhanded, and pressed himself against the wall.

A kick now, and this time the table slid into the room, and a rectangle of light hit the far wall, framing the form of a guard whose gun was aimed the wrong way. The Healer swung around, catching the man in the chest with his blade; the man jerked violently as the impact ended his life. Without a pause, the Healer moved forward, as the wood behind him exploded, gunshots hitting the back wall harmlessly.

The Healer pulled the dead man's gun from his hand, came round the corner so fast the second guard had no time to react. The flow of bullets hit the guard ruthlessly in the chest, and he dropped to the ground, his face still in a state of shock.

A quick movement later, the Healer was on the other side of the door again, watching bodies pile in front of his exit.

He flicked the light on. Paused. Then off.

He listened, heard nothing. Staggering silence. He looked down at the man with the severed arm, saw he was looking back around the corner, his whimpering all but stopped, his breathing calm. Emboldened.

The Healer grabbed him by his jacket, and with a pained grunt, yanked him out of the doorway and into the room. The man screamed hysterically, his arm nearly coming off; at least one set of boots outside pounded loudly, coming to his rescue. The Healer held the man close to him, and then, trying to think past his pain, threw the man out into the hallway.

A barrage of gunfire shot out and sprayed the poor wretch with bullets, and he bounced off the wall and onto the ground, dead before he could continue his screaming. The Healer used the moment of confusion to point the stolen gun round the corner and fire in an arc, and he heard the quick thuds of hits, grunts, yelps, and then heavy thumps as bodies landed on the ground.

He pulled his arm back into the room, stayed tight against the wall, held the pain in his shoulder at bay. There were no sounds but the ringing in his ears, the whining noise he couldn't escape. His suit was warning him, warning him to calm down.

"Are you alive?" called Anouma, somewhere in the distance.

He paused.

"Yes," he answered simply.

He heard the sound of tentative footsteps.

"They're all dead," she said, voice trembling.

He carefully walked into the hallway again, saw the damage all around; Anouma standing by the front door, just beyond the first sentry, stalled by the sight of so many bodies. He nodded to her painfully.

"You should leave," he told her. "They are not interested in talking."

"Yes," she said quietly, and she stepped away, back outside.

*　*　*

Crew hit the brakes too late, and the car skidded sideways, slamming sidelong into the dark sedan, sending the two of them sliding on the ice, until the sedan came to a rest just inches from the side of a building. When the cars stopped, Crew threw himself out, chest puffed and angry.

"What the hell was that?" he shouted. "Learn to drive, you maniac!"

"Me?" yelled Sobotka, kicking her own door closed, Pyotr cuffed in the back seat. "What kind of idiot speeds around in these conditions?"

"It's November!" Crew blustered. "It'll melt!"

Sobotka laughed, checked her car for damage. It was dented lightly along the side, but otherwise fine. The Aston-Martin was somehow in pristine condition.

"Nice car," she cracked. "where you going so fast?"

Crew checked the house numbers, frowning. He settled on the one Sobotka's car had nearly crashed into. He motioned with his chin.

"This one right here. You?"

Sobotka frowned, checked back to Pyotr, then back to Crew.
"Same."

Crew cackled madly, doubled over from the effort, while Sobotka scowled.

"Oh this is rich! So what, your kid is teamed up with my Healer or something?"

Sobotka shook her head. She was about to speak when the side door to the building opened, and into the street came Eva, her mother, and an incubator. They made it a few steps before Eva noticed Sobotka and Crew, arms folded, obviously amused at their own good luck.

Eva set the incubator down, held her mother upright.

"This isn't what it looks like!" she pleaded.

"Oh, then you've *got* to tell me what it *is!*" Sobotka cackled.

"Found your mother, I see," said Crew, nodding to his partner. "Good luck, that."

"Yes indeed," said Sobotka gravely.

Eva looked behind them at the running car, saw Pyotr's face pressed close to the windshield, trying to spy. She sneered at them.

"How's your snitch working out?" she said bitterly.

Sobotka grinned.

"Not the best snitch, but he'll do," she sneered. "I think you and your mother have some big things to explain to us. Like where you're hiding your boyfriend, and how to stop the outbreak at the hospital."

Eva backed up, then heard the sound of crashing glass, and a second-storey window in Daniels' compound broke outwards. A man in a black suit flew backwards and down, down into the windshield of the car, cracking it horribly. Shards of glass stuck out of his already-mangled body, and he crumpled there, blood seeping out.

Crew, Sobotka and Eva all looked at the dead man in shock.

"Thank god I didn't park there," Crew said.

Crew and Sobotka looked back to Eva, then the window, then back to Eva again, exchanged glances.

"I think you want to check in there first," Eva offered.

"Hell yeah," said Crew, turning and running back to the front of the building.

"We'll be in touch!" called Sobotka, following her partner with her gun drawn.

Eva paused for a moment, looking at the man on the car, then picked up the incubator and pushed onward, back to home.

48

The Healer retrieved his machete from the chest of a fallen guard, wiped the blood off on a stray leg, then swung it lightly, getting the weight back. The upstairs hallway was deserted now, but for the sounds of two men slowly dying of their wounds. Ahead of him, a room beckoned cheerfully, pleasant lighting nearly hiding the shadow of another person.

He stopped for a moment, listened. The broken window behind him was whistling faintly as the wind outside blew by, and he heard the drip, drip, drip of snow melting inside and onto the floor. A very quiet shuffle called from ahead.

He started forward, involuntarily clutching his injured shoulder, squeezing the pain away. He heard another soft shuffle among the crackles and the drips, and he held his breath so he could hear better. There was a very calm and deliberate breathing, very close. Very calm. A professional.

In a moment, they were engaged. A sharp sensation sliced into the Healer's left arm just above his elbow, and his suit screamed out with his senses, and he knew he'd been cut. He spun himself around, his machete swinging, and the other man barely dodged. A bloodied axe wrenched from the wall.

The two of them faced each other, far enough apart to be safe, but not enough to release any tension. They began again: the axe swung forward, and the Healer side-stepped, swung with his machete, but both missed; the Healer received a kick to the stomach that sent him flailing backwards, trying to keep from landing off his feet.

The axe came back towards him in a broad arc, but he let himself fall backwards, avoiding it. He landed on the ground and without a pause to think, dangerously swung his arm and weapon out towards the other man's legs; felt a tug as he sliced the Achilles tendon.

The man growled at the pain, tried to continue on, but his leg wouldn't hold him anymore. He dropped downward onto one knee, roaring under his breath, refusing to give in. The Healer's arm was still exposed from the attack and his enemy knew it, lurching forward with his axe, but only managing to hit the Healer's cloak behind him.

Pinned down, the Healer tried to escape, but the man grabbed his machete hand and started beating it onto the ground, trying to break his grip. The Healer braced himself with his other hand, his cut arm stinging sharply as disinfectant shifted in the wound. His opponent was breathing heavily, and the blood from his leg was forming a pool under them.

The Healer's suit wailed: his heart rate burst forward, his wound seared, the blood around him creeping ever closer… his vision blurred momentarily, shook his head frantically. His hand was slammed into the ground, his index finger letting go slightly, giving up under the beating. The man was panting heavily now, moving in for the kill.

When his hand was lifted off the ground again, the Healer used the clearance to spin the blade around backhanded, and then, before he could lose the advantage, plunged it into the man's good thigh.

This time the man screamed, gripped down towards his legs, and choked as the blade was pulled free. The Healer rolled to his knees and grabbed the axe's handle, pulled it from the floor and unbound himself. As the other man started to curl into a ball on the floor, breathing heavily, the Healer got to his feet, holding his blade and the axe loose by his side.

The man looked up at the Healer, eyes narrow with pain and anger. His eyelids drooped slightly as the blood loss made him dizzy. The Healer watched him for a moment, trying to calm his own heart.

Then with visible effort, the Healer swung the axe back and threw it across the room, embedding it in a wall. He looked back to the man on the floor, shook his head no.

Struggling painfully, his suit still calling out for him to stop, to slow down, the Healer dragged his battered body towards the staircase.

*   *   *

Carey listened carefully from the centre of Daniels' bedroom, cuffs half-latched, frozen in fear. There were no noises anymore, but the silence was terrifying. Behind him, Dmitri was rechecking clips for his pistol, repeating something to himself in Russian that Carey couldn't understand. Daniels was back on his bed, quiet, waiting for word.

The dresser they'd propped in front of the door was thick, but it wobbled slightly when Dmitri leaned on it, making Carey shiver. And then, there… a creak outside the door, a soft pacing.

Carey moved further away from the door, back towards the bed. Dmitri reloaded his gun and took aim, his eyes narrow with intense focus. Carey stumbled as he paced backwards, never taking his eyes off the danger.

Knock.

Knock.

Knock.

No one moved, not even to check each other's expressions. Carey felt miserably hot in his mask, panic setting in, fumbled suddenly with the latches by his neck, but couldn't get to them. Dmitri made a quick sideways glance at him, obviously annoyed at the distraction.

The latches were so tight, Carey couldn't get a grip somehow… his fingers felt numb… and — *knock!* — he pulled uselessly at a strap, the metal links clinking quietly but so very deafening some-how. He heard a gurgle, gasped for breath, trying to take the damn thing off!

"I can't breathe..." he gasped. "I can't breathe in this thing..."

Dmitri glared back, looking ready to waste a bullet on Carey. But instead, his eyes were wide and he half-turned, his gun lowering, face blanching.

Carey thought something must be wrong with him, a sudden panic took hold. He jerked around, trying to get free of his mask, but then he heard it again: the gurgling. A gurgling noise...

He looked around and saw Daniels, flopped over on his side on the bed, blood running out of his mouth, his ears, his nose... his eyes were bloody, crying red. He gurgled again, a crimson bubble forming at his lips, and twitched slightly. Carey gasped, staggered back.

"Oh my god..." he whispered. "His blood was clear. His blood was *clear*..."

Then there was a loud metallic crunch, and Carey saw a beaten blade knock the doorknob out of the door, twist round and disappear. Dmitri wasted no time: he fired into the door seven times, backing up slightly as he did so, putting distance between himself and whatever might come through the door next.

There was a moment of silence, and the sound of the shots echoed in Carey's ears. Then, with a slow start: a bump, and then he watched with horror as the door started to slide forward, pushing the dresser with it.

Dmitri moved into the corner of the room and started firing again, unloading his clip into the door. He quickly re-loaded again and repeated the process with another ten or so bullets before stopping, watching in horror as the door kept moving. The light through the holes beamed through uninterrupted, and yet somehow, the door was still moving...

Dmitri motioned for Carey to stay still, and he slowly moved up and to the right of the door, staying flat against the wall, and aiming carefully at the space the intruder would need to come through. He was safely out of sight, ready.

Carey realized with a jolt that *he* was *not* out of sight, and stumbled backwards, next to Daniels' limp body, and tried to stay still.

There was a moment of silence, no one moving, no sign of life from any quarter. And then, slowly, Carey saw the tip of a long battered blade climb up along the crack in the door, and across towards the light switch. He looked to Dmitri urgently, willing him to see it, but it was beyond the door, out of his line of sight.

Carey swallowed slowly, and then the room went dark.

* * *

The Healer knelt down next to the door, wood chips on his back. Beyond, the room was dark, silent. No movements, no shadows, no gleams or reflections. He held his breath, tried to quiet his suit, but it screamed at him, warned him of the cuts and bruises he already felt intensely.

He took a deep breath, closed his eyes a moment, and then dove through the door, into the room. He rolled to his feet and stayed low, checking his surroundings: a large bed, and on it, one man covered in blood… not breathing, and behind him… behind him…

The Healer gasped, got to his feet as if in a daze, and stumbled forward. Across the room was another Healer. The mask, the suit, it was unmistakable. He reached a hand out towards his comrade, slow and dazed, and before he could react, he heard a crack, and his arm erupted on him, sending him tumbling forward, his blood spraying out in front, hitting the goggles on his mask.

Without thinking, he spun round with dazed ferocity and threw his machete out in an arc. He stumbled to one knee, shocked by the sight of a thick and rough-looking man, hidden behind the door, gun smoking slightly, the machete planted deep in his chest.

"Shit," he muttered in quiet Russian, and slumped back against the wall.

The Healer got back to his feet, turned towards the bed, towards the other Healer.

"How are you here?" he said, voice wavering with pain. "I am still on schedule. I can still clear this up before the deadline..."

The other Healer shook his head urgently, climbed up on the bed, away, like he was *scared*. The dead man slipped sideways, down off the bed, onto the floor. The Healer stumbled to his knees next to the body, checked the mouth, the red eyes, the blood on the shirt. He looked up at his comrade, faint.

"Was he the vector?" he asked, the room starting to spin.

The other Healer shook his head so urgently now, held his hand out to say no. And then he spoke, and the Healer jerked backwards at the foreign sounds. He shook his head as if to clear it, then heard an entirely different language again. And again, painfully, a third time, and this time it made sense to him:

"Please don't kill me!"

French. The Healer tried to stand, but slipped over, barely catching himself on the bed.

"Who sent you here?" he asked in French, quiet, desperate.

The other Healer still seemed terrified, and it looked odd.

"I... I am from the Containment Office," he said, his voice distorted through his mask. "I was sent to arrest this man."

"Arrest? What Office?"

"The British Containment Office," came the reply. "In London. England."

It took a moment, but the Healer laughed. He lowered his head and felt the world go black, and then pulled himself back up to his feet. The British man moved further away, terrified.

"What happened to this man?" the Healer said with increasing intensity.

"I don't know," said the other, shaking his head. "He just started bleeding... out of his mouth, his eyes... it...there was no warning!"

The Healer looked at the dead man, saw the look of shock on his face. No warning.

"Did you inject him with anything?" he said, stepping closer to the British man.

"No! No, I just came and tested his blood. He had no diseases. Nothing that could cause *this*!"

The Healer reached back towards his bag to remove his testing vials, and the other man screamed, covering his head with his arms.

"There were others!" he shouted. "The wife and the stepdaughter!"

The Healer stopped, thought, then grabbed the British man by the neck, threw him off the bed, onto the ground. He loomed over, felt the blood seeping inside his glove, warm on his skin.

"Were they sick?" he boomed.

"The stepdaughter was. I don't know what it was… it wasn't registered…"

Then they heard it, both looking up towards the door at the same time. Distant, probably on the stairwell, two voices calling to each other, the same words repeated.

"Police," the Healer said quietly. "They will be here soon."

He grabbed the man's head in his large bloodied glove, lifting him up, making him pay attention.

"Where did they go?" he demanded.

The British man feebly shook his head.

"I don't know! Believe me, I don't!"

The Healer tossed the bureaucrat to the ground, marched towards him, and the man scattered back, standing, slipping and hitting the curtains of the far window, and he pulled them round him for protection.

"*Where did they go?*" he asked again, bearing down.

The man cried, the sound so pitiful in his mask, and shook his head, holding on to the curtain so tightly it nearly ripped free.

The Healer punched him in the throat, and the man bounced back into the window, the glass cracking, and he dropped to his knees, gagging, trying to get air. The Healer placed a menacing hand on the man's head, squeezed, and then let the bitter fury within him take over.

*   *   *

Sobotka saw the door first, riddled with holes, blood seeping through the hinged corner. There were no lights on inside. She nodded to Crew, motioned him forward.

They stood on either side of the door now, guns at the ready, trying to get a sense of what might be inside. Crew tried nudging the door a bit further open, but it was blocked by something. They exchanged glances uncertainly.

"This is the police!" Crew shouted, shrugging to his partner. "If you move, we'll kill you."

"Put your hands above your head!" added Sobotka, and Crew nodded appreciatively.

There was a loud crash, and a pained scream, and then the sound of glass breaking, falling, and Crew's eyes opened so wide Sobotka had to put her hand out to steady him. There was scraping, some clunking, and then, an uneasy silence, punctuated by gasps.

Sobotka took her hand from her gun and gave Crew a silent countdown:

3… 2… 1…

Crew moved into the room quickly, scanning left and arcing right, and Sobotka covered him, checking for hostiles. There was a man covered in blood just by the bed, the window was shattered out, the curtains fluttering in the wind, and the only thing left was what Crew was now closing in on: the Healer, bloodied and beaten.

They circled him carefully, checking for weapons. He was on his knees, his cloak soaked with blood, his hands in the air. He looked broken, almost sagging down, swaying slightly, near death.

"Move a muscle and I'll blow that mask off your head," Crew said, completing his circuit. Sobotka finished checking the room and joined him there.

"You're under arrest," Sobotka said sternly, and Crew shot her an angry look. She squinted it away, motioned to the Healer. "I hope you've enjoyed yourself tonight, because you're going to pay for it for a long, *long* time."

The Healer spoke, his voice weak, raspy almost, impossible to understand. He gasped after a bit, stopped trying to talk, seemed too tired to continue. His arms were slowly drifting downwards, his whole body collapsing in slow motion.

"Don't *move!*" shouted Crew, and the Healer sat up straight again, shook his head slightly.

"You're being charged with, what… nine counts of murder?" Sobotka asked, her gun not moving from its target.

Crew nodded to her.

"I'm going to check the window," she said, and he nodded slightly again. She backed up, keeping her gun ready, and as she reached the window, the curtains brushing past her, she peered outside, saw it was snowing thickly now. She glanced down onto the street below and saw a body there, red around it, lying distorted on the ground.

"Make that ten counts," she said, and looked back at the Healer.

He started to shake his head again, moved his hand down towards his chest, and Crew backed up, kept his gun ready.

"Don't do that!" he shouted angrily. "Don't move any more!"

The Healer kept shaking his head, reached down, touched something on his belt, and started pulling it forward, something rectangular, something…

"Don't!" shouted Sobotka, but it was too late, he was pulling it up. Before she knew what was happening, the dark room flashed brightly with gunfire, and she saw Crew's face flinching with satisfaction, fury and a bizarre kind of justice.

When the sound stopped, Crew and Sobotka stayed perfectly still and watched the Healer crumple backwards onto the floor.

49

Eva tore into the box, dropping a long tube into her trembling hand, rushing back into the living room where the incubator had finished booting. She popped open the lid, pushed the tube into place, and reloaded the file she'd been working on, the cure to Nuremberg-6.

"It doesn't matter if you kill me again," Rhodri called to her from his spot on the couch, his black jacket and trousers blazing against the fabric. "I'll be here in person soon, won't I?"

Eva ignored him, pulled up the cure, and planted a finger on the start button. The incubator began to churn, humming softly.

Then, from the bathroom, Eva heard a smash, a scream, and she dashed away from the table, down the hall. Rhodri paced ahead of her, trying to put himself in her way, and she shoved past, dodging this way and that, but he wouldn't leave her alone until she slammed into the door frame, catching her breath.

Her mother lay on the ground, cowering against an invisible foe, broken mirror shards everywhere.

"Mama!" Eva said, rushing over. "Mama, you need to be careful here."

Her mother looked up with watery eyes, reached a hand towards her daughter, and then swivelled around, turning on the tap to the bathtub. Blood from her cut arm dripped into the stream, making the base briefly pink.

"Shh, mama. Come on, we need to get back now," Eva said, lifting her up.

Rhodri stood by the door, leaning with a smirk on his face, faked a yawn.

"Won't be long now," he said as she passed. "I'm about ready to reach out and touch you. Are you looking forward to it?"

Eva sat her mother down on the sofa, wrapping her arms in bandages she found in the closet, pushed her head down gently, trying to urge her to sleep. Her mother sighed, rolled back and forth like she was having a nightmare, though her eyes were open.

"Somebody find Eva... my poor Eva..." she gasped all to herself.

Eva checked the progress on the incubator: nearly done. Warm hands once again stroked her neck, her shoulders, and she hit them away, refusing to pay attention.

"I'll be here soon," Rhodri said softly. "In the flesh, where you can't avoid me. Any minute now..."

Eva squeezed her eyes shut, pushed the voice away in her mind. Then she heard a knock at the door. *A knock at the door!* She froze, hands clasping the desk desperately. She stayed perfectly still, listened, waited.

The knock returned, more urgent this time.

"Come on, Eva!" sang Rhodri. "I'm waiting! Let me in!"

Eva pressed her head against the door, afraid to look. She heard noises from outside: feet shifting, pacing. She peered through the peephole, trembling, afraid. At first she saw nothing... and then... she saw a woman, black and just as scared as she was.

"Who is it?" Eva called out. The woman turned, pushed both hands against the door, seemed so relieved to hear a voice.

"I'm from the hospital," she replied. "My name is Fanta Anouma. I'm a doctor there. We... *I* need your help."

Eva slammed her head into the door, grit her teeth.

"Go away!" she shouted. "I can't help you! Just go away!"

Anouma shook her head, seemed so desperate. She pushed a feeble fist against the door.

"Please! I saw you with the incubator! I need your help! My brother is dying and there's no one else who will help him!"

Eva turned her head from the door, saw Rhodri. He shrugged, disinterested.

"What makes you think I can help you?" she called out, and there was a long pause before Anouma answered.

"Maybe you can, maybe you cannot. But that incubator has the power to cure my brother, and maybe stop the outbreak that has quarantined half the hospital. I have to try!"

The door popped open a touch, Eva looked out nervously.

"What outbreak?"

"We don't know. It seems to cause hallucinations. Bad ones. Virtual insanity in the afflicted."

"Hmm, sounds familiar..." hummed Rhodri, running a finger down Eva's cheek.

Eva opened the door wide, ushered Anouma in, closed and locked them in. She paced towards the incubator just as it finished processing, and it spat out another container with the orange lid. Eva took it in her hand, held it up to Anouma.

"This will cure your outbreak," she said, confident.

Anouma reached a cautious hand out, incredulous...

"But how did you..."

"Never mind that. I'll make more. But first, I need to give this to my..." Eva turned, saw the empty sofa, and nearly dropped the container. "Mama? Mama!"

She saw a streak of blood on the wall near the bathroom, and took off. She and Anouma tripped into the bathroom to find Eva's mother, face-first into the full bathtub, arms floating loose at her sides.

"Oops!" Rhodri cackled.

"Mama!" Eva screamed, and pulled her mother out, laying her on the floor. Anouma pushed in, leaned close and listened.

"She's not breathing. Tilt her head."

Eva pushed behind her mother's neck, and Anouma began CPR, pumping, breathing, pumping, breathing, until Eva lost track of it all, just sat back and cried while her mother lay there, unconscious and fading further away.

Rhodri ran a hand down her thigh, and she pushed him.

"Leave me the fuck alone!" she screamed, and Anouma paused, looked at her, concerned.

"Who are you…?" she began.

"Just help her," Eva begged, filtering Rhodri out as best she could. "Please!"

Anouma pushed down on the chest again, and this time, suddenly, water bubbled up and out of the mouth, and Eva's mother choked, gasped, spat and was rolled to her side, and she vomited bile and water onto the floor. Anouma rubbed her back, eyeing Eva cautiously.

"Mama? Can you hear me? Are you okay?" Eva pleaded, down on her hands and knees next to her pale mother.

"Eva?" came the reply. "Eva, my baby… she's in the tub. Somebody has to find her, please!"

Eva pushed her forehead into the ground, let out a rattled breath. When she looked up, Anouma was staring at her seriously.

"You have the virus too," she said. "You both do."

Eva nodded weakly, said nothing.

"Are you sure this cure works?" Anouma asked.

"I'm sure," Eva said seriously, getting to her feet. "And I can prove it to you."

She ran out of the bathroom, down to her mother's office, throwing junk aside until she found a box of needles. She ran back to the bathroom, uncapped the container, filled the syringe, and without a moment's hesitation, injected her mother with the cure.

*   *   *

Crew and Sobotka sat on the bed in the dead man's room. Sobotka put her gun in her holster, rubbed her temple, trying to massage out a pending headache.

"That went well," she said, gloomy.

Crew snorted, then laughed. He got to his feet, stretched out and sighed loudly.

"Let's do a quick check and get back after the girl," he said. "I'm all done with *my* case now, so we might as well do yours too. We can leave this mess to the crime lab."

He bent down over the Healer's body, peeled back bits of fabric, investigating the body. Sobotka got to her feet, did a brief look around, nudged some things with a pen, but didn't touch anything.

"God it stinks in here," she gagged. "Too much blood."

She pushed out to the window, leaning into the night air, the curtains flapping at either side.

"So you really think the Healer was behind this? I mean, he did kill a lot of people here tonight, but if he's going to do that, why would he bother making a virus at all?" she asked, leaning out, looking at the body on the sidewalk again.

"Maybe he's just a nut job," said Crew, tossing bits of paper from the body, obviously not concerned with disturbing the crime scene. "Anyone that dresses like this has got to be at least a little bit nutty."

Sobotka laughed, turned back to the room, but then did a double-take, spinning round and looking out again... there, a glint on the drainpipe outside. She looked further down, saw a clear streak of red down the drainpipe. The body in the snow. The drainpipe again. They weren't in the same direction.

"Those two don't connect..." she muttered. "Uh, Crew... I think we have a problem here."

She turned round to her partner, stopped dead. Crew's face was white. He looked up at her, blinking.

"Oh yeah," he said. "I think so too."

He held out a small leather wallet, flipped open to a bright white card. Sobotka couldn't read it, but didn't need to. In the top left corner was a very obvious Union Jack.

*   *   *

The door exploded open, showering the room with fragments of wood, and the Healer stumbled in, his arm bandaged with red-soaked gauze, clutched by a desperate hand. Anouma got to her feet, pushing Eva back, away.

"I told you to stay in the stairwell!" Anouma said, urgently.

Eva shot a confused and horrified looked to the doctor.

"You're *with* this monster?"

"Oh, this is getting *good*," chuckled Rhodri.

The Healer shoved Anouma aside, into the refrigerator.

"Talking is too slow," came his weakened voice, distorted and delirious. He walked past Eva without effort, kneeling down at the edge of the sofa, where her mother was laying, eyes open, almost alert. With his one good hand, he grabbed her by the chin, tilted her head up, looked at her eyes. His hands were shaking, and although he was bandaged heavily, he was still dripping bright red blood on the floor.

Eva stepped forward aggressively.

"Stop that!" she shouted in French, clenching her fists. The Healer turned his head to her, and her confidence melted.

"Where is her blood?" he demanded. Eva glanced to Anouma, then back to the Healer, and sneered.

"Why do you need it?" she asked, defiant.

He let go of her mother, lurched into a turn and bore down on Eva. She clenched her jaw, kept her eyes on his, and held her ground. He looked at her, a blank fury growling from his mask.

"I do not have time to play games," he said, his voice faltering slightly. "Give me her blood or I will take it myself. My way."

Eva's eye twitched.

"You leave her alone," she said to him, a warning.

"I will do as I please," he said, and Anouma stepped forward again to protest, but he held his hand out to her to stop her. "Give me the blood *now*!"

"It won't do you any good!" Eva yelled. "I've already cured her! There's no virus left for you to diagnose!"

Behind her, the incubator deposited another container of serum. Her eyes darted towards it very carefully, trying not to show.

"Who is that for?" he asked her, ominous.

Eva watched him carefully, then made a mad dash for the incubator, grabbing towards the container, trying to get it before... the Healer pulled her shoulder, threw her onto the floor in the back of the kitchen. Her sprained wrist screamed out at her, and she cradled it urgently.

The Healer loomed over her, pulling a grey device from his pack.

"Give me your arm or I will cut it off and test it that way," he said.

Eva looked to Anouma, who seemed just as scared as she did. She held out her arm, terrified, and the Healer placed the device to her. She felt a prick, a tug, and her blood seeped away, into the machine that purred softly as it worked. He turned away, watching it intently.

Eva got to her feet, shaky, and Rhodri was there beside her, whispering in her ear:

"The knife, Eva. The knife. Cut his heart out with a knife, like you would for me."

Eva saw the knife there beside the rotting carrot, and she reached a cautious hand over, slipped it away, kept it close. The Healer fell against the counter, stood straight again, leaving a red mark where he'd been. He kept watching his display, waiting. Oblivious to anything else.

Finally, the answer came, and Eva watched him carefully as his expressionless face stayed locked down. Slowly at first, he started to shake his head more broadly, and then she heard the creak of plastic in his hands, and he savagely ripped the empty vial from the bottom and threw it across the room, into a mirror, which shattered loudly onto the floor.

"A new strain!" he shouted, coughing at the force of his own voice.

Eva acted: she flipped the knife around in her hand and swung it in a quick, precise arc at the Healer's neck.

He caught her arm in mid-swing, did not even turn to look. Eva trembled at the force of his rough glove on her wrist, her hand unable to move in for the kill. She ground her teeth, tried to will it forward, but it was no use. She watched him, helpless.

He turned his head, looked at her calmly.

"I am done with games," he said, and squeezed her arm, her hand releasing the knife against her will. She didn't make a sound; he made no more movements, just stayed there, holding her tightly.

Anouma came to his side, put a hand on his shoulder, carefully, like she was scared what he might do to her, too.

"Please don't," she said, her voice soft and trembling.

He shook his head, slowly, dizzily.

"No, she carries a new strain. It must be contained. I have my directives…"

"But I found the cure!" Eva exclaimed, tears in her eyes. "I've already saved two people, and I can do more! You don't need to do this!"

The Healer froze, he let go of her arm, but she didn't move it, not sure what he might do. He looked slowly to the incubator, then round at Eva, his bloody goggles still a frightening sight.

"You cured the man Daniels?" he asked, and Eva's breath stopped in her lungs.

"How did you…?"

"Did you cure him first?"

"Y-y-yes, maybe an hour ago…" she said, tense. "What did you do to him?"

The Healer looked away from her, stared at her mother, didn't move.

"Nothing," he said, and she breathed again, feeling less tension, less anxiety. "He was already dead."

The ground spun for Eva, and she fell backwards against the counter, slid down it, put her head in her hands and tried to get her breathing back under her control. There was a thumping in her ears and she couldn't focus. The Healer stood over her, blood dripping from his arm onto the ground next to her.

"Was he bleeding before you treated him?" he barked.

Eva had trouble focusing. She shook her head vaguely, unsure.

"I must see your cure," said the Healer, his voice gaining strength. He pulled the container from the side of the incubator, held it towards Eva. "Is this it?"

Eva didn't look, just nodded blankly. She felt so cold.

He put the vial into his device and pushed another button, staring at the display as if were the only thing in the world to see. Eva's gaze shifted from the Healer to her mother, then to Rhodri, who sat next to her, kissing her ear softly. Then... then back to her mother. She was staring past her at the countertop, blinking, somehow different than before.

Suddenly, the Healer dropped his device on the ground, and it cracked on impact. He made no other moves, just stood there, his hand open, frozen. He spoke something to himself, a hiss, that Eva had no concept of understanding. He clenched his fist, lowered his head and shook it.

Anouma looked up to him, reached a hand up to his.

"What is it?" she asked.

He looked past her, at Eva.

"She will die too," he said without inflection. "Same as Daniels. Massive hemorrhaging. It cannot be stopped. Your cure is too effective."

And with that, he straightened himself up, groaned, and grabbed the last of the serum off the table. He grunted as he slid it into his belt, and then with a deep breath, lurched towards the door, his body giving out on him so quickly he looked like he might disintegrate at the threshold. Eva leapt to her feet, started after the Healer, shouting: "Stop! You have to *do* something!"

The Healer turned, his breaths uneven and wheezy while he looked at her.

"I have no solutions," he said quietly. "Only the one you do not want."

Eva watched the Healer as he stood there, patiently delaying his own death for her, and she nodded to him, horribly.

"End it," she pleaded quietly. "Please."

The Healer nodded gravely, turned and stumbled back to the counter. He removed a blue pouch from his pack and placed it on the countertop and unrolled it carefully, leaving bloody prints all over it. Eva looked away, and Rhodri moved in to kiss her. She closed her eyes at it, and felt the brush of his beard on her lips, the softness. She buried her head down, gasped for air, trying to block out whatever sounds she might hear.

"Eva," said her mother quietly. "It's done, Eva."

She opened her eyes, blinked. Her mother sat on the sofa, a gentle smile on her face, her arm still out where the Healer had killed her. She motioned for Eva to come, and she obeyed, sitting on the sofa too, as if in a dream. Even Rhodri stayed distant, giving them space.

"Mama, I'm so sorry..." she sobbed, pushing her head into her mother's arms. "I'm so sorry..."

"Shhh now, Eva. It's not your fault."

Her mother put her hand on the side of Eva's face, brushed her cheek softly, and she met her eyes, calm and forgiving.

"I'll be fine," she said, her smile radiant, comforting. "I'm just glad I got to say good-bye first."

Eva cried, gasped for air.

"I should have said no," Eva said darkly. "I should have trusted my instincts. I knew this wouldn't work. I didn't know what I was doing, and it killed you! I *killed* you!"

Her mother closed her eyes now, seemed to be feeling something, her smile faded slightly. But she spoke:

"The reason... the reason I kept Richard from hiring you, Eva, was because I knew how terrible it can be to make mistakes in this field. It's not what I'd wish upon you. It's not what I'd wish upon anyone. And you've already suffered enough for the mistakes you've made in life."

Her mother began to shake. A low, subtle shake, but it shook her whole body, and Eva held tight.

"Eva," she gasped. "You did well. I'm proud of you. Don't let my death crush your spirit. You have to live on... you have to learn from your mistakes and do better... promise me..."

Eva cried, nodded.

"I promise, mama," she whispered.

"Good," said her mother, a slight smile on her face, but her eyes seeing nothing. "Good."

And then she jerked slightly, then again, backwards onto the back of the sofa, and started to seize more violently, her eyes rolling back in her head and a few strained gasps coming from her mouth. Eva tried to hold her, somehow stop it, the sounds ripping her apart. And then her mother calmed suddenly, she exhaled, and Eva did too, her lungs aching from the endless pause.

No one moved for a moment, and the sound of the room took time to come flooding back. Eva's hands were shaking, and she squeezed them together to try and regain her composure.

She looked to the Healer, who stood by the door, leaning on it for support.

"I need to destroy that cure," he said. "It's too dangerous."

He shook his head, took a step backwards in the open space of the doorway.

"Make a new version," he said, swaying slightly. "You can stop the outbreak if you hurry. Check the cure against your own blood and you'll see."

"But what about…"

"I will keep this one," he said, and it was not up for discussion. "I have one last use for it."

50

1 PISECKÉHO, PRAGUE, CZECH REPUBLIC
NOVEMBER 30

"What are you going to do?" Anouma called to the Healer as he made his way down the back stairwell at Eva's building.

He lost his balance briefly, hit the wall and left a dark red smear. He put his other foot down to the next step, but it missed the edge and he stumbled down, landing on his weakened elbow, and the spots overtook his vision. He shook his head again and again, trying to regain control.

He got to his feet, used his good arm to guide himself down the steps, watching his footing carefully.

"What are you doing?" Anouma shouted, stopping a few steps up.

The Healer came to a rest, turned to face her, but missed her face.

"I am going to cure your brother."

*   *   *

The blood trail led to the front of a building Sobotka and Crew knew well, so when they came within a few houses, they leapt out of Crew's car and sprinted the rest of the way, guns drawn. An old woman stood in the hallway around the corner, staring at fragments of a broken door. She was dressed in a night gown, slippers, seemed confused and concerned.

"I haven't called you yet," she said to them.

"Go back inside, ma'am," said Sobotka, edging closer to the door.

"She really is a nice girl," the woman said, her mind switching gears and tones suddenly. "Just like her mother. A real beauty."

Sobotka nodded to the woman, trying to be patient, but Crew had no tact left: he grabbed her night gown and dragged her back, threw her into her apartment, and closed the door. The two of them stayed by the broken door, guns ready.

"Police!" Sobotka called. "Keep your hands in the air and *do not move!*"

"I'm alone!" cried Eva from inside, and they checked each other, confused.

Sobotka peeked around the corner cautiously, then led herself and Crew in, making a sweep of the rooms. Eva's mother lay dead on the sofa, blood all over the kitchen, a knife, footprints and water everywhere... and there sat Eva at the coffee table, hands flying madly across the trackpad of an incubator.

"Ms Kolikov, what are you—"

"Listen," Eva said, eyes glued to the screen, "I need you to shut up. You can arrest me and beat me up all you like, but I've got to finish what I'm doing."

Sobotka put her gun away, edged around the side. Crew kept his weapon out, but aimed at the floor, frowning.

"What *are* you doing?"

"There's an outbreak at the hospital, I have to cure it before it spreads."

"How do *you* know about the outbreak?" Sobotka asked.

"One of the doctors told me. Now seriously, shut up so I can concentrate!"

Sobotka slid over next to Crew, spoke in a hushed voice.

"She's telling the truth?"

"Could be that Anouma woman I was looking for. She's a friend of the Healer's. Still, Kolikov and an incubator can't be a good combination."

Sobotka watched Eva a moment, twitched an eye.

"Call in to the hospital and see what their status is. I don't trust her, but I don't want to shut this down if it can help."

Crew nodded reluctantly, headed to the hall with his phone. Sobotka crouched next to Eva, watched her working. A tourniquet was still strung tight around her arm, a small drip falling around to her elbow. Eva was handling a small vial of blood, searching the side of the machine, probing with shaking hands.

"I can't figure out where this thing goes in..." she cursed, slamming her bandaged arm on the table in frustration and then cursing some more.

Sobotka took the vial from her, darted around the side of the machine, saw a port there, and pushed the vial in. It clicked solidly, then the incubator rotated the blood out of sight, and began to purr.

"Thanks," Eva said, eyes darting wildly. "I'm having a hard time focusing right now."

An alert popped onto the screen:

CUSTOM BLOOD SAMPLE DETECTED.

OVERRIDE LOCALE SETTINGS?

Eva accepted the change, and threw herself into cracking the virus code once more.

*   *   *

The Healer burst into Adjobi's room, Anouma close behind, and came to a sudden stop at the base of the bed. Adjobi sat up, wary and weary and somehow sicker than before as the Healer pulled another needle from his bag and started filling it with serum. His arm was stiff and awkward, and he struggled to hold himself steady.

"Do you know what this is?" he asked as he filled the syringe. "This is the cure to the disease you sent me after."

Adjobi seemed surprised by this, tried to sit up.

"Really..." he said, his eyes wide with curiosity, but still fear.

"Yes," said the Healer, pulling the needle free and holding it ready. "It has killed two people already. Let us try for three."

He plunged the needle into Adjobi's arm and pushed the plunger down, and Adjobi groaned loudly, jerked suddenly but couldn't fight the strength of the Healer.

"No!" Anouma screamed, pounding on the Healer's back, until he was done, pulled the needle free, and stepped back. Anouma collapsed to the floor, weeping.

The Healer felt a powerful release, he stumbled, caught on to the railing at the side of the bed, and leaned on it, transferring all his reliance there, all the strength he'd been drawing suddenly gone. His suit was whining in his ear that he was too excited, but he already knew.

Adjobi looked down at the needle mark in his arm, the blood dripping around and onto the sheets, and then looked up at the Healer with a calm stare. And then, ever so slightly, he smiled.

Anouma saw her brother, saw his expression, and her crying trailed off. She got to her knees, took his hand, but he pulled it away, his smile turning into a smirk.

The Healer stumbled, held on to the bed tighter.

"You have no vector," he said to Adjobi, faint and tired. "You *are* the vector."

Anouma looked from Adjobi to the Healer, then back, her crying stopped, her mouth ajar, trying to understand what was going on.

"What are you talking about?" she gasped. "He's sick, he was infected by... by someone else... he's the *victim*! And you've killed him!"

The Healer didn't listen to her. He was watching Adjobi, saw the sickly man start to laugh, laugh so awkwardly it was painful. And then, finally, when Adjobi calmed himself enough, he looked at the Healer with intense anger.

"You are clever," he said. "But I would bet you're too late."

*   *   *

Crew burst back in the room, eyes wide with fear or excitement.

"Sestak just passed down the order... they're going to gas the hospital! We've got to move!"

Eva and Sobotka both gaped.

"They're *what?*"

"Sestak's afraid of a major outbreak across the city. He's full-on paranoid from the sound of it. They've sealed the doors and the army is moving in to gas and burn the place down. The captain's ordered us there to provide backup. In case anyone makes it outside."

"Are they insane?" Sobotka yelled, getting to her feet furiously. "All those people… there are over ten thousand people in there!"

Eva kept moving blocks around, pushing the cure further, watching the antibodies in her blood react horribly to every option she threw at it.

"I can fix this," she said, mostly to herself. "Just give me five minutes. I can fix it, and we can stop the outbreak. I just need five minutes of quiet. Please."

Sobotka looked to Crew, who didn't seem keen on the idea. She looked back to Eva.

"You've got five minutes," she said.

Eva nodded, then flinched, jabbed her elbow out and to the side.

"Fuck off!" she spat.

Sobotka and Crew took a cautious step backwards.

"What's going on?" Sobotka asked.

Eva didn't look up, rolled her eyes as she worked.

"I'm gonna say some strange things for the next little while," she said darkly. "Don't worry about it. *It's not going to be around for much longer.*"

Eva ran the test, saw the familiar shapes falling and disappearing as her cure broke down Nuremberg-6. But instead of leaving no traces, the screen warned her:

ANTIBODY CONFLICT. SEE REPORT.

She clicked through, and her jaw dropped open at the sight.

"Oh shit," she gasped.

"What?" demanded Sobotka. "What's wrong?"

"The cure, it leaves stupid little fragments in the blood, stuff that doesn't do any harm. Simple compounds. See? These little grey squares. They shouldn't impact anything. They *didn't* impact anything when I ran this before."

Sobotka leaned in, couldn't see what Eva was seeing.

"So what's different?"

"There's something in my blood that's not in the incubator's base profile. Something I've got that isn't standard, or *wasn't* standard when they made this thing. Something my mother, Richard, and probably you and everyone else in this city... something we've all got in common. The cure is making things worse! It's too perfect... it's a trap, and I fell for it!"

*   *   *

The Healer threw the syringe across the room, tried to fight the urge to strangle the man.

"This is no game!" he shouted.

"No it isn't!" growled Adjobi, trying to sit up. "This is far too sad to be a game! You, all of you, worrying over these people, with their home-made sickness, hoping to God that you can save them, find them a cure! This is no game... *this is a farce*! And you need to see why!"

Anouma gasped, let go of Adjobi, looked to the Healer, her face so overcome she had no expression. The Healer composed himself, stepped back from the bed, had to focus.

"You created a virus, designed it brilliantly," he said. "So the cure, the treatment, would be lethal."

Adjobi smiled proudly now.

"It was not easy," he said simply.

"But it won't hurt *you*," the Healer growled. "Because your blood is missing the compound it needs to kill. The compounds that survive attach to something already there, create a new virus with them. A deadly one. A terrible one. What is it? What are you targeting?"

Adjobi closed his eyes, rested his head back, and took a deep breath. Anouma was now further away, looking shocked, confused.

"Four years ago," said Adjobi, his voice weaker now, distant. "Four years ago I met a girl. Beautiful woman, so perfect. So perfect I knew I must win her, marry her, keep her close. You met her, Anouma. Do you remember? Nowa?"

Anouma nodded, like in a dream.

"We were happy," he said, his eyes still closed. "For a time. And then, one day, one day she got sick, and the doctors told us: AIDS. Can you believe it? AIDS! But I... I don't know, we were so young, so naïve, we thought it would be all right. There were drugs, weren't there? Treatments? They'd had them for years, hadn't they? We'd be all right."

Adjobi opened his eyes, looked straight into the soul of the Healer.

"She died," he said, his voice a whisper. "she died of AIDS, a disease dead outside Africa, all because the vaccine stopped being made. It wasn't vital anymore! There were new threats! Greater threats! And my Nowa died in her bed for nothing! Nothing but weakness and greed and throwing a whole continent to the dogs!"

Adjobi pointed a trembling finger at the Healer.

"A disease is not dead until it is wiped from the face of the *whole* planet."

He clenched his hand into a fist, shook it slightly, and exhaled, his long, painful secret finally gone.

"The cure targets the AIDS vaccine," gasped the Healer.

*   *   *

Rhodri held her tight, caressing her body as he nuzzled her ear. Eva didn't even flinch, pushing blocks around, watching the fallout, watching the changes as they shot across the screen. Stroke, paralysis, kidney failure... they came and went as fast as her hands would move.

"Why don't you give it up so we can have some fun?" Rhodri whispered. "I can make it worth your while."

"Stop yakking. I'm busy here."

He cupped her breasts in his hands, kissed her neck.

"I wonder how long until you can't see the screen anymore, and you're mine forever?" he said, licking gently.

Eva dropped a blue square into place, and then the results came through…

WARNING:

PATIENT DEVELOPS MILD FEVER

She grinned, looked Rhodri clear in the face, kissed him back.

"Say goodnight, fucker."

She ran off, down the hall, into her mother's office, and pulled out the other two boxes of refill tubes, got halfway back to the living room when she noticed they were damp at the bottom. She stopped midway, mouth gaping, dumped the contents. The tubes were nearly empty. Cracked. Leaking. Lost.

"Oh no," he gasped as Rhodri held her from behind.

"What's wrong?" Sobotka asked, getting to her feet. "What are those?"

"The refills… we don't have any more refills. I can only make one more batch of this stuff."

"How many can it treat?" asked Crew.

Eva lowered her head, felt Rhodri on her neck, felt a shiver.

"Just one. The fix is contagious in its current form, but there's no way we'd cover everyone fast enough. There's just no way…"

They stood in silence. Rhodri held her tight, so tight, she felt it hard to breathe. The room started to grey around her, disappear into her mind like a dream she was waking from. She stumbled forward, onto her knees, and Rhodri was before her, kneeling too, white shirt undone, biting his lip, his dead eyes shining with glee.

"Can you feel it, Eva? Can you feel the end? It's coming. I can tell it's coming. Soon you'll be mine forever."

"I've still got the last dose. I can use it and burn you alive."

"You're not going to use the last dose on *yourself*, are you? And let all those people die?"

Eva stared him dead in the eye, and he kissed her. She tried to fight it, but it was so… so… she felt herself kissing back, felt his hands on her cheeks his body pressing against hers, and she shuddered, let him run his lips down her neck.

"Can you feel it?" he sang softly. "There's love in the air…"

And she paused.

"The air!" she gasped, and shoved him off, scrambling to the table, pushing past the grey, dancing fingers on the trackpad as he pulled her waist, tried to draw her back. She scoured the screen, found it under the 'Advanced' menu... down at the bottom... "Make Aerosolized".

*   *   *

"Every man, woman and child in Europe, the Americas, the East... they're all targets!" boomed the Healer. "You would kill a whole world of people out of revenge?"

"Their suffering's just as real to me, as mine is to them."

The Healer didn't say anything for a moment.

"Adjobi..." said Anouma, stepping closer. "you couldn't..."

"No?" spat her brother, giving her an icy stare. "No? I would *gladly* fear the poison I made if it meant I'd been protected like the others in this wretched city! I'm dying of AIDS, Fanta, and there is no one in the world that will help me! Oh, I made the trigger, but *they* made the weapon! Let them burn, I say! Let them all burn!"

The Healer's temper flared suddenly. He smashed one of the heart monitors against the wall so hard its casing shattered, and he threw the wreckage to the ground savagely.

"You made me your accomplice!" he shouted. "Kwong's blood was tainted too! You set a trap and let me poison my own people!"

Adjobi laughed a bit, looked at the Healer, sickly again.

"Don't worry," he said. "You're not alone. I've been working towards this for months."

Anouma gasped, trembling.

"What do you mean? I thought we were here to help, Adjobi... I thought we were—"

"Oh, we were. And at first, I was like you, Fanta. I thought this was the most noble calling in the world. I knew my time would run out, but I wanted to die doing something good for the world. I had no regrets.

"But then one day, I met a man with a different sort of mission. He wasn't content to just treat the symptoms, he wanted to cut the viruses down, here, in the field. We worked together, this Daniels and his partner. We found things nobody else would see for months, and we *fixed them*, Fanta. We saved so many lives.

"He had an incubator, and as I learned to use it, I realized I had it in my power to cure my AIDS, to patch your blood and save us both. Daniels was a pharmaceutical executive, so he'd have access to the vaccines. I asked him over and over again, and finally he told me he couldn't help... he *wouldn't* help, because it would get him caught, and our whole operation would fall apart."

The Healer bowed his head, drifting. Anouma backed further away, terrified.

"I couldn't stand it, Fanta," Adjobi continued. "I couldn't stand that he had the cure there, within his reach, and he denied it to me. It was too much. So I began learning the second function of the incubator, learned how to mix compounds badly, learned how to create poisons out of vaccines. I produced flawed results at the start, but I learned and improved.

"Their agents abroad, I took their compounds and made subtle tweaks. I broke their solutions and sent them back, ready to kill. Then they came to me, they asked: 'How did this happen, Adjobi? How did it go so wrong?', and I pleaded ignorance, said all was well when I saw the files last.

"Really, I was hoping Daniels would do as he promised, send my cures back to his company's database, have them distributed around the world in one of those godforsaken boosters. Think of the carnage. Think of the justice!"

"That is not justice!" roared the Healer, staggering backward. "That is genocide!"

"Oh, that's rich, coming from you! I'm not half the monster you are! Even when the outbreak downstairs claims half the city, my conscience is like untouched snow next to yours!"

"The outbreak..." Anouma gasped. "That was *you?*"

"It's not a long walk to the supply room, Fanta," he smiled. "And all it takes is a few millilitres of the virus to do the trick. In the coffee of a co-worker, a nip in the arm, a small prick in the IV bag."

Anouma lowered her head, crying now.

"This was all supposed to take a very different path," Adjobi said, sighing. "But I knew my time was running out, and Dr Kolikov saw the signature from those fools at the university in my work. The ones I hired to cover my tracks, and it lead her right to me. She started to investigate… I had to change things. I admit, I was afraid I wouldn't be able to see this through to the end… but I didn't expect I'd get such a gift as you," he said to the Healer, who stared at him, ragged. "You gave me a unique opportunity to become a very *powerful* vector."

He grinned uncontrollably.

"I hope I will live to see the cure," he said, faking his earlier, weaker voice. "Oh, how I *pray* I will see the cure."

The Healer stepped back from the bed, looked at Anouma, then back at Adjobi. He faltered, fell to his knees, slipped forward, but clung to the bed rails, pulled himself up, sliding the blue pouch out on the bed.

"I'm ready now," Adjobi said, lifting his arm up to the Healer. "Finish your duty before you die, Healer. I am ready to go."

*   *   *

The car slid sideways through the turn, almost hitting a lamp post, Crew spinning the wheel furiously, punching the gas, trying to get back on track. Ice shot off the windshield and into the buildings around them, smashing into a bright mist.

"Slow down, idiot!" shouted Sobotka, gripping the passenger seat door desperately.

"It's November!" Crew yelled. "I don't slow down till January!"

Between them, Eva sat, doubled over, hands on the sides of her face, pulling her skin down madly. Rhodri was curled around her back, arms moving fluidly over her body, his mouth across her skin, everywhere, exposed or not, drawing her into the grey again. She trembled, muttered into her lap, soft and urgent.

"It's all in my head. It's not real, I know it's not real."

"Are you sure?" Rhodri asked smoothly as he licked her neck. "I seem real to me."

"You're dead. I killed you, and you're dead."

"Richard said I was still alive. And I'm coming for you. You should be happy..."

He held her tighter, and she felt warm, shuddered, leaned her head back and let him kiss her shoulders, her neck, feeling so warm... She squeezed her eyes shut to push him away. She heard nothing but him, but refused to lose sight of the world around her.

The car shot forwards, around another turn, and they saw it: barricades ahead. Four soldiers in full masks, guarding the entrance to the hospital. Sobotka winced.

"Is there another way in?" she asked.

"Yeah," said Crew, switching gears. "*Faster.*"

The soldiers didn't have time to react. The Aston-Martin shot through the single-beam barricade, throwing wood and yellow lights in all directions. Crew didn't check the mirror to see what they'd done, he just pushed his foot straight to the floor they careened into the old emergency bay, skidding in a large arc, coming to a halt right next to the doors. Sobotka knocked her head on the car frame as the inertia left, looked to Crew with wide-open eyes.

"Don't do that again."

They got out of the car, hearing shouts in the distance as the soldiers gave chase, grabbed Eva by the arm and pushed into the foyer. Crew motioned to the great wooden doors, wrapped in yellow tape, a padlock across the handles.

"Shit, they're competent all of a sudden!" he cursed.

"Stand back!" Sobotka yelled, pulled her gun out, took aim and the padlock exploded off the doors. Crew wrenched them open, stumbled into the mass of hysterical and dying patients, all clawing off their beds, trying to escape, falling apart at the sights and sounds of their worst nightmares. Sobotka staggered back, watching a nurse flail desperately as five bloodstained figures tried to drag her into a side room, wailing madly.

Bastien stormed towards them, mask nearly off his face, bloody slashes on his cheeks.

"You fools! Get out of here! It's not safe!"

Crew held him back before the old doctor could reach them.

"They're going to torch this place, doc. You know that, right?"

Bastien barely registered the news, nodded gravely.

"If they must. We're ready to make that sacrifice."

"Well I'm not!" shouted Sobotka, and then a staggering patient threw her off her feet and onto the ground.

Eva stumbled forward, Rhodri tugging at her pants, punched him away, but missed. She gasped, half-seeing the mess in the room. A lunatic like the beast from the university came at her, and she hit him across the side of the head, and unlike Rhodri, he collapsed down, scampering away. She fell onto her back, felt Rhodri climb on top of her, lean over her, feet pushing her legs apart.

"We never did have that last afternoon off," he said, his voice quiet yet somehow louder than the pandemonium around them. "But now's as good a time as any..."

Eva tried to turn her head from him, but he held her jaw with clutching hands, slammed her skull down onto the floor once as he kissed her, clawing angrily, holding her hostage. She fought, but he pinned her hand, kept her legs spread, and she couldn't win, she couldn't... she...

... she saw them.

"Sobotka!" she yelled through Rhodri, through everything, though she couldn't see anything but him. "The fans! Use the fans!"

Sobotka pushed past Bastien, running to the row of switches by the door, pushed them all on. The lights above came to life, bathing them in a warm glow... and then, slowly, creaking, all the overhead fans began to move... swirling faster and faster.

Eva pulled the container from her pocket, fighting Rhodri's strong grip, held it out with a trembling gaze towards Crew, who kept an uneasy distance, not understanding what she was seeing. She pushed against Rhodri, knocked him off, held the container up further.

"Hurry…" she whispered, and he took it.

"Sobotka!" Crew yelled, twisting the cap off the container, hands trembling. "Ready!"

"Go!" she called, and he threw the container into the air, over the beds, into the centre of the room. Sobotka watched it float, almost weightless, for what seemed like an eternity. And then, like a dandelion in the wind, the white dust inside began flowing out and into the air.

*　　*　　*

The Healer took a weak step back.

"Kill me!" Adjobi screamed. "I'm dead anyway! Do it!"

The Healer steadied himself, hand gripping the blue pouch, the deadly serum.

He stared evenly at Adjobi.

"No," he said, and the sick man froze. "Mercy is not my commission."

Adjobi started forward, but the Healer shoved him back into bed with a bloodied hand, suddenly strong again, suddenly dominating. Terrifying.

"You will die here in this bed, as slow as your disease takes you. I will not be an instrument in your game any longer. I will not be an instrument for *anyone's* lunatic fantasies!"

Anouma stepped towards him, hand out, pausing…

"You *will* die. Your end will come slowly, and painfully, and there will be nothing you can do to ease your suffering. Because when all your caretakers are dead and buried by the carnage you wrought, there will be no one left to help you."

And with that, the Healer turned, and walked towards the door. He heard a quick sob, and then Anouma ran after him, catching him in the hallway. She put a hand on his shoulder, and he let himself be turned around.

"I must warn my people about Kwong's blood," he gasped, faltering. "I cannot stand your tears now."

She looked at him so sadly. She placed a hand on his chest and lowered her head, and whispered to him: "I am sorry for what he did. I am so sorry..."

The Healer took a deep breath, and the pain all over his body gripped him like a dull vice.

"You are not his master," he said. "Do not let him be yours. I must go now, before... before..."

He slipped onto the floor, his vision blacking.

*   *   *

The dust caught the light as it fell in swirls around the room. Eva saw it through Rhodri's strong embrace, and she smiled at it, breathed in heavily, smelled his sweat, the smell of that summer in Nuremberg.

He saw her smile, and his expression changed, angrier, deranged. He wrapped a callous hand around her face, lifted her head off the ground, even as his other hand stroked her gently.

"You like this?" he asked. "Is this good for you?"

"Yes..." she whispered. "Yes, it's good."

He slammed her head down on the ground, leaned in close.

"Then why did you leave me? Why did you kill me, Eva? Why?"

He slammed her again, but the pain passed through her, and she started to laugh. His hands were becoming fainter, his face less opaque. He noticed it, too, grabbed her head with both hands, leaning in close, furious, nose to hers.

"Eva!" he seethed, then suddenly his expression changed. Desperate, scared, alone... he started to cry, stroked her cheeks gently, rested his head on her chest, holding her, holding...

"Eva, please... please, I love you. Please don't do this... please don't..."

She lay there, unmoving, felt his hands dissolving, the breaths fainter, the weight of him on her melting away.

"Eva, I love you... I love you..." he said, his voice a whisper.

"I know," she said. "I loved you too."

Just then, a patient fell over her, legs smashing her ribs, and she rolled to her side, the sound of the room coming back full-force. The screams had been replaced by quiet whimpers, calls of pain, strong commands from the medical staff as they ran through the aisles, putting things back in order. Eva got to her feet, unsteady, and was caught under the arm by Sobotka.

"You okay?" she asked, and Eva nodded.

"It'll take a while to go away completely. Plus the fever. But I'm fine. Thanks."

Crew strode up, tossing a blood-stained patient out of his way as he went. He surveyed the damage.

"So I guess it worked," he said. "We knocked the disaster down a notch."

"I guess so," Eva smiled. "If you happen to see the Healer or Dr Anouma again, tell them thanks for me."

Crew nodded agreeably, staring off into the back of the room. His gaze shifted back to Eva, at the same time Sobotka let her go, frowning seriously.

"*Them*," they said together.

*   *   *

The Healer pushed himself to his feet, staggering forward, Anouma pulling him back, or trying to help, or... he stumbled again. Then, down the hallway two lights trained themselves on him. He couldn't understand the words, but knew what they meant. He stayed perfectly still, swaying slightly.

Anouma called to them in Czech; they yelled something back, and she held out both her hands towards them, but they dragged her away.

They grabbed him by the back of his suit and threw him, face-first into the wall. They kicked his legs and he fell to his knees, his arms pulled up — he coughed out a gagging cry as his shoulder was moved — and he heard the sound of a gun clicking behind his head.

There was more talking, Anouma's, and the armed woman, and a deeper, angry man. Anouma was frantic in her foreign tongue; she was telling them all the deeds he'd done, all the killing, about her brother's plight. He blinked slowly, nearly fell.

"Forgive me," he said softly in his native language. "May there be future generations left to curse my name... please..."

And then the Healer felt another grip under his arm, and he was lifted from the ground, turned towards the stairwell, and shoved so suddenly he fell onto the floor, his body exploding with pain, it was as if he'd been shot again. He stayed there for a moment, his suit deafening.

But now the silence was different. He heard his own mask, heard the breaths he took, but nothing else. The sounds of the two police were distant, were fading away, and when he opened his eyes, their lights were gone, too. He lay there in the dark, felt his heart beating.

And when he blinked again, Anouma was leaning over him, her hand on his back, rubbing him gently. Her eyes were wet, but the look on her face was not disgust... concern. Concern?

"Can you walk?" she asked quietly.

He nodded, slowly.

"I told them," she said, her voice wavering, her awful confession reluctantly coming forth. "I told them you need to warn your people. About Adjobi's virus." She bit her lip, tried to keep from crying, refused to look back towards her brother's room. "I told them why."

She helped him to his feet, and he started towards the stairwell, slipping in his own blood. He stumbled again, and she tried to catch him, but the weight was too much, and he fell down, face hitting the floor... he heard her around him, calling him back, but his vision blurred, echoed softly, and the darkness slowly soaked him away.

DECEMBER 1

51

At the edge of the field was an old wooden fence, a set of splintered logs stacked on top of each other, marking a passive border no one respected anymore. The snow was untouched, smooth and perfect, a light blue colour in the shade that was the hue of a perfect summer's day. The kind that seemed so alien now.

The winter sky was grey, clouds slowly ebbing into the west. And in the distance, down by the city, the smoke reached upwards, out of sight.

Eva watched the scene a while longer, the cold on her cheeks freezing the bandage she now wore. She squinted at the brightness of the day, adjusted her backpack over one shoulder. She reached into her pockets, pulled her mitts out and put them on, the thick wool tingling on her fingertips like a wave of needles.

She looked back to Sobotka and Crew, their car still humming quietly behind them, the windshield fogged.

"Thanks for the ride," she said, smiling weakly.

Sobotka didn't make eye contact, looked off into the distance like there was something to see. She sniffed loudly, uncomfortable.

"Anything to get criminals out of town," she said, then glanced over, smirked. Behind her, Crew shivered, stomped his feet in the snow, trying to give a hint. His breath flowed out of his mouth like smoke.

"What about Pyotr?" Eva asked.

"You want us to fetch him for you?"

Eva thought, smiled.

"No, no that's all right."

"It's what I figured," Sobotka snorted. "Besides, in the prison he's at, he's somebody else's girlfriend now anyway."

Crew chortled.

Sobotka reached into her bag and pulled out a brown paper bag, taped shut along the top. She handed it over to Eva, tentative.

"You sure you don't need anything else?" she asked. "I think we owe you more than this."

Eva held the bag tightly, shrugged.

"I think we can call it even," she said, stepping backwards a step.

Sobotka nodded, turned and lead Crew towards the car. She stopped, glanced over her shoulder, watched Eva leaving into the snowy fields.

"Take care of yourself, Ms Kolikov!" she yelled. "You're more useful than you look!"

Eva said nothing, just smiled.

As the sound of the car receded into the background, Eva opened the bag again, pulling out the contents as she walked down the train tracks, off towards a distant farm. It was all there, and she nodded happily.

A sketchbook, some pencils. A photo of her mother. A beginner's guide on growing your own food.

*   *   *

"Home to Green Four," came the voice, a distant crackle among the static waterfall. "Your signal is faint, Green Four."

"My suit is damaged."

"What is your status? Have you located LS-411?"

Static.

"LS-411 was a trap."

"Green Four, please repeat."

"It was a trap. My earlier samples are also tainted. Do not release treatments for those samples."

Static.

"Green Four, our engineers discovered the flaw in your earlier samples. They were discarded."

Wind.

"Green Four, what is your status? Can you make the journey back?"

Cold. Bitter cold.

"No," he said. "I am done."

And before he heard more, he dropped the phone into the snow, and continued on his way.

NOTES

Writing a novel is viciously hard work. I've written screenplays and picture books, but nothing has ever come close to being as difficult as writing this story, start to finish.

It all started with an article posted to Slashdot in 2002, which read (in part): "Scientists have assembled the first synthetic virus. The US researchers built the infectious agent from scratch using the genome sequence for polio. The most amusing part is this snippit: 'To construct the virus, the researchers say they followed a recipe they downloaded from the internet and used gene sequences from a mail-order supplier.'"

http://science.slashdot.org/article.pl?sid=02/07/11/2352202

The resulting discussion got my brain working overtime: imagine what would happen if biotech tools were put in the hands of "script kiddies" — hackers with no real understanding of what they were doing, but a strong desire to do harm. How fast would civilization fall?

The first real incarnation of this book was as a late-night brainstorm back in the summer of 2003. I pitched the idea to a bunch of friends during a 36-hour work marathon: the world is ravaged by disease, and this lone "healer" travels the countryside, finding the causes of infection, and kills them with his machete.

"A machete?" asked Chris, my long-time creative foil. "Why'd he use a machete? Isn't that more dangerous?"

"Yeah," agreed Jeremy. "He should just inject them with a poison. That way he doesn't have to worry about getting infected blood on him."

"He could make them think it was the cure, but it's not!" agreed Chris.

"Shut up and get back to work!" growled Lucy (Jeremy's wife, and ruthless taskmaster).

Three years later, I was ready to give it a try. I constructed a story about the Healer, intermingled with the story of a Russian kid named Pyotr who was trying to find his mother while being hunted by the police.

Suffice to say, quite a lot has changed since that draft.

There are two footnotes I want to cover, in response to critiques I received along the way. They're elements that I couldn't fit into the narrative without resorting to painful exposition, but I still contemplated endlessly:

The Healer doesn't use a gun because guns are not a limitless weapon. If you're sending an agent into a dangerous environment like that, you don't want to weigh him down unnecessarily. He already needs to carry a tent and enough food to sustain him for weeks at a time (between airdrop deliveries). If he had to carry bullets too, he'd never make any progress, and would be in deep trouble if he used up his stock too early in the month. A machete is small, tough, and never runs out.

We don't hear about America because when you're dealing with a tragedy in your home, you don't often care what's happening halfway across the world. It's unimportant to you at that moment in time. Is the U.S. in as bad shape as Europe, or did they keep things under control? Have they erected a wall between Mexico? Canada? Has democracy failed in the face of multiple concurrent plagues? All interesting questions, but none of which impact the world of Eva or the Healer.

The shaping of this book took a lot of hard work from a lot of different people, who I will now thank in absolutely no order whatsoever:

Slashdot. Okay, that's not a person, but I think it's obvious that without my "news for nerds", I wouldn't be half as interesting as I am today.

Chris Gully, my partner in crime. Chris read draft four of this book and said to me: "You're telling, not showing. Didn't you learn anything in high school? I'm not reading any more of this until you fix it."

Jeremy List, for helping me realize that a machete is a weapon best saved for special occasions. And also **Lucy List**. Because if I don't thank her, she'll kill me.

Don McMillan, genius space nut and very good friend, who read draft 3 and said in as polite a way as I think is possible: "Hmm. It's very good! Thanks!" That told me I needed to write a few more versions.

My parents, because they actually read draft 6, and whereas *your* parents may just say "Oh my dearest! That was wonderful!", *my* parents gave me 25 pages of highly critical notes, which I couldn't fully resolve until draft 9.

Mary Anne Mohanraj and **John Scalzi** for their fantastic posts about race and writing: http://whatever.scalzi.com/2009/03/13/mary-anne-mohanraj-gets-yo u-up-to-speed-part-ii/. Although I talked mostly about Chinese attributes in my comments there, I was (and still am) deeply concerned about writing "other" people (racial, cultural or even just regional) than myself. I think I treated everyone with appropriate respect in this story, but if not, I'd love to hear your thoughts on how I could improve.

Ken Kehl and **Robert Lambert,** who butchered draft 5 so severely and so well that it saved me from myself. And of course all the folks at **Critters** (http://critique.org) who do a fantastic job honing raw materials into something great.

Kyle Newton, who not only found a few dozen typos that everyone else missed, but did it while reading on a PSP. Oh, and he also helped me discover my unintentional affection for asyndeton. He saved you all from great suffering.

Tim Pollak, my editor extraordinaire, found more glitches and oversights in this book than I could possibly imagine. He didn't get to read this section, though, so any mistakes are on me!

And I want to thank my wonderful wife, **Rie**, who read draft 6 in a big blue binder over the course of a week, and said to me at the end: "Well, at least it didn't suck."

That's the nicest thing she's ever said to me!

Yes!

— MCM
mcm@1889.ca
May 2009